CELLAR DOOR PARALLAX

Parker J. Duncan

CRANTHORPE
—MILLNER—
PUBLISHERS

Copyright © Parker J. Duncan (2023)

The right of Parker J. Duncan to be identified as author of this work has been asserted by him in accordance with section 77 and 78 of the Copyright, Designs and Patents Act 1988.

All rights reserved. No part of this publication may be reproduced, stored in a retrieval system, or transmitted in any form or by any means, electronic, mechanical, photocopying, recording, or otherwise, without the prior permission of the publishers.

Any person who commits any unauthorized act in relation to this publication may be liable to criminal prosecution and civil claims for damages.

This book is a work of fiction. Names, characters, places and incidents are either products of the author's imagination or are used fictitiously. Any resemblance to actual events or locales or persons, living or dead, is entirely coincidental.

First published by Cranthorpe Millner Publishers (2023)

ISBN 978-1-80378-106-8 (Paperback)

www.cranthorpemillner.com

Cranthorpe Millner Publishers

For my uncle Shannon, a marvel of the human spirit

TABLE OF CONTENTS

LIST OF TRILOGY MAIN CHARACTERS
SEPTEMBER 7TH 2098 – YEAR OF THE HORSE
XXXIX EFFECTUM UTOPIA
XL BENEVOLENT DIVINE
XLI WHEN PLANETS SPEAK
XLII SERAPHIC YOUTH
XLIII SILENT SCREAM
XLIV BLACK WIDOW
XLV SUB-HUMAN DEFECTORS
XLVI RITUAL SATANICO
XLVII CHILDREN OF THE SUN
XLVIII THE APPALACHIAN FRONT
XLIX LOCUST REIGN
L SIBERIAN ASYLUM
LI FELLOWSHIP OF MISFITS
LII WOMB RAKER
LIII RETURN OF THE TRINITY
LIV LUX MAXIMA
LV TITANOMACHY
LVI ARTEMIS
LVII PHARAOH'S FLOWER OF DEATH
LVIII THE SURGE
LIX DOOM ASCETICS
LX THE MONARCH
LXI OBLIVION
LXII GENESIS
ACKNOWLEDGMENTS

TRILOGY MAIN CHARACTERS

Ezra James Beller (2001-2033) – first Sararan who passes on the Sararan gene to Ingrid and Michael.
Name meaning: God helps (Hebrew).
Mythological counterpart: Marchosias – winged wolf demon who gives true answers to all questions.

Ingrid Eleanor McAdam (2005-2053) – wife of Ezra who passes on the Sararan gene to Melody.
Name meaning: beautiful (Old Norse).
Mythological counterpart: Pavonis or The Peacock – the constellation of salvation/Mother Earth.

Michael Ian Beller (2033-) – son of Ezra and Ingrid and Emperor of the Western World.
Name meaning: one who is closest to God (Hebrew).
Mythological counterpart: Archangel Michael – the angel who defeats Satan in the war in Heaven.

Melody Bakr (2035-) – Michael's lover and Empress of the Western World.
Name meaning: song (Greek).
Mythological counterpart: Gaia – personification of the Earth.

Lillian Sage (1980-2052) – human midwife to Ezra/Ingrid and Michael's caregiver.
Name meaning: pure (Latin).
Mythological counterpart: Lucina – Roman Goddess of Childbirth.

William Cane Beller (2008-) – Ezra's human brother.
  Name meaning: helmet, protection (Germanic).
  Mythological counterpart: Ares – Greek God of War.

Queen Parvati (2047-) – Queen of the Eastern World.
  Mythological counterpart: Parvati – Hindu goddess of fertility.

Vishnu (1817-2033) – the first Aradian.
  Name meaning: one who supports, preserves, sustains and governs the universe and originates and develops all elements within.
  Mythological counterpart: Vishnu (Hindu).

Shakti (1933-2053) – Vishnu's first apprentice and Queen of Earth under the Zurvan Order.
  Name meaning: empowerment and cosmic energy (Hindu).
  Mythological counterpart: Shakti (Hindu).

Lakshmi (2004-) – Vishnu's fourth apprentice and Lord of Neon City.
  Name meaning: material and spiritual wealth (Hindu).
  Mythological counterpart: Lakshmi (Hindu).

Sandraudiga (Cassandra Larson) (2001-2053) – Shakti's general.
  Name meaning: 'she who dyes the sand red' (Germanic).
  Mythological counterpart: Sandraudiga – Germanic goddess.

Mayari (1949-2053) – Vishnu's apprentice and twin of Tala
  Name meaning: Goddess of Stars (Filipino)
  Mythological counterpart: Icarus – 'The one who flew too close to the sun'.

Tala (1949-) – Vishnu's apprentice and twin of Mayari
　　Name meaning: Lunar Goddess (Filipino)
　　Mythological counterpart: Ganesha – deity of removing obstacles.

September 7th 2098 – Year of the Horse

"A snake's poison is life to the snake; it is in relation to man that it means death."

Jalāl ad-Dīn Muhammad Rūmī

CHAPTER 39 – EFFECTUM UTOPIA

A small hand rose from beneath the cellar door. Like a flower unearthed, a young girl plucked herself from the damp foundation and leapt into a maze of grass. Singing in her splendor, she sprawled under the rising warmth of morning, cured by the evaporation from the sun's half-life. She stood and combed her hair with a bird's rib cage, pulling spider webs and dead leaves from the long dark strands. She slipped the canary skeleton into her pocket. The flowers and trees seemed to smile back at her as her teeth gleamed at the prospect of that waking September day. She stood up and began running, pulling her dress up so she wouldn't trip as she sped around the old stone house. After turning the corner to the front porch, she came face to face with a woman standing in a white robe, her arms crossed like a statue blocking the way.

"Devonia, where have you been? You're going to be late for school again!"

"Sorry, Madam Bedisa! I was exploring beneath the house and lost track of time."

The woman grabbed Devonia's hand and began walking down the dirt road with haste as she spoke.

"You shouldn't be playing in that filth! There are poisonous spiders and nasty things down there."

"Actually they are venomous. That means they put toxins into your body by biting you. Poisonous things only make you unwell if you eat them. But mostly the spiders don't bite you unless you mess with them, and then you probably deserve it. How else would they defend themselves? People poke at them and poke at them and they don't have any way of saying 'stop it!'," Devonia exclaimed.

"Well at least you've been doing your biology homework."

"I did all my homework by the creek yesterday afternoon. Then I took a nap and looked up and there was a toad sitting on my belly. I asked him – well, I think it was a 'him', I'm not really sure – but I asked him if he was a prince, because I read a story where a frog turned into a prince when a lady kissed him, but he didn't answer so I kissed him, and he didn't... he just tasted funny."

"You shouldn't be kissing toads, Devonia," Melania said, rolling her eyes.

The road they walked had been slightly beaten down by travelers, yet small craters in the stones, filled now with moss and grass, alluded to ancient violence.

"'You shouldn't be kissing toads, Devonia'," the young girl mimicked. "You're always telling me what NOT to do, it's so boring. Why can't you tell me something interesting? Like where the best places are to hunt for insects? Or why different frogs make different sounds? Or why some insects fly and others have hundreds of little legs?"

"That's enough, Devonia. You're eleven years old. You can't continue to spend all morning out in the wilderness or the cellar. If you keep arriving late for school, you will fall behind and all the other children will laugh at you."

"Let them laugh, I don't care! Laughing is good for the soul."

They walked down the road, past the baker and the shoemaker, past the butcher and the tailor. A stack of fresh vegetables towered above the bed of a farmer's cart, parked next to a stone wall to allow the mule pulling it to nibble at the apples drooping from the branches that hung over its threshold. A small incline led Devonia and Melania to the schoolyard, where pink rose bushes lined the white fencing and rowdy children were being called to their morning sessions.

"You're lucky you're not late, now hurry to class! I'll see you at the market for lunch," Melania said as she tapped Devonia lightly on her backside.

Just as she walked through the gates, a large centipede crawled up Devonia's back and Melania reached over and flicked it away, shivering with disgust.

"What am I going to do with that child?" she asked herself as Devonia entered the school, oblivious to the dungeon dweller that had hitched a ride on her once-white dress.

Softly but suddenly, a voice came from behind her.

"You could always place her back in the orphanage, but then she wouldn't have the wonderful life she has now, would she?"

Melania turned to find a young oriental woman in a humble brown and white silk robe, smiling brightly as she bowed. Her black hair was tied in spirals of tight golden weave, subtly marking her as a noble figure. She had magenta eyes and a look of humorous generosity, as if she were on the verge of laughing at any moment.

"Melania Bedisa, pleasure to meet you. And you are?" Melania said, bowing in return.

"What an extraordinary name. I am Xiang Yu, daughter of Chen Yu, Seventh Princess to the Holy Shrine of Queen Parvati, and currently Ambassador to Empress Melody. I'm pleased to meet you as well."

"Your graciousness, please forgive me!" Melania said, bowing again. "I was unaware of your visit. I'd have organized some kind of festival, or perhaps a feast in your honor—"

Xiang chuckled. "Your hospitality is beyond flattering, but the attributes of your wonderful village more than suffice. The gardens here are some of the most splendid I've seen outside Geneva's palace. Perhaps you could oblige me with a tour of your lovely community while we walk and discuss young Devonia's future?"

"Oh dear, what has she done this time?"

Xiang laughed again, shaking her head in amusement. "Ha! Why, she's done nothing terrible at all. I am in love with this place already. How utterly wonderful," she said, as she led Melania down the road toward town, the brilliant Black Sea glistening to the west.

"The Caucus mountains are a majestic region. I'm not sure why it took me so long to come to Georgia. Did you grow up here, Melania?"

"No, I am from Armenia. My father fought in the Post-Eruption Wars but was killed by Shakti's troops soon after they invaded. My mother and I were transferred to a refugee camp in Eastern Georgia when I was very young. Too young to remember. Devonia, however, was born in this town. She's been moved around to different foster homes for causing her host parents too much stress. They often lose her and find her wandering in the woods, miles from where she is supposed to be."

"Yes, I've been informed of Devonia's exploratory nature. Her parents would have had their hands full with such a wild young girl. She seems well though?"

"Despite her disregard for authority, she is a remarkable young girl. She always wants to learn, especially about the natural world. The dangers of life do not illicit fear in her. This morning I found her crawling out of the cellar beneath her host-parents' house, covered in muck and webs. Most girls want to play dress up and tease boys. Devonia just wants to find the strangest organisms she can and learn everything about them."

"How wonderful! It does not surprise me that I have been sent to fetch her then."

"Fetch her? You mean... you're Devonia's new host parent?"

"No, Empress Melody is."

"Oh my goodness!" Melania exclaimed, stopping in front of a café momentarily, her heart skipping a beat.

"DNA samples and annual testing data from your region have revealed that Devonia's lineage has special qualities that the empress is particularly interested in. She's been carefully selected from thousands of girls her age to join an advanced learning program. I hope this news doesn't upset you?"

"Not at all! I am just surprised that she has been chosen. I mean, yes, she's brilliant, but her behavior... I mean... did the empress tell you why Devonia specifically was selected?"

Xiang shook her head with a half-cracked smile, "No, she did not." She tipped her head towards the vine laden building in front of them. "Shall we have a refreshment at this adorable café while we wait for Devonia to be excused for lunch?"

"Of course, yes... pardon my manners."

They sat on the patio as the sun rose high above them. Curious eyes watched the ambassador keenly, for they hadn't seen any nobles in their lands since Queen Parvati visited years ago. At the time, she had brought a security team of rifle wielding Mongols wherever she ventured, so seeing a royal ambassador wandering around their town unaccompanied was a rare sight indeed.

"This a peaceful town, but we do have thieves and petty

criminals from time to time. Forgive me, but are you not at all worried for your safety here without even a bodyguard?" Melania asked.

"I'm more afraid of losing track of the afternoon," Xiang said brightly.

The waiter set down a bottle of white wine and an oak board dotted with soft cheeses, fig jam, and fresh baked bread that steamed in the rays of light coming through the tree branches. Xiang poured Melania a glass and let Melania pour hers, a courtesy paired with the eastern traditions Xiang was accustomed to. They said 'gaumarjos' and clinked glasses before Xiang took a sip and elaborated on her answer.

"The moment I dress in fine clothes and surround myself with armed men, criminals suddenly think there's something of high value at stake and they begin plotting. The highest testament of modern nobles is identifying with the common folk around us, to the point where they desire our presence rather than detest it. Besides, we have little to offer the common thief. We aren't wealthy aristocrats. We're servicemen and women. We want to be approachable and a positive extension of society. Even a step over that line could lead us once again into a convulsive vampiric bureaucracy. We were chosen to lead by fate, so we lead, just as Devonia may someday."

"So you'd let yourself be..." Melania found it hard to find the words, "... relieved of duty?" she asked, drinking from her glass of golden liquid as a butterfly tip-toed around the bottle's mouth.

"The empress can replace me far more easily than she can wage peace in faraway lands. That may be the nature of my undoing and I accept the possibility of such a fate every day of my life. The tradeoff is peace for the people."

"That's gracious of you. It seems the world is finally balanced because no one seems challenged by poverty or the lack of education or energy or food. At least in our community, the numerous wars of our past are but a strange and distant memory. I want to swallow my breath, for fear of the devil's ear, when I speculate how long these times of grace can truly last."

Xiang nodded and elaborated, "The empress has made sure to provide the creatures of Earth with the proper environment to be self-sufficient on a community-based platform, much like yours. Over-population and greed almost destroyed our planet. Too few commodities for too many people only ever leads to hardship, competition and corruption. Balance is key to a fruitful existence. Of course, there are those who don't see it that way, or would have it their own way altogether. Beyond the rare but inevitable homicide, if someone truly becomes a problem for our communities and habitats, such as influential males becoming dictators, terrorists taking hostages, pirates annexing sections of the ocean, or even small-town gangs committing repeated crimes and disturbing citizens daily lives… well… that's when the emperor's detachment gets deployed. Emperor Michael's forces have only had to neutralize eighty-nine people in the last sixty-six years. And he may have saved tens of thousands in doing so. Peace is a worthy ideal worth reaching for, but it's not a sustained reality. Some form of defense does need to be in place or someone else can and will bring us back to the dark ages of patriarchal imperialism. Luckily, Michael and his detachment are so precise and deadly that no one on Earth has the power or resources to become a threat. Crime, conflict, and pollution are at an all-time low. He has scared the aspiring warlords world-wide into submission. More people die from mountaineering now than murder. If a human is unfit for society, it is because he has chosen that life, and the community itself can usually handle those situations, which is why you don't see as many police on the streets."

"Sounds like we're safer than ever," Melania said, taking a sip and tipping her glass towards Xiang.

"Like I said, I'm more worried about my inability to deny the insistence of our charming waiter," Xiang chuckled.

A few hours later, Xiang and Melania watched as young Devonia skipped down the street with her chaperone close behind. The rest of the class dispersed to the various food carts in the area as the chaperone watched them closely, especially Devonia.

"Devonia, sweetheart! Over here!" Melania yelled from their shaded patio.

The small girl walked up and curtseyed them.

"Hello Devonia, my name is Xiang Yu. Are you having a good day at school?"

"I guess. Too much desk time if you ask me."

Xiang chuckled as she held a napkin to her mouth. "Oh dear... I know exactly how you feel. However, those lessons in the classroom are just as important as the ones outside of it."

Devonia nodded reluctantly. "What's going on?" she asked, annoyed by the air of secretiveness she could sense surrounding the two women.

"Well, Devonia, I have been sent here by the empress herself to offer you a new home, and to escort you there, if you agree. We will leave this evening, if that's alright with you," Xiang said, leaning down and looking at Devonia closely.

"Where am I going?"

"To the empress's palace, in the heart of Almuruna. The empress herself wishes to be your legal guardian."

Devonia gave Xiang a skeptical glance. "Really?" she asked, half excited.

Xiang nodded and smiled.

"Can I at least say goodbye to Boris?"

"And who is that?" Xiang asked.

"My tortoise," she said with a sad face.

"I'll tell you what, you can bring Boris with you."

Devonia smiled and flung her arms around Xiang's middle, much to the woman's surprise. Then she reached for Melania's hand.

"Will you come too, Madam Bedisa?"

"I have to stay here, Devonia, but it will be okay. I'm sure you will be able to visit me someday."

"Of course you will," Xiang said, turning to Devonia, "We can come back and visit in a few months, does that sound okay?"

Devonia nodded and smiled before grabbing a mushroom off Melania's plate and eating it.

"Manners!" Melania griped as she slapped Devonia's hand.

"Sorry, I'm starving!"

Xiang laughed and they ordered more food, eating and telling stories until it was time to leave. When they left, there was mink fur, silk, and Imperial Travel Credit on the table as payment.

Later that evening, Melania helped Devonia gather her things for the trip. Devonia said her goodbyes to Melania and her host family, who were both relieved and yet sad to see her go, before Xiang and the young girl mounted the noble's beautifully embellished horse-drawn buggy and headed west, with Boris the tortoise ambling by their feet.

CHAPTER 40 – BENEVOLENT DIVINE

As they roamed the countryside leading away from her home, Devonia looked out at the Black Sea dazzling in its wake. She could feel the tropæan breeze soft against her cheek as the green pastures and clumps of lights in the village quickly turned to pastel paintings in their receding view. Devonia looked up at the clear night sky.

"Beautiful, isn't it?" Xiang commented.

"I've always wondered what all that is above us. Are there beings up there, looking down at us? Like my parents in heaven maybe?"

Xiang just smiled and put her hand on the child's knee.

"Heaven exists above, below, here, there, inside you, everywhere. That's where your parents live. Everything you've inherited from them in body and mind lives through you, and you honor them by placing them in your own heaven."

"I guess I can understand that. They're like energy, right? But what's out there, then? Above us, in outer space?"

"Emptiness. Loneliness. Cold worlds and blazing suns and quiet violence on an unfathomable scale. But no life. The empress has studied our solar system and beyond. So far, it seems life is exclusive to Earth, and we don't know why. That's why it is so important that we nurture and take care of our planet."

Devonia looked into the oceanic abyss above as she swallowed the light with eager eyes, unknowingly edging past the furthest point she had ever been from home.

They travelled for months, sometimes joined by

diplomats or random travelers, all equally kind and helpful in their journey west. As they journeyed through the deserts of Turkey, Devonia marveled at the millions of solar panels, erected in circular patterns far reaching to the horizon's reflection. Xiang explained that enough light reached the plates of crystalline silicon to store and power all of Almuruna, what was once known as Europe. Xiang also lectured Devonia on environmental sustainability, permaculture, clean energy, the use of fungi for waste management, and other modern solutions endorsed and orchestrated by the emperor and empress. She told Devonia that the empress's goal was to steer Almuruna toward social reconstruction and an environmentally and energy conscious society, rather than one dictated by religion or industrial growth.

They rode through farms in Serbia during harvest season, beyond massive hemp fields whose stalks were of both material and pharmaceutical value, and on to the low vineyards where agricultural lords hosted the royal ambassador with a feast in honor of both autumn's waxing and their savior, Pavonis. Rapturous music played long into the night and Devonia could not understand how the musicians' instruments made sound, for the outputs of their synths and guitars were wireless and the speakers were hidden in the ceilings as if to disguise the technology altogether.

They continued through hills of heavenly air as Xiang led Devonia into Croatia, a land of beautiful mountain streams with sapphire-colored waters. Everything there resembled a gem to Devonia, from the ruby flowers dripping with golden nectar to the emerald leaves sprouting from round rocks polished by nature's steady work. Deeper into the mountains they ventured, until at last they reached a great castle jutting from the mountainside on a cool November afternoon.

Devonia awoke to see the western world's capital; a landscape of snowcapped mountains and sub-alpine forests covering the lower altitudes of the range. Their carriage entered the valley before the great peaks, where small houses spread about the landscape and folks prepared for winter by chopping wood and reinforcing their houses.

"Where are we?" Devonia asked, making sure Boris was still snugly wrapped up in her sweater.

"We are in the heart of the Kingdom of Almuruna, in a place once known as Geneva, Switzerland. It has long been a place of prosperity and neutrality, fitting for the empress and emperor of our Earth. We will meet them today, or at least the empress."

They hopped out of the cart and walked down into the valley's center, through the markets and by small power stations between venders, where the only byproduct of their generating was steam escaping their composite exhaust pipes. Devonia saw people of all ethnicities. Voices she'd never heard were like music to her young ears, and the fanciful outfits of so many cultures made Xiang hardly notable in the myriad of so much color and extravagance: African men with big gold hoops in their noses and long purple robes; covens of women with green face-paint and bright white dresses, marking them as late disciples of Pavonis, and whole troops of gypsies that juggled flame and performed dances in their dusty velvet attire.

Xiang and Devonia rode a magnet-propelled speed train to the palace at the foot of the mountains, zipping past all the city's wonders. As they sped along, Devonia stared in awe at the oddly shaped buildings with gardens on every other floor jutting from their walls and windows. When they exited the train, Devonia was nearly sick, her legs shaking and her head spinning as she looked up at the castle. Tall white columns stood above a wide stairwell, leading to a set of grand doors painted with golden weave from their base to their apex. At the top of the facade was a statue of Lord Pavonis, the sacred Tree-of-Life carved at her feet as she stood rigid and pearl white in the evening's glow.

At the palace doors stood robed guards, without weapons save for bow staffs, sitting with relaxed poses. They smiled and nodded slightly with approval as Xiang urged Devonia up the steps before the massive oak doors.

"Go ahead and knock, Devonia."

Devonia walked up to the intricately carved doors, but before she could reach them, they swung open with a deep groan. Xiang cleared her throat, hinting for Devonia to bow.

"Oh, sorry," Devonia whispered.

She set her tortoise down on the ground and they both bowed low, rising after a few seconds. When she looked up, Devonia's eyes lit up at the sight of the being before her.

In a dress as white as polished ivory stood the gracious empress, her dark skin and green eyes softer and more beautiful than Devonia could have imagined. She wore a diamond laurel that glistened in her long hair, a halo of subtle yellow light shimmering around her perfect Sararan skull. Empress Melody bowed in return and rose with a smile that swept the pavilion with wonderful nuances.

"Good evening, my loves. I trust your travels went well?" Her hypnotic voice echoed through the hall.

"Very much so, Empress. I'd like you to meet Devonia Ketevan, and Boris the tortoise."

"It is an honor to meet you, Empress. I love your dress!" Devonian exclaimed, excited to meet one of her heroes.

"Thank you, Devonia. It's wonderful to meet you, and your tortoise as well. I'm sure you're all hungry. Come in and get settled. The chef is preparing a delightful dish."

"Will the emperor be joining us this evening?" Xiang asked.

"I doubt it, but he has a history of surprising me. Please come, before the cold follows you in."

The oak doors shut behind them, and Devonia entered her new home; the capital of Earth and domain of the world's leaders for the past forty-three years.

Devonia was shown her new room in the East Wing of the palace, a luxurious suite with stuffed toy animals and large pillows strewn all around. Her bed was so big that a step ladder was built so she could climb to its plateau safely. She set Boris down on the plush carpet and the tortoise looked around slowly before scuttling under a pillow. Devonia peeked out of the door into the hall. No one was around. She quickly sprinted off down the corridor and rounded the corner to a part of the palace she had not visited yet. She twirled across the carpet, laughing and making faces at the sculptures she passed. Suddenly, Xiang walked out of her room. She smiled at Devonia.

"Doing some exploring are we?"

"Yes, Ambassador Yu."

"I don't see a problem with that so long as you behave and get to bed at a decent hour. But first, we have dinner to attend, are you ready?"

She nodded with excitement.

They made their way to the dining hall and Devonia tilted her head curiously at the sweet autumnal fragrance that permeated the room. As she settled in her seat, she noticed several bouquets were set on the table – the source of the delightful smell. Warm cider was served with cinnamon stirring sticks as the ambassador and Devonia were joined by figures of the emperor and empress's council. They introduced themselves to the shy child as they entered. First came Councilwoman Sage Valor, the head of the Department of Energy, and her assistant Ronaldo. Then came General Ziven Fredrickson, Chief of Defense, and behind him, Councilman David Beller, the boy who had been famously adopted by Michael and Melody after the fall of the Zurvan Empire. Though his parents were older, David aged as any human would, and was now a middle-aged man doing his best to moderate the spiritual conflicts of the new age as one of the justices to the royal court.

"Good to see all of you," Xiang said. "It's been too long. Sage, my dear, how are relations with Queen Parvati in the East?"

"Very positive, Ambassador. Complete sustainability has been achieved in China's southern range. I trust they'll maintain their systems lest we make them wait another decade for the programs upgrade." She winked as she held her glass up and drank, her short purple hair quivering in the warm golden light.

"Splendid. And Ziven, you aren't too busy I hope?"

"Not currently, but that's not to say the world's gone quiet. The emperor is operating in Africa as we speak."

"Are you not the second in command of the armed forces? With all due respect, why did he not bring you and your team?" Xiang asked.

"Emperor Michael thinks it's best for the nation if one of us stays in Almuruna for defense purposes while the other is deployed."

"Perhaps he enjoys the sensation of battle. War is a drug,

is it not?" Sage said.

The general shook his head. "The emperor is, when needed, a covert agent to mitigate liability. He trains and deploys his task force but faces much of the danger himself."

"But if he is killed... who will protect us?" Sage asked.

"Protect us from what?" Devonia asked.

Everyone looked at the child. No one had an answer. David looked at her with a wise smile. Just then, the empress entered the room, and everyone stood.

"Good evening friends and council members."

"Good evening, Empress," they responded.

"Please, sit. Dinner should be served shortly. So... what did I miss?"

They sat and Sage stirred her drink. No one spoke until David finally spearheaded the awkward air.

"We were just discussing the radical nature of the Emperor Michael's defense program."

"I was not criticizing the emperor's methods," Sage said.

"No one said you were," David went on, "But I've spoken with the people of this kingdom and, if I may convey their concerns, it seems many do not fully understand or appreciate the sacrifices he has made in these long years since the dark times."

"They're just afraid of toxic masculinity, something we all should be wary of," Sage said.

Ziven looked at her with disconcerting eyes. The empress nodded but did not speak.

David continued. "Those of us who lived through those hellish years under Shakti know the dangers of feminine power as well. It matters not the condition of a person's gender. We cannot resort to that kind of sexist bigotry."

"Bigotry... right. And yet you think religion should be illegal?" Sage said with an annoyed tone.

Then the empress spoke. "Only public practice of certain religions will be forbidden if the new mandate is passed, and it was I who pushed for this new legislation."

"With respect, Empress, doesn't the emperor also need to agree with this new policy?" Sage asked.

"I'm sure he will agree. He understands better than anyone the power religion can have and the evil it provokes. Please, friends, let us save this conversation for our next council. I promise to answer all your questions and fulfill your needs in due time."

The food came and everyone ate. More drinks were poured, and laughter soon broke the room's thorny ambience. David and the empress spoke the least, their opinions on worldly matters solidified in their history of violence.

After dinner, Devonia was sent to bed. When the lights were shut off and the door closed, she got up and peeked out into the hall, her thirst for adventure unquenchable. Creeping through the long halls, lamp in hand, she left the East Wing and made her way to the main hall, then up to the highest tower overlooking the vast mountain scape. She intentionally got lost in the mysterious South Wing, which she had been explicitly told not to enter. She gazed at the marble walls, where acrylic paintings of Lord Pavonis and the divine couple had been set inside intricate gold leaf frames. She grazed her fingers over the masterfully crafted portraits and as she turned to walk away, she bumped into someone. She yelped with fright.

"And who might you be?" the stranger asked in a low tone.

He towered over her, his dark clothes covered by ballistic body armor. His face was splotched with charcoal and his long, black hair was messy, cascading over his blazing orange eyes. He smiled, his irises burning like suns in the darkness.

"I'm Devonia, I came with Ambassador Yu from Georgia. I'm one of the empress's new apprentices."

"Welcome, Devonia. I am Emperor Michael. Excuse my untidy appearance. I've just returned from a long trip and need to wash up. Do you need help finding your way back to your room?"

"I'll find my way. Thank you."

"Have a good rest, Devonia. Be safe."

"Good to meet you, Emperor Michael," she said hesitantly.

The man walked on through the darkness, his cape of black chainmail clinking softly as his flaming eyes lit the way. As soon as he had departed, Devonia took the short way back to the East Wing. When she entered her quarters, she found Boris and took him to bed. She snuggled close to him, still shaken by meeting the Sararan Emperor in the hallway, who had smelled of burning Earth and looked at her with eyes that held a hidden anger.

Michael walked into his room and sloughed his heavy kit with a loud clunk.

"You're back later than expected. A promising venture, I hope?" Melody asked.

Her lashes spoke to the candlelight and with her hair tied back there was nothing but her green nightgown to impede the glow of her golden skin, shimmering with ten million scales of solar super-cells.

Michael walked over and kissed her on the lips, before

walking back to the entry to take his boots and clothes off. She looked into his eyes, but they were silent.

"What troubles you?"

"Nothing troubles me. What trouble I've found has been of another's undoing."

He took off his undershirt. His muscles were bruised and bloodied, his body still healing from some insidious barrage. Lacerations, still purple from pipe-bomb shrapnel and homemade hand-cannons, pulsed and expelled shards of copper and steel onto the floor. Slowly but effectively Michael's cells regenerated, as they had so many times before.

"When was the last time you slept?" the empress asked.

Michael sighed and thought for a moment. "Eighty-six moons ago."

Michael looked at his hands for a moment, as if feeling incompatible with their primitive shape. Melody shook her head.

"You need to dream, Michael."

There was a pause. Michael finished undressing and walked naked to his lover.

"I know," he replied at last. He kissed her again and ran his fingertips along her shoulders, delicately calming her with his soft caress. "I have not slept because I've been without you."

"You were only gone five weeks," she said.

"And yet my work leads me farther from you all the time. Even here, I feel spiritually separated, yet my body remains. Your embrace passes through me. There is something missing." He shook his head, angered suddenly by his own words. "You're right though. I will sleep tonight. At least until dawn."

"You are much too hard on yourself. The world is ours to gift but do not feel obligated to become these humans godhead. We are just guardians doing our best to protect the Earth your mother left us. Look at what we've achieved with nearly fifty years of peace."

"Just the same, the world is changing faster than the humans can keep up with."

"I know why you do what you do."

"I know you do. You were in the Valley of Banff; you witnessed the madness of war, where my mother laid to waste the last protectors of the free world."

Melody looked at him with a solemn gaze. She touched his scarred chest. "I can almost see your weary heart. Where have you been, my love. What happened?"

Michael sighed and wiped her bloody tear with his thumb. "We were in the Horn of Africa, looking for poachers and merchants making exchanges via the re-established ivory trade. A twelve-man team plus myself. We found a trading outpost in Northern Ethiopia. It was supposed to just be a routine check in with the trader. I scanned the area and took all the precautions. One of my men stepped on a carefully hidden IED: very small, precise, and meant for a single person. I think someone had anticipated Xiang's inspection. She would have been your third assassinated ambassador."

"My God…" Melody shook her head.

"I take full responsibility for not identifying the threat. That soldier's death is on my hands. Soon after the explosion, we entered a large-scale fire fight. We killed everyone in the compound except for the trade boss, who told us he hated hunting the endangered animals. He said he did it to support his family. After further investigation, I found that radical tribal leaders had profiled his family and exiled them from Somalia. Without his farm, he had to resort to the only trade that would put food on his family's table."

"Why didn't he go to the nearest co-op?"

"The poachers have already seized the state sponsored co-ops, from the headwaters of the Blue Nile to the Indian Ocean."

"Which ones?" she asked.

"All of them."

Melody's head sank with disbelief.

"I am fully committed to your objective of waging peace, but I've learned something crucial. No matter what we do, men will become beasts, and those of us who seek a moral high road will find obstructions at every turn, until we descend to the ways of men who treat other men as lesser beasts. It's as if we're meant for it."

Melody shook her head, irritated by his pessimism. "You talk like you're still a man. You're more than that, Michael. You're a Sararan emperor. You can see beyond this heresy, can't you?"

"Sometimes, I'm not sure if I can. I still crave what all men crave."

Melody looked up and smiled sensually. "Prove it."

Michael walked over and sat down on the bed, pulling Melody with him into his lap. The empress wrapped her arms around him and they kissed deeply, drawing opium circles on each other's spines. As they cuddled and laughed, Michael began to undress Melody, his movements becoming increasingly frantic as more of her skin was revealed. When she was finally as naked as he, they seized one another, their warm bodies heating the room while Michael's eyes burned with urgency. The royal couple's intimate lovemaking shook the nightstand by the bed and a small figurine of a woman tipped over. As the mammoth-tusk icon fell to the floor, Michael orgasmed inside of his empress, focusing on the thought of a son forming in her womb.

The next morning, Devonia had breakfast in the dining hall with Boris while the council attended their morning meeting in the royal court. The empress and emperor sat atop the court's mount, with their department heads sitting below them in a large half circle. Many issues were discussed. Overall, the humans championed in their ability to make compromise and heed the people's wishes. Michael, however, was not so pleased with their efforts.

"Councilman Hyman, several years ago you claimed that your committee had eradicated the threat of Chagas disease using the Sub-Sararan Proxy Gene SARV14 on your patients, but new reports are coming in with varying statistics of fatalities. Can you explain?"

"You are correct, Emperor. The follow-up procedures will be far more comprehensive than in 2079, when we had initially thought to have expelled the parasite from the tropics. Due to warmer temperatures and temporary housing, the disease has returned to Central Pavonia. The Disease-Control Committee will have an updated outline of our strategy in the coming weeks."

"Very well. Does anyone have anything else to say about this matter for the time being?"

The council shook their heads.

"The next order of business is the new Imperial mandate affecting our whole kingdom; in Northern, Central, and Southern Pavonia, Africa, and the provinces of Almuruna," the empress stated, driving the discussion forward. "Councilman Beller and I have constructed an amendment to the constitution, Amendment 113, which decrees that all ancient orthodox religions are illegal to practice publicly, with exceptions being made for natural and pagan practitioner's. This order is for the sake of peace, and shall not infringe on an individual's wellbeing. All who oppose this legislation please inform the council."

Several council members raised their hands. To everyone's surprise, Michael raised his hand as well. The empress turned her head in disbelief. Council members began whispering things to their neighbors.

"Emperor Michael. As chief speaker of this council, you have the floor," Melody said, her face tight as she tried to keep her embarrassment and confusion from showing.

Michael stood and leaned over the bench, his strong arms flexing as he gripped the corners of the podium.

"The wreckage that caused the great catastrophe decades ago was partially yet undeniably caused by religious fanaticism. And yet the subject of spirituality is something we must regulate with the utmost delicacy and tolerance, lest we are seen as sectarian rulers in the public eye. Councilman Beller, you believe in God, yes?"

"Whole-heartedly, Emperor," David said.

"You're of Jewish faith?"

"Yes, sir."

"Do you wish to practice your religion in public?"

"No, sir."

"Why not?"

"It's not necessary. My relationship with God is a personal one."

"Is it? What about those who find God through communal prayer?"

"There are churches and synagogues and mosques for that. The mandate does not affect sanctuaries of worship. Only public worship."

"As one of the architects of this legislation, I'm sure you mean to eradicate the extremists, correct? Yet have you considered that these institutions may be empowered by this amendment? In my experience, most radical idealists originate from minority groups that the governing authority have attempted to subdue in some way. Even if we lock up all the people who 'incorrectly' follow the old religions, some disturbed druid pardoned by this mandate will be screaming my mother's name through the streets in vain, parading their stupidity without any concept of what actual sacrifices she made to save this world. The basic message I would like to convey regarding this issue is that either all spiritual practices must be allowed or none of them. And I think we all know which of those is more reasonable. Anything else would be social suicide."

"Excuse me, Emperor, but is your personal association with the ancient Zoroastrian cult affecting this council's motion? Pavonis was a prophet, yes, but Moses did something very similar for his people. I think, if anything, this mandate is generous to those who believe Pavonis—"

"Pavonis did not need 'belief' to become a goddess!" Michael snapped, his eyes enflamed. "Nor was it offered. The evidence of what my mother has gifted us with is all around you every day of your waking life. Do not abuse your privilege to speak in this court by countering me with your offensive accusations, Councilman!"

"Then admit the real reason you don't want this law to pass, Michael!" David demanded.

Several council members whispered to one another. The empress spoke above the new commotion arising from the heated conversation.

"For the sake of the council's neutrality, I will suspend the mandate until a consensus has been reached by all members. We will re-visit this subject tomorrow with an appropriated outline. Councilman Beller, you are excused from this council until you have had a full psychological evaluation and no less than three hours of music therapy."

David stood up and walked out quickly. Michael watched him with eyes aflame. The empress moved on.

"The last subject we will speak of today concerns a message sent to us by the Crow Tribe in Northern Pavonia. Councilwoman Valor, you have the floor.

"Thank you, Empress," Sage stood and began. "During a routine maintenance upgrade to the geo-thermal power stations outside the Yellowstone Caldera, my team and I were given a letter from a tribal member who lives there. This is his message:

To our Holy Empress and Emperor,

My name is Falling Bird, and I speak on behalf of my tribe. We are grateful for the empress's support and everything she's given us here. We are grateful for Lord Pavonis, whom we praise for returning the Spirit of the Earth to all. The rivers are full of fish. The woods have many deer and birds for us to hunt. Our children are healthy. The water is clear. The sky is clear. Everything that our ancestors fought to protect is now here with us, and they are with us too. But a new evil has alerted the medicine man in our tribe. They have felt a buried demon beneath the Earth. The Caldera holds a dangerous entity. For fear of losing our lives, we will not enter its realm. I plead that the emperor himself come here to find whatever lies in these lands. Perhaps it is nothing but sour air trapped under the dirt. But if it is something more, this evil may once again spread over the Earth as it has before."

"As Chief of Defense, I expect you to provide a briefing within a week's time about this issue," Michael told General

Fredrickson.

"As you wish, Emperor. Perhaps we can have a summit as soon as tomorrow afternoon."

"It will be so."

Empress Melody knocked her rose quartz gravel and concluded the council.

"For the sake of the public's safety, the subjects of today's discussion will be kept confidential until remedied. Tell the press only what you know to be true and remain vague. Thank you, councilwomen and councilmen."

Leaving the council to disperse, the empress returned to the dining hall where Devonia was kicking her feet on the bottom of the table, eating toast and dripping jelly on herself.

"How did you sleep, Devonia?"

"I slept okay. I had nightmares."

"Yes, well, going into the South Wing can be a scary affair."

"I'm sorry, Empress. I shouldn't have disobeyed Ambassador Yu."

"Just know that sometimes dark places can harbor dark creatures. So... are you ready to begin your apprenticeship?"

"Yep, and so is Boris!" Devonia said, picking up her tortoise and holding him high over her head.

CHAPTER 41 – WHEN PLANETS SPEAK

Devonia stood at the feet of Switzerland's snowy peaks. The wind howled across the ridges, raking the fresh snow off the tree branches and sending small flakes back into the air. She pulled her coat in close to her body, with Boris tucked tightly under her shirt. She shivered as Melody looked down at her.

"Have you ever heard of kulning?"

Devonia shook her head.

"It's an ancient method of calling livestock down from the hills. It also serves as an alarm to predators… and is sometimes used to perform magick."

"Magick is real?"

"Yes, very much so," Melody smiled.

"Do you think I could use magick?"

"You probably can. Though to use it well takes years of learning and practice."

"Let's start then! I want to be able to cast spells and make potions!"

"There's a lot more to magic than spells and potions, Devonia. Watch."

Melody began the hymn. Her high voice sliced the air and the birds scattered from their nests for miles around. Through the mountains the eerie, beautiful song reverberated and called back. Suddenly the wind stopped, the clouds parted and the sun lent its light. Devonia rested her shoulders and relaxed as she became wrapped in the sun's warmth.

"Now you try," Melody said, nodding in her direction.

"Okay…" Devonia inhaled deeply then let out a raspy,

dissonant screech that came back with an insulting echo. "Yikes," she cringed, her teeth clenched.

The empress laughed. "That's all right. You're not going to be perfect your first time. Try again, this time using your breath as the vehicle for your sound. Do not force it. Let the song flow from your abdomen and carry through your vocal chords."

Devonia heeded her words and took another breath. Melody touched her apprentice's throat as Devonia began singing. Springing from her throat was a sharp and voluminous sound, untamed and yet harmonious. The mountains sang in distant return. Devonia stepped back with a baffled look.

"Whoa! How did I do that?"

"With some good listening skills, no doubt," the empress said, surprised by the quickness of Devonia's progression during her first lesson, despite the touch of help she'd provided.

They watched the herd of sheep come down from the hills and Melody continued kulning, her voice inspiring her young and eager apprentice. The snow blew over them and clung to their stray strands of hair as ice crystallized on their brows and lashes. Devonia shivered in the dawn light.

As if it were nothing at all, Melody heated her body, melting the snow around her as she levitated and called the sheep towards her aura. Her halo dilated, and Devonia reached out to the goddess's shimmering radiance, her hand thawing as if she were inching toward the sun itself.

As the sheep began feeding around them, Melody let Devonia mingle with them as she continued the lesson.

"These animals carry an energy," she began as Devonia pet a small lamb. "All living things have energy. From the smallest microbes inside your intestinal tract, to blue whales diving deep below the ocean's depths. This energy can be transposed, like the musical notes we used. You can shift whole herds, or spread fungal networks in a desired direction. With words and with your energy, you'll eventually hone this power to a level that can physically alter their very essence."

"What about people?"

"People can also be swayed by energy. Have you ever entered a room and felt someone's anger before you even knew why? Or hugged someone and felt their love travel between both of you?"

"Yeah, I see what you mean... hey Empress? Did you know your parents?"

"No, actually. I became an orphan at a young age, like you. The closest thing to a parent I had was Ingrid Beller, or Pavonis as you know her. She saved me from certain torture and became my teacher. But I had to learn much faster than you're learning now. She challenged me daily when I was barely surviving in the mountains of Canada."

Devonia spoke with a cautious tone. "I overheard a councilman saying that your father was an evil man; that he was one of the reasons the country of Israel was bombed. They made it sound like... well... they said a lot of your political opinions come from your own fear, and that your policies are there to protect David, since he's a Jew."

"Is that so? Well, each councilman and councilwoman has the right to believe what they wish, but just know that fear and my love for David are are not the reasons I implement certain policies. Everything Michael and I do is for Almuruna and beyond. We were shaped by war and we do not wish to see it again in our lands. Organized religion brought much pain to the world; you may not see it in our recovered world, but its shadow still haunts many souls."

"I believe in God, I think," Devonia said.

"That's wonderful," the empress said.

"But I believe she's a mother. A kind woman, like you. And all the creatures are her children. I like to think of her like that... I don't know if she is or not, or if she even exists, but that's what I want to believe."

"I believe the same thing, Devonia," the empress said, caressing the child's hair.

"Is that what Pavonis was like? Like you? Kind and gentle?"

"Pavonis loved and cared for Earth's creatures immensely, but no. She had a side to her that was truly ruthless. It's only because she was able to fully accept who she was and maintain balance that she was able to save the world. We all play a unique role in this life. You just have to find what gives you purpose and fulfill that role as best you can."

"Do you want to be a mother, Empress?"

Melody laughed. "Oh dear, I've considered it, but never wanted children myself. It would take away from my work as a leader."

"Since you adopted me, I'm kind of your daughter though, right?"

"Well yes, it is my aim to raise you and love you as my own."

"Awesome, because that's what I want too. Thank you for everything," she said, hugging the empress. "I've never had a parent who actually listened to me and wanted to talk about the things I want to talk about."

Melody hugged her in return. "Just remember, Devonia, you can talk to me about anything. In a few years you'll be experiencing some pretty wild changes, but that conversation is for another time. Let's get back and have some lunch now, shall we?"

They finished feeding the sheep and walked back to the palace when Devonia suddenly asked an awkward question.

"Did you ever kill anyone in the war?"

Melody looked up, thinking about the moment she stabbed Pavonis through the heart in a series of events that would set off the world's rejuvenation. She relived that moment every day of her life; the sinking of the blade through god-flesh, the feeling of betrayal toward her master, all while crossing the threshold to become her own master. Decades had passed, and yet the feeling never got easier. She was held to that cursed memory forever, and now her own apprentice was prying it to the surface.

"We all made sacrifices during the post-eruption wars. Someday, when you're older, I'll tell you more about them. You must be getting hungry, Devonia. Save your questions for the next lesson.

Devonia hung her head, feeling she had crossed some kind of line.

"It's fine, sweetheart, just know that as adults it is our duty to keep some things from you until you're ready. And you're just not ready yet."

Back at the palace, Xiang and Sage were enjoying brunch under the portico of the palace's southern entrance. They wore thick arctic fox coats and warmed themselves with a heat lamp above their table. The sun shone down on them weakly as winter's malady approached. Their discussion pertained to that morning's council meeting.

"If Michael and Melody did not agree on the mandate prior to the council, then it proves she really is handling certain issues autocratically," Sage said.

"In her defense, when Michael is absent on his campaigns, she has to work with what she has," Xiang argued.

"True, but aren't Sararans able to speak telepathically at almost any distance?"

"It would seem Michael has not slept, therefore has not answered his empress's calls."

"How strange... there must be more going on than meets the eye."

"For sure. But remember, despite our gracious leaders' sagacity, they are still subject to the same emotional strain that humans are. Their tolerance for fear is much higher than ours of course, but they bear one hundred times more responsibility as well. We cannot expect them to take on the world's endeavors forever, no matter their titles as Immortals. Their reign must end eventually."

"Why?" Sage asked, sipping her steaming coffee.

"For the same reason Parvati's reign will end. For the same reason every great leader's time comes to pass."

"Is Devonia aware she's the empress's only apprentice? The Royal School of Sciences was decommissioned over ten years ago. Perhaps she is the next great leader of the Western World."

Xiang smiled. "She is a delightful girl, isn't she? The title will have to be passed on to someone eventually, but it is only natural to desire an heir of one's own bloodline... we'll talk about this later. The empress approaches."

Melody and Devonia came outside and greeted the women.

"How was your first lesson this morning, Devonia?" Sage asked.

"It was so great! We practiced kulning, which is when you

sing to the mountains, and all the sheep came to say hi to us! I wasn't very good at it to start with, but I'm learning."

"That sounds very exciting. You two are just back for lunch, I presume?" Xiang enquired.

"Lunch, and then reassignment. Xiang, I'd like you to take an airship to South Africa and bring Devonia along with you. The trip will only be a few days but there are important diplomatic matters there I need your help with. Devonia could learn a lot from a mission like this," the empress said.

"Very well, Empress. Are you ready for another adventure?" Xiang asked, taking Devonia's hands.

Devonia said nothing but jumped up and down excitedly. They all laughed and smiled as they watched the child hop around the portico, doing her best impression of a tribal dance.

Later that evening, Michael sat at his desk reading a book on the First World War, his eyes feasting on the details of Verdun, his mind entering the terrified men's experiences as if he were there. He thought of the demolition workers in France still digging up the shells the Germans had fired by the millions, which would at times kill farmers tilling their fields, as if such a battle of attrition could never actually end and that swathe of Earth was therefore set apart, its very soil saturated with arsenic and young men's souls, beyond hope of becoming anything but an unquenchable grave; a serfdom for the damned.

Beside his quill stand was the Venus of Hohle Fels, gifted to him by Queen Shakti. He looked at the artifact with great obsession, as he always had. This mother figure, birther of all living things – what divinity is required to enact your essence? he wondered. He touched the carved mammoth tusk with his thumb and stroked its shape. As he watched it, a shock suddenly rang through his body and he jumped to his feet. A vision of a woman with blinding white luminescent eyes flashed before him. He jumped from the desk and the carving fell to the floor as Michael breathed heavily and stared at it.

"Is everything alright, my love?" Melody asked, entering his chamber quietly.

"It can't be her," he murmured.

"Who?"

"My vision... someone broke the wall of my subconscious. But it can't be."

"You killed Shakti a long time ago, Michael. This is what happens when you wait so long to sleep. It was just a bad vision."

"She was real, whoever it was, I'm sure of it."

Melody rubbed his back and touched her hand to his face.

"I wonder if the tribes of Pavonia are correct in their suspicions of a revived Zurvan witch..." he said.

"The Zurvans are no longer what they were," she reminded him.

"Then perhaps it is some new evil."

Melody coaxed him to the bed. He laid down and stared at his lover's irises, moving in swirls like leaves in the wind.

"Something troubles you beyond this vicious harkening. Beyond what you saw in Africa."

Michael nodded. "Today I went to the prisons and talked with the inmates. What I found there disturbed me. There were good men in there, men who had been wrongly accused of domestic violence and had their children taken from them."

"Those men had their chance to be good fathers."

"I could see the men's souls, Melody. They were pure of heart."

"Then why were they in prison?"

"Because the system you've created gives total power to the mother. Because the rage within the hearts of men is there to last, and in a utopian socialist society they have nowhere to put it. It was there when the first man threw a spear and will be there until the last man is killed by its inglorious thrust. We must embrace the nature of men; their visceral need for violence must be brought out in some other way. Without war to expend their vitality, men bring the war home. We must find another way to channel their nature."

"Or quell it altogether."

"Such a thing would come about as easily as one might douse the flame in my eyes."

"Do not forget what patriarchy once did to the world," Melody warned.

"And yet patriarchy made humans what they are. When women are pregnant and vulnerable and children are small, who protects them?"

"Protects them from what?"

"Threats both temporal and celestial. There will always be an enemy. You don't bear the sensation of hunting these jackals as I do."

"Are you saying I'm apathetic?"

"On the contrary. I'm saying you're more sensitive now than in the days when you'd kill your own master to save the planet."

"There's something more, isn't there?" Melody prodded, her jawline sharpened from grinding her teeth.

Michael looked at her longingly, as if hoping the pity in

his complexion would bring them to an understanding and resolve his buried grief.

"I want a son."

He stared passionately into her eyes. She turned her cheek.

"Michael, you know how I feel about having children."

"Why do you not even consider it?"

"Because we are Immortals, Michael. Tala herself said there can only be two divine beings and they must be lovers."

"And yet she sits atop her ice throne above the arctic circle orchestrating the climate beyond the council's authority."

"It is because she presides there that our climate is stable. Without her it would take hundreds if not thousands of years to re-balance our atmosphere after the eruption."

"If it is a rule given by the prophecy, it is a rule that died with Shakti's Empire. Do you not desire children?"

Melody stared at him with a solemn gaze.

"It doesn't matter what I want. I must do what is best for the organisms of Earth. That is my destiny; my one and only responsibility. Are you not happy with me?"

"I am happy with you and I love you dearly. But perhaps it is because I never had a father that I desire to be one so badly. You can understand that, can't you?"

"Of course I can. We're Immortals. We have nothing but time. I'll consider it, my love."

They kissed and held each other, though inside Melody's thoughts swirled anxiously. She knew well these issues would soon spill over into the council like a cauldron of tar if not handled carefully and secretly.

After a while, Michael broke himself from her embrace and headed towards the horse stables. There he saddled his trusted steed and rode off into the night, galloping swiftly along mountain passes, through wide rivers and down into low crevices, where dormant raiders cowered as he and Apollo rumbled past like ghosts of the frigid night, gone again as soon as they'd come.

CHAPTER 42 – SERAPHIC YOUTH

As the sun rose the following morning, so did the morning air from the composite tarmac at Almuruna's airport. Devonia and Xiang entered the terminal and walked into the express line leading to their craft.

"Is flying scary?" Devonia asked.

"It's safer than driving a car."

"What's a car?"

Xiang laughed. "Every ship at port here is made of recycled parts and runs on sustainable aviation biofuel. But don't be fooled by their affordability. These ships are faster and more efficient than any plane before the Eruption Wars. They are suitable for transporting both foreign dignitaries and everyday passengers all across the globe. Though most technology these days is used sparsely, airships are utilized primarily for farming, emergency rescues, and commercial flights."

"So they're safe, then?"

"Very safe, don't worry. This is going to be fun," Xiang reassured her, smiling.

They boarded their ship, which had been painted sparkling white and fitted with two massive engines on either wing. With only fifteen passengers, the small vessel could zip through the skies with ease and go from central Almuruna to Cape Town South Africa in less than six hours.

The ship taxied out and when the lane was clear, they blasted off. Devonia felt the sudden thrust and gasped with excitement as she looked out the window with wonder in her eyes as they rose into the sky and glided above the thin clouds with ease.

"It's beautiful!"

"Wait until we fly over the Pyramids of Giza on the return journey!"

"No way! That's one of the Seven Wonders of the ancient world!" Suddenly, Devonia furrowed her brow and her expression became more serious. "Ambassador Yu, why do I get to see all these fantastic things? I'm only eleven but I feel like I'm being treated like royalty. Where are all the others I'm supposed to be training with? Don't I have to go to school?"

"Why go to school when you can see the world and experience it first hand?"

"I guess that's true but... I just miss my friends is all..."

"I'm sorry you miss your friends, but you'll make new friends during our travels, I promise."

"I hope so!" She paused, then looked over at Xiang with wide eyes. "I hope you don't think I'm being ungrateful, Ambassador Yu. I really am happy to be here. I mean... Empress Melody is my hero and to be learning from her is the coolest thing in the world."

"She is very fond of you too, Devonia."

The child gave a relieved smiled and looked out the window. The mountains of northern Italy were already receding behind them.

Mists cascaded up from the ocean's curls and wafted across Devonia's face as she breathed in the pure, salty air of Cape Town's coast. The tide crashed and gnawed at the cliffs beside her as she wiggled her toes in the sand. She cupped a hermit crab in her hands as Boris scuttled around her feet.

"Look Boris! He's got a shell too!"

One hundred statues lined the ridge behind her, all dedicated to the holy mothers and doulas of the new world: African women who'd birthed newborns on Creation Day. The sun dipped into the western horizon and nearly all the clouds were beaten away by its settling, casting the stone monoliths in a soft pink light, those relic goddesses, their tall figures bathing in the evening's tender wash. Behind Devonia, Xiang stood with Yemaja, Protector of South Africa and Third Princess to the Holy Shrine of Queen Parvati. They stood with Yemaja's guards looking out at the crisp blue deep.

"Thank you for coming so quickly, Princess Xiang. You must be very busy as the empress's ambassador," Yemaja said. Her long black hair fell over her ebony skin, and her eyes were wide and beautiful, one blue and one brown like gems or sister moons.

"I am busy, yes, but as you said, I am the empress's conduit, so I am pleased to help you whichever way I can. What can I do for you, sister?"

"There are men making weapons, to the north near what was once our border with Namibia. They've diverted water from irrigation culverts to their mills and are forging swords, axes, and crude guns. Sometimes armor when they can find the right materials."

"Do you know what for?"

"They say it's for defense."

"Against?"

Yemaja pulled a dagger from her waistband and handed it to the ambassador. On its ivory hilt had been carved an image of a lion-headed man coiled by a serpent.

"Mithra. One of the Zurvan deities," Xiang said.

"Apparently there is more evidence where this was found, and some even say they hear strange rituals being performed in the wilderness."

Xiang held the blade in both hands, inspecting its details for hexes.

"They wanted you to find this," Xiang said.

"So it's a threat of some sort?"

"More like a warning. I wonder why they would come so far…"

"I'm not sure. But as Protector of these lands, it's rather troubling."

"The Zurvans made a treaty with the emperor and empress nearly forty years ago. They have reverted to their origins of spiritual healing. The days of Zurvan domination are long behind us."

"Would you trust them?"

Xiang looked at Princess Yemaja and thought about the question, but did not answer.

That night, Devonia came down with a terrible sickness. She cried and vomited as they travelled to the hospital, clenching her stomach all the way. Xiang left her there with the doctor, promising to check on her later the following day.

The next morning Devonia woke up to the sun shining through the curtains. Her nausea had passed – the anti-viral medication had worked – and she had managed to sleep for at least a few hours before the rest of the ward had risen. Nurses bustled about and were handing out breakfasts. Devonia sat up in her bed and looked around the ward. More children lay next to her, some still stirring awake in their beds.

"Hey! Pssst!" an African girl the same age as Devonia whispered next to her.

"What?"

She lifted the sheets on her bed and unveiled Boris, chomping on some lettuce.

"Hey! That's my tortoise!"

"I know, dummy! I'm trying to hide him from the nurse!"

"Oh. Thanks."

"No problem. Sorry for calling you a dummy. But we got to be quiet."

"He's cute, isn't he," Devonia whispered.

"Oh yeah, he's super cute."

"What's your name?"

"Uhlanga. Uli for short. What about you?"

"I'm Devonia. I got really sick last night, that's why I'm here. What are you here for?"

"I was kidnapped. My parents think they were Zurvans but no one really knows. My parents sent me all the way here from Namibia so they wouldn't find me. The hospital wanted to check me out in case they messed with me. They didn't though. I feel fine. How do you feel now?"

"I feel much better. That's insane that you got kidnapped! Was it scary?"

"It was really scary at first, but when I behaved well they stopped watching me. After a few days I escaped in the middle of the night and ran for miles until I found someone who could help me."

"Why did they want to keep you?"

"They said I was special, that I was the reincarnation of their ancient master."

"That's kinda cool."

"Yeah, it's pretty of cool I guess. I don't think it's true though."

Just then, the nurse walked up to Devonia.

"Glad to see you're both up. How do you feel young one?" she asked, turning to Devonia.

"A lot better. What happened?"

"Oh, just a stomach bug. We gave you some medicine and you should be okay now, but we want to keep you here for the day just to make sure."

"Do I have to stay in this bed all day?"

"No, not at all. There is a cafe downstairs and a courtyard where you can go to read or play. Just take it easy, okay? You had a long night. Ambassador Yu should be here in a few hours to visit you."

"Okay. Do you want to go play outside?" Devonia asked Uli.

"Sure!"

"Not too long Uli, you have an assessment whenever the doctor is ready."

"Okay!"

They leapt from their beds and Uli handed Devonia her tortoise. As they ran out of the room, the nurse furrowed her brow and yelled.

"Hey, what is that turtle doing in here?"

"He's a tortoise!" Devonia said as she giggled down the hall with Boris and her new friend.

"Boris the tortoise!" they yelled, laughing all the way.

Xiang flew to southern Namibia where the sand cathedrals towered over the desert and spiral-horned ungulates pursued grafts of flora between vast stretches of dunes and feldspar formations. She found the village at the center of a shallow valley. The mill in the distance spewed a grey smoke as she walked from the craft to meet the tribal leader. He bowed to her, and her him, and they retreated to his vista to drink tea.

"Come sit, Ambassador. Welcome to my homeland," he exclaimed, grinning widely and coaxing her to her seat. He lifted his hands to the view like a composer and opened them, proud of his country.

"Thank you, Chioto. You have a beautiful village. I can see why you are so adamant about protecting it."

"Yes. Yes. We've had many years of peace here, so you can imagine the heartache the last few weeks have caused us. Kidnapping and other nefarious schemes have cast a shadow upon my lands. Many people are worried this will keep up if we do not do something, but I fear we have done all we can."

"I appreciate your independence and self-sufficiency. However, are you aware that you can call upon the emperor's detachment, who are specifically trained in counterinsurgency? You don't have to put your own people at risk."

Chioto drank his tea and contemplated his next words for a moment.

"I am gracious that His Holiness would do that for us, but there is a part of me that does not want foreign legions entering our land."

"It is only a small contingent—"

"But they are not from here, Ambassador. Nor do they have the connection with my people that I do, and my soldiers do."

"Yes, well, you do know that arms production is illegal—"

"We are only building weapons to protect ourselves. We

do not have enough people here to invade anyone. I am a family man who's only crime is being prepared to defend myself against attackers."

"I understand, Chioto, and as long as your words are true, the council will have no need to take legal action against you. Right now, I am more concerned about the presence of the Zurvan clan in your area. I saw the dagger, but I need more proof."

"There is a young girl from this village who was taken a few days ago. She escaped and came back to us. For fear of her being found again we sent her somewhere she would be safe."

"They didn't harm her?"

"Not at all. She said she was treated better than she would be here, like royalty."

Xiang sipped her tea. She gazed over the orange desert as she speculated, watching the sun burn the Earth lethargically.

"Shiva is the current leader of the Zurvan clan, and resides in Nepal. I doubt he would come this far for something of that nature. They must be satellites of the order, shaman scouts scouring the planet for new apprentices."

Chioto nodded. "I will pray that God does not let our world be destroyed by them once again."

"Perhaps that is not their motive. Maybe they want to help protect it," Xiang speculated.

"Regardless, I think the Zurvans know something we don't, Ambassador."

When they had finished tea, a brewing sandstorm forced Xiang to say her goodbyes and depart back to Cape Town. As she flew her craft up and away from the storm, she couldn't help but wonder if the tumultuous winds were in fact orchestrated by those desert witch-doctors moving her out of the way, like keen pawns against bishops across the global chessboard.

○

Xiang returned to the South African hospital where she found Devonia and Uli using a soccer ball to play keep-away from Boris. The tortoise had hidden in his shell to protect himself from both the hyper girls and the sun's relentless rays.

"Hello Devonia, you seem well."

"I feel great! This is Uli."

"Hello Uli, I am Ambassador Xiang Yu."

Uli waved shyly.

"Come here for a moment both of you, if you would."

Devonia and Uli ran over to Xiang. The tortoise made a dash for the water dish.

"We're going to stay one more night, then leave in the morning."

"But we just got here," Devonia groaned.

"Yes, well, I have a feeling we will be back very soon," Xiang said, smiling.

"But what about Uli? Can we write to each other? Please?"

"That's a marvelous idea. I'm sure we will see you soon, Uli. You ready, Devonia?"

Devonia gave Uli a firm hug, sad to be leaving her new friend so soon.

"Goodbye Ambassador Yu. Goodbye Devonia. Don't forget Boris!"

Devonia ran over and picked up her tortoise before

waving goodbye and leaving with Xiang.

The next morning, Devonia chatted almost all the way back to Almuruna.

"Slow down, child, you're going to run out of breath!" Xiang chuckled.

"So when I woke up Uli was there – apparently she was kidnapped, can you believe it? – and she helped me save Boris from the nurses and we ran outside and then we played tug of war and then—"

"Did you say Uli was kidnapped?"

"Yeah, she said she was kidnapped by Zurvans."

Xiang's face turned white as she realized who Uli was.

"Ambassador Yu, what's a Zurvan?

"A very powerful person. Like the ones who destroyed the world over four decades ago."

"Oh…"

"They aren't like that anymore, at least they say they aren't."

"Well I hope she isn't kidnapped again. Even if she is the reincarnation of some ancient master person… do you think I could be a reincarnation of an ancient warrior? I'm really good at fighting."

Devonia stood up and pretended to punch and kick while making what she considered to be battle noises. Xiang smiled, briefly writing something in her notebook, before leaning her head back and listening to the rest of Devonia's story as she drifted to sleep, knowing that another worthy apprentice was well within reach. The bidding war for the next generation of golden children was underway.

C

Upon their return, Xiang and Devonia had a few days to rest from their travels. Empress Melody was informed about the Zurvans and their obsession with the girl Uhlanga, named after the goddess of swamp lands. She didn't take immediate action. Instead, the Empress decided to meditate on the findings and send a transmission to Master Shiva himself.

One evening, Melody lay in bed, looking up at the ceiling where each constellation sparkled brightly, the diamond inlays surrounded by gemstones of dark blue and black.

Michael walked into the room naked, as he most often preferred. In the right light one could see the four faint red lines across his chest, carved by the bear he'd slain in his youth, where shredded human skin had been cauterized by a sword dipped in flame, forever engraved in him as his Sararan cells refused to fix what wasn't broken.

"You didn't tell me you were considering a second apprentice."

"I know you want a child yourself, Michael, but these girls have something special, I swear it," Melody pleaded, hopeful that he would not plunge them into another argument.

"My love, it's alright. I understand what you are trying to do, and I fully support you."

Melody sat up in surprise as he came over to her.

"You do?"

"Of course I do. Just because I want a son doesn't mean you can't have apprentices. You could open up a whole school for gifted children."

"Yes, well, we tried that and it didn't work."

"Only because you didn't have the right students. Maybe now you do."

"Maybe," she said, smiling softly at the thought.

He smiled fondly down at her and moved in to kiss her neck.

"What are you doing?" she asked teasingly.

"Kissing you."

Melody leaned into him, her eyes fluttering closed as he continued to press hot kisses down her neck and across her shoulders. As he nipped her pulse point she gasped, reaching for him and twining her fingers through his hair, pulling him down towards her breasts, barely hidden by her robe. Pushing the fabric aside, Michael teased her nipples, making her squirm for more.

"Melody, my love."

"Yes," she panted, moaning as he began to circle the apex of her thighs with his fingers.

"My goddess... my queen."

"Yes!"

"Make a baby with me," he breathed, nudging at her entrance with his hardness.

"Yes... now... please, I need you!"

Michael captured her lips with his as he thrust inside her, swallowing her moans of pleasure. He kissed her roughly, plunging into her at increasing pace as their pleasure built.

"I want a son!" he yelled, his rhythm becoming erratic.

"Yes!" Melody cried out, her head thrown back in pleasure. "Give me your seed! Give it to me!"

Melody's legs wrapped tightly around her lover, gripping him to her and locking his seed inside her as they came together. Michael gazed into his lover's eyes, knowing this was it; they would finally be gifted with a child; a third generation Sararan to rule the world forevermore.

Melody smiled softly as they both came down from their high, wrapping her body around him like a snake entwining her victim as Michael lay there, elated, more in love with his wife than ever before.

CHAPTER 43 – SILENT SCREAM

Xiang was walking Devonia to breakfast when she noticed the main entrance of the palace was surrounded by monks, warding off the press with their bamboo staffs.

"What's going on?" Devonia asked.

"I'm not sure," Xiang said, wondering herself.

"Ambassador Yu! You've been called for an emergency council!" an advisor shouted from the bottom of the large stairway.

"I'll be right there! Devonia, go to the dining hall and I'll meet you there when I'm finished, okay?"

Devonia saluted and went off with the advisor as Xiang walked through the halls at an anxious pace. When the white doors of the royal court opened, the council was in chaos. People were yelling out of turn and throwing papers in the air angrily as the emperor and empress sat in their seats calmly, watching the free-for-all and listening to the arguments, deciphering for themselves what to make of the mayhem.

"What happened?" Xiang asked.

"Councilman Beller was assassinated this morning. A copper plate charge was placed outside his doorway. Sliced him clear in half... left a scene for the whole neighborhood."

"What? When?"

"About two hours ago. There aren't any leads yet; everyone's on high alert."

Xiang looked up with wide eyes. Several people were screaming at once.

"We should have never redacted the mandate!"

"The mandate is what caused this!"

"He was surely killed by antisemites!"

"How are we going to keep the peace with people murdering council members?"

Michael stood and requested order. "Would the council settle down so we can have a decent discussion?!"

His voice was drowned out as the arguments continued.

Finally, Melody whistled loud enough to clear the room of sound. The piercing echo blasted the walls and no one spoke as she stared them down like ill-behaved children. The ringing in their ears would not subside for some time.

"May I remind each member of this council that assassination is something you all risk by being here. By overreacting, we provide leverage for whoever committed this hellacious crime. I promise you that justice will reign down upon the person or persons responsible. There will be a far-sweeping investigation with our best agents working on the case."

"Then let it be you, Empress," Sage requested, "Are you not a goddess of divine clairvoyance, who can see through the world's mantle itself?"

"I cannot be everything to everyone, and neither can Emperor Michael. If it would please the council, I would like to solidify the mandate during this meeting."

"At a time like this? That very proposition is what caused all this chaos!" yelled a flustered council member.

"Silence! Let the empress speak," Michael said, scowling at him.

"All in favor of the Religious Freedoms Amendment, raise your hand."

More than half the council raised their hands. As Michael's hand rose high, Melody winked at her lover and hammered her gravel.

"From this day forward, it will be illegal to practice ancient monotheistic religions in the open air, as directed in the 113th Amendment of the New World Constitution of 2060. All symbols and practices of such religions henceforth shall be hidden from sight on public property, both on clothing and buildings that are not specified places of worship."

Many people clapped. Some frustrated council members were already leaving before she had finished.

"I hereby end this council until tomorrow's weekly meeting. By then we will surely know more about our dear friend David, who would have been happy to see this mandate passed in the wake of his death. A funeral service will be announced soon to honor his legacy."

Melody and Michael left the council together. As Melody walked out of the room, she burst into tears, the crimson streams painting her face with woe. She collapsed in the hall and Michael knelt by her side to hold her.

"Sweetheart," he attempted to console her.

"David was like my little brother," she wept. "I loved him so much. He helped us save the world!"

"How could I forget? Only when he handed Shakti the flower did she let her guard down, and it was then my arrow found its way into her cold heart. Without his bravery we would not have been able to make this world what it is today."

"And yet some people would rather spit on his grave!"

"We'll find who did this, and when we do, they will be punished."

He held her close as she crouched in a fetal position. Maids and royal dignitaries walked by with fearful reactions. Most had never seen a goddess have a nervous breakdown, but as rarely as it appeared, her humanity had never truly left her; in her grief, she was human: a wounded animal taken hostage by its own fears, vulnerable as the day it was born.

On the same day as the funeral, General Fredrickson and a team of twenty men flew across the lands of Northern Pavonia. They passed over the great plains, where vast stretches of farmland replaced the blanket of ash, and through the mountains, snowcapped and gorgeous, to that land of eternal volcanism where boiling pools, geysers and mud pits could still be found in the young forest that grew after Creation Day. Caldera was much like it had been a hundred years before, lying dormant like a sleeping dragon.

The team split in half and scoured the basin, hiking through Shakti's former domain in search of anything suspicious. Even something as insignificant as an oddly shaped cloud was to be noted. They flew multiple passovers, scanning three thousand square miles for energy levels matching Sararan or Aradian auras. Nothing came back. After ten days of deep reconnaissance, the team went back to Almuruna empty handed, claiming the native man who had requested them was just heeding the warnings of his elders, as they feared the echoes of the past catching them unawares.

Although the native chief had explicitly requested Michael's presence, the emperor never went to Caldera. Instead, Michael took a leave of absence and traveled to his uncle's residence in Germany. When he arrived at the small mountain village, the streets were bustling with cheer as snow fell and accumulated on the alpine settlement. Many in the town were steadily preparing for Christmas, though the word was not mentioned. People were strolling and gift giving in the most religiously ambiguous way to appease the new laws. Children wrapped trees in lights and ornaments, but no angel was set atop. Women who'd once worn burkas donned dark blue and green robes, their hair tied back, their long lashes reaching out like tree branches catching large snowflakes. Michael walked through the streets without royal dress or insignia, for he was a man of the people. Still, the citizens of Bonn saw his unmistakable eyes and bowed.

"Schöne ferien, my good people," he said, walking with a placid smile and patting children on the head as he passed.

People continued to bow as the musicians and dancers played on behind him, a wave of honor granting him righteous passage. A six-year-old boy holding a menorah hid the brass lamp behind his back as Michael walked up to him. His parents looked at each other, worried they would be fined, or worse.

"Hello young one. What do you have there?"

"It's our menorah for Hannukah. I'm not supposed to have it, am I?"

Michael crouched down to the child's level.

"Is tonight the lighting of the first candle?"

The child nodded. Michael put his hand out and upturned his palm. The child handed him the eight candles that branched from a single stem. With the tips of his thumb and forefinger, Michael rubbed the wick of the first candle and made fire from their friction. He smiled from behind the small flame, and the child smiled back in wonder.

"May your candles burn long and bright this Hannukah."

His parents hugged Michael close and thanked him.

"Amen. Ha'el sheg'molkha kol tov."

"Amen," Michael said. Then he turned and kept walking through the festivities.

C

Michael entered a home of some of the world's oldest survivors of the Post-Eruption Wars, tough as nails and treated luxuriously as ordered by the empress. Poinsettias had been placed on the mantles by the entryway and the hall smelled of fresh cinnamon and spices. The caretakers greeted him and led him up the stairs and through the marble halls to the study on the top floor, where William spent his afternoons.

The old man turned his chair slowly as Michael walked into the study.

"Nephew! How the hell are ya?"

"I'm well, William. How are you?"

"As well as a ninety-year-old man can be, I suppose."

Michael walked over and crouched beside him, hugging the frail old man. Will was wearing a green sweater, the outline of his dog tags visible under the soft wool.

"How's the place?"

"Yes, yes, everything's fine here, although they don't let me wander around like they used to."

"I didn't know you could 'wander' much at all these days."

"Oh is that so, smartass?"

Michael smiled briefly at the old man's humor. But the reason for his visit could not be avoided, and his fond expression soon wavered.

"You heard about David, I'm sure."

"Yes, I did. Do you know who did it yet?"

"Not yet."

Will sighed as Michael sat down on a chair across from

his uncle. The books reached high to the ceiling, illuminated by the soft gray blue light from the windows. The room was cold, but neither of them minded.

"There are new evils at play in the world, Uncle. David's assassination is just the beginning. The Zurvans are reaching far and wide to find new apprentices."

"The Zurvans aren't a threat anymore. If what you say is true, this is something else. It probably doesn't help that your council is disintegrating over the new amendment to the constitution."

Michael nodded.

"It is for your wisdom and knowledge that I come to you in these times of uncertainty. Are you still averse to becoming Sararan, so close to death's door?"

"You'd piss off Tala like that? Isn't there a rule that there can only be two Immortals?"

"Yet she herself is an Immortal," Michael grumbled. "Besides, I don't take orders from that Aradian witch. I will kill her without hesitation if she ever leaves her post."

Will took out a picture of his wife from his pocket and looked at it longingly.

"I thank you for the offer, Nephew, but Lakshmi is waiting for me. I do not wish to live forever. Everything must die. Even you."

"I know, yet the very thought evades Melody. She thinks it will be she and I ruling Earth forevermore. She fails to realize the irrational goal of blessing all mutants, people, and species at once. Eventually someone will become envious, and eventually downright malicious in their envy. Melody is trying to rewrite nature's laws, disregarding the fact that the laws of nature are fixed beyond our control."

"Is she still reluctant to have a child with you?"

"I gave her my seed. She claims to finally want to be a

parent. But I am skeptical. I don't believe she wants children. A personal choice, no doubt, but one I cannot stand any longer. A deep anger swells within me, as if I have been infected with some nameless hunger. I come to you for guidance, Uncle."

Will looked out the window. Snow fell silently in clumps on the cobblestone below.

"You look like you did the day you graduated bootcamp. You still have that knife I gave you?"

Michael unsheathed the blade from his boot and handed it to Will. He gripped it tightly and gazed at it with soft eyes.

"My grandfather told me a story about this knife once. It has Eugene's initials, but it was his father who gave it to him. Your great grandfather, Samuel, forged it from an old railroad spike, and was the first one in the family to take it to war. He turned nineteen on his way to Germany to fight the Nazis. This knife carried him through many battles, and I speak genuinely when I say it has a certain power to it, like an instrument of rituals. Well, after they'd killed about every damn thing in the country, he stayed to serve as a military policeman. One day he was walking down the street in Frankfurt when he found a wounded German officer who'd surrendered, sitting on the side of the road selling his last possessions in an attempt to start a new life. Samuel was fascinated by an accordion the man was selling. He asked where the man had purchased it. The man said he picked it up from a dead Italian soldier in Naples. It was apparently a beautiful instrument, with elephant ivory keys and a sleek black finish. Samuel could have just taken it. Spoils of war. But he traded the man two cartons of cigarettes for the accordion. The cigarettes were valuable enough at the time to feed the man for a month. Before he shipped the accordion as a Christmas present to his wife back in the

States, he carved his child's initials EEB into the knife handle and put it in the instrument's case as a present to his newborn son. Not long after, some crazy Hitler die-hard stormed his base and shot him before being torn to pieces by GIs, and the accordion didn't make it back to the States. But strangely enough, the knife showed up one day on his wife's doorstep, delivered first class from a U.S. military transport."

"Whoever stole the accordion didn't steal the knife, or couldn't."

"Precisely. Somehow, they knew the knife's power, consciously or not."

Michael interjected, "Power objects, especially weapons, can trap the souls they take, particularly in times of demonic flourishing."

"Right. But likewise, Samuel saved that man's life by giving the man the cigarettes. He could easily have stolen the goods and then expected the man to limp up to the door and open it for him the next day. But Samuel was not that kind of man."

"Did his virtues serve him in the end? The war had only technically ended. They had not yet entered the humanitarian phase."

"Yes, but that phase never truly happened until the wall came down in the '80s, decades later."

Michael thought for a moment before responding. "Imagine how long it took for Germany to stand on its own two feet after the war, after already rebuilding from the First World War, and then look at our post-eruption world. How much have humans really changed? How much can they change? Genocide or Utopia... the nature of man is a devious constant. It's all determined by how much and how long we're willing to lie to ourselves."

"But there aren't any diseases; there aren't any wars. Everything is near perfect."

Michael nodded and looked at his uncle with a serious demeanor.

"Maybe that's what I'm afraid of. The more beautiful something is, the greater the desire to violate it."

"Why are you suddenly talking like this? What makes you so paranoid?"

"A woman has plagued my dreams of late. Her eyes are as bright as the surface of the sun, and she speaks blasphemy through flaming lips. I feel as though I have seen her before, that she's gazed upon me in this life, and I her. Perhaps it is this mysterious witch who targeted David and alerted the Zurvans."

"For both your sake and the world's, I hope you find out soon."

◯

For a time, Devonia's curriculum was reduced. She explored the palace grounds, read through half the books in the palace library and walked by the riverside with Xiang, though only when the ambassador could part from the political upheaval erupting at Melody's helm. Her lessons continued but at odd intervals. Luckily for everyone, Devonia's intense curiosity made her eager to learn in whatever form she could, and her ability to absorb and retain knowledge proved to equate with persons almost twice her age.

It was four days after Christmas when she and Xiang were laying poinsettias and white lilies in the gardens for fallen heroes. Each small bronze plaque mounted on the cobblestone wall stood for the sacrifices of the volunteers during the Post-Eruption Wars. A large circular golden plaque for all the nameless veterans spread wide under them as Devonia swept the fresh snow from its icy surface.

"What was that sound?" Devonia asked.

The ground shook slightly and Xiang looked up. Her velvet blue hood fell behind her nape and her cloak rustled with urgent movement.

"Come with me child. Now!"

She took Devonia's hand and quickly led her down a path away from the palace. A monk nearby saw them escape and coaxed them his way.

"Here, Ambassador!"

They dropped under a stone henge and crept through the sanctuary of the catacombs, the monk lighting a torch to lead the way. Moments later, they reached a chamber, the walls lined with monks, meditating quietly with candles lit in small spirals neatly set atop their wool robes.

"Send someone to retrieve the empress!" Xiang ordered.

The monk who'd led them nodded, and as if reading his master's mind, a young monk stood from the back of the chamber and hurried into one of the dark passages.

"What happened?" Devonia asked.

Xiang kissed Devonia's forehead then sat and closed her eyes, running her fingers along her wrists to let her bones breathe. The sensation calmed her anxiety, and as she looked back up at the confused, frightened face of Devonia, she remembered the empress's wise words and let them imbue her with strength.

Beneath blankets of mink fur and royal silk, the empress

slept, breathing the air filled with frankincense and sweet burning herbs. She dreamed her way to salvation, recharging her constantly evolving brain cells. In an instant she awoke, as the furious cry of her lover pried her from her astral temple.

"What have you done with my child?" Michael screamed. He surfaced from the shadows with eyes burning like the belly of hell. His hands and fingers were out-stretched to the side – a threatening stance – for he was volatile sorcerer unable to contain his wrath any longer.

"What do you speak of?" she asked, attempting to counteract his anger with quiet words.

"I can smell him on you! Our son you killed, MY son!" he screamed, sending a blasting heatwave into her, slamming her body against the bed's headrest.

"Michael, please!" she wailed, leaping from the bed in panic.

"All I wanted was a family for us!" he exclaimed. "For the future of our planet! But you had to silence life! You had to abort our unborn son without my approval!"

"It's my body, Michael!" she sobbed, sliding her foot across the floor and unleashing a wall of bamboo in thick rows. She ducked behind them and ran into Michael's study, toppling the large desk and hiding behind its barrier. "I'm not ready to be a mother. Please, Michael, calm down! What do you accomplish by harming me?"

In a burst of anger and fire, Michael shattered the bamboo poles and stormed into the study. Flaming leaves fell by his feet.

"You don't want what's best for us or the world. Your fear reflects just how selfish and cowardly you've become," Michael snarled, his face disgusted, his soul rotting with delusional obsessions.

"What's come over you? What haunts you?" Melody cried.

"You will pay for this!" Michael bellowed with both his voice and his mind; all his heart and all his hate.

He pushed his hands forward and a wave of blue and orange flame rolled toward Melody. She cried blood and wiped a crimson splotch across the desk, propagating ponderosa pine branches and stems to block the heated front. Sparks rained down on her as she cowered under Michael's wrath. The stems grew thick into branches and trunks and no matter how hot the fire became, Melody's blood thickened the bark and resisted consumption. After some time, Michael retreated the grounds altogether and Melody was left in a dome of solid wood, smoldering in the center of the world's largest library. Ash and burning pages fell to the floor like dead doves, their toxic ink once again spoiling the halls of an empire in bloom.

After realizing her torment was at an end, Melody broke through the crackling softwood layers and crawled over the glass shards left scattered from the shattered windows, letting the falling snowflakes melt on her half-charred skin. Bloody tears fell down her body, but she let the wind contain her cries of grief, sobbing silently beneath the white sky.

After the violent disappearance of Michael and amidst chaos in her kingdom, Melody fled to the northern-most part of the globe, where almost no living thing dwelled. The white drifts of ice spread vast like frozen waves in that desolate arctic desert. The wind howled in icy currents, pouring itself around eddies created by the deity at large. Through the blasting gusts of ice shards, Melody could detect Tala's aura like a hot needle in a dry haystack, for where there is only death, life becomes a sacred beacon. She walked on through the blizzard and suddenly stood at the step of Tala's ice throne, tall and carved with geometric fidelity, where the infamous Aradian sat, her crown of glacial blue ice reflecting the light from her animate eyes of past memories. The small and beautiful being stood and bowed to Melody, who bowed in return.

"Goddess of the Moon and Sun, I come to you in great peril!" Melody exclaimed.

Tala spoke telepathically, for her energy was nearly entirely focused on her aeromancy. "You fear your lover's body has been overtaken by a vile specter. You have come to me to help find him. Look back, Empress, the clues are there. David's assassination, the surprising skills of your new apprentice, the reinvigoration of the Zurvan clan. All occurrences are contained in the plan of this unknown diviner."

"Do they relate to the prophecy?"

"None can say. What authors remain are translating the scripture as we speak."

"What does Devonia have to do with any of it?"

"Everything. She is the reincarnation of Pavonis."

"How do you know for sure?"

"Using the moon as a repeater, I've routed the parallax of the Pavo constellation. The red dwarf Gliese 693 was extinguished the same day she was born."

"That star is over eighteen lightyears from Earth."

"I have felt its death before the light has reached us. And so has she. You forget she is Queen of Borrowed Light." Tala smirked, her child-like smile deceptive.

"How did it die?"

"The star was bleeding it's hydrogen slowly. It should have lived another seven billion years. The spirit of salvation has been called upon yet again to relieve the world of this new burden. When the photons of its last light finally reach us, Devonia's soul will germinate. This cosmic sacrifice was made to honor us."

"By who?"

"God, of course."

"So Uli..." Melody whispered.

"Uhlanga is quite possibly the reincarnation of Zou Cheng, for her astrology hints to that of a grand teacher. But Zou disguised his soul with another so that sorcerers of the future could not distinguish him."

"That would explain why the Zurvans were in Namibia trying to kidnap her. Since you are so wise and clairvoyant, Lord Tala, do you know where to find Michael?"

"If Michael is possessed, his possessor has been steeped in dark magick and has reduced their ionic signature beyond my line of sight. Like Pavonis, this witch is using astral camouflage."

"There must be a way to detect them!"

"One cannot see what isn't there. When Pavonis brought David and you with her on her journey, I could finally track her because your human bodies acted as antennae for her frequency. Until that point, she was intrinsically merged with the species around her."

"What kind of divine cloak could mask your sight now?"

"You ask the wrong questions. There are those who performed under Shakti's orders only to rise up themselves."

"The Zurvan priests?"

"No. Someone far more sinister. Someone who feeds off others pain for the sheer sensation of it. For power; for pure obsession. I will not say its name, for the ears of the demonic are beckoned by their own title. In word and in mind, they can hear it like a bell ringing in the empty sky, and you will be under their spell before you can initiate your defenses. I do not fear this malicious foe, but for the sake of slowing its progress, let its name never be uttered. This being lurks in the trenches of space-time where it seethes an endless hunger, a cosmic bottom feeder clenching and devouring souls taken adrift by rogue dimensions."

Melody stared at Tala for a while, remembering well the titanium plated war machine she once was, and how she murdered Lily in cold blood along with billions of other innocent people.

"Go to where the only true shroud of darkness exists. There you will find your sorcerer."

"The sunken palace of Caldera... there is not a more pitch black place beyond the void of space. You will help me destroy her, if it comes to that?"

"It will come to that, but I cannot yet go. To leave the climate at this time of year would disrupt the planets weather patterns indefinitely. This task is for you and you alone. Perhaps you should start teaching your apprentice to be both a divine healer and violent nomad. The world will need her to be both."

A vision of Tala and her sister Mayari meditating played through her eye, a memory of the day she was reunited with her sister and met her new master who guided the estranged twins and would change the Zurvan Order forever. Melody looked into her eyes and bowed as she walked away, knowing something drastic would happen to her kingdom if she did not act on Tala's words soon.

CHAPTER 44 – BLACK WIDOW

On January 2nd, 2099, under increasing pressure from the council, Empress Melody held a summit to discuss Michael's desertion. Many members were curious and concerned about his absence, having heard rumors of violence in the South Wing. Xiang sat patiently in her seat, watching some members shake their heads in anger as the Empress spoke.

"I speak to you with a heavy heart today, councilmen and women. Our beloved emperor has left the palace and may not return. His whereabouts are unknown, but we are seeking information regarding his location and motives."

"Can you not detect him with your Sararan sensibilities?" someone asked.

"I'll open up the council for discussion once—"

"Can you not detect him with your Sararan sensibilities?" they asked again.

"I cannot. He has clouded my foresight and ability to consciously or subconsciously distinguish his presence."

"Empress Melody, was there a domestic dispute between yourself and the emperor recently?" Ziven asked. He tipped his brow and hunched in his decorated uniform.

"If you mean to accuse me, I will admit no fault. Michael is ill. His mood swings and violent outbursts are the result of his increased subjection to deployments by the program you are directing, General," Melody argued.

"You know as well as I do that Michael volunteers for those operations. He is nearly impossible to kill. Why wouldn't we utilize him as an asset? At least Michael has always been willing to get his hands dirty, while you sit and make policies behind the backs of both our citizens and council members. Why don't you tell the council the full story, Empress?" he said, standing suddenly.

"How dare you insult the empress in such a way! This council has rules against speaking with such disrespect!" Sage yelled, pointing at him sternly.

"Rules implemented by her and her alone. No wonder Michael left! How many other laws did you pass while he was away fighting for your poisonous reformation?"

"General!" Melody exclaimed and stood. Her eyes darkened to a murky forest green. Her hand clenched her quartz gravel tightly.

"You've gone too far, Empress. I will tolerate this council's concession to your regime no longer!"

"General Fredrickson, as long as I am Empress of Almuruna, you are dismissed from this council. Leave at once, or you will be arrested," Melody stated firmly, nodding to the monks to escort him out.

"Fuck you, you conniving bitch! All hail Emperor Michael, our true king!"

As he was escorted out, a few other male members of the council followed, already frustrated by the Empress's new mandate. Xiang and Sage remained in their seats, shaking their heads in disbelief as the council crumbled before them. Melody's head sunk, and from her crimson tears she grew a shroud of vines to hide behind, unable to look up at those who still remained loyal to her.

Three days later, Xiang came to the empress's meditation room, where ancient musical instruments lined the walls and fresh plants reached high to the open ceiling.

"Empress?"

"Come in, Xiang," Melody said calmly. Her long hair was draped over her shoulders in a weave of black and gold strands. She sat at the center of her mandala and hummed a blissful tone. The snow fell upward as a slight vibration resonated through the room.

Xiang cleared her throat. "There has been a bombing in Montana. Ten wounded. Pavonian investigators ruled the incident an attack by foreign forces. A broadcasting center was taken over then neutralized. Here, take a look. An image of one of the suspects has been captured."

She handed the empress a series of photos. Melody shuffled through the sharply focused images.

"This is the person in question? The one retreating the scene in the grey robe?"

"Yes, Empress."

"What do you know about them?"

"The facial recognition matches an individual known as Avestan, a transexual military commander and demolitions expert for the Zurvans. Avesten was the daughter to the Queen of Siberia but was kidnapped and replaced with a clone early on. Their 'transformation' came later, as a means to cloud their identity."

"Did you know this person well?"

"Yes, Empress. As daughters of the nine queens, we trained together at a young age."

Melody nodded and thought for a moment.

"Shiva has denounced any foul play by the Zurvan Order. If he is lying then he's not being careful about covering this up, and Shiva is no fool."

"Should I call off the bounty for Avestan?"

"No. Due to the public's opinion about the Zurvans I must

take a hard stance. Do, however, make sure the bounty is retrieved alive."

"It will be so, Empress."

"In a few days I would like you to go there and see what you can find. Leave Devonia to her studies and bring security forces with you."

"I will bring what I can, but you will need guards here too, surely."

"No I won't, and I'm leaving before you anyway."

"Where are you going?"

Melody slowly levitated into the air as dust floated around her like an asteroid belt circling her robe. A halo of snowflakes became suspended in her flaxen radiance.

"The march to Caldera ended when Pavonis defeated Shakti on Babbs Mount. When the dreadful queen had been slain, we assumed all was right with the world. But when we abandoned our conquest; when the slaves of Caldera fled and the black palace sunk into the Earth, its evil was neglected and forgotten. Someone returned to that hollowed obsidian palace and remained there for decades, plotting. They must be stopped before they become a malignant cell and fully take over my husband's mind. I alone will go to Caldera and face this foe."

"As your ambassador, I advise we switch aircrafts, so that I may act as a decoy. We must be extra careful in these troubling times."

"This is why you're my ambassador. I hope this conflict never reaches you, my dear."

Melody dropped from her pose and kissed Xiang on the cheek before hugging her deeply.

"You are my best friend and hero, Empress. I am loyal to you."

"If whatever happened to Michael somehow happens to

me, I ask that you relinquish that virtue and do whatever you must to stop me."

"Is that how you will deal with Michael when you find him? Will you kill him?"

"I will use every ounce of my being to try and bring him back to us. But if my love cannot turn him, nothing can, and his mind will devour itself. He will be as expendable as a feral dog."

Melody stepped back and allowed Xiang to see how serious her face was before walking away, leaving the snow to fall downward again quietly on the cobblestone mandala.

A string suddenly twanged loudly. Devonia stood next to a mounted koto as if frozen mid sprint. The instrument's note was sustained for many awkward seconds.

"Oops."

"Eavesdropping are we?" Xiang asked.

"I heard... well... almost everything."

"Then you're going to have to be a good spy and keep the information to yourself."

Devonia nodded rapidly.

"Okay then, young one. Let's go have supper."

As they walked to the dining hall, Devonia's expression became contemplative.

"Ambassador Yu... do you think if I got better at using my magick I would be able to make Emperor Michael all better again?"

Xiang smiled and subtly wiped a tear from her eye. "Maybe, Devonia. Maybe."

Through the estranged lands of Caldera, the empress crept

on feathered feet, denouncing her presence. Like her master had taught her long ago, she mimicked the organisms around her. Cactus and white pine bark protruded from her skin, doubling as armor. She wielded no weapon, but instead would use the minerals around her to construct one of the millions of biological weapons plucked from her vast genetic quiver. She felt a small quake beneath the crust and cursed the cauldron of boiling mantle already accumulating pressure for its next eruption, still thousands of years away.

Bogs of hot clay belched and steam from adolescent mineral pools rose into the cool air. No birds chirped. The snow was nearly void of tracks. Only the deep murmur of the volcano sounded in the desolate land where almost no animal ventured.

She walked down into the valley where the city of Caldera once stood. Little remained to remind the world of its holocaust. The very crust of the Earth had been scraped and resown, then violated again by the vents of magma beneath it. A massive crater had formed where the palace had been submerged underground, and the red stained-glass roof was only half windblown with sulfuric dunes, providing whatever was inside with a beam of diluted scarlet light.

Melody walked down the pitch cautiously. She slipped through a sliver of the obsidian's brittle decay and dropped to the floor with a light tap. The main chamber of the dreaded palace was mostly intact, lit brighter than she'd thought through the glass above. The ominous red light cast over the large chamber, and Melody slowly walked up the white hexagonal tiles toward that abominable throne shaded in infinite dusk.

Suddenly aware of a faen's presence, Melody's hairs stood. She stopped, and as she scanned the blackness she caught a pair of cat-like eyes staring malignantly back at her.

"Empress Melody. Queen of benevolence, life, and all things precious to life. I was beginning to wonder if you'd ever come."

"And with whom am I speaking?" Melody asked, stepping forward slightly to assert her dominance.

"You should have killed me when you had the chance. All the best conquerors in history made a point to exterminate their enemies highest ranking officers. A poor choice on your part."

"We couldn't kill them all."

"Of course not, especially since Michael would be considered one of them. He never told you about how he joined the Zurvans, did he? How he fucked Shakti and lost his virginity to her instead of you, his supposed lover."

"You've a deceitful tongue, faen," Melody spat, realizing the identity of the woman before her. "Shakti had many despicable generals but none fouler you, Fraus. You managed to slip past while your cohorts were destroyed by Lord Pavonis."

"Cohorts, bait, cannon fodder: call them what you please. Shakti's council was just a stepping stone for me. I will have more than her someday."

"Not as a human, you won't."

"I can barely be considered a human now, Empress. And once I coax your emperor into my web and make him my cock slave, I'll become the greatest Sararan to ever live, perhaps beyond the Aradians. I can't wait for him to pleasure me in ways you'll never know."

"Is stealing one of the remaining vials of Ezra's modified blood from the Zurvans somehow more difficult than luring my husband from me?"

"No... but watching your soul implode will be worth it."

Her psychotic smile was slight. Melody stared at the

solitary sorceress, ready at any moment to attack her.

"Where does this hatred come from?"

The woman's eerie eyes closed and reopened, as if grasping the memory with difficulty.

"I suppose you have the right to know, since your end will be at my hand. I was born in Kiev, in 1955, and when I was of age, I joined the Soviet Army. I became a helicopter pilot, to follow in my father's footsteps. In April 1986, I was called to the Chernobyl nuclear disaster two days after the explosion. I was one of the first to fly above the crater. Fire was still burning below tons of rubble. The government were concerned that all of Europe would be a fallout zone, deemed uninhabitable, if a second explosion occurred. We began to dump sand into the reactor, but the radiation sickness was already claiming our lives. One night I snuck away from the base, knowing I'd be court marshaled for desertion if I was caught. I was vomiting and robbing the hospital for medicine. My bones burned and my skin peeled with a sour decay. I knew I didn't have long to live. I went back to the base and stole a plane. There were rumors of a clan of healers in the mountains of Nepal, so I went there. They brought me to their monastery where I was taken in by the Zurvans. They used ancient magick to heal my wounds, but they couldn't expel the radiation from my body. Instead, I am cursed with it eternally, but every curse can be a gift if you follow where it leads. I went back to Soviet Russia to fight ghost wars against the United States. But instead of re-enlisting me I was imprisoned and faced the most atrocious treatment a human can undergo. It made me who I am. It filled me with hate, yes, but I found an identity all of my own in those wretched prison halls. I eventually escaped and trained with the Zurvans until I learned immortality, channeling the radiation to fuel my body just like you do with the sun. The twins were always a step ahead of me, but I knew that although my path to power would be a tedious one, I would triumph in my becoming. My body is a nuclear reactor, and once I harness the Sararan gene, nothing will stop me."

"I will stop you. And if I can't, Tala will."

"Ha! She is bound to her stupid experiment of stratospheric manipulation. You foolish amortal dignitaries want to ameliorate the world and yet you alter nature's cycles and species as if you know what is best for them. Nature is wild, violent, and unimpassioned. The strong prey on the weak, which is how Tala used to be before her sister committed suicide. It's almost romantic actually, how she could kill off half the planet's humans and yet you and that kike boy somehow managed to win her heart."

"ENOUGH!" Melody shrieked.

She threw up her arms and shot thick vines from her palms. The streaming green tentacles wrapped around her adversary like snakes and pulled at the woman's limbs. Fraus screamed and heated her body, burning through the vines and crawling up the shattered rock like a spider along the wall. The vines followed Fraus and struck her, breaking her jaw and cracking her ribs. Finally, she leapt from an arch and broke through the stained glass, leaving the shards to fall on Melody below. An explosion rocked the palace and massive chunks of razor-sharp boulders pelted Melody to the chamber floor, burying her as the palace crumbled and the thick soil filled its deepening sinkhole.

Fraus watched the smoking pile of rock from the surface. She threw the detonator for the explosives on the ground and stood for several minutes, watching the crater. Once she was satisfied Melody wouldn't be moving anytime soon, she whistled to the hills, her face broken and bleeding. A pale horse with undead eyes came to her. She mounted the ghoulish stallion and galloped north like a pestilent wind, driving a pulsing spear of electro-magnetic energy through the engine of the empress's ship as she went.

Minutes later, a hand reached up from the remains of Shakti's palace. Melody unearthed herself from the smoldering rock, her muscles filleted and bleeding and her hair burnt to the extent that her head was charred bald. Her lashes still singed and glowed orange with a subtle flame.

"If it's war she wants, she'll need more than that," she muttered, spitting blood onto the rubble and walking back to her sabotaged ship with a whole new initiative in mind.

On the foothills of the Rocky Mountain front, Michael led his undaunted steed through the deep snow and up into the high woods. The stormy winds howled and scraped along the range, pulling the tops of the trees and forcing the frozen dead ones to the ground like splintering epitaphs. He pressed forward, riding naked save for a bear fur he wore over his shoulders. He cut through the thick wood where no trail led and neared his destination, for he could sense the magnetism of the holy shrine of Pavonis. As he came upon the place of his mother's passing, Michael dismounted Apollo and knelt, breathing deeply the spirit of that place. A stone statue of Pavonis stood before him with an engraved prayer beneath her. She was wrapped in rose vines and yet even in winter's hollow scorn, the beautiful flowers grew without remission. The soft pink outer petals drifted in the wind as snow collected in their ovaries. Michael closed his eyes and prayed.

"Oh Holy Mother of Earth, who hath beckoned the sun with harmonies thrice woven, and came to us a lioness in a land of snakes, may your memory grace thy tortured soul, for I am without thee in flesh."

The wind died and Michael became aware of an unsettling presence. He looked behind him, knowing someone was standing there.

"Hello, Michael."

A woman stood tall in a maroon robe, smiling beatifically down at him, her voice soft and alluring. Her cut up ears and tattoos were mostly hidden by her long hair, but Michael knew her by her voice alone.

"Fraus... but it cannot be?"

He stood, ready to attack.

"Please, Michael, I mean you no harm. I come here to pray often, as you do."

Michael looked at her angrily but settled his stance.

"Do you pray to Pavonis or Shakti?"

"Was it not both divine forces that brought our world back to balance?"

Michael turned again, shaking his head and looking down at the snow.

"I spent more time with Shakti than my own mother. I was closer to my captor."

"When you became a Zurvan, you were just playing Shakti's game."

"Of course I was. I didn't offer my soul in blind loyalty as you did."

"Don't be so sure of your accusations. I was using the queen as well. I'm the only one that wanted the marines alive. Even your mother didn't want that."

"She did what she had to do."

"And she abandoned you, Michael. So did your lover

when she aborted your child."

Michael's head sunk, his body forcing him forwards to shove the snow off the trees, unable to contain his rage.

"A livid fire grows inside me," he growled.

Fraus smiled and nodded, orchestrating his emotions without him even knowing.

"What will you do with such a flame? If you contain it, you will self-consume. You must burn those who oppose you."

Michael turned to her with eyes of tinder.

"Those who have disrespected you."

He nodded.

"Those who have said your name in vain. Those who do not recognize the strength of your divine masculine nature."

"That is what I crave. I cannot live this lie anymore. I am a Zurvan prince."

"No Michael. You are a Zurvan king. You can be the one to reimagine the Earth however you wish. Enough of this pacifist, failing democracy. The oligarchy you left is a pathetic group of hypocrites living lavishly at the expense of the working class. Turn the working class into the warrior class. It's time to start the world."

"You will help me in this new movement?" Michael asked, giving in to his new obsession.

He walked up to her and she smiled deceitfully softly, placing her hand around his neck.

"It is your movement, Michael. I will do anything you wish. Anything."

She locked eyes with him, trapping him in her passionate gaze, then turned and called to her steed. Michael mounted Apollo and the two of them descended the ridge. At the base of the mountains, where the vast prairie met the tree line, a contingent of a few hundred men had been summoned by General Fredrickson to honor the new alliance, having received a message from Fraus about the dangers of Melody's administration.

Once Ziven and his cavalry had saluted their commander, the general and the sorcerers stepped away from the contingent and exchanged a few words: a congregation of demonic tacticians with nothing to lose and everything to gain. They spoke of Empress Melody's corruption, the changing of times, and the new breed of Immortals. Apollo sniffed the ground for the scent of blood and tipped his head south with eyes alight like his masters, the hell horse leading the brigade as they rode on, raising black flags of autonomy with their spears pointed forward like lion hunters. Michael remained beside Fraus at the front of the legion, glancing every so often at the sensual sorceress. The poison of her possession was already coursing through his veins, mixing with his wrecked emotions and revitalized Sararan cells, severing the last thread of decency that tethered him to his once beloved wife.

CHAPTER 45 – SUB-HUMAN DEFECTORS

Weeks passed and the empress had still not returned. But despite the conflicts unfolding, the government hid what details they could, and instead focused the people's attention on a parade. The musical extravaganza started by the lake and continued through Geneva's old town district. Drums, bells, and horns of all ancestry played whimsically alongside dancers and crowds waving with holiday cheer. The cold was pushed away by so many bodies, and the late afternoon sun beamed across the joyous celebration, where folks in thick coats drank cider and jokers dazzled children. Devonia clapped and danced beside Xiang as they entered the festival.

"Why aren't you dancing, Ambassador Yu?"

Xiang looked around at all the people enjoying themselves despite the emperor's desertion and the empress's disappearance. She thought too of the Zurvan terrorist, and how a place concentrated with so many people would be an easy target.

"We'll be going back to the palace now, Devonia."

"What? But we only just got here!"

"It's time to go. Come now," Xiang said sternly, leaving no room for further argument.

When they returned to the palace, there were a number of advisors whispering to each other in the main hall.

"What's going on?" Devonia asked loudly.

Xiang shushed her, guiding her swiftly up the stairs to her room. Once they were safely inside, Xiang crouched in front of Devonia, clasping the little girl's hands in hers. She knew the child was getting tired of all the white lies about the unfolding drama around her.

"Devonia, please, look at me."

"Are you angry with me?" the girl mumbled, her bottom lip trembling. "I just wanted to dance with everyone…"

"No, Devonia, I'm not angry with you. I'm sorry I made you feel that way."

"Then why did we have to leave the party? And what's really going on? Is it about the empress? I'm worried about her… she was so sad when she left…"

"Empress Melody is sad because she is in love with Emperor Michael, and he is very sick right now. To make things worse, he doesn't want her help. He thinks it is the empress who made him sick. You might not understand now, but you will someday. Now take off your coat and boots and go get some cocoa."

Xiang stood swiftly and left, heading back to the main hall to talk with the advisors they had seen earlier.

Devonia grumbled to herself in frustration. "I thought Sararan's couldn't get sick? How many more lies is that woman going to tell me before she realizes I don't believe any of them? Ugh, why is it so embarrassing being a kid?"

Just then, Devonia heard a commotion outside. Ignoring Xiang's request, she pushed open the door to her room and raced down the stairs.

The doors of the palace had been flung wide open and the empress stood in the main hall, orange light pouring through the doorway behind her, illuminating her halo for a brief moment before the monks closed the massive doors and the shimmer faded. She was dressed in a kimono and her head was bald, with the faintest remnants of scarring.

"Empress! What happened?" an advisor gasped.

The empress walked in and said nothing, simply smiling

and bowing to each of them as any humble sage would.

She walked up the stairs and everyone looked at each other inquisitively before turning to Devonia's bright face.

"She... looks... AWESOME!" Devonia exclaimed, delighted to see the empress home again.

Having once again sent Devonia to fetch herself a hot drink from the dining hall, Xiang now stood with Melody, looking out at the city and mountains from the hallway of the South Wing. Melody told Xiang about Fraus and her lair of deceit, and about her intentions with Michael now that he'd become fully possessed.

"So this is what it has come to?" Xiang asked quietly.

Melody fought back tears. She looked at Xiang with her sunken emerald eyes. "I don't want to lose him... I don't know why this has happened. It's the worst thing imaginable."

She wept in such pain, it physically hurt for Xiang to stand there and listen. But she had to. "I'm with you sister," Xiang said.

"It just all makes me so damn sad... Why couldn't he and I have just talked it out? Now he might be possessed... it's all so tragic."

Melody and Xiang embraced for a moment, then the empress stifled her emotions temporarily while she continued.

"Thank you, Xiang. There still may be a way to avert further conflict, but it will take immediate action. You will go to the relay station where the bombing attack took place. Bring a security team and investigators, and I'm assigning you a qualified clairvoyant. I would go myself but I need to stay and protect my kingdom. I underestimated this demon's abilities."

"I understand, your highness. Who is the clairvoyant?"

"A Zurvan called Caspian. He is a young man with extraordinary talents."

"A Zurvan? Aren't we investigating a terrorist attack whose primary suspect is a Zurvan?"

"Not anymore. Avestan was not there to commit some heinous act against the people of Pavonia. Shiva responded to my message; Avestan is working alone and has been for some time, so not even he knows the exact details. However, he assured me their intentions are good, and I believe him—"

"Empress?" Xiang asked as Melody was suddenly struck by a vision.

The empress touched the window and stepped into the evening sunlight, her halo aglow. "The relay station," she surmised. "The witch was using it as a repeater. The palace was a capsule of pure obsidian hiding her identity, but it also limited her range of spell casting. She used the relay station as a mass-frequency transmitter. Perhaps Avestan knew about Michael's possession before I did and destroyed the station to prevent the lurid transmission."

"Was it worth wounding ten people?"

"In comparison to potentially saving the world's population? Absolutely. Our primary objective as of today is to destroy this conjurer and to bring Michael back into his own self."

Xiang nodded, contemplating what she believed. Just then, a maiden came walking briskly from down the hall.

"Empress, Ambassador Yu... I'm sorry to disturb you but Devonia has become very sick suddenly."

The three of them walked through the halls and into Devonia's room. She lay on the bed, hugging her tortoise and sobbing.

"What happened?" Xiang asked, stroking the girl's head.

"I feel like I'm dying."

The maiden stepped forward. "She said she wasn't feeling good. Then she collapsed, so we took her here."

Melody walked over to Devonia and looked into her eyes. She put her thumb on her chin and opened her mouth, looking inside. "She has respiratory syncytia virus. Hand me her glass please."

The maiden handed Melody a glass of water from the dresser top. She rubbed her fingers together above the glass, fragments of her skin falling into the water.

"Drink up," she said as she handed Devonia the glass.

The child's face twisted in discomfort but she listened to the empress and gulped down the powerful anesthetic.

"That should expel the virus but she will require hospitalization for a time just in case. See to it, maiden."

"Yes, of course Empress."

"Feel better, Devonia, I'll check on you tomorrow when I have time."

"Thank you, Empress," the girl said, her arms still clinging to Boris as she coughed and wiped her eyes in quiet misery.

The empress and her ambassador walked out into the hall again and shut the door behind them.

"I want you to leave as soon as you can get your things together. I'll be in close contact. Be near the ship's communications and keep me informed on your progress."

"I will, Empress," Xiang said as she bowed and walked away to gather the monks and the shaman.

Caspian awaited the ambassador in the entrance hall and Xiang was immediately relieved to discover that they had common ground: he was from the same area as Devonia and had even helped to build the school she went to. Not only that, but he was also young, handsome, and cordial. Xiang couldn't help but blush when Caspian exclaimed that he refused to believe she was still unmarried and yet so beautiful. Eight armed monks joined them soon after, and they quickly boarded the fastest ship in Melody's fleet.

They flew for several hours, but somewhere over the Atlantic, Xiang was awakened by a monk.

"The pilot requests you, Ambassador Yu."

"Thank you, I'll be right there."

She dressed and walked to the flight deck. The pilot looked up from his position.

"Sorry to wake you, Ambassador. You've got an urgent message from the empress."

Xiang picked up the transmitter.

"Good evening, Empress."

Melody answered instantly with a sense of panic in her voice.

"You're being redirected. There's a situation developing northeast of Temuco, Chile. We are getting emergency signals from all over South America. You will have to refuel in Brazil. Stay alert and on standby for further information."

"Thank you, Empress."

The transmission ended and they modified their route, speeding south with nothing but the prospect of danger before them.

A swell of purple light gleamed over the Atlantic ocean's horizon as Brazilian birds sang with dawn's awakening. Xiang and her spiritual warriors had landed and walked over the tarmac to greet the local dignitaries at the gate.

"Bom dia, embaixador!" a happy and well-dressed Brazilian man yelled as he walked out to meet them.

He hugged Xiang warmly and the monks raised their staffs in caution as she returned the hug, then relaxed their battle ready poses.

"Posso pegar café?"

"No, thank you. Just looking to get some fuel."

"What kind are you looking for? We are out of everything except bio-aviation fuel, and even that is running low. All over the country fuel has been stolen and re-routed."

"Do you know where its being re-routed to?"

"The rumors point to central Chile. Whoever 'they' are stole all the most volatile octanes, which concerns us. It is an unusually hot and dry summer here in South America. The forests of Chile and Argentina are parched. I hope whoever is stealing all this fuel is very careful with it."

Xiang nodded. "Well, if it's all right with you, we will take what bio-aviation fuel you have and continue our investigation."

"Do you need weapons, embaixador?"

"Why would we need weapons?"

He looked at her as if she didn't understand the question, then smiled and nodded.

"Safe travels, embaixador. I'll see you on your return journey."

"Thank you. See you soon."

In the depths of Xiang's gut, a knot formed and pulled itself tight. She wondered if perhaps she should have taken the guns.

As they flew over the mountains of Chile, the sun was rising high and the heat of the day rose with it. One of the monks was looking over the scape through the window.

"Ambassador, come see this."

Xiang walked over to his window and looked out.

"Oh my... Pilot, fly around that smoke at your ten o'clock and reduce speed."

"Your call, Ambassador," he confirmed from the cabin.

"I sense danger ahead, Ambassador Yu. Be careful," Caspian said, with his finger on his third eye and his eyelids closed.

The ship dipped and slowed toward the rising smoke. As they approached the ridge, Xiang's eyes widened. To her horror, she saw a line of men holding torches. They were spaced an eighth of a mile between one another, stretching as far as one could see, the line of smoke reaching over the horizon and toward the sun as if the morning star itself were the farthest ignitor. Trucks with heavily armed troops crawled on the dirt roads and in the valleys below, refueling the torches and swapping out tired men for fresh ones.

"This isn't a sanctioned burn unit. This is... madness," Xiang muttered. "Fly close to that ridge!"

They sped toward a mount where the flames licked over the ridge's edge, spewing sparks and flame onto the other side. From the wake of scorching Earth, a brutish warrior emerged. He stood tall with his hair whipping in the wind, singing and regrowing all the time with infernal strands. His eyes burned hot like the bushes and trees around him. Michael's hands raised as he pulled in the coastal winds and beckoned the continent's funeral pyre. He wore black armor with a long sword sheathed on his back. On the hilt of his blade a tassel of human ears had been tied and sewn with sinew.

"It's Michael. He's going to burn his way north with the shifting of the seasons. He's trying to take Pavonia!" Xiang yelled.

Michael looked up at them from his high perch as the ship circled his position.

Caspian suddenly opened his eyes and screamed. "She's entered my mind. How did she... PLEASE!"

He wobbled on his feet, clenching his skull as if it were self-destructing.

"Caspian?"

"KILL ME NOW! BEFORE SHE—"

He lunged toward Xiang and gripped her neck. His maddened face was red as he slobbered over her with livid concentration. Xiang kicked and choked until the monks pulled Caspian off her and applied immediate hits to his pressure points to submit him. He wrangled with the monks like a tameless beast until one of them silenced him with a twist of the neck and a loud crack. Xiang stood breathing heavily, her neck bleeding slightly with scratch marks. They looked down at the dead Zurvan.

"Pilot, we're leaving now!" she wheezed, "North to Sao Paulo! Go!"

The ship sped away and Michael watched on until it disappeared. Fraus joined him on that scorched mount and they kissed hungrily as the forest crowned behind them, the flames galloping toward villages unaware of the fire storm coming their way.

An eerie fog hung in Geneva's air that evening. Nurses walked the halls of the hospital whispering rumors and secrets to one another. Despite their occult conversations, Devonia's curiosity was quelled once again by her weak immune system. She lay in her bed, looking at Boris on his tabletop perch at the other side of the room. Outside, the streetlights burned the moist air, the articulations of trees and buildings blurred by the layers of fog.

A nurse walked in wearing a mask and holding a tray of needles.

"Good evening, Devonia."

"Where is Nurse Lidia?"

"She had to leave. I am your PM nurse."

"Okay…" Devonia said, looking quizzically at her new caregiver.

Their features seemed both male and female. Their jaw shape matched the angle of their shocking brows, and their shoulder-length hair was black as night. They donned surgical gloves and picked up a large needle.

"We're going to make you all better."

"But the empress already gave me medicine, I'm just staying here in case I get sick again."

"You will never get sick again, my child."

Devonia reluctantly let the nurse tie a tourniquet around her arm before they poked her with the needle and injected a scarlet liquid.

"Why so much?" she asked as the concoction burned in her veins.

"We have to make sure it works."

The nurse finished up and put a band aid on Devonia's arm.

"We're going to transfer you to another room now."

"But why?"

Without answering, the nurse gathered Devonia's things and put them in a bag.

"Where's Ambassador Yu? What's going on?" she asked as the nurse picked up Boris.

They tipped their brow and hesitated, before neatly tucking the animal inside the bag. "Come, child."

They left the hospital and disappeared into the night. No one saw them leave. An amber alert was immediately sent out, and Empress Melody was notified. All ships, transports and commuters in Almuruna were stopped and inspected. Many citizens who were already skeptical about Melody's mandates considered it a false-flag operation; that she was lying about the kidnapping in order to find goods being traded illicitly with Asia. All over the world, more people were losing trust in the empress, and in spite of his wicked game, Michael was gaining followers every day, each gang of impressionable young men more devoted than the last.

Xiang and her monks returned to Almuruna that night with a body bag containing the dead Zurvan. She walked up the steps and her solemn eyes matched Melody's, who stood in a light rainfall under the awning's dim glow. Each knew of the other's tragedies and no words sufficed exchanging. She and the monks bowed as they walked past the holy empress on the way to their sleeping chambers, for it had been a hellish day and the hour of the wolf was upon them. Melody stayed with the casket for some time and let the rain roll over her hydrophobic skin, knowing that all chances of diplomacy with her enemy had died with Caspian that day.

CHAPTER 46 – RITUAL SATANICO

The next morning, an emergency summit was held at the palace with the remaining members of council. Only Xiang, Sage and few others remained. The abbot spoke first. The subject was war.

"There are four hundred monks in this palace, willing to do what they must to protect the peace. But we are not a viable offensive force when it comes to this new enemy. I will remind you there are fully trained Mongol troops ready to be dispatched by Parvati at a moment's notice. We must call on her for aid. If we do not send for help now, the demon will cross the Atlantic and be at our doorstep before any support can reach us. There's no harm in turning them back toward their homeland in the spring when provisions are plentiful."

"As gracious as I am for the abbot's safeguard, in this dire time we need gods, not soldiers. Why won't Tala help us?" Sage asked.

The empress shook her head and answered. "Because if she leaves her post she'll destabilize the climate and the Earth will experience an incredible famine, and famine breeds more conflict. This witch is not as powerful as Tala, but she is clever. She understands the positions we Immortals have created for ourselves. Even as a Sararan, I do not have the strategic mind it takes to fight and lead in warfare. But you do." She turned to Sage. "While I stay here and use my magick to try and protect as many as I can from the witch's influence, I want you to lead our armed forces into Pavonia and stop Michael and his possessor. Then, I want you to destroy them."

"Even Michael?" Sage asked, surprised at both her promotion and objective.

"It wouldn't be easy. First you must destroy Fr—"

The empress winced. She saw the despicable woman's face in her mind's eye and cursed herself for nearly twisting her tongue with the devil's. The witch had dug into Melody's subconscious and attempted to lure the empress into saying her name. From beyond the crevices of time's most sodden refractions she'd infiltrated the astral plane and entered the empress's mind like a spider trickling into her ear canal in the night, sinking its caustic fangs into her brainstem with an icy sting. Melody gathered herself quickly as she shook her head and adjusted her jaw.

"As I was saying… first you must destroy the demon so Michael is freed from her possession. If he does not turn back to his normal self, he must also be destroyed. I understand none of this will be easy."

Sage then spoke with a concerned voice. "With respect, Empress, what advantage do our forces have that these two sorcerers do not? Michael has over four thousand men behind him, with more joining every day. Not to mention a witch who can possess nearly anyone in her vicinity and beyond. She can control the minds of multiple subjects at once which is only possible by hijacking higher dimensions and exploiting their mercurial bias. Not even the Aradian's were psychotic enough to tamper with such energies. She's a celestial terrorist. If you say you will not help us fight on the front line then… what do we have?"

The empress nodded and spoke with promise. "There is an underground hanger containing a fleet of fighter jets. They will be fueled, armed and tested over the next week. They were staged here years ago as a potential final course of action; as Michael's secret air defense program to protect us from extraterrestrial threats and anything else he alone could not defend us from."

"And what makes you think Michael won't commandeer his own airships?" the abbot asked.

"That is why we have to beat him to the skies," the empress said, looking out at the half-melted snow of winter's atrophy.

"And do you have pilots for these relic fighters?" Sage asked.

"I have a list of ace pilots, the ones who are still alive at least. All twenty-two are en route... all but one."

"Who?" Sage inquired. "I know every fighter pilot on this planet."

"Galen Fox."

"Good thing too! Galen Fox is a hobo and a drunk. He quit flying years ago," Sage scoffed. "Anyone who drinks a fifth of vodka in a single sitting is a liability, not an asset."

"As long as he doesn't drink and fly, right?" Xiang said, shrugging.

"Trust me, you don't want to be on a gunship while he's piloting. We're better off without him."

The empress stood, signaling an end to the summit. "Ambassador Yu will leave immediately to find Devonia. If what Tala says is true and the child is the reincarnation of Pavonis, we'll need to recover her and speed up her training at once. Xiang, you have my permission to do whatever it takes to get her back. I've uploaded an intel feed to the computer onboard your ship. I ask that you go alone, and make sure you carry a lot of fire power."

"It will be done, Empress."

Xiang bowed and left the room.

"Won't she need assistance?" the abbot asked.

"Despite the ambassador's sweet demeanor she is

excellent at tradecraft and combat operational tactics. She'll multiply her forces where she needs to. When she finds Devonia, which I'm confident she will, I'll have her join General Valor on the Pavonian front to help lead our forces."

"And what about your security, Empress?"

"I'm going to keep half of your monks here and send half with you and the general to Pavonia. Once the pilots and other reinforcements arrive, we will mobilize our forces. Have you ever shot a gun before, Abbot?"

"It is forbidden, Empress."

"Not anymore it's not. I suggest you begin training. That goes for all of you. If we are to protect this great kingdom, we must all learn to fight. May God be with you all."

She dismissed the council, waiting until they had all departed and silence filled the room before collapsing into her chair. Melody's head sank and she began to weep. So much had happened so quickly. She felt completely alone. She missed her husband's sweet touch and his warming voice. And though the thought of him becoming such a despicable creature gnawed at her soul, she prayed to Pavonis that some buried light in him was salvageable. She thought of the decades they'd lived with one another since the fall of the Zurvan Empire, and how they'd rebuilt the world so beautifully as Pavonis had wished. Such astounding equilibrium had taken place over those years of peace.

She wondered where it all went wrong; if her self-induced abortion was truly the catalyst for Michael's betrayal, why hadn't the issue come up earlier in their marriage? Melody deemed the witch to be behind all of it, slowly tempting Michael by planting ideas in his mind while instigating enough violence throughout the world to feed his addiction to war, persuading him to drift farther from his empress and the council. Still, those first few years after the fall of Caldera were so peaceful. She remembered living in Montana before they moved to Almuruna, before they became world leaders. Those long, wonderful summer days by the river were akin to how Ingrid and Ezra had lived before the fall. And like the famous duo before them, their dream of tranquility was just that; a temporary island of bliss isolating them from the stark reality that awaited them.

Michael's blitz moved northward. Smoke from the immense fires wrapped around the world and pain and war bred heathens beyond the drape of red western skies. Young men eager for the call of conquest left their pliant lives to follow Michael's promises of glory. Like a puppet master, Fraus kept him focused on his hatred and let the brutality inside him come untamed. Casualties mounted and eventually the unprepared civilians surrendered to the demonic pair and their army of savages. Those lucky enough to flee boarded boats and ships and embarked on the long journey across the ocean to Almuruna. Hundreds perished at sea. More would soon follow them into their watery graves.

After easily triumphing all of South Pavonia, Michael sent a small contingent of his troops through Mexico to lay waste to its inhabitants in preparation for the siege of what was once the mighty United States. He established his new base camp in the ancient city of Mayapan and lined the jungle perimeter with spears erect, stabbing the Earth with the skewered bloodied skulls of those few who bravely but foolishly chose to resist his scourge.

On a clear hot night, when all the stars shone blue and bright upon those crafted steps of Mayan artisanship, a great ritual was about to take place. War drums rang out loudly and seven large fires burned around the base of the Pyramid of Kukulcan. Michael approached the stone monument naked and glowing, holding in his hand an obsidian dagger. The light from the fires was absorbed in his burning eyes, for fire attracts fire, and where once he felt love he felt only a sinful urgency boiling through him. He walked past the drummers between the fires, each as naked as he, for his warriors were innately unclothed with spirits as pure and barbaric as their ancestors who'd abandoned that city long ago. They returned to their mecca for the resurrection of the Kukulcan; the feathered serpent.

Torches were mounted at the base of the weathered temple, and he passed through that invisible gate of ill magick in his ascension. Up the stairs he walked steadily. The fires raged beneath him and he let the sparks wash over his thick skin. Higher he climbed, until he reached the last step, a tomb rising from its pinnacle. With a great lunge he leapt up to the mount and there lay his malevolent mistress, exposed and tied down with heavy ropes and chains. She squirmed, a demon in heat, thrusting her hips toward him and licking her lips. Michael stood before her and watched her fuck the wind.

"Do it Michael. Cut me," she moaned.

He stepped forward and pointed the blade to her throat. Fraus yelped with masochistic excitement as the cool of the knife touched her burning skin. He gently guided the steel edge between her breasts and down to her dripping vagina.

"Fucking cut me!" she moaned.

Michael flicked the sharp blade across her swollen labia and blood splattered her face, her mouth hanging open in ecstasy. He then held the blade to his own erect cock and cut a gash in one of the pulsing veins. The tip of his phallus dripped with sacred blood as he leaned over his bound succubus.

"Fuck me," she moaned, "Give me your cock as you would plunge your sword into your enemies. Fuck me while I bleed," she beckoned with teeth clenched.

Michael thrust into her, gripping her throat as blood dripped down his legs. In their violent fornication, his Sararan blood mixed with her radioactive cells and both knew the propagation of some spectacular new creature would come of it, transforming the witch in the process.

Michael growled with a deviant hunger as the succubus screamed with delight. Faster he fucked her until they shook the stars from the sky and the tomb beneath them rattled with some unholy awakening, the men below beating the goatskin drums with climactic incantations. Deeper he ventured into her, her face wet with sweat and blood, her thighs tight and succumbing. At the height of their orgasms, Fraus howled and Michael pumped his seed inside the demon witch, and through his cruelty and vigor she came as well. The Sararan eyes of Fraus lit like the white flash of a hydrogen bomb as she became that cursed species that all creatures fear. With the transformation complete, Michael cut the ropes and let her ravage him. All night they gave into their lust, violently copulating to the beat of the jungle long after the drummers waned their pulsing. Into dawn they played their morbid games until insects rose to feed on their sultry bodies.

Michael's savage affair had broken Tala's rule, and though the Aradian knew well of their blasphemous union, she would give Melody a fair chance to stop them before she would intervene. With half of Pavonia already conquered in a matter of weeks, the time wedge for a solution to the grand massacre was thinning. Michael's mind was enslaved. The further he fell into Fraus's trap, the more formidable she became.

CHAPTER 47 – CHILDREN OF THE SUN

When Pavonian spies informed Empress Melody of Fraus's metamorphosis, she officially declared war against Michael and the Luciferian Army. The empress deployed spike teams behind enemy lines who fought in every direction, calling in air strikes on Luciferian Army forces in those vast jungles where confusion and lack of experience on both sides caused mass casualties. Most of the untrained Almurunan soldiers were wounded or killed within the first week, their limited air force already exhausted of fuel and bombs, their own reinforcements decimated. The captured faced a terrible bargain of either death by fire or enlisting in the Army. Those beaten-up recon platoons and downed pilots who narrowly escaped told the council of their experience. They gave reports of large-scale attacks, murder, genocide, rebellions, counter-rebellions, unlimited warfare, gas attacks, mutilation and all brands of torture emanating from the possessed king and his legion. These events led scribes and historians to write about what would later be known as the first battles of World War IV. The fighting raged, and carbon dioxide poured into the atmosphere with Michael's scorching spread, contradicting Tala's efforts to balance the already precarious climate. And as refugees began to pour onto the shores of Almuruna, another crisis was unfolding eleven thousand miles south in Namibia.

It was a calm night when some nameless rebel army invaded Uhlanga's village. The men set fires to houses and rounded everyone up.

"Give us de golden child!" one yelled.

Uli looked over her village in flames and shook her head in disgust, unwilling to exploit herself to the obsessed thieves who'd caught wind of her supposed divinity. The eleven-year-old left her hut and hopped on a small motorcycle that leaned against the light pole beside her home. The engine popped and revved and the owner yelled at her to stop but she sped off into the night, leaving him holding his hands up in disbelief. She bolted east where she was free from the raiders but at the mercy of the wilderness, climbing through desert canyons and across plateaus, down hills and through valleys. She rode all night until, just before dawn, her bike sputtered and died and she dropped the exhausted machine before looking up at the wall of trees before her. Uli was at the edge of a jungle, where strange birds were stretching their wings in the blue light of early day, and small conversations could be heard in the forest of many faces. Uli took out the charms from her pocket and spilled them onto the sand, already a novice witch blossoming on that cusp of bio regions.

"Which way to go, which way to go," she muttered quietly. She stood back and looked at the artifacts from a wide angle. "What the heck? Why would I stay right here?" she asked, scratching her head.

Just then, she heard some distant commotion. She picked up her stones and trinkets and left the trail, sneaking quietly through the bushes toward the sounds. After a few minutes she came upon a gathering of robed men and women around a small fire. The discussion pertained to a serious topic. Uli recognized one of the voices.

"Zurvans!" she whispered.

Just as she was about to tuck and run, she saw a small girl held by one of the women. It was Devonia. Uli gasped and stayed to watch and listen to the strange meeting of her former captors, who'd stolen Devonia in place of herself.

"Shiva we must meet Michael head on with or without the help of Queen Parvati. Each day he gains strength."

The wise man sitting opposite the woman who had spoken stood and looked at her.

"See this child?" he said, pointing to Devonia.

The young girl looked solemnly at the ground, frightened and mute.

"Even though Avestan injected her with divine blood, it will not engage until she has matured. It could be another six to seven years before she becomes Aradian. Until then, the Queendoms of Pavonia, Almuruna and Mongolia will have to combine forces. We are already too late to stop Michael and his mistress with our group alone. I will visit Parvati soon to discuss negotiations of arrangements and an alliance with our clan. But first we must find Uhlanga as well."

Uli dipped her head down, thinking hard about what to do. With a plan forming in her mind, she tip-toed over to the fire and positioned herself behind a tree, on the opposite side from Devonia.

While the Zurvans continued their discussion, Uli threw one of her charms at Devonias feet. A small silver crocodile fell by Devonia and she looked at the charm with wide eyes.

"Can I go to the bathroom?" Devonia asked one of her captors.

The woman reluctantly agreed and ushered Devonia away from the gathering.

Devonia squatted by a bush as the woman stood close by. Suddenly, a large stick swung from behind a nearby tree and struck the woman in the jaw. Uli dropped the stick as the woman fell to the ground.

"Run!" she whispered to Devonia, grabbing her hand and taking off down the hill.

The woman stood and hollered to the rest.

"Only four of you go!" Shiva demanded, making sure to keep his unit intact.

Avestan and two others joined chase. So began the hunt for the two most valuable children on Earth.

The sweltering Kalahari desert proved a difficult adversary for Xiang. She walked for many miles through its red sands and parched grasses, venturing through treacherous sandstorms, her shawl wrapped tightly around her face; her eyes collecting dust. The relentless winds pushed against her, and a fierce armament of sharp rocks pelted her body. Though she'd learned at a young age how to survive in nearly every environment on Earth, Xiang knew the conditions were but one of many threats as she searched for Devonia. The mission given to her by Melody was the most open-ended assignment yet, with almost no rules of engagement and a single objective to maintain. At least she was outfitted. She had a suppressed carbon-fiber barreled rifle, with six magazines strapped to her chest and more on her hydration pack, and on her hips she wore two automatic pistols. Hidden under her deceitfully fashioned Tswana garb were thirty-six razor blades and a tanto knife.

She walked for many miles until the storm settled, arriving in Uli's village that same evening. The charred remains of the straw huts lay about and the mud buildings had been smashed. Glass from windows lay about and from the black smoke lingering in the air Xiang could smell the sweet sizzle of cooked human flesh. The tracks of those who fled were swallowed by the storm. Only children remained.

A small boy came up to Xiang as she looked around at the devastation.

Xiang knelt slowly and looked into the eyes of the adolescent sage, for he'd developed a knowing beyond his years since the raging men had cast their shadow of horror over him, never to be unseen.

"What happened here, my child?"

"Men came with swords and torches. They burned everything looking for the holy child. Many fled, but the desert will kill them if the raiders don't. I stay to help those who wander back."

She touched the boy's face gently and continued on. She walked through the village, through the massacre. A man's head stood on its neck in the middle of the street as if placed there as some abject amusement. Blood had dried around the base of his severed neck, and his half-open eyes looked toward the sun.

Xiang felt unsettled leaving the orphans behind, but she had to keep on. She ventured into odd lands, where cliffs distinguishing time's erosion jutted above the desert flats: towers insinuating time's cataclysm.

That night, Xiang crossed some tracks leading into a large chasm, and she slowly crept into the low canyon where stinging creatures hid, not wanting to be found. She had the means to fashion a torch but the risk of detection was too hazardous. She would simply rest unseen, just another creature that did not want to be found.

○

With a small noise, Xiang awoke the next morning to a rifle barrel pointed at her face.

"Vuka, lady," the man pointing the rifle said.

"What do you want?" Xiang asked, her eyes flicking to the armed raiders surrounding the area.

"Siyazi ukuthiunayo ingane. Uhlanga."

"I don't know what you're saying," Xiang said. She reached slowly for her pistol.

"No, no, no!" he shook his head and made clicking noises like a bushman. "Siphe yena futhi akukho okubi okuzokwenzeka kuwe."

Xiang shook her head.

One of the raiders spoke English for him. "He said we know you have de child. Give her to us and no harm will come to you."

"Are you the ones who pillaged that small town to the west?"

The leader continued to point his rifle at her.

"What does it mattah? Soon all de world will be on fyah if we do not give back its muddha."

"Then why would you so foolishly fan the flames?" she said angrily.

Just then, a rock from seemingly nowhere hit the man in the head. He whirled about to identify the perpetrator. Up above them on the top of the canyon, a group of black hooded figures stood and circled them, like points on a deadly crown. The Zurvan clan had arrived heavily armed, outnumbering the desperate thieves three to one.

One of them stepped forward and Xiang gasped in recognition.

"Avestan..." she whispered.

"To threaten an ambassador of Almuruna warrants a life sentencing," Avestan declared.

"But she will hide de golden child!"

"From savages like you!" Xiang said as she stood and held her gun to him.

He dropped his rifle and put his hands up slowly.

"So where are they, Avestan? Or is this another one of your clandestine opportunities outside the bounds of your queen?"

Shiva stepped forward to make his presence known. "Avestan has done nothing outside the bounds of law in this or any other kingdom. Our attempts to give the world back its mother is our reaction to the lack of maneuvering by Empress Melody. The witch will consume us all if we do not stop her. As for the children, they've managed to escape us and are somewhere in this labyrinth of rocks."

Xiang sighed. "You lost two eleven year old girls? Were you playing hide and seek?"

"They're a clever duo, I'll give them that."

While the Zurvans rounded up the raiders and tied their wrists behind their backs, Xiang spoke with Avestan and Shiva directly, making breakfast from a lizard she'd killed and cooked.

"Despite the extreme violations committed by the Zurvans, I will vie for your clemency if all kidnapping attempts and terrorizing of the world's citizens ceases immediately and you help me find the children."

"It will be so," Shiva said, bowing. "It was not my direct intention to distress the empress nor to cause harm to the children. We only wanted what is best for the Earth in this dire time."

"As do we all. The empress is well aware of Devonia's

divine lineage and understands how crucial her progression is."

"I would ask that Avestan and I come to Geneva and train her, since the Zurvan training regimen is time-tested and proficient."

"A formal request at an earlier date would have been less problematic. Perhaps you can recall the Treaty of 2055 when the Mongol Queens could have destroyed the Zurvan clan forever but chose a peaceful alliance instead? For now, let's just find the girls before they die of dehydration." Xiang mounted her pistol and spat out a leg bone.

"What about us?" the raider asked.

"Start walking. If the little punks set any traps, you'll be the first to know."

"But our hands are bound."

"Sucks to be you," Xiang shrugged.

Shiva smiled. "So the children have been briefed in counter-tracking?"

"No. In order to escape you, it seems they've already begun opening facets from their past lives."

The odd company divided themselves between the canyon's fissures and fanned out. Xiang watched the raiders closely from above and used her keen vision to sweep the vast mirage of mid-morning, looking closely for a momentary speck between the rippling heatwaves.

Just before noon, the first raider screamed. Xiang hurried along the cliffs toward the commotion. Two men crowded a wounded man.

"Move aside!" Xiang said as she approached them.

The men stepped back. A large man was lying on the ground holding his knee and wincing.

"What happened?" she asked.

"A boulda hit heem! When he crossed de trench it rolled

down de split in de rock."

Xiang couldn't help but smile. "Surely not on its own. Everyone spread out, they're close!"

As the bound men timidly dispersed, Xiang climbed high on a rigid formation and peaked out from its mount. She crouched on a lofty overhang and gazed across the baking crust, beyond the purging chrome horizon where the heat swallowed the sky, sound, time, all. Two beings scurried their way through the canals below, moving parallel to one another but without pattern or set pace.

"There to the west!"

The raiders moved in on them. With no shadow beneath her, Xiang hopped from her perch and skidded down the scree, landing in a dusty heap in the arid pit below. As she ran through the narrow corridor of rock she heard another scream. She stopped to listen. A low chatter grumbled under the high-pitched screech of a child. She ran to where they were and found another casualty. The men surrounded the two girls in a natural rock quarry.

"It's alright girls! Back away, you imbeciles," Xiang ordered the men.

She walked past the man who lay fetal. He held his testicles in his hands, murmuring something in his native tongue.

"Ambassador Yu!" Devonia cried as she and Uli ran up and hugged her.

"Are you two okay?" she asked them.

"Yes. So thirsty though. We thought these were bad guys chasing us so Uli kicked a big rock from the cliff on them and busted that guys leg. Then I kicked this one right in the junk!"

"Don't apologize to him, he's a criminal. Though for helping myself and the others find you two, they may get a more lenient sentencing."

"Who are the others?" Devonia asked.

Just then, the Zurvans walked up from behind a pillar. The young girls gasped.

"It's okay girls, they've agreed to play nice. They're going to help us fight the war."

"What war?"

"The war for Pavonia. Emperor Michael has been possessed by a witch who seems set on global annihilation. The reason all these people have been trying to find you two is because you have some very powerful souls. Perhaps not now, but someday, the world may need you. You will be trained in martial arts, learn new languages, and be tested in a myriad of trials. It is something you must choose willingly, for as much as each here wants you as an apprentice, it is not in our hands any longer."

Devonia spoke first. "Before we decide any of that, I need to know where Boris is."

Everyone looked at each other with confused faces.

"Your turtle?" Xiang asked.

"He's a tortoise, actually," Uli reminded her.

"Where is my tortoise?" Devonia screamed, using Melody's vocal techniques and leaving the surrounding raiders and Zurvans jumpy and wide-eyed.

A Zurvan pulled the small animal out of a satchel and held it up to let her see.

"Boris! Can someone get him some water, please? Quickly!"

Her demands were met with multiple hands holding out partially full water canteens.

"Thank you." She took one and poured some water into Boris's mouth, then turned to face her captors-cum-rescuers. "I hope you all feel ashamed of yourselves? That wasn't cool.

I was so scared when you took me, Avestan." She glared at them. "I know you were doing what you thought was best, to keep me safe, but you could have at least EXPLAINED first." She tilted her head and have them all a haughty look. "Now that we are apparently all together in this fight... maybe there is a chance to stop what's coming. I will accept the offer of training. It feels like we already started anyway."

Uli nodded in agreement. "The smoke from Michael's fires reached my house before the raiders did. All the way across the ocean. I don't think he will stop until the world is barren like in the times of the Great Eruption. If we don't help, more people will die. I also accept your invitation."

"On one condition," Devonia added. "If we do this, we don't want to be deceived anymore. No more lies and talking behind our backs about 'grown up' things like we're idiots. Also, Uli and I are to be council members and briefed daily by the security board," she said standing on her tiptoes with an upturned chin and arms crossed.

"It will be done, Devonia," Xiang said, trying to hold in her amusement.

As Uli tilted her head graciously, Xiang could not help the smirk that escaped onto her lips.

"Come girls, we must return to Geneva post haste."

"Can I say goodbye to my family before I go?" Uli asked

A shadow crossed Xiang's face as she answered hesitantly. "Of... of course."

They all left at once. The raiders, though likely guilty of the crimes against Uli's village, could not be held on suspicion alone, and without regional judges to support or deny their claim, they were sent away without their weapons; godless hungry men, banished to their primal origins in the wilds.

The Zurvans escorted Xiang and the girls out of the area,

carrying the raiders weapons – at least two rifles each – their brass necklaces and shotgun bandoleers slung over their shoulders like advanced infantry marching into the heaviest battle imaginable, and soon they would be. Though they'd planned and executed their mission with the 'well-being of the common people' in mind, the Zurvan elite owed the empress for their soft crimes. They knew it. Xiang knew it. And the empress would expect it. They were now Almuruna's shock troops, ready to reinvigorate the human spirit by showing the world what humans were still capable of.

On the trip back to Geneva, Xiang spoke with Avestan.

"It is good to see you again," Xiang said softly, still unsure how her childhood friend might react.

Avestan turned from looking out the window and smiled. "And you as well, sister."

"How are you? It's been so long."

"Very well, I suppose. I'm a full-time assassin for Shiva now. Business is good. It's about to get better."

"I'm curious if you can help us find David's assassin while you're in Geneva, since you know the art better than most."

"Whoever killed David was part of the political opposition, I'm sure of it. The copper plate charge placed in the entrance of his home. The timing and execution. It's obvious they were a critic of the empress's mandate. I'm sorry for you and your nation's loss, but I don't think finding this perpetrator matters now as much as you think it does."

"But we must know! He was an important diplomat."

"Diplomat... sure... but you of all people should know the meaninglessness of titles and positions. David's shining moment was on Babbs Mount forty-six years ago. Sure, he became a scholar and councilman, but nothing will compare to his role on Creation Day. I think if you were to step back and really take a look at what's been going on, you'll find the events unfolding less surprising. Just wait until you see it."

"See what?"

Avestan did not answer but rather peered out the window as a gathering of cumulus pulsed in the west like a dark omen. They looked at Xiang with wise eyes, knowing no words could prepare her for the level of human suffering she would soon witness.

It was a foggy morning when Michael rode up on the Alamo. The stirring of a crow's nest somewhere on the dusty yellow sand broke the silence. Soldiers on horseback came through the fog's veil, gently clopping against the ground with a staggered hum. Michael halted them and shifted his head away from Apollo's stinking and bloodied dreadlocked mane to smell the wet air. He whispered something to the Earth as a horse came galloping from the cavalry division. General Fredrickson slowed his pace as he approached.

"Sir, our scouts are reporting four battalions ahead. They have heavy artillery and mortar cannons. It might be better to wait until Fraus and the rest of our troops return from the Northlands to attack."

Michael smelled the air again. "We will meet them head on. We will break the line."

"Why sir, when we could easily conserve our men and pick them off later after they've dispersed?"

"Two hundred and sixty-three years ago, Antonio Lopez

de Santa Anna sieged this place and left no survivors. For two weeks the forces of the Republic of Texas held them off until they were finally over run. I am obliged to honor that legacy. Más ultra, amigo."

"But the men who defended the Alamo lost the battle, sir."

"They won't this time."

"But sir—"

"Haven't you ever desired to lead your men into a battle of this magnitude, General? We have five thousand cavalry behind us. Strong men, fasted by their pace, eager for the bloodletting. Those who fall in battle will become legends to those who live, forever binding these men to a higher calling."

"Even you could be cut down by their mortars, sir," Ziven said. He pulled his horse another step forward to make clear his affection, lest his maniacal king took his words for insubordination.

"Even so, Ziven, I cannot think of a more glorious way to end my life."

They looked up as a voice pierced through the morning air, beyond sight in the low desert haze.

"Emperor Michael! Angel of death and curator of Hell's legions! Surrender now… or die!"

The other commanders of Michael's divisions hurried to his side, standing like mounted statues while they awaited orders. Michael inhaled deeply, then with a quick utterance he let loose some foul spell into the mist. The fog began to dissolve and slowly one could see a mass of soldiers spread out beyond and above a line of ash trees. They were outfitted with Eruption War-era military weapons and wore varying colors of fatigues. The native forces were separated into four distinct groups, with five to seven hundred men in each. Despite their heavy armament, they were all infantryman, and they were without reserves.

Michael coaxed Apollo forward and pulled his sword from its sheath. He raised its razor tip to the cresting sunlight and emptied his lungs with an ear-splitting lion's roar as he spoke to his own troops.

"Men of no nation! By right of conquest the natives have allowed us to send them to the afterlife! Spare them no mercy! Whether you live or die you will earn your place in history today! Go forth and rise to your highest selves!"

The troops rode up behind him and passed Ziven's arrested pose, who saw the operation as nothing but a slaughter for both sides.

Michael whispered some insidious order into Apollos ear and the massive steed flared its nostrils and burned the air with its fiery breath in anticipation. Apollo heightened his pace to a gallop and the men followed quickly. Behind them, snipers took positions on the roof of the Alamo. When they rode past the line of ash, the Pavonians opened fire. A line of cavalrymen were shot and dropped from their horses as the animals behind them sped toward the line, undaunted by the explosive bursts. Apollo zig-zagged across the field, shaking off the copper projectiles like flies as they ricocheted off his armor and body. When the two forces met, an explosion of screams and gunfire rang out with a thunderous clash. The Luciferian Army's cavalry opened fire while trampling the front line of infantrymen. Heads flew at the whim of Michael's large German blade and as bullets entered his airspace he would detect and block them, sending them back into the swell of the fighting, impartial to whose flesh they entered. Many horsemen fell at the initial strike, but as Ziven's men flanked the dispersing infantrymen, the battle shifted dramatically in the conqueror's favor.

Snipers on the Alamo killed the Pavonian forces heavy gunners. Another thousand horsemen poured onto the battlefield and flooded the natives with pulverizing force. Without sufficient ammunition, the axe wielding townspeople fell quickly to the armored cavalry. Some knelt and prayed for forgiveness while the savage men sustained the massacre, beheading the surrendering men mid-pose and once again feeding the Texan soil with rivers of blood. Loud hoots and yips of victory rang through the air as the last of the infantrymen were chased and trampled. A wounded man was shot in the head and smoke rose from his ear, ridding him of his final thoughts.

"You see Ziven!" Michael yelled, his face shining with arterial blood. "You make a man feel invincible, and he becomes it!"

Ziven nodded and breathed heavily, having nearly been knocked out with a hammer. He looked around at the vast array of slain corpses as his brain bled.

"Get the wounded medical attention, then we'll mobilize northward."

"What about the dead, sir?"

"Leave them for the buzzards."

"I meant our own."

"The order sustains."

Ziven watched his king reach into a fresh cadaver and pull from its chest a still beating heart. He began eating it like an apple before mounting Apollo and riding over to the other commanders who were converging with their divisions. Ziven followed behind him slowly, sublimated by his leader's passion and madness. His men were intoxicated by it. They lived for it. The mere sensation of war vitalized them and gave purpose to their crusade. They'd follow him into certain death so long as Michael pointed his sword toward their fate with confidence. As they treated their wounded and gathered enemy weapons, a mass of condors and vultures flocked from the west, the cadence of their screeches amplifying the death around them, for this was just the first of Michael's movements in he and his mistress's symphony of brutality.

As Michael's wave of dread spread over Pavonia, Almuruna's population grew. More refugees arrived daily to the shores of Portugal and France. They came on battered ships with the frozen bodies of their dead friends and family in the hulls. From all over Northern Almuruna, volunteers came seeking to help those in crisis, bringing with them food and medicine. There were people from placid lands who came to volunteer to fight, having never been in so much as a scuffle. In Melody's mind, any soul brave enough to stand against Michael would be honored in both life and death, for Michael was now a god of war, driven by perpetual hatred and a thirst for human blood.

Xiang promptly returned to Geneva with the children and the Zurvan clan. When they arrived, an arctic front had claimed the land with clear skies and sub-zero temperatures. Uli stepped off the ship and immediately scrambled to get back inside.

"Nope! Nuh-uh. Not doing that."

"Come now Uli, you'll get used to it," Xiang assured her.

One of the Zurvans gently pushed her back out the door as she pulled her arms in tight.

"How cold is it?"

"Negative thirty-four degrees Celsius. It won't always be

this cold, Uli. Come now. It's time to meet the empress."

As they walked from the ship to the palace, Devonia packed a snowball and threw it at Uli.

"Hey!" She picked one up herself and tossed it, but the ball fragmented into pieces.

"You have to pack it better because it's so dry," Devonia said.

"Snow is weird!" Uli said

As the children continued their snowball fight, Shiva spoke to Xiang.

"Perhaps we have been too rigid in dealing with them. Though they must prepare for their roles as god-hunters, we cannot let their youth diminish."

"We will do what the empress asks of us. You may be under Queen Parvati's jurisdiction in your homeland, but here you are under hers. They will have a more regimented weekly schedule and training program starting tomorrow. What they will miss of their youth is but a small sacrifice compared to what they will save for others. Why do you think Tala and Mayari were so capable?"

"The manipulation of Tala and Mayari by their masters at such a young age may have made them powerful, but it also damaged their souls. Let these girls run in the woods. Let them play with other children. Let them dance. Teach them the lessons of old. If we conform them to the principles of their quest too early, they may turn on us someday."

"I will heed your words, Master Shiva."

As the group entered the palace, the empress welcomed them into the dining hall. Uli was ecstatic to meet Melody and spent all evening telling her stories of Africa and how much she loved her homeland, despite her losses there. After the meal, Melody sent the children off to their rooms and dismissed the Zurvans, save for Shiva and Avestan.

Xiang poured them all more wine, and Melody insisted they all drink the 'fine vines blood', to loosen the tension between the cult that had once destroyed the world and the Sararan queen who had helped to save them all.

"For the sake of our people and planet, I ask that this hearing remains confidential. General Valor will be the only other member of the council informed. Do you all agree to this procedure?"

Everyone nodded in synchronized acceptance.

"Good. Then I will begin. Why, Master Shiva, did you take the children when we could have easily discussed reforming their education and training programs?" Melody asked, drinking the cool cabernet slowly. Her hair had grown back to half its original length, and she had tied her short bangs with green and blue braids.

Shiva answered. "We took the children because we felt we had to implement our plan before you had a chance to dismiss it, which you might have. Two weeks ago, we gave Devonia an injection containing Aradia Complex-C, the most advanced form of the Aradian formula, constructed carefully by Shakti and reformulated in the halls of Master Zou Cheng's tomb. Uhlanga was also given the mutative gene at an earlier time. According to the prophecy, these two girls will one day bring the world back to balance."

Melody let the information sink in, less surprised than the others thought she would be. "But the prophecy says there can only be two divine beings, and they must be lovers."

"Yes, and for the longest time we were convinced it referred to you and Michael. But we cannot rely on that assumption because of what has happened. Since Michael has given the witch the Sararan gene, we must take this union seriously, lest they alter the prophecy for their own ends."

Melody nodded, wishing what Shiva was saying was not true.

Xiang spoke up. "Michael's connection to the Slavic witch has increased... but to call it love? Are you insinuating that Uli and Devonia are destined to be lovers and will someday defeat them?"

Avestan intervened, smirking. "What makes you so sure they couldn't be lovers?"

Melody shook her head with frustration. "Perhaps we are all assuming too much. The witch, who shall not be named, has clouded my premonitions. My clairvoyance is useless now. She's jammed all celestial frequencies with her violent flourishing. We must rely on our physical capabilities and bring down the weight of our forces on them."

"It is unfortunate Tala cannot help us," Shiva lamented.

"Tala is neutral, for now. If she leaves, she may end the war, but could potentially cause a famine, which would have dire consequences for all life on Earth."

"And yet if she stays," Shiva intervened, "Michael and his possessor may spawn an infinite breed of ultra-modified beasts, equating the mass to our planet, our galaxy, and eventually the whole universe. He and that thing will synchronize their bodies to dark matter and become a disease of death inking its way through the marrow of time and existence. A Sararan pandemic: seamless, quantified and irrevocable."

Xiang's eyes grew wide with terror at the possibility. "What could prompt Tala to rise up and fight?" she asked, breathing deeply to calm herself.

"I don't know," Melody said.

Silence swept the room. Avestan put their hands to their ears, as if to listen to their own thoughts, while Melody turned to Shiva with betrayal in her gaze.

"You took those children like a thief in the night. You are aware of your debt to me now and why I must enforce it?"

"I am, Empress. I offer up the Zurvan clan to your armed forces. Our blood is your blood. Expend it at your will," Shiva said.

Melody nodded. "Your clan of warriors will be most welcome in the ranks. I look forward to seeing what you and Sage have in mind for our first offensive."

She slid a piece of paper to Shiva. The agreement outlined the military contract in explicit detail with an imperial golden seal smudged at the top to declare its resiliency to future altercations. Avestan uncupped their ears as Shiva signed the contract and passed it back.

"This resolves our hearing. Shiva. Avestan. I expect to see both of you at the council meeting tomorrow morning, to discuss the invasion of Pavonia. Sleep well, friends."

The Zurvans bowed and left but Xiang stayed, drinking her wine and staring at the center of the table with a glaze over her eyes.

Melody stood behind her. "How are you holding up?" she asked, touching her ambassador's neck softly sending endorphins directly into her bloodstream.

Xiang sighed with relief. "It's been a long week," she replied.

"Get some rest, Xiang. You deserve it."

"What do I deserve?"

"Happiness."

Melody stood up and said goodnight before leaving the room. She wondered who else in her council was having manic episodes. The witch had sunk her teeth into the astral sphere, while a wailing choir of new ghosts screamed in Melody's amaranthine mind like parasites, unable to penetrate her perfect cells. Just there. Screaming. Whatever the case, she had no choice but to remain optimistic. With the rest of the Zurvans and the pilots arriving in a few days' time, she would soon have everything she needed to launch her war against Michael and his succubus mistress.

Early in the stages of the Palace of Geneva's development, Michael had worked with Tibetan monks and Chinese architects to construct a superbly designed dojo in the East Tower. Using traditional styles of architecture within the narrow perimeters of sacred geometry, the training space was deemed a Kamiza, where martial artists from around the world would come to spar and learn from the modern bushi. Michael and the monks had trained future members of council since their birth. Even Ziven and Xiang had traded black eyes on the canvas mats well before their indoctrination to the council. To become an Imperial Operator meant becoming an advanced Samurai first. Though most would never use such skills in combat, their abilities wrapped their bones in steady movement, like the arms on a clock carefully ticking toward synchronicity. As the twenty-second century loomed, the dojo lay in quiet wait for its next generation of students. All two of them. The abbot and his monks in residency were capable of teaching the children, but since the girls were to be Aradians they also needed a teacher of sorcery, though it would be some time before they reached that tier in their progression.

One morning, as the sun shone through the high windows of that articulately shaped room, Devonia and Uli sat on the faded blood-splattered canvas in white gis and waited for their masters.

"Where are they?" Devonia asked, bored already.

Uli shrugged, watching as Boris walked the edge of the mat and toppled over lethargically. Uli reached over and flipped him right side up before laying back and yawning.

"Tatsu!"

The girls scurried to their feet and stood behind the canvas seams as Avestan and Shiva appeared. Shiva's eyes shot to Uli and she scooted her toes behind the seam.

"What is that?" Avestan asked, looking at the lazy reptile.

"That's Boris."

"From now on, no pets in the dojo."

"But he's training with us," Devonia argued.

Shiva spoke quickly to dismiss her sarcasm. "To start, myself and Avestan wish to apologize for what happened. We need you to trust us. We hope that by aligning ourselves with the empress we have shown you that we are all on the same side. In order for your training to be efficient, we need your loyalty and your approval."

"You're forgiven," Devonia shrugged.

Uli nodded in agreement.

"Are you ready for your first lesson?" Avestan asked.

"One question..." Devonia said, raising her hand. "Are you a guy or a girl?"

Uli couldn't help but giggle as she hid her mouth with her hands. She stopped after receiving a grueling scowl from Shiva.

"Let me ask you this, Devonia. Does it matter?" Avestan asked.

"I guess not," she shrugged.

"Then all you need to know is that I am the teacher, and you are the student. Understand?"

"Yes," the girls said simultaneously.

"Good. I want twenty pushups on your knuckles followed

by a three-minute wall sit, go!"

The girls dropped to the mat reluctantly and fixed themselves into a modified push up position, beginning the reps.

"This hurts!" Uli said, shaking out her knuckles.

"It's supposed to hurt. We're conditioning your fists," Shiva said, pointing to the mat with a stern gesture.

"Where's Ambassador Yu?" Devonia asked, looking up.

"I didn't tell you to stop, Devonia!"

The girls finished their push-ups then leaned against the wall, their faces contorted with discomfort. After thirty seconds, they plopped to the ground. Uli laughed.

"Okay, okay, let's try this," Devonia said.

They got back up into position and dropped again, laughing and rolling on the mat.

"This is going to take some work," Avestan admitted quietly to Shiva as he approached them.

"Were you any better? We all began as seeds," Shiva said.

Avestan sighed and nodded. "Again!"

The abbot watched from afar, behind a crack in the door. With a slight smile, he closed his eyes and thanked the sun for the return of Pavonis.

Later that evening, a small ceremony was held for the apprentices by the shores of the lake. The girls were dressed in silk robes and made to look like royalty. The abbot and Xiang stood in ritualistic red garments across from Avestan and Shiva, with the girls kneeling at the water's edge facing the palace. Melody approached, holding two pillows with silk sheets over them. Upon one of the pillows was a polished silver scrying mirror, which she gave to Uli, giving her the power of foresight. The second pillow held Ezra's knife, which she gave to Devonia. Both were entry level instruments of magick, marking the beginning of their careers as psychological warfare operatives. The ceremony concluded with a blessing from the empress, whereupon Melody drew the most divine protective energy she could muster from the depths of the old lake.

A week later, the ambassador for Queen Parvati of Mongolia arrived, binding at last the reformed Council of Almuruna. Sage introduced the ambassador to council, then rose to speak first. The subject was not a pleasant one and she spoke slowly, so that all could absorb her words well.

"In the last five weeks, more than thirty-five thousand men, women and children have been slain by Michael's Luciferian Army. More than ten thousand wounded are without aid, and all humanitarian efforts to Pavonia have been cut off by his expansive network of militants. He is primarily using guerrilla tactics and moving quickly across the land with nothing but horses and light vehicles. There have been numerous reports of rapes, torture, hangings, disemboweling, dismembering, beheadings and scalp collecting. These men have violated every human rights clause outlined in the constitution of 2060, and these tragedies continue as we speak. Some resistance has been met by Pavonian natives, but they've retreated all the way to the Northern Appalachian region. The area in direst need of aid as of now is Southern and Central Pavonia, where a cholera outbreak is spreading quickly and without containment could be more damaging than the casualties of these massacres."

Melody stood and spoke with certainty. "Michael is

reinstating the international law of Right of Conquest. Based on the evidence of the recent human rights violations and direct attacks against the Kingdoms of Pavonia and Almuruna, I have officially declared war against Michael's legion and all those involved in his regime. This goes for any followers or supporters in this very city who would rather he take the throne of Almuruna. We must stay vigilant and warn our civilians of this threat while the preparations for war commence."

"What is your prospective timeline for the offensive?" Sage asked.

"Michael and his troops are infiltrating the Rocky Mountains as we speak. It will take weeks or months to work from West to East, which is his plan according to our sources. He will meet more opposition there than he's faced yet. The children who survived the fallout of Caldera are the most hardened people on the planet. Michael will defeat them, but it will take time. In the meantime, we must finalize preparations."

Sage nodded. Xiang looked at the ambassador for the Mongol nation, a daughter to one of the nine queens, as she was, their mothers abducted by Shakti long ago; kidnapped and made into royal assassins, who in turn taught her and Xiang, just like Devonia and Uli would be taught too. She returned eye contact with Xiang as Melody addressed the small oriental woman.

"Ambassador, what message from the Mongolian Empress have you come so far to tell? What was your holy leader's answer to my request for troops?"

"Queen Parvati sympathizes with your losses, and is deeply concerned with the situation in Pavonia. She will not, however, be sending her forces to Almuruna to reinforce this kingdom's borders. If Michael's strategy shifts and he crosses the Pacific instead of the Atlantic, he could easily invade the Mongol empire if we send our forces to the wrong end of the continent. I'm sure you can understand how critical it is for us to be patient and plan ahead should our own kingdom come under attack."

"Though I am disheartened by this news, I understand, and will be in close contact with Parvati should she need our support as well. For now, we are taking volunteers from all nations, yours included. We thank you for any further support you can give us."

The ambassador bowed slightly in her seat.

"As for this council, General Valor will be directing our newly established military while Master Shiva has offered to take up training and organizing her troops. Avestan will be the caretaker for my apprentices and will serve as both their master and guardian. Ambassador Yu will remain in Almuruna until international threat levels have lessened. The abbot will remain Sensei and divide his monks into security forces for the palace and send the rest of them to train with the Zurvan clan. Does anyone have any questions about their duties before the next movement?"

No one spoke. The abbot closed his eyes, as though he could feel Melody's emotions flickering across his own face as she suppressed them as best she could.

"Michael's wrath has seeped into domestic affairs. Two days ago, former councilman Fernando Vesper was arrested and charged with the assassination of David Beller and treason against the Kingdom of Almuruna. He pleaded guilty at his hearing and awaits his verdict in solitary confinement in Geneva's prison. Though I can hide him from the world, the inmates who trust him know he's there. They're talking. They will spill his sermon to the outside world; in the markets, offices, taverns and store fronts; on the fringes of our fields and mountain communities. These quiet revolutionists claim I am a tyrant and must be stopped. For now, I have temporarily suspended an order that would result in Vesper's immediate execution. But I fear these factions will gain momentum by his pardoning. What does the council say?"

"We cannot stoop to Michael's level. I say absolutely not," Xiang said first, confident in her answer. She looked around for disputants.

"Without a swift act of justice, more killings will surely follow. You must break your pacifist traditions for the sake of this kingdom's future," Shiva said.

"I agree. Kill him," Sage said with certainty.

"All in favor of the execution of Fernando Vesper, raise your hand," Melody said, raising her right hand high as she spoke.

The others agreed save for Xiang, who shook her head in anger as if she perhaps saw why the revolutionists had begun to question their long-held leader.

That night, an Italian's head was severed and placed in a wooden box in the basement of the palace, like some cursed thing to be forgotten, as if no one knew where to put it. Despite his hellacious crimes, in time his death would become the symbolic catalyst for a proxy force of Michael's legion, the very problem the execution was intended to extinguish. He spoke his last words in eloquent prose.

"Il Figlio di Dio si è fatto uomo per diventare Dio."

'The son of God became man so that we might become God.'

Preparations were finalized for the massive invasion as refugees poured ashore. Almuruna teemed with volunteer fighters and medical practitioners and aid workers, all filtering through Geneva on their way to the French coasts where large ships would soon embark on a treacherous voyage. The pilots soon arrived from their various corners of the kingdom and Melody was most relieved at the sight of them. She welcomed them with a great feast in the palace two weeks before the offensive. Those dining consisted of the pilots and the council, who were eager to meet one another at last. The candlelight illuminated a bittersweet rejoicing as introductions lessened and Melody spoke. None there had been to war except the empress, since such things had barely existed in almost half a century.

"My friends! Let me begin by thanking you for coming here to our aid. It means a great deal to me that you've come to help us in this fight against the Luciferian Army. I know we have a myriad of pilot classes—"

Melody paused as an old man walked into the room. Everyone looked over to see the legendary William Beller enter. He wore his Marine Corps officer uniform, his hat primed, his white pants ironed and his jacket fashioned neatly with a plethora of medals. He used a cane to walk over and sit himself down.

"Good evening, Empress. Sorry I'm late. Those damn steps beat the hell out of me."

"Welcome, William," Melody said, her eyes alight with a green aura as she glimpsed Michael in his uncle's features.

"Am I? Well how come I didn't get an invitation for re-enlistment?" he asked.

Sage smiled and turned to him. "My apologies, William. I assumed you'd retired from flying a long time ago."

"I might be ninety years old but I can still fly a damn

plane."

"These are re-commissioned fighter jets that can go two thousand miles per hour and bank up to nine Gs of acceleration."

"You have helicopters, don't ya?" he said.

"A small fleet."

"I can at least be an instructor, damnit. Do you have anyone else out there that can do it? I hate to be the bearer of bad news, but your best pilots left with Michael when he lost his damn mind. These folks sitting at this table might run better than me and see better, and even fly better, but they're no warriors. You're going to at least need my help training them if you want this to succeed."

Sage nodded, as did Melody.

"I will see to it, William. Your wisdom and leadership will be greatly appreciated."

William stood then, turning to speak to the group as a whole. "My nephew has left us. He left his loving wife and his kingdom. He left everything he had for the fruits of conquest. I've heard about this witch and I don't give a shit who she is or what her plan is. They both need to be destroyed. Even I, who loved Michael like a son, understand what must be done now. I have seen ordinary people pull together to save the planet once before, and I believe we have more than enough good men and women to accomplish it again. Let us raise a toast. To a better world."

The room raised their glasses and Melody smiled, raising her glass towards William. He smiled solemnly in return. A string quartet began to play in the corner of the dining hall and the mood brightened as conversation commenced. Will shoved his wine away and gestured to a serving maiden.

"Hey, you got any brandy around here?"

"Yes... umm... I think there's some in the cellar."

"And what kind of food is this."

"It's Swedish meatballs, sir."

"Well put it in a box and send it back to Sweden!"

"I'll make sure to do just that," she said, walking away hastily.

A handsome young Italian pilot sitting next to Will looked at him oddly.

"What do you fly?" Will asked him.

"Fighter jet, M-Class. What did you fly?"

"Blackhawks mostly, and a few of the relic fighters Michael would let me take for a spin. Haven't done either in about sixty years or so and I've never flown the empress's M-Class fighters, but I thought: what the hell? If anything, I'll just fly straight into those sons a bitches."

"You mean, you'd be a kamikaze?"

"Hell yeah! For the right target, absolutely."

"But that's suicide."

"Hey kid, my wife died five years ago. I'm ninety years old. I don't even buy green bananas anymore."

The woman returned with the brandy and a different meal.

"Sorry for being a grump, miss. Here's a tip for your troubles." He handed her some vintage paper money.

"Thanks... I guess," she said, walking away holding the mysterious green bill.

He poured a healthy glass of whiskey for both himself and the Italian.

"Here's to winning," he said as he clinked his drink against the man's glass, gulping the liquid and pouring another before the other pilot could drink his first.

CHAPTER 48 – THE APPALACIAN FRONT

In an effort to combat Fraus's northward push, Tala pulled together opposing fronts in the Pacific, creating a swell of storms barreling towards the coast. She sent arctic winds from the north, causing a devastating series of blizzards to form when they met the ocean's warm precipitation, crushing western Pavonia. While the locals thrived in the March storms, Fraus's contingent pushed downward to lower elevations and quickly thinned out by snipers whose nests were kept occupied by the survivors of Shakti's terrible reign, those mixed-blooded sixteenth generation Americans who never took sovereignty for granted. The Sararan witch herself could not be halted by bullets or blizzards. She kept on alone, using her new body to draw in the weak minded, making faithful pale zombies and marching them through snowy mountains, their limbs black and frost-bitten as they heeded her every thought and direction. She would steal the minds of more than just humans. Cats and raptors fell easily under her spell, following the insane posse with a rabid hunger, their selfish natures fulfilled by her wishes as they viciously attacked anything that breathed.

Villages fell easily to the undead brigade and once harmonious communities dispersed, abandoning their homes at the first sight of the Slavic demon. She blinded those who dared gaze into her eyes, those poisonous irises as complex as a star system and nearly as lethal, nestled within orbs of decaying uranium. The veins on her hands bulked like snakes gliding under horse hide, her hatred ever flowing as the burning white gloss of her stare turned the living to stone. She was a modern day Medusa, complying to the devil's bidding, materializing her vast string of sins like a web as any arachnid would. For sheer enjoyment she would rape the most resistant men, clubbing their skulls the moment she orgasmed, leaving their naked bodies to freeze, discarded and forgotten in the accumulative drift.

She went further north into what was once Canada and even further into the Yukon and Alaskan territories. By the time she'd peaked Denali and risen above the inversion, no threat remained in Pavonia save for the natives scrambling to build up their defenses in the Appalachian Mountains. The only other creature worth hunting was Tala, but without Michael's help, she'd have no chance of confronting the Aradian. She looked north but made no other motion that way. Instead, she turned south, letting her forces of soulless corpses die off in the cold and dark.

Whoever crossed paths with the shadowy reaper was killed as quietly as the wind, their brains instantly infected with disease, a tender treat for the murder of crows that followed her like a black cloud. She took her time on the return journey as she followed the microscopic breadcrumbs left by Pavonis's war path, for she believed the holy witch had known some secret beyond the knowledge of any Aradian divination. With some careful approximation she at last discovered an old cabin deep in the woods. Someone had buried an axe in the floor, and beneath the creaky boards, the witch unearthed a hidden treasure.

"So this is where Ingrid became Pavonis," she spoke aloud.

She picked up the occult book and wiped off some snow. All the pages were blotched with ink save for a single page, where instructions for a hex had been drawn, so despicable and unstable it was little wonder that the redemptive goddess had never used it. Yet she had not chosen to destroy its formula either.

Fraus smiled and slipped the page under her breastplate, before leaving on winged feet, eager to report her findings to Michael and to tell him the news of the son growing in her womb, his soul yet undecided.

○

The French coast was becoming overcrowded. Those who had fled Michael's atrocities and were arriving from distant shores met those coming from inland, about to embark on an invasion like none other. William Beller walked through the crowd of lost Pavonians, their hair caked with sand and grease as it dried in the salty air, their faces strained with sorrow and uncertainty. His tall figure rose above those around him. A woman saw the patch on his flight suit and kissed his hand.

"Estar bien, piloto," she said.

He looked into her eyes and saw his late wife in them, a beautiful dark woman following the same path of hardship as Lakshmi had early in her life. William did not pass the physical requirements to become a pilot in Sage's ranks, but was ordered to be a reserve fighter pilot and flight instructor. Many times before he'd felt confident he'd be killed in battle, never to return. This time he would be required to.

Sage came behind him, wearing her general's coat with trepidation as she walked aboard the aircraft carrier. The massive ship was surrounded by hybrid destroyers and an array of speed boats mounted with large artillery guns. The refugees offered carved bones and other power objects as the general passed them.

"Gracias, gracias," she said as she nodded to the victims.

The rest of the pilots came walking with the mystique of astronauts about to embark on a perilous expedition into the unknown. Behind them, thousands of volunteers from all over Almuruna anxiously awaited their turn to board. The ships cast off shortly after as an audience of thousands watched them leave at the cusp of twilight. Fireworks exploded with clapping and cheering as the steel ships churned the sea and drifted toward the lawless continent.

As the people waved their loved ones off, Melody watched on with Xiang by her side.

"Fare well, heroes of Almuruna," Melody said.

Her ambassador wrapped her arms around the empress, abandoning formalities for compassion. The empress smiled and returned the embrace.

"I love you."

"I love you too."

"Do you think Sage is ready to confront the belligerents?"

Melody sighed, perhaps feeling a sliver of guilt for staying behind.

"She'll have to be."

The armada crossed the horizon, halved by the bowed circumference of the Earth as they drifted, wave over wave, toward a shore already lined with blockades of oil rigs fueling Michael's war machine.

After the long journey across the cold sea, the maritime soldiers prepared their kits and made their peace with God on all decks. There were Almurunan monks, Mongol irregulars, Zurvans, Royal Marines, the French Foreign Legion, Russian mercenaries and whole divisions of North African teens. There were ships filled entirely with criminals who'd been given the choice of prison or war, drafted to be minesweepers and to take on all the most grueling infantry undertakings.

A thick mist hung over the Pavonian coast as the ships neared the shore. It was morning and darkness was shedding to light, just as winter had shed to spring, and the once-chemist Sage Valor had shed her former trade to become Almuruna's General of the Armed Forces. Though Sage had reached willingly for that new rank, her training and preparation would now be tested in full, and she fidgeted with a pen as she watched the radar screen surmise. Nothing came up.

"Halt the armada. Send out scouts. Let the empress know we've arrived."

As the engines ceased their grinding, the ship's anchors were tossed into the deep and labored for some time along the murk until they caught on the steel graveyard of New York City's sunken shattered remains. Deployed first and quietest were a myriad of smaller boats holding the world's best trackers: scouts of the Nine Tribes; a special contingent developed by Queen Parvati, trained from birth and explicitly taught the way of the Paleolithic hunter. From the first gentle rise of the tide they fell and disappeared below the sea foam. Without fins or suits they swam unseen, using small reeds for snorkels, crawling onto the beach like fish growing limbs and scuttling into the woods. They wove through the forest and spoke raven's tongue, cawing through the thick to insure total coverage. After they'd swept the area for enemy movement, one of them popped a flair. A green light shot into the air leaving a smoke trail behind it.

"That's a positive signal, General. We're all clear," a woman spoke from the observation point.

"Confirmed."

Sage turned as Will came to stand beside her with his arms crossed.

"I thought for certain he'd have the coast guarded north of the barricade," she said, nervous about the quiet.

Will shook his head. "Why would Michael do that when he can just wait for you on his own chosen piece of ground? He's well aware of our intentions. He's halted his troops further inland so we have to waste more resources getting to him, and if you decide to seize his refineries that will split our forces and slow us down further."

"How do you suggest we expedite the invasion?"

"The one advantage we do have is that the Pavonian forces are between him and us, and they have not yet been attacked since Michael dug in more than two months ago."

"We need to integrate them. Do we know their strength?"

Shiva, who'd been pacing near the window, spoke with some disparity. "There were five-thousand soldiers last time there was a census taken. But the winter has been brutal and long and many have died from wounds and complications. Deserters have fled by the hundreds. Those who remain are the most dedicated. We will need them."

Sage nodded and spoke with a greater confidence than before. "We'll set up a base of operations, move west, then tie in with the Pavonian forces in three days. Make sure the pilots are ready to scramble in case Michael decides to make a move. If this plan is going to favor us, we need to act."

"Will you be staying with the ship?" Will asked.

"No. I've delegated Shiva to stay behind to command the fleet. I'll be on the ground with everyone else who doesn't want to be here. They need to see me at the head of the march."

Will smiled and nodded. "Now I see why Melody chose you."

○

Three days later, the forces of Almuruna and Pavonia broke bread on the Potomac river and marched as one army on the old roads of war, their tanks and small vehicles treading on the decaying asphalt highways that had been punctured by trees and plants ripping through the rocky tar. By that evening all the remnants of the last apocalypse lay behind them, as they once again found themselves deep in the wild where time could not be referred to by any shape made or unmade by man.

Wilderness: Michael's preferred battle grounds.

When they awoke on the fourth day, the scouts returned with reports of a large enemy encampment. The allies moved forward and found themselves at the head of the Appalachian front, only a half mile from Michael's troops. The ancient mountains stunk with fungal propagation and an eerie silence fed their fears of the foul demon. Sage thought perhaps she would see enemy campfires, but no smoke rose into the morning mist.

The general had shaved her head into a bleached white mohawk and spiked it with tree sap, leaving two tufts of long purple and black hair falling in front of her ears. Her armor was white and silver and engraved on her chest was the crest of Pavonis outlined in gold. She mounted her horse and walked toward the edge of a cliff to overlook the fog covered hills.

"What is the report?" she asked her second in command.

The man walked up to her. "They have twenty thousand strong, twice as many as our forces. But they have no heavy equipment, no tanks, no ships... at least none that we've found."

"With his abilities he doesn't them."

"Let's just be glad he can't fly."

Then, from the mist, a hollow drum could be heard like a giant's heartbeat. Its slow rhythm brought the others to the crest. Those who had not yet awakened were pulled from their sleep by its ominous pulse. Sage looked around for the source. The drum's origin could not be seen, only heard. More joined until a line of percussionists boomed through the canyon.

"Fall into formation but do not let anyone past the creek. I'm calling in close air support."

"Roger that, ma'am," he said as he got on his radio and ordered his forces back. "You're all clear ma'am."

The drums continued to play as Sage got on her own radio.

"Shiva, this is Artemis Actual, go ahead and put two birds in the air."

"Copy that, ma'am. En route. What are your orders?"

"I want two sequential napalm runs from northeast to southwest between these coordinates: 31 degrees 41'51.83 minutes north by 79 degrees 02'30.16 minutes west."

Shiva read back the coordinates for confirmation.

"Targets confirmed," Sage said as she looked out across the low mountains, trying to spot any sign of the supposed army of enemy soldiers. Only drums could be heard; not a single sighting of anyone.

"All personnel are cleared of the blast zone. Perhaps we should get into position and off this crest," her second in command suggested. "There could be snipers and I'd hate to—"

Just then the distant crack of a rifle sounded and his head exploded, his body smacking the ground with a wallop.

"Take cover!" Sage screamed, as she moved behind the ledge and darted down the hill away from the gunshots. She picked up her radio as she breathed heavily, wiping the splattered blood from her horse's snout. "This is General Valor! Enemy snipers are in the area. Get in position and take coverrrr—"

The radio made modulating electronic noises before popping and burning up in her hand. More cracks from the rifles could be heard in the distance over the drums. Yelling and chaos erupted around them.

"God damnit!" she yelled, dropping the burning plastic sizzling to the wet forest floor.

"What the hell was that all about?" a soldier standing nearby asked, looking at the fried communicator.

"She's here."

"Who?"

Sage looked straight up and pointed through the branches. Far above, Fraus flew dragon-like on leather wings, jamming all communication signals and hindering Sage's conversation with Shiva and the pilots.

"Fire!" Sage yelled.

The soldiers pointed their rifles at the sky and shot in vain as the succubus spun and dodged their shots before disappearing back behind her line.

"No one cross the creek! We have a napalm run coming at any moment!" she yelled out as her soldiers fled the gunfire haphazardly.

The drums continued to pulse at a faster rate and Sage looked around at her troops gradually falling into place behind the trenches.

She heard the jets screaming toward them in the distance. For some of the troops it was too late. The aircraft came in low and dropped several barrels of the volatile octane, scorching man and woman and Earth in one felling. The fires burned high despite the morning humidity, the shrieking of those who'd been caught in its fury echoing across the landscape.

From the myriad of sizzling human bodies, a war god rose from the flames, his wings as broad as his counterpart's; his transformation into his most wicked self now complete. Michael's black armor shone against the orange light of dawn, his eyes a window into the blaze behind him. His massive wings fanned the flames and he smiled at Sage as he let himself become swallowed by the fire's crowning, disappearing into a more active section of the front.

Sage retreated to gather her troops and order a charge. Behind her she heard more screams and return gunfire. A second napalm drop blasted the hillside and Michael's men were charred into oblivion. The sound of artillery and cannon fire shattered the air. With so much screaming and gun fire, Sage could hardly talk with her third in command standing next to her. She screamed in his ear as allied attack helicopters flew above them.

"Get third company to flank from the south where the men are less concentrated! I want the rest of our forces to push forward once the fire has cooled down! Just keep firing at their positions!"

"But all our comms are down!"

"I know! Pass the order down the line! Hurry up!"

She looked up to see one of the helicopters hovering above the fire. Gunners shot at the enemy machine gun nests on the opposing slope and bullets ricocheted from the belly of the aircraft above them. Suddenly, Fraus flew up from the flames, grasping a large fiery log and throwing the torch at the chopper's tail rotor. In a blast of sparks, the helicopter spun out of control and fell into the forest, exploding and throwing shrapnel and burning metal into the conflict.

"Come with me to retrieve the wounded!" Sage ordered, swiftly dismounting and hurrying toward her ground troops.

Her infantrymen reluctantly followed her, bringing with them a few stretchers to carry out their fallen brethren. An array of bullets zipped by Sage's ears as she ducked behind a trench. The men behind her had been shot, save one who crawled up next to her, trembling. She looked across the canyon and watched her artillery pummel the trees to pieces.

"This isn't that kind of war," she said, suddenly less afraid. She picked up one of the machine guns and threw the belts of ammunition over her shoulders.

"What do you mean?" he asked.

"The ones you hear about in stories," she said, as she wrapped her ankle in some cloth to stop the bleeding from some shrapnel she'd received. "About glory and fighting for what is right. None of this is 'right'. This is about who is better."

"So what are you saying?"

"Be better!" she yelled.

She turned and rose slightly over the berm, spraying the oncoming soldiers with bullets. Four of them dropped with their chests full of lead as the other enemy fighters took cover. They immediately returned fire as Sage ducked back down. Dirt sprayed her mohawk as the bullets dug away at the bank. The soldier next to Sage took one of his grenades and threw it. With a terrific boom, the dead men and their limbs were strewn about the creek. The rest of the platoon had moved elsewhere. Sage looked up to see the fire losing its ferocity.

"FOR ALMURUNA! FOR PAVONIA! CHARGE!"

She ran back to her horse on the hill, and after mounting her steed she met with her forces and charged head on into battle, against cavalry and infantry alike, amidst the blaze and shelling and gun fire. As she shot and sliced her way through the battlefield, she realized suddenly that she might die that day, but through her battles, at risk of entering the cage of purgatory, perhaps she would become something greater in death. She shoved down those thoughts and settled on the task at hand. She was alive, and the demons circling overhead in the battlefield's air space were the only diviners.

More fighter jets came to aid the allies but all of them crashed into the mountain, their brains imploding from Fraus's mental hijacking. Michael directed his troops as he entered the slaughter. He picked up allied soldiers and dropped them from disastrous heights, watching their bodies fall on their own spears.

Eventually, the enemy overran the brave but disorganized allied troops. Michael chose not to pursue them in their retreat. He killed his own wounded men just as they had requested, for they believed they would enter Michael's version of Paradise, a place he had marveled over and preached about to his men like a religious converter who honors the will of men alone.

Sage left some of her wounded to die, afraid the witch would put spells on the medics and infect the remaining troops with her possessive powers.

In the dark of night, the cries of the wounded buried all other sound. A medical camp had been erected far behind the line and welcomed all who'd been maimed in battle, with the worst being sent to the naval fleet once communications had been re-established. Sage limped through the camp, holding a smudge of the plant after which she was named, its pungent smoke warding off Fraus's abilities.

A young man whose face had been badly burned lay on a blanket. He reached his hand out to her. Sage stopped and knelt by him.

"General..." he wheezed.

"What is your name, soldier?"

"Thomas Lundberg. I come from Cork, in Ireland."

"Thank you for you bravery today, Thomas. You must be in so much pain. I'll make sure you're on the next transport home."

He attempted to laugh but faltered into coughing. "Don't waste your space on me. Just give this to my mother. She always wanted to see Pavonia."

He handed her a smashed white Laelia flower, wrapped in a hand-written letter. Sage squinted her eyes.

"This came all the way from Mexico... how did you—"

"I joined Michael's brigade earlier this year. My father was wrongfully imprisoned for practicing his religion in public, but he was never intrusive or offensive about his beliefs. The local governors were cracking down on men of all kinds because of the empress's new mandates. They only ever imprisoned men who broke the law, never women. I wanted to resist the empress, for what she had done to him." The soldier coughed again, his face twisting in agony. "I joined Michael, but I immediately regretted my decision. I deserted only when I knew I could get away safely. I was tricked. We all were."

Sage smiled and put her hand on his chest. "You will be taken to a medical ship and transported home, Thomas. You can give this to your mother yourself. You're going to be okay."

He attempted a chuckle. "Michael and the witch cannot be defeated. We will all die here. They will take your ships, your weapons... they will spread their disease through the world. No one can stop them."

"Empress Melody can stop them."

"Then why isn't she here?"

Sage sat with him for a while, listening to him breathe, the rattling reminiscent of cancerous lungs of a man twice his age. The napalm had burned his insides and he had two bullet wounds in his left shoulder. By the time the extraction ship arrived, Thomas had passed. The medics found Sage weeping, her head on his chest.

No one slept that night, and the scouts stayed close, for fear of the smallest whispered spell floating eastward on a foul wind.

It was dawn when the monsters attacked.

Sage awoke to the sound of severed human heads falling from the sky and rolling through the allied camp. A woman shrieked, alerting the rest to rise. From the shadows of morning's infancy they came like cat-people, some winged and some not, descending upon the camp with maniacal folly. They were resurrected soldiers from the battlefield of yesterday, their bodies entwined with animal DNA and given the souls of angry Patawomeck ghosts, creations drawn from Fraus's more morbid forms of magick.

The infuriated demons crowded and clawed at the allies like vengeful beasts, creating a scene of horror for all who were still shellshocked from the First Battle of Appalachia.

Soldiers rose to arms and fought the creatures as they swept through the valley, the fiends taking gunshots to their abdomens and chests without disruption, for although their blood ran hot, they were not easy to kill. Some held scepters and skewered the allied soldiers mercilessly as they croaked ancient war chants from their hollow chests.

For many hours the forces bulged and pushed one another back. Hatred for either side rose, as did the ditches with rivers of blood and the air with a putrid calamity of screams and explosions. Sage led her forces east and away as Michael's cavalry suddenly flanked the camp. The Pavonians and Almurunans were quickly becoming outnumbered and outgunned. Their vehicles and tanks stopped dead under the exposed and terrible sky as they became trapped by the disgusting charade. The commanding officers called for a full retreat, but behind them the camp was being demolished as horses and men and creatures of some cruel sorcery crushed everything in their path, leaving none alive.

As if to nullify the sky's beauty, Michael and Fraus circled above like raptors; Hell's royalty watching the massacre with satisfied glances, admiring the dominion of the powerful over the weak. As much as Melody had empowered Michael to be great, Fraus empowered him to be a god. Their wide bat wings acted like solar panels, absorbing the rising sun's casting, though they were already beyond saturated with its energy. Rising high above the cirrus clouds to greet the unfiltered light, they flapped their enormous wings and stretched out their muscular bodies. Michael grasped the faded epaulettes inked on Fraus's shoulders and kissed her as the pure light hit them, invigorating their skin as they sent their energy downward onto the battle. The possessed demons on the ground suddenly combusted into flame and burned everything around the allies, cutting off Sage's retreat in a scorching circle. The few hundred survivors that remained dropped their weapons and stood before the cavalry, who slowly approached the circle from all sides, their armor making them appear as mechanical warriors on metal-plated horses as the skin walkers lay in smoldering ruin under their hooves.

Will and Shiva watched the battle from the carrier. They'd sent up a reconnaissance plane and had been following the attack from the start.

"We have to leave," Shiva said.

"Like hell we do! Scramble the ships!" Will declared, "Send 'em up! We need to rescue them!"

"Anyone who gets close to those sorcerers will die. We need to save our resources and get back to Almuruna as quickly as possible to come up with a new plan. Brute force will not defeat them. We need a different strategy."

"I'll go then. Give me a ship. I'll hold them off while you get the fleet moving."

Shiva tipped his brow. "What if you don't return?"

"I don't plan to."

The old man went to put on his flight suit one last time.

He walked up to the deck and breathed the salty air. A fine day for flying, he thought. He entered the cockpit of his craft and started the massive engines and his life flashed before his eyes; of growing up with his brother Ezra in Missouri, his time in college and the military and those vital years of becoming a man. He recollected the day when his world was changed forever as Ezra's turmoil swallowed their lives whole.

He thought of the darkness of the Post-Eruption Wars, the epoch in the bunker, his exile into the arctic with his men, and the long winter that followed. He remembered finding Michael in the mountains and training him to become a Marine; how he had fully bloomed, for Michael had now become a master of warfare in his own right, disregarding the virtues he was distilled in exchange for might. He remembered nearly assassinating Lakshmi, but instead loving her and marrying her, living many years in peace despite their former lives of woe and uncertainty. He remembered his loving wife and wept for her, for she was the one who had risked everything to rescue Michael and let the pieces of the new world fall into place on Creation Day. He took out a picture of her and slipped it behind the altimeter. Her beautiful soft brows complimented the shape of her smile, and as he gazed at her face, he muttered some prayer his mother would say, and vowed to do one last good thing before meeting her in the afterlife.

The allies stood as prisoners of war on that field of silence, and the glowing duo of death descended slowly before them. Sage stood at the front, her hands raised in surrender. The Luciferian Army troops backed up and widened the circle around the captured forces.

"Sage Valor. Your name does not suit you so well. Are you... shaking?" Michael asked, retracting his wings so they rose like a black spires behind him.

His eyes glowed bright with fire as they always had, yet the ring of flame around them had lessened with the humidity of the morning.

"Step forward, General."

Sage took a few steps forward and knelt, her body shaking terribly as she cried without sound.

"A beautiful spring morning, isn't it? The way the sun has risen to rival Cassiopeia in the Northern Sky..." He looked at the constellation and smiled, a laceration on his chest had healed, and yet behind it the scars of the bear attack remained.

Sage looked up slowly. "Do you remember the cave, Michael?"

He stared back, his eyes taunting her.

"For behind the constellation of beauty which you describe, Ursa Major lumbers faithfully in tow, and as the world turns so does the bear, crawling along the ridges of your dreamscape; reminding you of your greatest feat, of becoming a man, something you'll never be again since you are but a slave to your own mutation, a betrayer of friends and lovers. You are the lowest form of life, not the highest."

Fraus licked some blood from her bottom lip as she squinted painfully, her eyes brighter than the sun. Sage dared not look into them.

Michael snarled. "Gunners! On my command!"

He raised his sword and held it for a moment, looking into Sage's eyes before thrusting the blade down into the dirt. A burst of gunfire erupted and Sage closed her eyes and winced. Behind her the screams erupted with the firing squad, and just as soon were muted. The hundreds of guns barked on, sputtering out until all were turned to pulp. Sage dared not look behind her at the pile of bodies. The smell of open flesh and gunpowder filled the air. Michael took a deep breath with his nose and exhaled calmly. Sage looked up.

"Cherish this triumph, you inglorious angel." Her voice

was shaky but determined. "For in heaven, God and I will have a common foe. I may die today but you will forever live with this pain. A rotting mind in a perfect body. Today my destiny crystalizes, but you will never be remembered. Those who you have won over with your scheming will die; even your fiendish mistress will betray you in time, and you will live on, alone forevermore with nothing to show for your conquest but the blood on your hands. Even now, you look at me with your enflamed pupils affixed like abandoned stars, with nothing but rage left inside them, corrupted with consumption and nothing else."

Michael spat.

"You're just one little calf in this cattle drive," he said, smiling. "Surrounded by wolves, on the fringe, careful not to step too close to death, just like your empress. See how she has pushed you into the pit of war while she clings to her satin throne? You've come all this way only to be abandoned yourself. Pity doesn't even describe it. While your maimed body is left to rot in the sun, I'm going to take your ships and your aircraft and I'm going to invade Almuruna. Soon, tribal warfare will cover the Earth as if it were the elixir all along, and I'll be recognized as King until a more powerful being claims my throne, as any right man would have it."

They stared at one another in silence for a moment.

"Are you ready to die?" he asked.

"If death is my punishment for standing against your treachery then I welcome my end."

Sage shivered and knelt as Apollo came from behind his master, wet from battle and leaking blood from a stab wound in his leg. He began to kick his hooves into the stirred dirt. He snarled, a carnivorous man-eating stallion, snapping his topaz-like teeth and rearing up on his hind legs, screeching with callous cadence. He dropped back to the ground and galloped toward the wounded general. Sage shrieked. Fraus laughed. With menacing kicks, the steed's hooves trampled Sage into the soil as she screamed and gargled with struggling breaths. She tried to curse but her jaw was shattered; her cracked skull seeping blood. Michael spat on her crushed body then mounted Apollo as the horse's rage lessened. He looked at Sage's disfigured body seizing like a squashed insect. Fraus came up and kissed him.

"If only she'd fought to her end like she spoke to her end... we might have had a quality adversary."

She flew back into the open blue sky, seeking those who'd fled the battle – enemy or defector – killing all with equal prejudice.

The Luciferian Army moved forward, past the bodies and charred skeletons, into large open fields where Michael picked flowers and slipped them into Apollo's barbaric braids. As the last of the soldiers walked past the dying general, they spat on her bloodied flesh, leaving her still-twitching body for the vultures and ravens to finish off.

There was a fierce storm developing a few miles offshore, with hurricane weather coming in from the north by Tala's hand as Will Beller entered the enemy's airspace. The sonic boom accompanying him alerted Fraus, who flew upwards to meet him, instigating a vicious dogfight between herself and the seasoned Marine pilot. They wove through the sky like hawks in a death dance as both missiles and hexes were hurled through the turbulent atmosphere, only succumbing to the storm's intensity when a thunderbolt struck between them. The bright purple jolt hit nearest Fraus and she disappeared into the clouds, leaving Will to try and regain control of his aircraft.

He looked at the ejection handle, then to the picture of Lakshmi. Time stopped for a moment. Then he turned back to the controls with conviction, shutting them all down and letting the cockpit go silent as gravity drove his jet straight into the enemy cavalry below.

It struck the ground with a mighty blast, killing over fifty men, proving that humans could still inflict damage to the enemy with or without the Immortals. His death was felt by Melody the moment it occurred, and for Michael, some feeling of sympathy for his uncle stirred in the depths of his possessed soul, no matter how hard he tried to fight it.

Almuruna's sea-borne fleet had retreated long before Michael's forces reached the coast, but the furious duo would not be out done by a throw-together Navy. Shiva had sensed what was coming and left in a submarine, diving deep and sending smaller drone-submarines off course to confuse any pursuers. Those on the ships weren't so lucky.

A shot rang out on the main deck of the carrier. The clinking of feet on cold steel. Hurried conversations and the gathering of weapons as everyone scrambled to their stations. Too late.

By midnight, Michael had the crew blindfolded, gagged and lined up along the edge of the aircraft carrier. His men kicked them into the frigid water one by one, letting them drown: bound, blind, and mute.

Michael and Fraus celebrated their continental takeover with an orgy, satiating their carnal desires with their captured slaves; all the most beautiful women caught in the warpath, drugged and possessed and eager to worship Michael. None of them would recover from the poisonous spell, but rather become sirens of their own unfulfilled desires while pleasing their masters completely.

Distracted by their cravings, Michael and Fraus failed to track down the escaped Zurvan leader. Through the oceans low trenches, Shiva crept along in his craft, desperately trying to message the empress to begin the exodus of Almuruna.

CHAPTER 49 – LOCUST REIGN

The cries of a wounded angel filled the halls of the palace. A voice so heavenly yet piercing; echoing loud for the ears of the children, the maids, advisors, and monks to hear. As the fear of the looming army befell them, it was less their uncertain future that made her weep, but rather all the lives she'd wasted attempting to quell an enemy she knew could only be defeated by another Immortal.

The palace had become Melody's self-made prison cell, and she realized that to be truly free from her torments she would need to free herself from her fears of failure. She wondered if Michael would still be there if she had kept her son, loving them as a family. Yet she knew Michael's own abandonment as a child played into all of it. Fraus knew Michael's past and had used it to double down on her spell against him, creating an alluring avenue away from what he was already running from. He could never trust Tala after she had killed his godmother, so the only one left to align with was Fraus. The more Melody thought on this, the more she became convinced a new order would have to be established to protect her kingdom. A shift would come, but only at great sacrifice, something her master knew well.

Shiva entered the palace like a cold wind bursting through the doors.

"Where is the empress?" he asked, his long hair greasy

and chaotic.

A council was summoned, but there were few. Sage's seat held flowers and a picture of her. Before commencing, a moment of silence was observed for the general and the thousands of others who'd perished. Shiva spoke first. The subject was genocide.

"He moves with fire. He becomes it. The same hate found in his motion can be found in his men. They are not all possessed... no... some do not need persuasion of any kind. They follow him purely to conquer. And yet Michael and his centurions are but foot soldiers to the witch's might. Empress, Ambassador Yu, Abbot... we face a foe unlike the world has seen in a long, long time, for as much destruction as the Aradians caused, they had a purpose. This foe... she has no purpose. She is obsessed with killing, and I fear she will not stop unless stopped by another."

"Did we retain any resources?" Xiang asked.

Shiva sighed and went on. "All is lost. The fleet. The troops. Everyone and everything we sent is gone, save for a few Zurvans and myself. We no longer have an air force, but they do. And I'm not just talking about our jets and helicopters. They've grown wings: as wide as our aircraft and thick like armor. They've descended into the most lethal beings their evolutionary systems can allow, infecting others along the way with their evil by possessing the fallen on the battlefield and uprooting ghosts to join their brigade, mixing their genes with wild animals. I cannot imagine a more demoralizing enemy."

The empress spoke. "Based on the trajectory of their campaign, they'll take Almuruna, then Africa, then Mongolia... populating the world with unnamed monsters."

"What can we do?" the abbot asked.

The empress looked wistfully into the gentle old man's

eyes. "We will organize a grand exodus and let them take Almuruna in order to defend Mongolia."

Xiang's eyes widened in horror. "We cannot just let them—"

"I will not let anyone else die trying to defend what cannot be defended! If we push back to Western Mongolia, Parvati can set up defenses to insure our salvation. Do not think for a moment that I do not wish I could have done more. But my people and my kingdom must be represented by their empress or else we will lose all hope!"

"With all due respect, Empress," Shiva began, "your people would rather you be on the battlefield protecting them, since there are so few who are gifted with the advantages you possess. Think about it... what would Pavonis do in your situation?"

Melody inclined her head in acceptance. "Perhaps it is time I practice these advantages, so that my skills as a Sararan may be useful to our forces."

"Your skills are not just useful, Empress, they are crucial," Xiang reiterated.

"Then I'll begin at once. Send a transmission to Queen Parvati. Tell her she'll soon be at war. Request permission for our people to cross her borders unhindered, for tomorrow we begin our exodus."

"What territories shall we evacuate?"

Melody looked each of them in the eye, her heartache and determination visible in her gaze.

"All of them."

The next morning, the empress visited the dojo where the

children were training. Avestan yelled with vigor as the young girls kicked the stiff boxing bags.

"Maya-geri! Good! Now switch stances! Higher, Devonia. Again!"

As the empress came into view, Avestan stopped them.

"Mate!" Avestan yelled and the girls stepped back with their arms folded behind them.

"How is training going?" Melody asked.

"Well indeed. They're more intuitive every day. They're quick, good at remembering lessons, agile and exact. In time they'll be quite lethal."

The empress nodded and whispered to Avestan. "After this lesson, pack their things and prepare to leave. We're beginning the exodus at once."

"To where?"

"Russia."

The empress left and the girls continued their lesson, but Avestan struggled to focus, unable to comprehend how the empress intended to move fifty million people in just two days.

The ships landed in West Africa, France and Northern Ireland. Behind them, more came, cast from dredged-up ocean-floor wreckage and welded into war-boats carrying Michael's massive army. The ships were decorated with ancient symbols and flew dark flags that whipped in the air like streams of black smoke. As anchors dropped and boats jetted ashore, the invasion began with zero resistance. The coast had at least been cleared, but those unwilling to forfeit their homeland met their end in a despicable manner.

With Michael came the summer heat, and with the heat came the locusts. Swarms of billions ravaged the land, conjured in formation by Fraus, her abilities enabling her to hijack the insects' natural magnetoreception. The North African legions spread out and claimed the land, soldiers-turned-roughnecks feeding Michael's war machine with freshly siphoned crude oil. Contingents spread vast through Almuruna like they were insects themselves, and with hardly anyone in their path, they took the land by storm, stopping at the edges of eastern Europe.

With heartless deliberation, Michael bombed Geneva and slaughtered the monks protecting the palace. Some burned themselves as effigies before the bomb runs came, their poses crumbling to ash as the bombers gutted the palace until it stood as a ruinous sanctuary. The East Tower was scathed but still standing, with columns chipped and blackened by the rock splintering ordinance. It was atop this tall spire that Michael sat against the rubble on soft wings, playing a small guitar and watching the city burn behind him like Nero, the flowering despair given new meaning by his plucked melody.

Michael halted his expansion at the skirt of the Iron Curtain, so that he could drink the purity from the land, and the refugees who'd fled into Mongolia would forever be thankful that the empress had saved them from his summer of atrocities. Rapid industrial growth. Demolitions of shrines and churches. Round-the-clock bombings over the Curtain. Untamed forest fires. Pachyderm hunting expeditions. Pollution and degradation of nature. Systemic genocide. Concentration camps. Crucifixions of traitors. Mass rapes. Orphan labor. Spiteful resurrections. Blood orgies. Human taxidermy. All this occurred while a Sararan fetus grew inside

Fraus's radioactive womb, eager to show the world the face of a true god.

CHAPTER 50 – SIBERIAN ASYLUM

In the depths of the Ural mountains, the children were hidden from the world. With vast tracts of forested mountains stretching in every direction, Melody knew they'd all be safe from invasion, at least for a while. Avestan had found a way to confuse the witch's astral navigation by planting Tiger's Eye stones around the abandoned homestead they'd acquired, creating an energy eddy to confuse Fraus's raven spies that scoured the globe.

The farm property where they resided seemed fairly well kept, but had evidently been abandoned. For months they stayed at the homestead, and would have enjoyed a nearly peaceful summer if it weren't for the daily reality that while they lived in harmony, Almuruna was being ravaged.

Xiang had left on a mission to augment forces with Queen Parvati, which proved a difficult task since the Mongol queen was reluctant to fight a war so far from her empire's most prominent population centers and resources, while the children continued their training with Avestan, come rain or shine. Melody often left them for weeks at a time, travelling deep into mountain passes where she sang powerful spells and began her transformation into her militant self. She came back each time slightly more rigid, with greenish skin and vines wrapped around her arms like ectodermal snares readying to seize and constrict. Her hair began to dread with moss and leaves, and with each passing moon she turned more into a Mother Earth deity, possessing the same need to save the planet as her own master had before her.

O

One afternoon, as the sun shone in vain over the dying world, the children were playing a game in the garden, laughing away their naive misunderstandings and unsaid agony. Avestan watched them without emotion.

Melody approached the Zurvan, a bouquet of life following her every step. "What is the matter, Avestan?"

The combatant shook their head. "I need to find Shiva. He leads the Zurvans to war."

"In due time, Avestan."

There was a long pause. They watched the children roll around in the dirt, their innocence preserved.

"When Xiang has returned from her mission, we'll both be leaving."

Avestan turned to face her. "To the front?"

"You will be, yes. I must consult Tala one last time. If she does not join us willingly, there is another way to pry her from her self-rooted throne."

Avestan nodded. "Love."

Melody looked at Avestan as butterflies landed in her hair.

"Love is what will move her. That is the only way to fool a god, or destroy one. All other emotions can be quarantined by rational thought. Love transcends the rational."

"Who or what do you love, Avestan?"

"I understand love from the other side. For it is love that has made my tribe, propelled our vision, given us purpose, and yet I myself am without hope for its most concentrated embodiment. I lack the animalistic urge to procreate, and I can neither give seed nor conceive in my current state. I exist purely as a guardian for others, so that they may experience this incredible life. I exist to kill and displace poisonous entities from this existence. I am both the savior and executioner, both Christ and the Devil, my right hand the truth, my left hand, deception. I represent the virtues instilled in me by my masters, but I am leery of the inner conflict of the human psyche. By letting the heathens of the world run amok we do not somehow rise above them. You refrained from hunting down your enemies after the fall and look what happened. Love can kill, just as hate can serve. The universe holds no distinction of right or wrong. Humans have set these perimeters, redefined them, and it seems the modern moral code has been hacked through our steady negligence of nature's laws. This witch is a disease, evolving beyond our cures. And she knows well of your moral limitations."

The empress studied the strange and beautiful assassin. "A malevolent enemy cannot be destroyed using its own evil without the attacker becoming that evil itself," she disputed.

"So be it! Why bother seeking a means for justification when the act itself proves the greater virtue? You labor too much for one human life. Let it go. We are lions. I know in my heart what is true, and you know it as well. This truth is sacred to the tribe and worth dying for. I can't imagine being anything else."

The empress studied Avestan like a passage. "Yet you are an anomaly to your species."

"As are you."

"And them..." Melody said, nodding to the children still rolling playfully in the dirt.

"They will live in a world without God, and therefore become divine creatures themselves. The age to follow will be the most merciless time since the end of the Cretaceous period. This is why I've stalled their training. Violence and chaos come naturally to them, and they've adapted well. But we need to invest in their adolescence while they have it. All the Immortals have a lowest common denominator of traumatizing childhoods. Which is also what made them so effective."

"Not all."

"Are you so sure? Vishnu was found on a scree field nearly frozen to death. Shakti escaped burning rubble after a fire bombing. Mayari and Tala were slaves for most their childhoods. Ezra was beaten and prodded into the military. Michael was a prisoner of war and mentally castrated at the dawn of his transformation. Even you, Melody. You escaped from genocide. You witnessed Lily's murder and then your hometown was bombed into oblivion. As future Aradians, I want these girls to be protectors of our world. But we must be careful how we go about it, for when has being an Immortal not backfired?"

"Pavonis."

"Yet she was an anomaly within an anomaly. Her heart was purest of all, and she never lost sight of what mattered most. All humanoids are but fragile autumn leaves carried away by a mighty wind. A collision with a blade of grass will destroy us. We float into the fray untethered, but we must not fear. There is no surviving the wind. The wind is life."

"I am an Immortal, and yet the fear of death came to me even in the fortified walls of my palace during peacetime. What drives you onto the battlefield, time and time again?"

"God gave our enemy the capacity to be cruel. Therefore, I must destroy them."

"God or the enemy?"

"Both," Avestan said decisively, looking at her as if through the eyes of a crow.

"I'll never be as good as Pavonis," Melody admitted.

"Anyone, human or Immortal, can be as good as her. I think that was part of her message. Life takes sacrifice."

The empress wrapped her arms around herself with an anxious trembling, for as much as she heeded the younglings in their ascent, her negative approach got the best of her and she saw her own spirit as nothing but another leaf descending to the forest floor, a life among others lives erased; wholly unaccounted for in the infinite ocean of this phantom existence.

The next day, Devonia was watching the sunrise from the barn's loft as Uli slept nearby against a pile of straw and Boris munched on some cabbage by her feet. The creak of the ladder behind her startled her to her feet.

"Ambassador Yu!" she cried out excitedly.

Devonia ran over and hugged Xiang, who smiled and held the child close.

"Why have you been gone so long?"

"I have been helping Parvati and my sisters prepare for war," she said. "How are you, Devonia? Is training going well?"

"Yeah, it's good... I guess. I can kick and punch through a wood block now, but I'm not sure what that's going to do against a god. Avestan makes us meditate a lot and sometimes I get bored. But then sometimes I think about different worlds beyond the stars and let my imagination wander to those places, wondering what our world would like from an alien's perspective. I'm nervous though, Ambassador Yu... I don't know if I want to be become an Aradian. I just want to be a normal human."

"Only those who do not deserve such power seek this metamorphosis. You were chosen because your heart is pure."

"I thought it was because I have the soul of Pavonis?"

"Reincarnation is not an exact science, but if they're right…" She paused, smiling at the apprentice. "Only you know who you truly are."

"I'm Devonia, Queen of Tortoises!" she said, looking at Boris as he scuttled under some straw.

Xiang knelt and placed her hand over Devonia's, looking lovingly at the child as if she were her own. "I'm sorry you've been through so much, Devonia. This has been a tumultuous year for all of us."

"I just want to help Empress Melody however I can. She's so sad. Is it true half the world is burning?"

"Yes. But we can still save the other half."

Xiang enveloped her in a hug as the sun rose above the dry grass, the evergreens that stood at the edge of the field swaying in the diurnal wind. The empress's aircraft sat at the field's edge, collecting pollen. Inside its cavity, Melody prepared the craft for Avestan's flight, planting every protective spell she could muster into the nanocrystals, hardwiring the vessel to overcome unholy dangers.

Though the children were saddened to see their empress depart, they understood perfectly well the severity of her mission. Avestan was leaving as well. The assassin bowed to their apprentices and promised to continue their training when time allowed. Xiang hugged Melody and Avestan and wished them safe travels, for she'd be completely out of touch with them while she and the girls remained in the mountain sanctuary.

As the aircraft rose above the field and roared up into the western sky, Xiang couldn't help but feel suddenly alone and vulnerable as she looked at the two girls.

"How long will we be here, Ambassador Yu?" Uli asked.

"As long as we need to keep you hidden."

"I don't want to hide. I want to help!"

"Me too!" Devonia agreed.

Uli thrust her scrying mirror above her head and pointed it toward the sun. Devonia pulled her dagger out and followed suit, holding it up close to Uli's mirror.

"We either fight, or wait to fight! So, what are we waiting for?" Uli asked.

Xiang smiled, impressed by the child's exuberance. "We're waiting for you to become of age. When you are both Aradians, you will have the advantages necessary to quell demons."

"Aradian-shmadian. I'm sick of sitting around while people are getting hurt and dying. Think of all those poor creatures! If Michael wants a war on nature, he'll have to come through us first!" Devonia said bravely.

They both stepped out into a clearing and began shadow fighting invisible enemies. Xiang couldn't help but notice their impeccable technique and developing muscles.

"They may not be ready for Michael… but they sure aren't your typical preteen girls anymore."

After their training, Uli and Devonia were feeding Boris some cabbage in the shade of the trees, when Uli spoke up about something on her mind.

"Hey, Devonia?"

"Yeah?"

"What do you think of all this? I mean, we didn't really get much choice in this. We were made immortals against our will."

"I know… I think about it sometimes, but I want to help the planet any way I can, so if this is the way, I have to accept it."

"I want to help too, I just don't know… what if they made a mistake? What if you and I aren't the ones that are supposed to get these powers? It all happened so fast."

"What do you love more than anything, Uli?"

"My home. Mother Africa."

"What would you do to defend it?"

"Anything, I suppose."

Devonia took Uli's scrying mirror and held it up to her. "Look into your mirror. It's you! You're the one that gets to bring balance back to your continent someday. You are the future Mother Africa!"

A frightened expression fell over Uli's face. "I don't know if I want that. I don't know if I can live up to it."

"You can! You're amazing, Uli. I can see why they chose you. You have the heart for this. You are a warrior goddess!

"Thank you, Devonia. I can see why they chose you too. I've never had a friend like you. I'm so connected to my people and my culture, and you're so connected to the wilderness and animals. We make a good team. Thank you for showing me the value in all lifeforms, not just people."

"Of course, Uli. I appreciate you and love you. Promise to always be my friend?"

"I promise," she said, hugging Devonia tightly for several minutes.

Nothing could phase them, no matter how bad things got. As long as they had each other.

That evening, once the girls were asleep, Xiang ventured upstairs to the bathing room adjacent to the main bedroom. As the tub filled, she lit candles and burned incense, before sinking into the warm water and slowly wiping from her body the dust and sweat from her travels through the unstable lands between the farmstead and the Mongolian capital. She'd hidden in the trunks of vehicles, walked through long canyons and ranges, and stayed in the salvation of people's houses to recuperate. She hummed a tune as she washed, hearing the lovely twang of a koto still ringing in her ear. Mongolia made her feel at home. The blissful weather. The enduring peace. The diverse culture. The enchanting lands it encompassed. The wisdom and love brought about by her sisters, her queen, and most importantly, her potential place as ruler of the eastern world.

She quickly attempted to dismiss the world's troubles as she relaxed and dipped low into the steaming water. She closed her eyes and laid there so only the front of her face was poking up from the water's surface. For some time, she was motionless, letting the water warm her bones and calm her mind. When she opened her eyes, a tall man was standing over her. With a large splash, she sat up and clasped her hands over her breasts.

"Who are you? What are you doing here?"

The man tilted his weathered brow, as calm as she was frightened. He smiled.

"I could ask you same question. This is my home." He

spoke with a thick accent, walking over and retrieving a towel from the wall hang.

"You surprised me," Xiang said, wrapping herself up in the towel. "We had thought it to be abandoned."

"We?"

"I came with a few others from Almuruna. My name is Xiang."

"I see... I'm Igor."

He shook her hand and walked into the bedroom, leaving the door ajar as he shuffled around.

"How long have you lived here?" she asked him.

"I moved here with my mother and sister after the war. My father was killed during Shakti's occupation, of course, and my sister moved south, so it was just me and my mother for a while. I've been living here alone since my mother's passing a few years ago."

"I'm sorry for your loss," Xiang said softly. Igor's story rang too similar to David's plight during that dismal age. "It must have been lonely for you."

"It's not so bad. I am very close with the trees and animals and I often spend weeks or months in the south with my sister, which is where I just came from. Tell me, why have you come so far out here?"

"I am Ambassador to Empress Melody. I'm on a diplomatic mission to save what remains of Almuruna. I didn't know anyone lived here; I just needed a place to stay for a while."

He paced the room slowly. "You are on a mission to save Almuruna, you say? I hate to be the one to tell you, but from what I have heard, it is not going so well."

"It's more complicated than you think."

"More complicated than I think? Shakti's General of Armies escaped after the war, Empress Melody chose not to pursue her, which led to this woman's rise to power, her possession over the emperor, and eventual domination through extermination. Is that not correct, Ambassador?"

Xiang sighed, hanging her head in shame. "Something like that."

"You are not to blame for the actions of your master, Xiang." Igor's voice had taken on a kinder tone. "You are welcome to stay here as long as you need to."

"Thank you, Igor. We will not trouble you for much longer. I was planning on sleeping in what I assume is your bed, but I'll—"

"It's all right. I sleep best on the ground anyway," he said as he lit a match and blew on some kindling in the blackened stone hearth.

Xiang clothed herself and watched him from the crack in the door. He made the fire crackle in sizzle into life and laid down on the bedroll Avestan had been sleeping on. Weary from his travels, he was asleep soon after. Xiang crept past him quietly towards the bed, then looked back at the lanky Russian man under the thin wool blanket.

Sighing, she walked back and slowly lifted the blanket, settling down beside him. Her need to be close to another warm body transcended her embarrassment; she needed someone to keep her dreams sweet. Igor opened his eyes and smiled, pulling her gently towards him, his eyes alight in the candling flames before him. But as he stared into the smoking coals in the fireplace, he saw in them a fleeting wraith, pitchfork in tail, whipping up the symmetrical flume with a thieving pace. For the sun itself had lent its power to the trees, and as all creatures do defy their creator at some point in their existence, so did the elm, its combusting heartwood in collusion with evil spirits, like eyes for the demonic, as mirrors are to the divine when all elements are at play.

While Michael and Fraus reveled in their new nation, the war raged elsewhere. The grisly men of the Luciferian Army, hellbent on conquest and unceremonious lust, gripped the Earth like sons of Eris, draining the women of their nectar and violating the fruit of the land. They had met little resistance on the warpath until the Zurvans intervened, New Rome being the ancient cult's chosen place of counterinsurgency.

General Ziven Fredrickson had become a puppet governor of Michael's empire, but he began to see himself as emperor, wearing a laurel wreath of gold leaves and a red satin toga, likening his image to Caesar. He established himself in the Temple of Saturn, with one hundred slave wives and enough riches to bury himself in gold and jewels many times over. Shiva vowed he would make it so.

Through shards of brick composite and old dust, Avestan walked in total blackness. The ancient city's catacombs stank with the foul essence of its immortal history, as if the cries of tortured Gauls still echoed eerily if one put their ear to the seeping walls. Two sappers with satchels of C4 explosives followed close behind the Zurvan assassin.

Avestan read the walls with soft fingers. "Place one of the charges here."

One of the sappers laid down the volatile clay charge and attached a detonator. They kept on, Avestan leading the way, dragging their hand on the walls and navigating the catacombs based on the map they'd memorized days earlier. They walked over puddles of acidic muck and felt the crunch of rat bones beneath their feet. The echoes of their steps became voluminous as the corridor opened into a larger chamber.

"And another here." Avestan felt a large crack in the column next to them as they dragged their fingers along the old carvings. "Place the rest of it here in the fissures so that it splits the column."

The sappers went to work, molding the blocks into the fissures like kintsugi artisans turned demolition anti-priests. When they were finished, Avestan pushed a golden denarius into the soft clay and led them discreetly through the miles of dark, dank corridors.

The temperate air wafted over Avestan's sweat stained face as the sappers surfaced into the open world and coughed up the dust of yore. One of the sappers looked back at the decrepit forum.

"We came that far?"

Avestan nodded and spit onto the beaten stone. More Zurvan warriors hid in the ditch behind them, ready to pounce like hungry lions.

"Get into position," they ordered the sappers.

To the west, the Roman Forum stood as a romantic epitaph newly reimagined by Ziven and his brigade of blood-drunk heathens. The midday happenings consisted of funeral marches amidst untamed revelry. Complacent in their unbridled occupation, thousands of soldiers swarmed the ruins, oblivious to the trap awaiting beneath them.

"Give me the coms," Avestan ordered one of the sappers.

The cloaked man handed Avestan a small device.

"Siamo a posto."

"In movimento," Shiva's voice replied.

The battalion of sacred assassins sat quietly for several

minutes. Though most of the Luciferian Army was inside the forum, a few sentries had been dispatched to keep eyes on the perimeter of the city. One of them approached the ditch as Avestan slid behind a wall of weathered brick.

The soldier walked between old craters where the Aradians had once pummeled Italy with their own arsenal, leaving the ruins standing to mock the people's modernity. The soldier slunk against the wall and pulled a small bottle of wine from his pocket. As he tipped his head back to gulp the Barolo, Avestan reached under his arm like a cobra and wrapped his throat with a rusty piano wire. The man kicked and struggled silently with bloodshot eyes, his one free arm flailing. The bottle dropped and spilled and as the wine returned to the soil, so did the man's soul return to its provenance. Avestan pulled the body over the wall and laid him in the ditch, searching his pockets and finding gold, silk, and a bright red apple. Avestan threw the gold and silk in the cut and bit into the delicious fruit as they gazed up at the orange overcast August sky. Beyond the brick hedge, far to the north, a single tree torched in the forest on the hill outside the forum. The plan had been ignited. While the snag smoldered and spewed smoke, soldiers by the forum's north-western quadrant left to investigate the burning tree and prevent its spreading, leaving a sizable section of the city unattended.

"It's incredible how invincible they think they are," one of the Zurvans muttered.

"Fuck them if they can't take an omen," Avestan said.

While the distraction worked its magic, Shiva and his battalion circled the guarded city to implement a focused insertion point. Avestan watched the city's movement, for it was a beastly swarm with its high commander in its beating heart. A chilling trumpeting of horns stung the air and soon the concentration of soldiers centralized around the temple of Saturn.

"Prepare for detonation," Avestan alerted the sappers.

The Zurvans emerged from the rocks equipped with Edo-era katanas and automatic rifles, wearing ceramic armor and black silk headbands, the patches on their left shoulders revealing their origins. Each carried holistic powders in small vials on their necklaces, some with hemostatic agents for clotting arterial wounds, or cyanide in case of capture, or morphine for pain. Some of the rail-gun operators carried a dangerous concoction for battle frenzy: a cocktail of methamphetamine, MDMA and tiger adrenaline to be huffed down in the heat of combat. The battle would be long, and those who had prepared their whole lives for this moment knew how outnumbered they were, just like their monk ancestors a thousand years before. There were one hundred enemy soldiers for every Zurvan fighter, and all of them had to die.

"Sapper One. Set?" Avestan asked.

"Prepared to engage," he responded.

The sapper dialed a sequence into a small device clipped to his chest harness and exhaled.

"Initiate," Avestan said sharply.

"First charge engaged. Fire in the hole."

With a massive boom, the eastern side of the forum exploded. Enemy troops were halved, severed, and swallowed by debris as chaos erupted. Trampling and chaotic discourse commenced. The Arch of Septimius Severus collapsed on the royal stable and freed Ziven's prized stallions from the calamity. Men fled without knowing where to flee.

"Sapper Two and Sapper One: detonate all charges. Send them all to hell," Avestan ordered, taking a large bite of the apple and crunching it in their mouth with satisfaction.

Twenty-seven carefully placed bombs exploded from under the forum, crumbling ancient pillars of wisdom onto the foolish men below. The black cloud of smoke and ash caused more death and confusion as troops began firing their weapons outward in response. Roman officers gave orders to cease fire but were drowned out by the catastrophe. The heavy dust was far from settling when Shiva and his battalion opened fire on the forum's western edge. With a sudden uproar of machine gun clatter, the Zurvans took the Stadium Domitiani and demolished the bridge across the river behind them. The battle for New Rome had begun in the Zurvan's favor, and Ziven didn't even know who was attacking them yet.

While the city was under heavy attack, Avestan led their contingent along the Tiber River, slaughtering any soldiers along its banks and pushing them into the watery slew. They used arrows to disguise their presence from the main enemy forces, but the noise of battle had grown to such mammoth ferocity that no one would have heard their shots.

Waves of men made their way towards Shiva's legion but they'd already lost their footing. Zurvan snipers and machine gunners were picking them off in groups and cover behind the ruins was getting crowded. When the occupying forces had finally dug into position, Shiva and half the legion had already moved towards another temple to the north, flanking the uncoordinated army. Avestan and their demolitionists entered the skirmish from the south, positioning themselves high on a plateau above the crumbling pillars of the Basilica Julia and firing shoulder-mounted rockets down on the enemy, squeezing the Luciferian forces between themselves and Shiva's troops like a death vice.

By late afternoon, though many Zurvans had been

wounded or killed, the Luciferians had suffered over two thousand casualties and an entire legion had retreated across the Adriatic sea, leaving Ziven and the remaining legion to fight the Zurvans alone.

The fighting did not stop at nightfall, though gun fire was sparse and intermittent as commanders from both sides tried to reconfigure their strategies. Fires within the temples raged and their livid general seethed with anger behind Saturn's wall, speaking closely with his officers.

"We have to try and oust at least one of their battalions," Ziven said sternly. "I don't care which one, but as we speak, they're rounding our position on all sides. Soon they'll close off our only route of retreat if we don't break the line."

"Without resupply coming from the river, we are limited to the munitions on hand," cautioned his second-in-command.

Ziven stroked the crystal ball in his pocket, his eyes cloaked in hatred.

"Would Michael not come to our aid, General?" another asked.

A few more shots rang out. The Zurvans were taunting them.

"If he has not dispatched himself or his bombers, there must be more prevalent matters at this conspicuous hour. The retreating legion is foolish and will be killed by the king if they return to Geneva. No... we stay and fight until this is over. I will not hand Rome over to those fucking gooks or accept any negotiation terms. What would you do, officer?"

"I would stay and fight for the king, General Frederiksen. As would all of us. We will kill as many Zurvans as we can until our last breath leaves our bodies. But General, we have limited munitions left. How should we ration them?" the officer asked.

"My brothers... we will run out of water before we run out of bullets. Go forth and breathe the glorious air."

Arrows dripping with flaming tar were shot into the trees below Avestan and their troops to try and smoke them out, the light rainfall doing little to extinguish the flames. Four Zurvans attempting to escape the burning overgrowth were shot dead by Luciferian snipers, who had so much practice splitting skulls they would synchronize Chopin's Op. 9 in B major quietly over their radios and execute command fire on the first note of every twelfth bar, confusing the Zurvans as to their distances and approximations.

Avestan crawled through the bushes slowly and met with Shiva in the early hours of morning. The smell of raw earth and human decay filled the air as an orange glow hung over the city.

"Master Shiva. That went better than planned, considering the losses," Avestan said, glancing towards a shell-shocked woman clasping a water jug in her shaking hands. Her ear had been shot off and wrapped with a scarf. She took out a vial of white powder and licked the rim to absorb into her cracked lips whatever chemicals remained.

"Well indeed. We have seventy dead and one hundred and fifty wounded. The rest can fight until we take the city. Maybe some of the wounded too."

"I've lost twelve. Forty wounded. There was a sniper that took a while to find. We had to shoot him through his scope. The rest of these bastards seem to be waiting until morning."

A few shots barked from a machine gun down below.

"They'll need to conserve ammunition. We should bleed the time as long as we can."

"Do you have eyes on the river in case that legion comes up behind us?"

"Yes, but I don't think they'll be returning anytime soon," Shiva said, spitting blood onto the ground, the dry air coursing through his nostrils. "If this lasts more than a week they'll return. But it won't. We've got them pinned. Once we break their morale, they'll perhaps be vulnerable enough to surrender."

"Would you accept Ziven's surrender?"

"No. We would kill them all. For now, keep guards on duty but get some rest. We might be here a while. I'll send food provisions come morning."

"Thank you, Master. God be with you."

"God be with you, Avestan," Shiva said, bowing.

The sexless warrior bowed low in return and climbed back to their perch, going to sleep with one eye half shut, envisioning the imperial city at its apex; with plentiful gardens, polished marble architecture, and finely adorned politicians walking through the courtyards to pontificate the fate of their Caesar, while one of the senators, stoic in his stature, listened to the whisper of the wind.

On the fourth day of the battle, the cityscape was reduced to rubble, and the space between the walls and roofs of the ancient temples amounted to more than what remained. The pillars between the sour air gave both the New Romans and the Zurvans limited cover beneath the cloudy, colorless sky. Ziven and the remaining four hundred men with him had been driven back to the Colosseum, their snipers still glassing the scape for the artful contingent slowly gnawing at their positions with their large caliber magnetic rail guns.

A crack in the distance. Some faint vapor trail approaching. Ba-BOOM! The top of the Colosseum shook as a rail round blew out two pillars, crushing a dozen soldiers and sending rocks and debris onto the scared, dehydrated men.

Avestan drank the clear cool water from their canteen and poured it over their face, out of range of the enemy yet performing their taunting act just long enough for them to see the clear liquid running down their neck through their optics. The more the Zurvans weakened their enemy, the more mistakes they made. To his own men's astonishment, Ziven walked out into the nucleus of the stadium's open field and spoke loudly for all to hear.

"Hear me, warriors of the Mongol Nation, sons and daughters of the great Khan! Your time has come to an end! The reign of Michael will last ten thousand years, for you will all fall at the hand of our supreme leader!"

The men chanted, their song of war growing louder and louder until, thirsty for Valhalla's fountains, they descended the levels of the Colosseum and ran bravely but futilely into no-man's land.

"Humans won't be remembered for destroying their species. They'll be remembered for creating their nightmares," Avestan said as they lay in a prone position nestled up to their rifle scope. "I am one of them."

Shiva nodded – their signal to open fire – and Avestan and the Zurvan soldiers mowed down the enemy as the Luciferians charged in all directions. Men's heads and chests were split open as their bodies dropped, creating a giant circle of gore wrapping the outskirts of the Colosseum like a bloody wreath. Silence followed.

When the Zurvans entered the amphitheater, they found Ziven's second-in-command laying at its center, holding a golden gun with a bullet wound through his mouth.

Avesten looked at the man without emotion. Shiva knelt by the false general and dropped a coin in his mouth.

"Should we pursue him?" Avestan asked, eager to hunt down the cowardly general.

"No. Humiliation is worse than death," Shiva answered, rising to his feet. "To Milan!" he yelled.

The remaining Zurvans responded with a thunderous war hymn, their stomachs as empty as their satchels and rifle magazines, their eyes dry like the bricks they prowled, their hearts greedy for kills as they treated their katanas with a stone polishing and drank the enemy's wine, taking the dead men's ammunition and leaving the empty bottles in the corpse's arms so they would be forever thirsty in the afterlife.

CHAPTER 51 – FELLOWSHIP OF MISFITS

It was a quiet, cloudless evening at Earth's north pole. The air was sub-zero and crisp, and the stars gleamed overhead an amethyst skyline, refracting through the aurora and mirrored by the crystalline snowpack. Melody walked lightly on the arctic turf. She could feel no wind, something rare for that land of wind magick. Tala's throne stood massive and empty, save the white drift that obscured its one hundred and eight steps.

Melody inhaled as if to sing, then stopped and held her breath in. As she gazed up at that throne of divine architecture, Melody saw past it, behind the shifting aurora, behind the stars so intangible, and she thought of a quiet heaven. A place that is many places, beyond all human versions of paradise, wherein after death her body and mind would disintegrate and reveal themselves for what they were: electricity unifying carbon and other elements.

The heart stops. The brain fades. And the body rests eternal on the shoulders of some slow and painless unsettling. Organic matter gives way to the expanse, its pieces cast out into the chaotic beyond, dispersing over eons, integrating with new compounds, until at last – by the blessing of fate – these particles cross old patterns; what was once flesh, bone, blood, emotions, memories, dreams become a partial reincarnation, creating new flame. Life, pure in its innocence and forgiven of its sins, born anew in the womb of a solitary sun.

Melody exhaled. Her icy breath fell to the ground along with a small seed. She turned slowly and began walking back in the direction she had come. A white flower grew from the icy ground behind her. The petals froze and fell one by one onto the snow. Then, from above, a voice spoke to her, synthesized in multiple tones and delicately rippling in an anodyne wheeze.

"You have supernal capabilities, yet you squander them on a dying gladiolus."

She looked up to see Tala hovering in the air like a cyber angel. She'd donned her polished titanium armor, not worn since the Post-Eruption Wars. The Aradian's eyes repeated her words, echoing the moment immediately before.

"I have every power I need to wage this war but one, Tala," she said, bowing to Earth's truest overlord. "I must learn flight. I've come to you for guidance."

"Why is it that Michael can fly but you cannot?"

"Because he is possessed by a more powerful witch than I—"

"You are wrong, Empress... on so many levels. It is a choice to fly, but a selfish one, which is why you have not made it. Michael is only partially possessed, and you are no less powerful than she who possesses him. She is not a witch, she is a demon, and she is pregnant with Michael's son."

Melody shuttered at the Aradian's words, but she knew them to be true.

"Will Michael's son be... a demon?"

"No. His genes will not allow for that kind of self-degradation. He will be something the world has never seen; a third generation Sararan, his mind, body and abilities equal to an Aradian's, perhaps greater."

Tala lowered her body to the snowy ground, stepping lightly toward Melody, their eyes meeting in subtle empathy. Tala's memory shone in her irises: of her sister flying into the sun like Icarus.

"Am I inferior to you?" Melody asked.

"You are inferior only to your former self; the young woman who sunk a sword into her master's heart for the sake of humanity has regressed into history's pages. A half century of pacifism has given you exactly what you feared: death and destruction on a global scale."

"Peace is all I ever wanted."

"Peace is a fabrication of reality projected by your mind to circumvent the fear of nature's root functions. Are you not a goddess of song? So sing! Let the universe dance in its blood. Without song, all life is massacre without meaning."

"And what was the meaning of your massacre?"

"I never had the privilege of being the world's respected shepherd, as Pavonis was; as you were. I was a military weapon used for a period of time for a specific purpose. I killed billions in order to save the world's species from extinction, including yours. I never felt the need to be vindicated for what I did. It was an impersonal admonition for the future of life, not conquest. When Shakti turned away from the prophecy and followed her passions, that is when I left her cause and began my own path."

"I have trained and practiced divination and meditated for months, but I need to know how to fly. I cannot win this war without knowing!"

"Let go."

"Of what?"

"Anything stopping you. Here... show me your stone."

Melody pulled from her hair a deep blue crystal ball and let it hover in the air above her hand.

"See how it floats above your hand? Make the Earth your stone; transfer all your energy to a more ionically absorbent object, and you can defy its gravity at the drop of a foot."

Melody nodded and watched the ball rotate above her

hand, spun by the slight twitching of her fingertips. Tala reached down and picked up the frozen flower. She pulled her shoulders back and looked at the Earth goddess with a proud smile.

"I know you've come to request my intervention in your war, but there is a reason I have been stalling. I sense something sacred in the radioactive child. When Michael's son is born, I will kill his mother and put him in the hands of Zurvans."

"And what will happen to Michael?"

"When the spell finally fades, he'll be an impotent Sararan; his body over-exerted from fighting cancers, his mind hungover with rage and sultry endeavors, his spirit dissimilated and unrecognizable. He will be a stranger to even himself, yet no one will forgive him. His fate is fixed. Once the demon is vanquished, I will leave this planet, taking my stone with me."

"You have a stone?"

She laughed at Melody's ignorance. "Every diviner has a stone, Melody."

Tala turned her head and Melody's eyes followed, their stares aligning with the broad glow of the moon as it found its dusk on the horizon.

"You wouldn't..." Melody stuttered. The cold air hadn't affected her skin, but the moment itself was cold with Tala's threat hanging in the frigid air.

"I'm taking the moon from Earth's orbit and placing it elsewhere in the Solar System. It will be a template for a new form of life, and I will be that world's creator."

"But the Earth will be devastated! There will be chaos in our weather and eco-systems; everything we've worked so hard for will be reversed!"

"By removing our planet's anchor, life will have to adapt

quickly as it once did, without governments and prophets telling Earth's creatures what to do and how to live. The world needs to return to savagery in order to remain viable for life. I shouldn't have to lecture you on this necessary paradox. Too easy is it to insult nature's laborious craftsmanship with our own, resulting in needless overpopulation and evolutionary corrosion. The absence of our moon will separate those who can survive on their own from those who depend on the state for protection, since the state has failed them. Those apprentices of yours are designed for the new world. They will one day be nobles, not by birth or their father's treasury or by privilege, but by their strength and intelligence proven time and time again through the arduous days of the world post Fraus."

"You speak her name as if it were not a curse."

"It is too late for that. Saying her name now is no more blasphemous than saying Vishnu or Marchosias. You could split the continent with your voice, Melody. Take counsel in your fears but do not let them control you. Face them and let your courage guide you to triumph over your foes. We have roughly four weeks until Michael's son is born. Bring every available asset to the helm of your kingdom and we will retake your city. As long as the demon dies and her son lives, this world still has hope."

"What about Devonia?"

"Gift her a talisman and she will continue where Pavonis left off."

"I gave her the knife of Ezra, but she's too young to wield it."

"She is not too young. She just hasn't had a worthy challenge yet. She'll soon be a goddess to be reckoned with and one day she'll sweep the world with a vicious bloom."

The Aradian slowly levitated above the ground and

opened her arms wide, stretching her fingers and tipping her head back toward Polaris. Melody watched her climb high until she seemed to be just another speck, gleaming in the perforated eternal cloth above.

○

Despite the strange homecoming, Igor welcomed Xiang and the children to his homestead. They worked together, preparing for harvest under the late August sun as Xiang wondered painfully when the empress would return to them. The girls were put to work in the wheat fields and she and Igor hunted animals nearby. Without any communication with the outside world, they didn't know anything about the state of Almuruna, or how far Michael's forces had pushed east. All they could do was live and wait.

One afternoon, Igor was out hunting when the girls and Xiang were going over language lessons.

"So who can tell me what an adverb is?"

Uli laid back on the grass looking at the sky. Devonia was even more distracted by a cow staring at her from behind the fence.

"Girls?" Xiang asked.

"Why do we need to learn this?" Devonia griped.

"Because when people can't communicate it is a recipe for conflict."

"It's a little late for that! I want Avestan back."

"Yeah me too," Uli said. "Can you just be our fun person and Avestan can be our instructor?"

Xiang sighed. "Come on... what's an adverb?"

"Ugh... a word that qualifies an adjective, verb, or other adverb or a word group, expressing a relation of place, time, circumstance, manner, cause, or degree."

"Very good, Devonia!"

"Now can we please go spar in the field?"

"Well... if you're not going to stay focused. But we're finishing this lesson after lunch!"

They'd already grabbed their hand wraps and began sprinting to the gate before she'd finished her sentence. Xiang smiled and shook her head in amusement. Suddenly, Igor came running from behind the house.

"Xiang, get children and get away from here! Men are coming!"

"Who? What men?"

"Not sure," he said panting. "Could be the Luciferian Army, could be hunters, but better to be safe. I'll grab the rifles, just get the girls and go!"

Xiang ran out to the field where the girls were karate fighting, oblivious to the coming attack.

"Girls, we need to go now!" she said.

Xiang looked up to see men with tactical gear closing in from the fields edge.

"Hurry!"

They met back up with Igor who carried a gigantic machine gun and belts of ammunition on his back. He handed Xiang an old Kalashnikov rifle and pushed her away from the house.

"Go now!"

"Aren't you coming with us?" she asked.

"No, go now! I'll distract them! Fucking go already!" he yelled as he pushed her again.

The girls sprinted down the road as fast they could while Igor propped up his massive weapon on a tripod and slapped in a belt of ammo.

"Come at me motherfu—"

His words were cut off by the burst of fire that came from the antique cannon. Gunfire blared through the late morning air as Xiang and the girls escaped further down the road, not knowing if they could outrun whoever was closing in on them.

Igor did not meet them that evening. They had kept running for miles until the girls were too tired to move, all the while looking behind them even after the gunfire had faded behind the mountain. Reluctantly, Xiang had eventually allowed them to rest under a rock crater next to the road while she kept watch for Igor.

"We'll keep going now," Xiang murmured as darkness finally fell.

"I'm too tired Ambassador Yu!" Uli groaned.

"Eat this," she said, handing them both a nectarine. "And be quiet!"

Xiang poked her head out once more from behind a spruce tree, hoping Igor would be driving down the road in his truck. No one came.

"Come now," she whispered.

The children scrambled to their feet, chewing their fruit as they walked swiftly behind the ambassador. No sleep was had that night. The moon led the way with its gentle blue glow as the road wound south through the boreal landscape, the hoot of nearby owls the only sound. It wasn't until the end of the second day that they meet someone; a person more-so displaced than they were. Darkness had fallen upon them completely when the strange man appeared. He was standing in a tree when Xiang saw him waving his hand.

"Hello travelers!" he yelled.

Xiang pointed the rifle at him without thought and clicked the safety switch off. The girls dropped behind two tree bases for cover.

"Please don't shoot! I am a friend!" he said, slowly dropping from the bough and bowing low, dropping his weapon before Xiang as hers aligned with his skull. His turban unraveled slightly, but he didn't seem to mind. He looked up at them with twinkling green eyes, smiling.

"Who are you?" Xiang asked, wondering what a Middle-Eastern man was doing so far north.

"I am Ali, pleased to meet you. And what a lovely flower you are!"

The girls giggled.

Xiang looked about her while keeping the gun pointed at him. "How many are there?"

"How many what? Alis? None quite like me, I can assure you," he said, winking.

Xiang thrust the gun towards him.

"I mean you no harm, madam," he said after studying her for a moment, his smile subtle.

"What is a Kurd doing out here alone in the middle of nowhere?" Xiang asked as she began pulling things out of his pockets and throwing them on the ground.

"I got cut off from my regiment in an ambush. I fled north."

"You were fighting the Luciferian Army?"

"Who else would I be going to war with?"

"So you're a Zurvan?"

"A what?"

"Never mind. Where are you from?"

"Kurdistan."

"That's not a country."

"Is an emerald flawed if no one admires its beauty?"

Suddenly, Ali looked frightened. Xiang turned to look behind her and swung her weapon around. Igor stood there smiling.

"I see you found a rat. Shall we roast him over the fire tonight?"

Ali spat. "If I am a rat, you are a worm!"

Xiang tossed the gun aside as the two ran at each other, holding her hands out and blocking the two charging brutes from cracking skulls.

POP! PA-PA-POP-POP!

A rifle sputtered behind them. They all ducked and looked at Devonia, who held the AK-47 high above her head.

"Everyone knock it off or I'll send you straight to Hades!"

"Fiery one, isn't she?" Igor noted, smirking.

"Whose child is this? What is happening?" Ali asked, wearing a skeptical frown.

"She's... Pavonis," Xiang said, standing and brushing off her coat.

"You mean..." the Kurd sputtered, "she... she... ahh! Praise Allah she has returned to us!"

"Devonia, put down the gun. Igor put down the rock, and Uli... please put away Devonia's dagger before anyone gets hurt."

Uli came out from behind a tree and sighed before sheathing the blade.

"We should kill him now while no one else can hear," Igor said.

"A bit late for that," Uli said, commenting on the gunshots.

"No! We're all on the same side here."

Igor spat and glared at Ali.

"I already told you, I was fighting the Luciferians when we got cut off."

"We?" Xiang asked.

Just then, a woman came walking up the path towards them. Everyone except for Ali grabbed their weapons and pointed them at her. Another woman behind her cocked her gun as the first woman stood motionless. Ali stepped between the standoff.

"These are my two sisters, Medya and Lilan. I was going to tell you about them." Ali shrugged. "Sorry."

That night, the odd fellowship sat around a fire, cooking some roots and grouse they had caught in the bush. The air was quiet, mostly because of the disdain Igor and Ali felt for one another. Though they had never fought a war against one another, their ancestors had, and the mood was awkward as branches creaked in the wind like old doors behind them. The commando-outfitted sisters whispered to one another in their strange tongue, unfazed by the stagnant air.

"Who attacked us?" Xiang asked Igor.

"Only the worst kind of men," he responded as he tapped a stick in the dirt.

Another long silence ensued.

"So what is the plan now?" he asked.

Xiang sighed. "Well... we've all been uprooted from distant homelands to fight this war and I'd bargain to say that each has their own fortunes waiting for them after it ends. Foremost, I speak of the young ones, who have a great power in them waiting to be unleashed on the world. To protect them would be to serve Pavonis in spirit and flesh."

"What makes them this way?" Ali asked.

"They've been given the Aradian gene. They'll begin their evolution sometime in their teens, we can only assume."

"The Luciferian Army is like a plague. Anyone who comes near them dies. Is there a way to speed up the process?" Igor asked.

"Engaging the dormant gene early would result in tumors. We have to wait. The best we can do for them now is protect them and get them safely to Parvati."

"We need to move quickly. Vehicle, mule, river. Doesn't matter," Igor insisted.

"Where is your next destination?" Ali asked.

"Nur-Sultan. From there we will have safe passage to Parvati at the Mongol capital."

"Nur-Sultan is long ways away. One of the empress's ships would be nice…" Igor mumbled.

"How has Michael or the witch not found these children already? Why did Melody bring them here?" Ali asked.

"These mountains have a unique blend of minerals and gemstones that refract the witch's astral reconnaissance. But we cannot stay forever. We have to reach Nur-Sultan before Michael's Army begins their next invasion."

"So what, we just find some reindeer and ride them one thousand miles?" Igor scoffed.

"By chance alone we have assembled a small but savvy cell of well-equipped combatants; a fellowship of people willing to sacrifice themselves for the greater good. You don't have to stay with us, Igor. But I implore you to do so, if not for the girls, then for the future of your homeland."

Igor laughed. "Trying to lecture a Russian on sacrifice… I think you need to re-read your history, Ambassador. From our resistance to the Golden Horde one thousand years ago, to the deaths of millions of Soviet soldiers and civilians fighting the Nazi's, I don't think there is a force on Earth that could break Russian spirit."

"What about the senseless bombing of children in Syria? Or the horrific atrocities committed against Ukraine? Perhaps your 'great nation' made itself too great in the wake of your resistances and you became tyrants yourselves, as all empires do when given the birthright to might," Ali spoke sincerely, his gaze sharp and discerning.

"As we both know, my new Kurdish friend, neither of us were responsible for those choices; we did not fight in those wars. I don't always agree with the conflicts my country has entered into. But you of all people should know, war is not black and white. My grandfather was a soldier in the Russian army. My father was only a baby at the time, but my grandmother said he was great man who felt his duty was to protect innocent people from the terrorists like the Daesh, something your ancestors felt similarly, no?"

Ali nodded in agreement.

"The Daesh were an enemy that eventually aligned our grandfathers' nations, so that they could quell a worse evil. Perhaps we are experiencing that now with the Luciferian Army."

With a hesitant alliance formed between the two men, they all laid down to rest. Xiang closed her eyes as she settled beside the children, both sleeping soundly at her side. They were growing every day, and though their teen years were close, they remained vulnerable to the harsh world closing in.

The fellowship awoke at sunrise and cut west from the road. The smell of rain was in the air as a gathering thunderstorm loomed then dissipated. They bush-whacked through the descent, feeling a magnetic sense of camaraderie growing between them, though there were those who would not openly admit this bond. The valley's contour forced them through scree and undergrowth, at times up to their waists in nettles and woodland debris. By mid-afternoon they'd reached the Ural river, and spent the rest of the day building a log raft to take them southward. Igor committed to taking the night shift as boatman, and they soon embarked on their journey across the quiet waters, coasting idly above the softened round rocks.

Through the night, the hills descended to the steppe, where a sea of antelope grazed and colored grasses swayed in the early autumn breeze. With dusks yearning, the blood orange moon was castrated by the planets crest as it retreated behind the distant smoke of some distant siege. As the days passed, the smoke crept east, the Luciferian Army's wrath a force of nature itself.

Three times did the fellowship have to carry their raft down waterfalls, until at last they reached a westward bend where they abandoned their craft and walked out onto the Central Asian steppe. Humans were scarce, and those they encountered were much less fortunate than they; tribal herdsman famished in the low yield of that ill season. The herders offered magick mushrooms to the fellowship so that if the demons of the steppe came to them, they would have the means to confront the apparitions in their own dimension. When Xiang asked if they were referring to Fraus, they shook their heads with confusion. After further conversation, Xiang discovered that they were so displaced from the developing world that they knew not of the Yellowstone Eruption, World War III, or anything that had happened since. Having resided in the desolate region for so long, they had outlasted the catastrophic events of the twenty-first century while proving their resiliency as deft falconers.

The fellowship kept on. Ali was last to walk by the tribespeople, and accepted their offer. He ate the psychedelic fungus before his afternoon salah, praying to Allah that their destination would provide good fortune to the fellowship. Later that afternoon he walked behind his sisters, a glowing shaman, recollecting his youth by the streams of Tabriz and stumbling through the grassy abyss with splendor. When his sisters looked back after tuning him out, they found Ali collapsed in a patch of white flowers.

"Are you all right, Ali?" Devonia asked.

"Did you eat that fungus they gave you?" Xiang asked angrily.

The sisters giggled.

"I am having a vision," he said.

"What do you see?" Uli asked, pulling out her scrying mirror and giving it to him.

Ali looked into the dish and spoke. "I see... a great monster of the abyss. But here. A fish of the land. As if the soil were its seas. So incredible... it rises against man, Immortal... the sky itself."

He laughed as they stood over him swaying like trees, wondering what had become of him.

A few hours later, Devonia walked alongside Xiang, whose disturbed expression was easily noticed.

"What's wrong, Ambassador Yu?"

"Oh nothing, just what Ali said earlier reminded me of something Melody warned me about when I took my first maritime mission."

"What was the warning?"

"She told me that years ago, when people ferried nothing but small wooden ships across the vast reaches of the world, sailors on the high seas would return with tales of sea beasts attacking them, often during storms. But over time the loud turbines of industrial crafts frightened them back to the depths, until the tales of these prehistoric creatures became only myth. She said that what swims beneath the deep blue is indeed a creature of prehistory, a testament to the ocean's sovereignty. Let's pray we never see it."

"Were the sailors high on drugs too though?" Devonia asked skeptically.

"Perhaps," she laughed, grazing the child's hair with her hand. "But perhaps not."

They walked for another day and a half along the steppe when they came upon a town called Karabutak. Horses and camels were tied to posts outside the stores and taverns along the main street, and it was apparent upon entering the town that a general lack of law accounted for the loud music and madness rising in the early evening air. It was a place of whoredom, gambling, pistol shooting and bandit rallying. The town had become a hub for traders, the Silk Road having collapsed for the umpteenth time since the Luciferian Army's disruption of it's westward passage. Arabs, Turks, Kurds, Pashtuns, Mongols, Indians, Aussies and Russians all gathered together in one hellhole.

The fellowship entered a tavern, the commotion inside lessening as Xiang led the group to the bar. She made no eye contact save for the barkeep. All around were thugs, scavengers, ex-military and drifters looking upon the beautiful woman and her mixed company in awe.

"We're having a shot," Xiang said to the group.

The tavern went back to their drinking games and gruff conversations in too many languages to reckon.

"But why?" Ali asked.

"A fish doesn't swim to find water," she said.

Ali looked at the ceiling, puzzled.

"Also... I need a drink."

"I'll drink to that," Igor smiled with approval.

"Five shots of vodka, please," Xiang called to the barkeep as the girls hopped up onto the stools beside the others.

"Those two old enough?" the barkeep asked, looking at Devonia and Uli.

"What do you think?" Xiang snapped above the commotion.

The barkeep shrugged.

"But madam, I do not drink," Ali said.

"Today you do," Xiang replied, standing with her spine rigid and her look fierce in that cesspool of men.

Seven shots of clear liquor were poured into scratched up glasses and Xiang handed them out. She looked at the shots for the girls then shrugged and handed them the glasses.

"To the fellowship!" she said as they touched glasses.

The young girls coughed violently as they attempted to down their drinks.

"What is this?" Uli asked.

"Tastes like bad medicine!" Devonia said, spitting the spirit onto the floor.

Medya and Lilan had also never consumed alcohol before and had similar reactions, though they continued tasting.

Igor drank his shot as if it were air, then took Ali's and knocked that one back as well.

"What's the plan?" Igor asked.

"Find transportation. Leave it to me," Xiang said.

After a few more drinks, Igor was playing a card game with a group of Russian militia while the others sat at the bar and watched the scoundrels of the old world wager their confidences. A man sitting next to Xiang recognized the emblem on her coat.

"Long way from Almuruna... figured you'd be busy negotiating with your enemies."

"You can't negotiate with a demon. You can only destroy it."

"And how do you destroy a demon?"

"With a god."

As she ordered another round, she noticed a rugged-looking man in the corner wearing a dusty cowboy hat and smoking a tobacco pipe, studying her and the fellowship closely. Xiang made eye contact and he walked over to her.

"Drinks goin' down easy after your trek, yeah?" he asked in a grimy Australian accent.

Xiang studied him, trying to work out where she had seen him before. "Who are you?"

"Galen Fox. And you must be Princess Xiang Yu. You're royalty in these lands, ain't ya? What's with the odd group of comrades? You haven't had it easy since the invasion, I reckon."

Xiang flared her nostrils and clenched her teeth. "You could have helped us, you drunk bastard! Call yourself a pilot? Pathetic!" she snarled. She took another shot and shook her head while looking across the bar.

Galen sighed. "There's a difference between bravery and suicide, Princess. Your empress sent those men and women to their deaths. Can't blame you for tryin' to stop the war but damned if I'll be one of those mugs gettin' their brains cracked open by that fuckin' demon... that's somethin' more terrible than dyin'."

Xiang tried to ignore his existence.

"Where you tryin' for?"

She didn't answer.

"A lot of folks come through here peakin' for somethin'. Don't always get it unless they know where they're goin'."

"Nur-Sultan."

A legless viola player had set themselves up on a stool in the center of the stage and began playing a melancholy tune, moving their shoulders with their instrument slowly as they stroked the strings with a tightened yaks-hair bow.

"Nur-Sultan... huh. That road's full of treachery. Just did it myself; barely got here alive. You walkin' it? That'll take weeks."

"We've got goods and money to trade for horses. Tomorrow morning we'll find some and make our way."

"You think anyone here's gonna give up their only ride?"

"It only takes one bad loss at the gambling table for someone to be desperate enough."

Galen laughed. "Don't I know it."

Xiang rolled her eyes. "I'm sure you do."

"Listen, Princess, I'll make you a deal since I refused the empress's conscription. I'll help guide you and your oddball friends to your destination if you can get the empress to pardon me for some crimes I've been wrongly accused of. That and well... help me get my plane back."

Xiang looked at him with a skeptical expression. "You're the last professional pilot on Earth and you don't even have an aircraft?"

"She was repossessed by some Pashtun thugs a year or

so ago after I failed to pay a debt. Tried to steal her back one time and almost got my head chopped off by a Taliban drug lord. Bloody savages, I tell ya."

"If you can lead us to Nur-Sultan, we'll help you find your aircraft. Can you get us some horses?"

"I'll see what I can do," he said, winking.

As Galen walked away and the adults continued to talk and drink, Uli and Devonia watched the viola player's emotional melody, apathetic to the noisy tavern drowning them out. Some geisha girls and drag queens began harmonizing with the tune and everyone stopped their current activity to watch the blissful song play out. Eventually, more musicians joined, playing through the night until the revelry died out and even the town drunk needed to sleep.

Just like the homeless scoundrels and outlaw merchants around them, the fellowship fell asleep under the barstools, leaving a lone wasted Mongol to continue his throat-singing to dawn's light on the old front deck.

○

That morning, Xiang awoke to Galen shushing her. She blinked with drunken effort.

"Wake up, Princess. We've gotta move," he said as the barkeep swept the floor around the bodies of other inebriated patrons.

Leaving the rest of her unlikely company to sleep off the excesses of the previous night, Xiang walked slowly out of the tavern and into the sunlight, shielding her eyes from the harsh brightness. A few folks in town had risen, but none were motivated enough to move with any particular purpose. Galen showed her to a corral at the back of an inn where five horses and a camel were tied up and saddled. He spoke softly.

"We're gonna take 'em but we gotta do it quick. In ten minutes, I'll create a distraction at the other end of the street. While I'm gone, you wake up the crew and get 'em over here, then leg it. I'll be right behind ya."

"Won't we be followed?" Xiang asked.

"You wanna get outta here or stay until all you got left to barter is your snatch?"

"I regret working with you," Xiang shook her head as she scowled him.

"Just focus on gettin' outta here while I do the dirty work."

He winked and walked off, pulling his wrinkled bandana coated in engine oil over his nose and dropping a crowbar from his torn sleeve.

Sighing, Xiang headed back to the tavern and roused the rest of the company. Together, they walked quickly across the town's main street and crept behind the corral. Ali launched himself over the gate and opened it, quietly leading the horses out. Uli and Devonia were pushed onto a single horse while the rest of them leapt onto their steeds bareback, all except Igor, who was left standing in a whirl of dust as they rode out. The only creature left was the panicking camel, attempting to squeeze itself into the corner of the corral. Igor pulled the camel's reigns toward him but the creature spat on his toe. Igor spat back.

"Of course I get the desert jack-ass!" he cursed as he leapt atop the beast and wrestled his way between the camel's humps.

Safely astride his mount, Igor sped out of the gate to catch up with the others, who were already far ahead. A commotion a few blocks away was escalating to gunfire and angry screams.

"Hurry the hell up, Igor!" Xiang yelled from the back of the pack, turning east around the edge of town.

Bullets flew by Igor's head and bounced off the ground, as a man from the growing crowd glanced into one of the many alleyways and saw his horses being ridden off. Igor's camel shifted from a trot to full sprint, nearly knocking the irritated Russian off while passing Xiang's Arabian in its fearful retreat.

"Thieves!" the man yelled with a vile rasp.

More gunshots pursued them as they rode off in a blur of hooves, robes billowing like ocean waves in the sweltering mirage that swallowed their horses with its deceptive merging of the landscape. The man and his gang of bandits chased the fellowship on foot in vain as sweat poured from their pores, their bodies tethered to that cursed oasis of a town of few horses, others greedy and unwilling to part with their own. As the crowd watched the gang fire at the retreating horse thieves, one more rider shot like a cannonball from a locked gate in the north end of town, where wood as old as sand splintered over the sordid steppe. Atop his magnificent black stallion, Galen bolted into the shadowless wasteland, disappearing rapidly on the fluttering horizon like a pupil shrinking in the eye of the sun.

They bedded down in a canyon far along the steppe's contours, the landscape strange to them all. Only the stars were familiar, for even their faces had become less recognizable as their hope dwindled in the small fire's light.

They had managed to commandeer horsepower, but in their quickness, water remained an elusive element. Igor's negativity was obvious, as was Ali's and that of his troubled sisters. Devonia's face drooped as she held poor dehydrated Boris in her arms. Xiang poked a stick into the dirt lethargically and Uli slept, a mild case of heat exhaustion leaving her tired but restless.

Only Galen seemed unaffected, spitting a tobacco wad into the flames and gutting its remnants as he sat back against his sleeping horse, still sweating from the over exertion of sprinting across the burning plain. He wiped the spit from his beard and looked about the fellowship, his scarred hands caressing the fingertips of the trembling fire.

"The world was made for this moment, an' others like it." Galen spoke quietly in the windless canyon.

Xiang shook her head slowly. "I can't tell if that's optimism or fatalism."

"Each of you here will persist in the same way you always have: through adaptation; through honorin' the paths given to each of ya... y'know... the archetypes; like tributaries that find a river to speed their descent, and yet waitin' to disperse at their destination. We were forced to partake in this sacred fellowship after committin' to some unconscious vow, an' what awaits is a far more vital quest beyond the trials of this world."

"Does this drunken ramble have a point?" Xiang asked.

"You don't think it's fate? I've been called on once before by your empress and refused, only to have that task forced on me in the last place I expected. That's God's work there."

"That's your personal perception. None of what you mentioned has materialized yet. Even the circumstances that have brought us together... mere coincidence."

"All the more reason to apply our combined assets to the

cause! In what era could a Russian an' a Kurdish fighter find themselves shoulder to shoulder? In what other way could an orphan from the Balkans an' a stolen African girl become the most treasured livin' creatures? We're at a crossroads of the human race. If by coincidence you've all come together, then by causality you'll succeed in winnin' your war."

"Can this war be won?"

"What you need to ask yourself is what you're willin' to sacrifice in order to win, regardless of the aftermath."

"But what if the aftermath is worse than the war?"

"That..." Galen pointed at Xiang, "is why we have to win."

Galen tipped his hat and sunk back into his horse's belly, falling soundly asleep within minutes of his rant. Xiang sat unmoved, slowly watching the others drift off, her cracked lips collecting beads of saltwater tears at their corners.

CHAPTER 52 – WOMB RAKER

Thick refinery smoke hung over Geneva's sky as an enslaved population trudged below the ruinous throne. The callous air stung their lungs as they labored before a red sunset bleeding a vulturous grain. What timber could be salvaged was cut. What rivers could be siphoned were absorbed. What fuels could be unearthed were fracked. All animals were herded and bred like swine in the river's gutter and slaughtered and distributed to the ever-consuming Luciferian Army. Women were toyed with and made for selling, their dead eyes like black buttons sewn into their soft skin; those unfortunate few whose forced marriage was the result of some apes clenching. For man's nameless hunger would be forever insatiable, like their king above, who ordered them to work, war, or death, eroding the hearts of those weary men who had descended to lesser fiends than their fathers.

High atop the spire of what had once been the empress's observatory, a dire screech pierced the air. It was the cry of a demon in labor, her child clawing towards its birth. She lay on a large concrete base between bent rows of rebar, where the world's most advanced telescope – now ripped off and recycled for bomb parts – had once been mounted, its lens peeking over the rim of the universe where the tide of existence met some unarticulated void like the fetus inching his way to the surface of their sanctioned world, intrepid in his birthing despite the sour air to come.

Michael stood between Fraus's legs, beating his large wings to cool his distressed warlock mistress. He smiled as the child crowned, and Fraus shrieked in pain, for even as a Sararan her body knew the shock of birth was crucial to motherhood; that rite which connects mother, child, and Earth.

"He's coming! Push harder!" Michael yelled as she wailed in agony.

Her cries reached an impossible frequency and split the column beside her. The rocks plunged below, smashing a group of slaves in their ascent to their master, limestone dust settling slowly next to the mangled bodies. After several forceful pushes, the boy surfaced in full, and before Fraus could hold her child he was raised up to the setting sun by his father, who smiled and held his newborn son in his left hand, slicing the umbilical cord with his razor nails.

"Seth, ruler of all living things, gaze upon your empire!" Michael cried.

The baby neither wept nor cried out; he simply gazed about with bright, niveous eyes, like a wise man settling back into infancy. Seth. Prince of the New World. Immortal from birth. And unlike any creature on Earth.

The next morning, the fellowship woke before dawn's light and continued their journey through the sutures of the land. They found a spring lower down the canyon and tested their stomachs on the marsh, human and horse drinking voraciously besides one another.

Galen then led the fellowship south, and when Xiang was finally about to question his navigation skills, they crested a hill and gazed upon an old weaponized compound in the center of a small basin. Rows of razor wire wrapped the perimeter and a large aircraft hangar extended from its southwestern corner.

"What the hell is this?" Xiang snapped.

Galen spat and gazed down at the compound, crow's feet forming at the corners of his eyes. "My sweet Sylvia is in there. Probably just a matter of time before the bastards strip her for parts."

"You selfish son of a bitch!" Xiang yelled.

The girls stood back and cringed.

"You led us straight into the lap of these scoundrels instead of keeping your word!"

"Ah come off it, lady. I ain't gonna be much help to your bleedin' war effort until I get my plane back, am I?"

Igor shook his head. "We don't have the ammunition or numbers to attack them. Who do you think we are?"

Ali stepped up and looked out, clenching his jaw as he felt an insurgency of anger rise within him. "These falsifiers of Allah... much as I am compelled to turn them over to God, Igor is right. Your plan is strategically flawed."

His sisters looked down at the compound with equal disgust, clasping their rifles closely.

Galen shrugged. "I'll do most the foot work, just create a distraction."

"You're an imbecile," Xiang hissed, her furious gaze resting on the golden orb now beaming over the horizon.

"Hey! Maybe they can help us!" Devonia shouted.

Standing opposite them, staggered laterally across the hillside, were an ominous contingent of warriors. They were adorned in black robes with no insignia, each carrying at least six hundred rounds and trauma kits around their waists.

Igor's eyes scanned the mystery fighters, his gaze sharp and discerning. "Taliban?" he questioned.

"No. They're Zurvans," Xiang said, her voice calm but

careful.

She signaled. They signaled back. After a few moments, the two groups cautiously approached, slowly recognizing one another as allies. Their leader spoke with urgency.

"Shiva ordered us to retrieve an aircraft here. This is your plane?" he asked Galen.

"That she is, mate! An' I'll tell ya, if you an' your troops help me get her back I'll land her right in the Mongol capital."

"Be careful about promises with him," Xiang grumbled.

"If you wish to speak with Parvati, she is not there," the Zurvan explained. "She left her chief of staff in charge. You haven't heard?"

Xiang and the others stood without gesture, as dumb as they were curious.

"Parvati is taking advantage of Michael's loitering. She's mobilized the entire Mongol army west to meet the Luciferian Army head on. Whispers from the north point to the return of Tala. This grand convergence is suspected to take place in Geneva's ruins and will be a triumph for Parvati if the witch can be vanquished, but none can guess the aim of the arctic goddess."

"What news have you heard of Empress Melody?"

"None so viable that it would offer you any answers. All her contacts have been killed or are on the run, like you."

Xiang shook her head in confusion. "So why has Michael stalled the Luciferian's eastern movement when he has had such unstoppable momentum?"

"He is expecting a son with the demon; the illicit newborn will be the first purebred Sararan. Michael is sparing his enemies lands so that his offspring may conquer them; so that he may earn his place among history's lords rather than be handed the world his father fought to dominate."

"Every powerful nation's third or fourth generation takes for granted the spoils their predecessors bled for, distracted by riches they don't deserve and protected by men who'd rather sever their tribe from the ailing body of the state, renewing the cycle that has plagued mankind since the beginning," Ali mused. "It is no wonder Michael left Pavonia unoccupied in the wake of his ravaging. He's left a power vacuum for future sport, and sport alone. By choosing not to invade Mongolia, he's left a worthy adversary to train his son in the art of war."

The Zurvan nodded. "Which is why we must take offensive positions immediately."

"But the child will not be ready to command an army for many years," Xiang argued. "If what you say is true, why not spend the time building Mongol defenses and reinforcing the borders of the last free nation on Earth?"

"Because Michael has already surpassed Mongolia in terms of technological advancement and resource acquirements, and the amount of research on pure-bred Sararans is non-existent. We must assume the possibility of rapid growth cycles due to the child's genetic paradigm. He may mature faster than we can prepare. With half the world's population already killed, enslaved, or displaced, the probability for a Mongol victory wanes each day. We need every possible asset. Parvati and her army. The Zurvans. Empress Melody. Any and all irregular servicemen and women. Even Devonia and Uli here, who may well be generals of their own armies someday."

"If the Mongols are victorious, perhaps they won't need to be."

The Zurvan scowled at her. "Have you not learned yet the dangers of peace-mongering? Even if the warlock's head is felled, the Luciferian Army is vanquished and our forces manage to deflect the witch's cerebral terrorism, the naivety of your notion that this world will somehow return to a utopia has already been humiliated. Avestan trained the children to be warriors, not because they must fight but because they should know how to, so that this knowledge can be relayed to the threatened citizens in the twenty-second century."

"There will never be peace," Xiang murmured, her voice sorrowful as the realization hit her.

The Zurvan nodded solemnly in agreement.

Xiang breathed deeply, settling herself, before focusing her gaze on the hangar before them. "So... when do we attempt the siege of this air strip?"

"This evening, if that suits your company. Our forces can infiltrate the compound and conduct the raid. Perhaps yours can set up a perimeter; station themselves at the choke points to capture anyone trying to escape?"

"That sounds like it will work. I will stay with the children to the west, should we fail our mission and need to depart."

Ali raised his chin and spoke. "Would it be too late if we waited until after evening prayer to conduct this operation?"

"Not at all. I would prefer it if we all partook in our rituals. May God bless our cause."

The Zurvans bowed respectfully and turned away, both groups seeking out hidden crevices in which to rest prior to their mission.

That evening, as the boiling sun set and Ali and his sisters laid their rugs upon the earth to pray, the Zurvans passed around a golden plate engraved with the Tibetan mandala, symbolizing life after life, kissing it and meditating together in a wide circle before preparing their kits.

When night had fallen upon the barren landscape, and the sun's fading light had been drowned by a million restless stars, the Zurvans moved in, like rats born of the sewer's crevices and released onto that perilous range. They crept close against the northern wall of the compound, with swift and silent motion slitting the throats of the sleeping guards.

With the guards down, the Zurvans set charges on the heavy gate and moved everyone back. The gate exploded in a cloud of grey dust as the soldiers stormed through, their charges crumbling the thin walls as if they were dry bread. Shots from the fellowship outside the compound rang out as they killed the sentries and lookouts in their nests, providing the Zurvans cover fire while the black-cloaked killers flowed through the maze of huts in a murderous blaze.

The Pashtun tribesmen screamed futile orders as more explosions rocked the Earth, and the smell of sulfur and gun smoke lay over the depression like a foggy pond with ill magick igniting under its opaque surface.

Igor waited patiently on the hill opposite the southern gate while a few Taliban ran scattering between the desert rocks. When enough men had spilled from the opening, he pulled the trigger on his belt fed PK machine gun he'd commandeered, tearing the enemy combatants to pieces as his night vision goggles showed pools of white liquid pouring from their heads and abdomens like spurts of milk. The gun fire around the compound gradually sputtered out until only a single Taliban lay shrieking somewhere in the ruinous remains. A single shot popped against the stillness and he was finally quieted.

After another half hour of clearing rooms, the Zurvan point-man switched on the lights in the hangar and illuminated Galen's massive gunship. He called to the others and they entered. Galen shed a silent tear as he beheld his aircraft. He walked slowly around the plane, feeling its exterior, probing it with a gentle caress and kissing it on the hull. He poked his head under the bomb bay and looked about in loving remembrance.

"We need to make sure it's not sabotaged, could be rigged with explosives," one of the Zurvans said.

"No... she's perfect. They hardly touched her," Galen said as he stepped up the ladder into the cockpit, passing a painting of a beautiful naked Spanish girl toting a machine gun on the ship's nose.

Seventy-seven small white bomb symbols were painted next to her, marked for all the sorties she'd survived. Galen jumped in and sat down, looking at the panel and touching the controls as if making sure he wasn't dreaming.

Xiang walked up the ladder. "I didn't know you had an AC-130. These old gunships are rare. How did you come by it?"

"My grandfather was a pilot in the Australian Air Force back in the day. He taught my father how to fly, who eventually taught me all about what she's made of: the wirin', the controls, the weapon systems, everythin'. When Shakti's troops landed on our shores, my grandfather thought it foolish to face the Aradians head on, an' disobeyed orders when given a sortie, takin' our family to safety and waitin' until the Aradians left to continue his missions. Been some time since I've seen her though... I'm just glad to have her back."

"What do you say we get the hell out of here?"

Galen dug around under his seat and held up half a liter of some wicked brown spirit.

"No time for a celebratory drink?" he asked.

She snatched it from his loose grip and held the dusty bottle behind her back. "Not until you fulfil your promise, you drunkard."

"Can't be a drunkard if you're not gonna let me drink," he muttered.

They topped off the fuel tanks with outdated jet fuel and the Zurvans, the fellowship and their horses filtered into the cargo bay. When the propellers roared awake, the passengers were reminded of just why Galen's noisy mechanical dragon, a relic from the mutinous skies of old, had put the fear of God into so many humans before their time. It was a gunship that fed on the blood of the Earth, harboring 40mm cannons on its starboard side that were designed to create a meteor shower of hot lead, decimating its targets.

Devonia and Uli hugged one another tightly as the massive aircraft turned out of the hangar and aligned with the runway, taking off into the clear and empty night air. Xiang could see the bodies of the Pashtuns laid out next to the runway, and asked Ali if they would at least receive a proper burial by the neighboring tribes. Ali answered solemnly, informing her that there were likely no neighboring tribes left to attend to their persecutors.

CHAPTER 53 – RETURN OF THE TRINITY

At dawn, the plane landed on a make-shift airstrip atop a flat section of the steppe, in what had once been West China. One hundred thousand soldiers stirred awake from their yurts, rising to gawk at the relic gunship of alloy patchwork: a man-made titan, oily and monstrous against the beautiful blue sky. Sylvia's tyres shot dust and rocks into the air before slowing and bouncing up to the wooden watch tower, creaking to a staggered halt when the engines finally ceased their rumbling.

The massive encampment around them was temporary but vast; all cavalry, with another hundred thousand horses waiting to replace the weary steeds of the riders who would soon join them, having ridden hard for days on end. Parvati's engineers had built a small tributary branching off from the river to nourish the horses and provide mobile gardens for the people. Her yurt was centered in that sea of tents, and a score of women guarded its entry: some disguised, some not.

Galen opened the cockpit and exited the ship, watching as the cargo bay opened and the Zurvans led the fellowship from its innards. Xiang walked up to him and hugged him.

"Thank you," she said softly, handing him the bottle of liquor she had swiped.

Galen ambled idly towards the nose of his beloved Sylvia and sat down against the front landing gear. He spat and uncorked the bottle Xiang had been holding captive and splashed the mysterious shine down his throat. The tribespeople, who had never seen an aircraft, noodled their way towards the metal bird as he sipped blissfully on the aged spirit.

Leaving Galen to his drink, Xiang went to join the rest of her unlikely comrades. A Zurvan commander met the fellowship at the edge of the runway, his golden nose ring shining brightly against his dark black skin in the orange morning light.

"Princess Yu, I knew you were an expert in social experimentation, but I think you've outdone yourself!" He looked pointedly at the Russian, the three Muslims, the children, and the pilot leaning against his last possession. "Welcome to Queen Parvati's camp. As you'd expect, she is eager to see you."

"You are kind to say so, but we have traveled for many weeks. May we refresh ourselves in the river before accepting Her Highness's blessing? I would hate to disrespect Her Graciousness by meeting her in this manner."

He chuckled. "There's no need for such formalities. We're all soldiers here. Please eat and drink while she speaks with you. The queen has just returned from a hunting party. I'm sure she won't mind a little sweat and dirt on her new general."

"General?" Xiang asked, looking around at the others.

Ali shrugged while his sisters both gave her a large grin.

"You're an ambassador with no nation to mediate. You've been promoted, General Yu," the commander informed her.

"But... that would mean... Empress Melody, where is she?"

"Come with me. Just you and the children for now." He turned to the others. "Go eat and rest, friends of Mongolia. Soon comes the return of The Trinity."

Xiang and the girls followed the Zurvan man through the camp, looking around at the soldiers who had been riding steadily toward the gloom on the western horizon. There were guerrilla jungle fighters, northern riflemen, steppe archers, snipers, sappers, engineers, hackers, men with robotic arms and artificial glass eyes, men and women who'd fought in ghost wars during the so called Age of Peace, and veterans of World War III, who were all in their sixties and seventies, their berets as clean as the day they were earned, smoking cigars and cleaning their rifles with arthritic, tattooed hands.

There were children digging up downed drones from the 2020's, using dogs to locate them. They unearthed the wreckages carefully with small tools and toothbrushes, like paleontologists excavating dinosaur bones, and reprogrammed them using hardware bestowed by their queen and rare gems collected from people's wedding rings. Shamans walked through the camps, burning incense and passing messages to one another, and a group of thespians were reciting verses in preparation for some unknown performance. A poet sat near them, writing as he smoked herb, watching Devonia walk by with a spiral gaze. There were all-female fighting brigades, Zurvan special forces groups, Taoist Monks, Russian troopers, and even Tlingit trackers, all supporting a bloodthirsty army of Mongols, who through some thread of lineage had tapped into the mindset of their forebears: the most brutal warriors the Earth had ever seen.

There was a distinct sense of culture melding, from the multitude of scents to the harmonizing of different worldly instruments, a carried culture not so different to that of the Mongol empire a thousand years before. A woman passed her baby to her daughter so she could reload recycled shells with carefully measured gunpowder loads and shiny copper bullets. Some children were being taught a language lesson behind them.

Xiang shook her head with dismay. "They should not have brought children."

Devonia's smile stretched wide across her face as she, Uli and Xiang entered the grand yurt. Candles were lit in the center, away from the walls of feathers and woven hoops that had been hung over large Buddhist tapestries, rescued from abandoned monasteries. Queen Parvati watched them from behind the flames. Her aged eyes were soft and welcoming, but Xiang could sense unease behind her façade of calm. The queen lifted her blue silk sleeves and raised her hands as if in prayer.

"At last, sister, you have come. And with you, the goddess redeemed… and perhaps another?"

Uli and Devonia stepped forward timidly.

"Come, girls," Xiang encouraged. "No need to be nervous."

Queen Parvati smiled kindly and walked up to them, kneeling as she gently took each child's hand and looked into their eyes.

"It is an honor to meet you both. Will you tell me your names?"

"I'm Uhlanga," said Uli shyly.

"And I'm Devonia. Pleased to meet you, Your Highness."

"Welcome to our great nation. I've been told Avestan has been training you?"

"Yes, they were. But we haven't seen them for some time now."

"Well, Avestan has been quite busy lately. I'm sure you'll

see them again soon."

She rose and walked to Xiang, hugging her closely. "It's good to see you again."

"My queen," Xiang said, returning the embrace.

"Budi told you of your new title then?"

"He did. But without Melody's permission—"

The queen gestured to the entrance as Melody walked inside, reaching for Xiang. They embraced warmly as the children ran to the empress's side.

"Empress! We missed you!"

"Devonia! Uli! It's good to see you both. You've been well?" she asked, her glow more astounding than ever; her hair braided perfectly and without false contour; her face splendid and fresh.

"Sort of... we've been on the run you see," Uli explained.

She and Devonia began trading honest claims.

"Yeah, and fighting Taliban..."

"And stealing from scoundrels..."

"And drinking from bogs!"

"Okay, children," Xiang said, trying to quiet them.

Melody and Parvati laughed; Xiang bowed her head in embarrassment.

"Well it sounds like you've had quite an adventure," Melody said. "I can't wait to hear all about it, but for now, why don't you two go find some breakfast? We three need to talk for a little while."

The children bowed and walked out, quickly joining some of the other children at the camp.

Melody watched them through the tent flap before tying the door shut. She turned and sighed with relief.

Xiang began to apologize. "I'm so sorry, Empress, I—"

"No. Please, Xiang. It's all right. This extended absence was my fault. I should not have put you and the children in such danger. I didn't expect to be gone as long as I was."

"Where were you?"

"Re-stabilizing Pavonia. There weren't many communities left to help, but I did what I could with the time I had."

"Did you meet any resistance?"

"Yes, but not in the way you'd expect. Pestilence has taken the continent. What humans remain are spread thin and are in immediate need of aid. Cholera is killing people daily. But we cannot be distracted by their turmoil at this time. We must liberate Almuruna before Michael's next wave of terror swells."

"I implore you, Melody, please choose someone else. I'm no general."

"Don't sell yourself short, Xiang. You are the daughter of one of Shakti's chosen. You were destined to shape this world and influence its peoples. We need someone who has your skills."

"Are you sure there are no others?"

"None that are alive."

Xiang nodded. "Where is Shiva and his regiment?"

Parvati looked to Melody, then Xiang. "They're in Milan," she answered.

"Lord have mercy," Xiang gasped.

"They're dug in and unable to move. As far as I know, they've lost half their forces but have managed to accomplish all their objectives so far. They've cut the Luciferian forces in half, but they'll soon reintegrate. Most of the enemy will return to Geneva in preparation for the Mongol invasion, which is why the pace of this army will increase over the coming days."

"So what's the plan?"

"Our only chance is uniting behind the chrome deity," Parvati continued. "Once the bastard son of Michael is safe in allied hands, we will destroy the demons and anyone who follows them."

"How will you avoid detection?"

"A sleeper agent has been planted in Geneva, posing as a palace guard. When the time is right, they will retrieve the child."

"Who?"

Melody shook her head. "No one can know. Even myself and Queen Parvati have not been informed."

"And how will you prevent the demon from possessing our forces and making them turn on us?"

"When I was in Pavonia, I was training myself to fly. Pavonis used to tell me stories about how the Aradians could fly as fast and deadly as jets, owning the skies as angelic overlords. Then I realized there was a much greater power I needed to master. I found a Mexican oracle who taught me counter-telepathy and I trained my brain to a transmit neural defense codes that can be broadcast when singing a low drone."

Parvati nodded and spoke to Xiang, "Now you see why everything is happening so urgently? Everyone has a specific role. I will be in charge of logistics, medical needs and support while Master Shiva and Commander Budi will be coordinating the infantry, cavalry and artillery. Melody will be weaving her spell to block any attempts at possession by the demon witch, taking up almost all her energy and attention. You will coordinate with our limited air force of drones and planes and provide key intelligence regarding the newborn's extraction."

"And the children?"

"They will be protected by Parvati's personal guard, far away from the battle. If all of us do our duty, Tala can swiftly destroy the tyrants and we can end their advance. She will also be our primary offensive resource after the abduction."

"That increases the chance of blowback," Xiang reminded her.

"A calculated risk we must take," Parvati said.

"I understand the objective. I'll need to be briefed again on air operations and communications when possible."

"There will be a briefing this afternoon," Parvati assured her.

"I see you've coaxed Galen into helping us at last," Melody said, smirking.

"Not exactly. He used us to get to his ship. He still owes us a favor."

"Naturally," Melody said. "But at least he helped us when it mattered most. Knowing what we know now, he'd be dead if he'd first agreed to the draft, and his ship would be nothing but scraps to patch up Michael's naval vessels."

"Will we have greater numbers than our enemy? The god to demon ratio is in our favor, but I fear for the mortal lives behind them."

"The possibility of mass casualties is high. There are infinite variables at play. One thing to remember, is that the Luciferian Army is just one of the witch's arms of war. I have been to the far reaches of Pavonia, and where there were once astral lands of deep wilderness, new evils lurk. Out there, beyond the scope of my understanding, a horde of mutant degenerates gather; a hideous swarm more ghoul than human, and yet somehow related to the humanoid. They are cyclops with half a brain, and they grow feathered wings and steel fangs. They hide well in the mountains and would watch me from afar, sneaking deep into the cracks in the rock like spiders if I came too close. I was often unable to locate them, much less eradicate them. We will have to show these creatures as little mercy as we can afford. Be it children, women, elderly… if they are not human and pose an immediate threat, they are to be cut down. Understood?"

Xiang nodded and cleared her throat. "I suppose we'll be mobilizing soon then."

"Tomorrow morning," Melody confirmed.

"And since this may be our last chance," Parvati added, "we will hold a festival tonight. You'll have access to my wardrobe so you can dress accordingly. We'll get you a clean outfit for tonight, as well as clothes and amenities for your new friends as well."

"Thank you, Empress. Thank you, my queen. You have my heart and my sword."

They three put one another's heads together: a triad of strong women united with a sense of matriarchal blessing. A common energy passed between them, augmented by the song goddess and transferred to the daughters of the Great Khan, who would soon be galloping thunderously towards their enemy, much like their ancestors; the weight of four hundred thousand hooves upon their warpath as they rode towards Michael and his fearsome army.

That night, the people congregated around their queen. The Mongol families centered themselves around that warm nucleus, unicellular and harmonious. Even those who strayed from its spiraling envelopment found breath in the cradling lung of the eternal sky above. Devonia entered the spectacle and walked through the happy maze of fire twirlers, knife jugglers and Siberian musicians. Acrobats performed flips like disciplined birds, and fairy-goddess children huddled in lotus-petal dresses, bowing in small circles then opening and closing with the blossoming rhythm of the music. Rockets with bright blue afterburners erupted over the camp, screaming toward the stars and coloring Devonia's insomnia-drunk eyes with one-hundred broken moons. She saw in them her own ghost's celeste wings urging to open again, but only time would tell.

Uli ran up behind her and frog-jumped over Devonia's shoulders, snapping her out of her trance.

"Come on, D! We'll miss the fireworks!"

Devonia grinned, grabbing her friend's hand and running across the camp. Xiang made no effort to chase them. Her silk dress tickled the grass behind her as she graciously kissed the hands of those few who recognized her.

Nearly every man had a family. Every woman, a child. Every child held some form of hope in their small callow hearts. The drums picked up and the dancers became wilder in their movements, their wiggling limbs barely able to express themselves to the amplified vibrations.

Melody emerged, and those around her bowed with respect before continuing their celebrations.

"I trust you're enjoying yourself?" she asked her new general.

"I am," Xiang said softly.

"I'm sorry I keep placing you in such challenging positions. The children should not have been kept in one place for so long."

"It's all right, I understand. Fortunately, the gods seem to be on our side... let's hope they stay that way."

They watched the glorious heavens alight with rainbow fire as the lotus children smiled and laughed with delight.

"Tala will be there to help us. At a price, of course."

"What price?" Xiang asked.

Melody looked up to the heavens. "Just... appreciate

what we have now."

"That's all we can ever do, Empress."

Melody smiled and kissed her friend on the cheek, welcoming the embrace she offered. For some time they sat together, watching the revelers, until they noticed a small crowd had gathered a short distance away. Edging closer, they recognized none other than Galen Fox – the last pilot; the castaway – sitting in the center of the group.

"... so, there I was, covered in blood an' muck an' racin' between the cockpit an' my wounded mate. Johnny'd been shot through his ribs, an' he was so far gone in his head he was singin' like Bruno Mars. I told him to save it for the stadium!"

The children laughed, waving as they spotted Melody and Xiang. They listened to the story with rapt attention, laughing and cringing and feeling the emotions of the tale unravel.

"We flew nine hundred an' thirty miles on limited fuel, coastin' in silence between mountains as tall as the sky before we crash landed in a massive valley. Lucky for us, the locals were good as gold an' patched ol' Johnny up. Told us to stay afterwards, an' we weren't gonna refuse. That valley was somethin' else, I tell ya. We lived there for years; found our true loves; married 'em. I told my story round campfires just like this one, with folks as beautiful and strong as yourselves, who lived the way our people always strived to live; in harmony, not tyranny. Leadin' with compassion, not intimidation. Allowin' any differences to be set aside. You're just like 'em, and you too will live to see betta days. God be with all of ya."

Some raised their drinks; others clapped. But they all celebrated Galen's sentiment.

As the crowd dispersed, Xiang approached him.

"You did a good deed there, Galen. These people... they may seem confident in their victory, but they know what they're up against. They needed that."

The Australian made a gruff sound of acknowledgment, looking down at the floor and reaching for his bottle.

"Forgive me for asking but... what happened after you left the valley? To your wife, I mean?"

"She was killed by insurgents three an' a half years after we married. They took my little girl too, but we never found her. Just two years old she was." He paused, his voice breaking as he tried to keep the tears at bay. "So I returned to the war. I hunted 'em. I killed as many as I could on my own before contractin' myself as a strategic gunship for Michael's peace keepers. One day I fired a missile at a buildin' we thought was an enemy trainin' facility, but it was a school full of kids."

"My God..." Xiang gasped.

"I redacted the contract and abandoned ship one night. I barely remember; I was drunker than an Irishman at breakfast. Went wanderin' through the empty parts of the world. The Gobi. Egypt. Back to Oz for a time to spend a year in the bush, before gettin' chased out by filthy feckin' lowlifes and robbed of everythin' I had. You wanna know why I drink so much? I suppose I'm already dead. Never findin' heaven, in this world or after. But I sorta become God with this fiery potion. It may be damn ruddy and near spent, but this twine around the bottle neck stops me from puttin' a rope around my own neck. It tethers me to my past, my future, an' may be the only thread I lay claim to in this life."

"I had no idea, Galen," Xiang said, hugging him.

"It's not your fault, Princess," he said, embracing her in return.

"But it is! The Nine Princesses of the new world were

meant to protect the Earth from such destruction! Michael should have—"

"You can't protect the world from madness, Princess. The world was born to be mad. You just have to make it mad with love."

They shared a toast and Xiang told him stories of her own as they walked together through the festivities, until they came across a private area with candles lit and a bottle of wine standing on a stump, perfectly unattended. They sat down with slight hesitation, and she looked at him oddly.

"Come on... you know it wasn't me who set this up..." he said.

"It wasn't me either! But maybe the hosts won't mind as long as we replace their bottle?"

Galen shrugged and sat. He uncorked the bottle while she glanced uncertainly at him from her seat.

"A wasted drink is a small tragedy. Tonight is for all of us. Why hold back now?"

"Do you think we'll overcome them? The enemy?" she asked.

"Goin' against the Luciferian Army and its hellish royalty will be no easy feat. But I reckon we'll prevail. It won't be over right away. The shockwave of this battle will continue into next century... which is why we've gotta celebrate life now!"

"That's why culture lives on through tragedy. We won't let it die."

"It never could die."

She looked at him warmly. He looked back, as if she reminded him of someone he knew. He averted his gaze.

"I want to thank you for everything. If you hadn't given me a chance, we would never have gotten Sylvia back. An' it would have been a very long walk."

"I'm glad we could help… and now that I outrank you, you'll have to follow every order I give you, or else its insubordination," she said smiling.

"What's your first order, General?" he asked with a grin, taking a sip of his drink.

She took a gulp of her own wine and set her glass down on the stump as she stood, reaching for him, her eyes entreating.

"I need…" She paused, taking his hands in hers and settling them on her waist. "Please, Galen."

Her plea urged him into action and he pulled her towards him, grasping her thighs as he dragged her into his lap. She brought her lips to his instantly, kissing him with desperate lust. He kissed her back, sliding them both off the chair and onto the ground as they continued to roam their hands over one another's bodies, yanking at clothes and hair pins until they both lay naked and Xiang's hair cascaded around her, free from its imprisonment atop her head.

They began kissing more aggressively, falling into one another's embrace as instant lovers, unable to restrain their desires. The whole universe harmonized with them, and what had begun as a dissonant arrangement gave back to itself a modest forgiveness. With their soft bodies they made love in the open air, a thousand million stars as witness, candlelight caressing their tingling bodies so coerced by the movement of their wanting; a movement that seemed to sync with the spinning of the Earth.

Groping at shoulders and chests, they became animalistic in their lovemaking. Panting. Thrusting. Moaning. Until they peaked, giving their love up to the night sky as the firework show climaxed and covered their ecstatic cries with bursts of predetermined victory mantras.

In that moment, a thunderstorm rumbled in the distance,

as if calling in return and challenging the humans with a message from the demon queen:

'Bring everything you have.'

The morning came, but the warm body Xiang had expected to find next to her was no more. She felt around the blanket for Galen, then sat upright and looked about in a whirl. His coat and boots were conspicuously absent. The flap on her yurt opened with her presence and slapped shut. The entire camp was breaking down and soldiers were preparing for demobilization. Armor was donned by those preparing to suffer most. Families congregated and wept together. Prayers were said to the fathers, brothers and sisters who'd been called to war. All kept a grim face.

"Where did he go? Galen? The pilot?" she asked a man nearby.

He shrugged and continued in his preparations. She crossed the camp towards the tarmac, past many a hurried crowd, breaking into a run when she heard the guttural engines churn.

"Oh no you don't!"

Xiang sprinted towards the tarmac with quick feet. She could see the rusted mosaic of Sylvia's exoskeleton as the plane taxied into position and she ran onto the runway, screaming for Galen to stop, but she was drowned by the blaring propellers. Desperate, she stared up at the cockpit, only for the old-world gunship to lift off towards the sun and fly away, blasting her face with wind and wrapping her skin with sideways streaming tears. She cupped her face in her hands and sobbed.

"You fucking son of a bitch, Galen! I never should have trusted you!" She wiped her tears furiously, startled when she felt a hand on her shoulder. She turned to find Melody beside her. "He's been nothing but a letdown. Why did you let him leave?"

The empress's green swirling eyes betrayed no emotion. "What kind of empress would I be if I forced people to do my bidding against their wishes? Shakti ruled in such ways. Galen served his purpose. He brought you and the children here to safety. That suffices for the time."

"Bullshit. He only came here to stock up on booze and get his dick wet."

"His intentions go beyond the simple characteristics you impose. I don't think we've seen the last of Galen Fox." She reached into her pocket and handed Xiang a letter. "He wanted me to give this to you."

Xiang took it and crumpled it in her fist. "Forget him. What time do we mobilize?"

"Ten hundred hours. And we'll be doubling our former pace. You have twenty thousand troops now under your command. Fall in with our pattern. Get to know your officers. But I do suggest you read the letter when the moment permits."

"I will follow you anywhere and exceed your expectations, Empress," she said, channeling her anger into initiative.

"The most important rule I cannot emphasize enough is that they cannot bring their families," Melody reminded her.

"No children."

"No children."

The tan tents collapsed and all around families wept and prepared for their own route back east in soft retreat. The warriors shed themselves of civil artifacts, save for those precious somethings they carried in their breast pockets: perfumed letters, pictures, hair, and worn cloth. Lances stroked the low morning fog in its recession and cannons lurched into motion, feathers hanging from their barrels and all.

The hoard gathered, clinking and thunderous upon the steppe's expanse, and those in the far rear, whose horses had been deafened or were untamed, or who had indulged in their chalice to an unworthy hour, were now being yanked back into the swell; hurried into the mass like lame sheep. The trailing officer was strafing the ranks like a cattle herder, barking at the lot of them. He made allies with an old woman, who could not separate her granddaughter from a Croatian irregular. But despite her grandmother's pleas, and the gruff demands of the officer, the girl continued to cling to her lover, kissing and holding him, handing him something small which he kept hidden in his fist, until they were pulled apart by impatient soldiers, their embrace denied. He was carried by the throng, bound west for the war, whilst she was shepherded east in retreat. As their union was cleaved, they finally gave up resistance, the mirrors of their watery eyes meeting with pained smiles, still clinging to the taste of their lips; a testament to the power of young love and other unsaid promises.

The immense army scathed the plains, a gross sandstorm raking the chest of the land as they trekked across the steppe of East Kazakhstan, past cities of sprawling squallers and run down refineries, where old, suspended drills swayed on rusted cables from bent beams like iron marionettes. One of the divisions crawled along the foothills of a great palace, its golden towers gleaming in the evening light, like the skins of divine animals pinned tightly to high pillars. The bulbous sapphire statues on their high mounts sat nearly hidden in the sky, almost transparent against the cobalt, refracting the dying horizon about their phallic edges.

The army did not camp that first night, nor the one after. They kept moving. Irregulars joined along the way. Almost all of Mongolia and Almuruna had taken up arms against the hostile king who'd betrayed his empire. Instruments of labor and agriculture were left to rust in the soil they had once tended, and as the army grew, so did its morale. Tens of thousands of troops from the north, south, and east pushed ever westward. By the time Parvati's army reached the Balkans, the Luciferian Army's divisions had fallen back to the stolen capital, abandoning their outposts on the iron curtain and burning them as they went, like feral coyotes leaving their half-eaten meal for the wolves. The unfinished wall Michael was erecting across Almuruna crumbled in the same streets where the Berlin wall had once stood more than a century before.

It was only once they reached the Alps that the invasion began to meet new obstructions. Melody's division diverted south and spent over five days liberating Shiva and his troops, who had been held down by enemy crossfire and bad weather for several weeks. As her soldiers battled to free their kinsmen, Melody focused all her energy on humming a spell for their protection, a song powerful enough to shift her army's consciousness yet almost inaudible to the human ear. The breath of the universe, she called it. When she sang, all became immune to those slithering demonic transmissions, those artificial parasites spawned from the radioactive drool of the succubus. As Shiva's troops rejoined the main army, no more did they feel threatened by Fraus's mind-hexes, but Melody knew the witch had more methods of catastrophe than there were stars in the sky, and with all the world against her, she was surely planning something grand.

Though the soldiers were free of telepathic diseases, the air contained a foul stench of decay and death no man could deny, and the essence of the witch was near and evident in the rot left in the wake of her vile craft. In preparation for the invasion, Fraus had ordered her soldiers to stack high the decaying bodies of slain Almurunans so the Mongol Army had to pass through rows of stinking, skin-wrapped skeletons, some still clinging to their families, having been cut down where they stood. Yet despite the horrors; despite the constant reminders of their potential fate should they fail, the fellowship did not fracture.

Even Devonia and Uli, young though they were, remained strong on the road to war, and their bond only grew as they continued west, the two girls often holding one another at night as they tossed and turned, cursed by increasingly horrific night terrors. Devonia had told Avestan that she was having dreams of Pavonis exclaiming that her lover had come at last, but no one except Melody understood the mystery of her nightmares.

As the army marched onwards, the fear of death became a daily reality, but all agreed that the cost of dying was lesser than witnessing the absolution of the world's evils. Demons existed, they had seen them, so God must also: the antitheses to damnation. God would guide them, and they would enact his virtuous justice using that same odious spark that exists somewhere in all living creatures, from the heart of a butterfly to the cornea's of Michael's scorching eyes.

O

From Geneva's high spire, Michael watched his general crawl along the mountain in his decent to the valley floor. Ziven staggered along the ice-encrusted granite like a blind sheep, his clothes ragged; his honor dejected. The sheer cliffs cut the open sky in half before him as if floating in the great tumultuous heavens, and his battered mind bargained for reference as a sickening carousel of lights sloshed around the pits of his eyes. In his stupor, the fires from the army camps were like reflections to the cosmos wheeling across the sky; a blazing hoop of white hot drips of fire, bleeding from the seed of something counterpart to nothingness, for all that is not illuminated belongs to an unnamed overseer, defying shape and material, that dictates what is and what is not and fingers its way into every chasm, shadow and nightmare.

Fraus approached Michael as he stood with his wings outstretched, like a hawk eager to dive.

"Are you going to kill him?" she asked.

"Not yet."

Fraus handed Michael a bundle of ash-stained cloth. Their son, Seth, had been bathed in fire, baptized by flame over and over until his skin was hard and splotched with burns. Michael pulled back the frail cloth and squinted at the bright white luminosity glowing from young Seth's divine eyes. Michael spoke calmly as he stroked the forehead of his son.

"Ziven deserves to know why he's being executed. And he may be an asset in the afterlife."

"But we have already brought back the one who matters most..." Fraus said, smiling and watching her Sararan son grasp for Scorpio's throbbing blue heart in the sky, her expression deceivingly content. "Is Melody still unaware that Seth is the reincarnation of your father?"

Michael gazed into his son's eyes, nodding his head pendulously. "Only Tala knows… for now."

"Melody will try to destroy us and take him. She will introduce him to that Balkan girl who houses your mother's soul and attempt to re-engage the prophecy."

"And this disturbs you?" he asked.

"Nothing disturbs me. I am disturbance." She stroked her son's forehead. "Wasted lives are wasted lives, but Ezra wasn't a weak man until he met your mother. He was betrayed; he had no way to augment his abilities as the Aradians did. One day, Seth's kingdom could be befouled by Pavonis. What you need to ask yourself is who you love more: your father, who sacrificed everything to protect you, or your mother, who abandoned you to chase fame in the Post-Eruption Wars? They are old souls; they will not deviate from their fates."

Michael nodded again, his eyes blazing. "From the moment his first word is spoken, Seth shall be an autonomous creature. His enemies and friends will be his to choose, and mercy will be a rare and precious virtue. He will walk a terrible road, and like a man outcast to the desert in search of an oasis, he will be made to go great distances to earn his crown."

Ziven dropped to his knees before the palace doors. Dawn was an hour out and the camp was rustling with a myriad of officers, kicking the boots of snoring men whose faces were stained with the grease of roasted fowl. Charcoal fumed from the nostrils of their desirous war machines to the north, and a thin smoke lay over the lake like a toxic apparition.

"My king... forgive me," he cried.

Michael opened the door and looked at him with blazing eyes. The general's withered body and ripped clothes were a disturbing sight to see; he had shed his armor, for the metal had caused frostbite, and his head was stained with blood, his face wet with tears. Michael wrapped his hands around Ziven's head, brushing his fingers against the dried, blackened blood that clung to his ears and burnt skull. Ziven looked up, the pain of guilt in his eyes reflected in Michael's own; the agony and isolation sustained by both their souls momentarily visible, unveiled by their mild exchange.

"Come and have some wine, General."

Michael turned, his massive wings tucked in tightly as he walked into the palace. They came to a dining table, which had been set with delicious food, but Ziven could barely eat and instead drank the crude wine in front of him. Michael sat across from the general and sipped a crystal glass filled with mammal's blood. Ziven shivered in the cold room.

Michael cast his flaming eyes upon the general, coaxing him to listen closely.

"There is a large void in the minds of all conscious creatures. Some succumb to their self-designed vendetta's for going against the evolutionary discipline of lethality. But you can find compassion in the best of them, and this is their weakness. The fires of hell may well be a remnant of biblical doctrine, but there are methods of wielding Lucifer's torch. The surface of the sun can be found in the heart of the Earth, and just as Vishnu bled the vein of its largest contusion, I will give this power to the world. By nature's laws alone, a rightful keeper will be chosen. Perhaps it is my son. But it is surely not you."

Ziven nodded. "Are you going to kill me?"

Michael laughed. "If I were to let you live, you would be forgiven. You would delegate all your duties to your officers and spend your wealth in the brothels, collecting warts in your mouth and gout in your feet, deeming your combat skills useless, your sense of victory dull and distracted."

"No, I would never—"

"SILENCE! You grossly outnumbered the Zurvans, General, and yet they annihilated your forces. I wasn't sure whether to be embarrassed by your leadership or impressed with theirs, but now I know. Since it is your life you wagered, and thereby submitted to me wholly, upon retreating the battlefield, you will hence commit your last objective here. You were the best general a king could hope for, but when I promoted you, you made a promise to me. A promise framed in loyalty. Escape was never an option."

Ziven did not speak.

"Tonight, I will oblige the enemy by ending your life. This is the way of our people, and you will honor them by crossing over now. If you can understand the beauty in that, you will have already arrived in paradise."

When Michael finished speaking, Ziven was slumped, his head cocked back, the poisonous wine dripping from the corners of his mouth and forming long purple lines down his neck. Michael toasted the officer once more and sipped his chalice of blood in silence.

Later that day, one of Michael's reconnaissance groups returned from the mountains to report the state of the

Mongol advance. To his pleasure, they also returned with a double agent who'd been working with both Parvati and the Luciferian Army for some time. They all stood at the base of the palace wall next to a trap door that steamed with a strange smell. A cool breeze shifted in the autumn air as Michael inspected the man. He was beaten and shackled like a crazed ape in a carnival, his clothes hanging from his dirt-smeared skin, his eyes blood red and quivering with an unnamed brand of rage.

"What is your name and rank?"

"Joshua Ishler the Second, Lance Corporal and loyal servant to Your Majesty."

"You are a defector."

"No, sir."

"You are worse."

"Please, sir—"

"You are a traitor! A weasel scheming against his own brothers. High treason permits a method I rarely have the pleasure of implementing. Tell me, were you the one sent to steal my son from me?"

The man dropped his head in defiance. They stood in silence until the cellar door opened and alchemists in ceremonial garb walked up from the dungeons deep. They came in a line, hooded as mock-Gnostics, burning incense and candles, lumbering up the dark steps like a clergy of devil-worshipping priests steeped in the black phlegm of the underworld. A massive blacksmith followed behind, carrying a boiling cauldron of liquid gold.

"Unclench his jaw," the king ordered.

One of the men stood behind the traitor and pulled back on his forehead, grasping his four fingers over his bottom teeth to force his mouth open. The man fought each motion, but the soldiers tipped his head back as he gargled with regret and panic. Michael gripped the large ladle and dipped it into the cauldron.

"Your thirst for new masters will be quenched."

The man lurched as Michael stepped towards him.

"Drink, traitor!" Michael proclaimed viciously as he poured the liquid metal between Joshua's lips.

The steaming gold cascaded down his throat and white smoke rose from the man's mouth as the metal burned through his gut and lungs. He croaked, drowning in the precious liquid, melted and solidified so many times throughout history that no one would ever know the full narrative of its composition: as a pirate's fruition, the headpiece of a forgotten king, a widow's ring, or its origins as creek-bed flakes dazzling like fragments of sun awaiting a dire renaissance.

The traitor collapsed in the dead grass as red-hot gold dripped through large holes in his chest.

"Cut off his ears and scalp him, then give his body back to the enemy."

Michael stepped away as the soldiers took out their knives and began slicing the man's head apart like mad surgeons insulting God's work.

Melody received the body of the agent the next day. From then on, she directed her forces but rarely spoke to them otherwise. She remained focused. Parvati did much the same, but from the back of her divisions. It was Melody who led the army from the front, just as her master had done. The path to Geneva snaked through the large mountains, and the Mongol army split into several legions that filled the massive valleys like blood rushing through shrunken veins. Xiang was certain that elements of Michael's forces would linger to ambush the scouts, but no living thing remained in that land save for scavenging birds and dogs that had become like dissatisfied hyenas in their savagery.

As they neared Geneva, one of the divisions was funneled into a tributary, tripping a hidden wire that had been placed at the canyon's entrance. A rumbling tide pulsed through the mountains and Xiang dispatched a medical team immediately. A shelf of granite had given way under the splintered rocks above and fell with crushing bombardment onto the trapped soldiers below. Hundreds died instantly as the boulders smashed the bodies like berries in a massive mortar and pestle. Horses hobbled out of the landslide screaming, their legs broken and eyes bulging in their swollen skulls. The shrieks of those wounded cut through the canyon and were not silenced by night's coming.

The entire invasion was held up for a whole day while the dead were removed and given proper ceremony for their sacrifices. Only the Zurvan legion continued to advance to foil any other schemes made up by the tireless enemy.

The closer the Mongol army approximated themselves to Geneva, the more soldiers died due to improvised explosion devices and other traps set by the enemy. Yet morale held, and even more irregulars came from distant lands and filled the rear divisions to support the immense counterstrike. On October 13th, in the year 2099, the Mongol army halted on the outskirts of Geneva and stabbed their flags into the ash and mud.

CHAPTER 54 – LUX MAXIMA

Night came with a light rain as a quiet blanket of fear settled over the battlefield. Rumors of different strategies and plans spread through the camp, but no one really knew what to expect. Some said Michael had hundreds of refurbished jets being fueled and could drop bombs on them at any time; some said nothing would happen for days, if not weeks, since both sides had Immortals to fight and protect them. Those who had been in battle before slept, or tried to. Those who hadn't stood anxiously in their uniforms and watched the fires of the Luciferian Army rise from great clay chalices, the shadows of their enemy flickering against the curved stone walls like thin dancing devils as they rolled cannons and rocket-batteries into position. The line of men spread as wide as the horizon, with artillery nests placed deep in the mountains.

The Mongols lit no fires that night and kept their squadrons closely organized and ready to engage. Xiang hid the children in the mountains with twenty imperial guards to protect them, then ventured to the command yurt. She walked by soldiers preparing their rifles and horses, some sharpening triangular trench knives: crude in their design and cruel in their intent, weapons outlawed by the Geneva Convention over two hundred years ago in that very place. It was midnight when she arrived at the yurt. She slowed and peeked through the deer skin flap. A subtle blue light shone through the door and Xiang gasped.

"It's all right General Yu. Please… join us," Queen Parvati said.

Xiang trembled as she entered. The blue light subsided and there sat Tala, Suzerain of Earth, in rebuilt and modified blue titanium armor and emanating a swirling aura from her chest. She sat facing Xiang from behind the fire, with a half circle of powerful leaders sitting around the burning olive wood. Empress Melody, Queen Parvati, Shiva, and the Mongol commanders watched Xiang as she walked up to them and bowed. Tala stood and bowed in return as Xiang sat and looked about nervously at the strange and powerful symposium of creatures; defiant angels on that desolate scrape of Earth. Tala spoke first, holding out her hands in prayer as she presented her revelations.

"This morning I left my post in the North Pole after twelve thousand days of sustained aeromancy. Without temperature regulation, our planet will experience a series of extreme weather events within hours. What that will entail, I cannot rightly say. Tomorrow is the beginning of a new era in our history, for the Earth is about to begin the purge of the human race. We're going to help her by starting with the Luciferian Army."

She paused and looked at Xiang, sensing her conflicted soul.

"If I may... what about post-war reconstruction?" Xiang asked, addressing Tala's threat to her own species.

"Reconstruction?" Tala asked.

Everyone turned to Xiang.

"Civilization. Society. Our culture. Our way of life. Is that not in your plan? Forgive me, Lord Tala, but you've already cleansed the Earth of man's evil once before. Is it so necessary a second time less than a century later, after we've come so far?"

Tala looked at her without expression, her eyes a bleak mirage of snow and ice.

"You all lost your privilege to lead those confederations when you chose not to defend them," she said, turning to the others, "What is about to happen is bigger than humans. It is bigger than Sararans or Aradians or whatever comes after. Every creature ultimately concedes to some higher power. Man tried to control the Earth, so Vishnu used the powers of Earth against man. Soon all life will be at the mercy of the planet. Had you not all stifled your imaginations with existential rationalism and scientific certainty, you would know ancient lore for what it is: a warning. A cautionary tale written by those who have witnessed God's purge against the monsters man is capable of creating. A grand trial awaits humans after tomorrow's inevitable apostasy, and the Immortals will judge and sentence man for his slow deformity, since he has been made into ape-swine with his obsessions and heinous inventions. Soon, the untapped spirits of the unborn will be free, and rather than settle into human form, they will take on the most lethal body of nature's variety."

"What could be worse than humans or Immortals?" Xiang asked.

"Their offspring," Shiva answered with a deliberate tone.

Tala then elaborated on Shiva's words. "Which is why Devonia and Uli, and even Seth now, are so important to our defenses. Never forget, the world's first Sararan was killed by a falling tree. Earth does not discern the importance of one soul from another in her expulsion. She will rid herself of the worthy and unworthy, the strong, the weak, the moral, the vile, the young and old. We are all here in Geneva for the same reason: to destroy a reckless demon. But I am not killing her only because she's committed genocide. Each of you had the chance to do that a long time ago when you pardoned Shakti's officers instead of executing them. This is about the child now."

Parvati nodded and spoke softly to the group. "Tala is right. The possibility for redemption has passed, but necessity has pulled us together: three variations of the human species, all with a common goal. The soul of the most powerful being on Earth is somewhere behind that wall. We must obtain the son of Michael and kill the demon. That is the primary objective. The secondary objective is to annihilate Michael and as many of their soldiers as we can until the primary objective is complete."

"Is there a way to complete these objectives without engaging the enemy forces with our own? It seems like a waste of life. If what you say is true, it won't matter if we engage in battle or not," Shiva said.

"Your troops volunteered to be here and help the cause. Are they not of the Zurvan cloth, devoted to the principles of The Order?"

"They are, Lord Tala," Shiva said, nodding.

"Good. Because I will need a great battle to distract Michael, for what he ultimately craves is to lead his troops in one of the greatest massacres in Earth's history. He'll likely leave Fraus alone to defend the child. She knows I am close, and she is expecting this. She will kill the boy and eat him if I take direct action. Fraus is an inferior sorcerer, but she's no fool. She'd rather curse her own soul forever than let us have the last word. Just be ready to improvise, withdraw and redirect your orders to your officers at a moment's notice."

"Once the child is recovered, what are we to do?" Xiang asked.

"Retreat at once. I will not wait long before I detonate a thermonuclear bomb over the Luciferians. It doesn't matter if you and the Mongol army are still tangled in with them. All will be destroyed who linger in the valley."

"There are slave fighters in their army… forced into the ranks… should we not try to free some of them?" one of the commanders asked.

"Risk versus reward," Parvati said. "Vetting is out of the question. You'll never construct a system clean enough. It didn't work in 2056 and it won't work now. I won't allow men like that in my Queendom."

Everyone nodded. They finished the meeting with a Tibetan prayer and Tala, the empress and the Mongol queen took a walk out onto the battlefield to discuss strategies while the military commanders ate breakfast and spoke amongst themselves. Shiva sat oddly quiet among them.

"Master Shiva… where is your second in command?" Xiang asked. "I thought surely Avestan would partake in the briefing."

Shiva looked over sadly. "I was informed this morning that Avestan was gunned down during a scouting mission yesterday in the mountains."

Xiang gaped at him in shock. "I… I had no idea. No one told me. I'm… I'm so sorry for your loss." She reached over and squeezed his hand.

"It was a loss for all of us. Avestan was an incredible fighter and a loyal companion. They will be missed." He smiled as a tear streamed down his face. "The ceremony will take place at dawn, before we attack. Some of their ashes are being poured into artillery rounds as we speak, and they will be the first ones fired."

As the sun rose, the soldiers in the camp slowly began to rise, congregating near the command tent as they awaited orders from their leaders. Parvati hoisted herself atop a horse and delivered a speech to the army in the grazing light of dawn. She reminded them of the ancient tribes who had fought for unity a thousand years ago, and told them that every person who had ever fought for justice in the history of human kind had unknowingly been working towards this one moment. She asked them not to die for nothing, but to live and die for everything; for the sake of their children's children, and those after.

The soldiers thrust their lanced rifles into the air and yipped and yelled war cries in all different languages until the hoorah transformed into a thundering, growling waltz that seemed to shake the Earth and distort the wind and heavens. Shiva carried a urn through the ranks of the infantry; through the artillery brigades; through the cavalry of war horses and harpoon mounted pachyderms brought from India and Africa, until the whole army had parted like the red sea and knelt to pay their respects to one of their most devoted and fearless warriors.

At the invisible line that separated the free world from a calamitous and tainted state, Shiva stopped alongside Melody. A vast stretch of no-man's land sprawled towards the enemy forces, now standing in perfect order with their thin flags waving silently above their standing figures; a black line that stretched from range to range like the edge of an endless forest, terrifying in its immensity. Shiva held the urn high as Melody lifted her arms, her aura stronger than ever, feeding off every transfer of energy within a hundred miles. She stuck her toes into the cold dirt and rooted herself there, singing a hymn under her breath that amplified with each moment, until at last the demon was roused from his lair.

At that moment, the field became so quiet one could almost hear the hooves clopping through the old stone halls at the foot of the palace. From deep inside the ruins, the fiery eyes of Apollo burned through the shadowed corridor, and the massive horse stepped out into the light, his winged master sitting naked upon his back, smiling at the challengers before him. He nodded at Melody, who could not help but evade his mile-long stare, for fear of possession. Every prediction by the allied Immortals had to be calculated, every reaction articulated.

Michael urged Apollo closer to the impressive support gathered to destroy him. He breathed in slowly, then let out a sky-splitting shriek that blasted the Mongols with a shockwave. Suddenly, Luciferian troops rose from the ground by the thousands, like coal-covered phantoms rising from graves, forming nearly as large a force as the mighty coalition before them. No-man's land was cut in half, and some allied artillery was already within range. Michael held his sword high as the Luciferian Army sung a song of their own, a cacophony of grinding metal and drums and screaming. It was the sound of ugliness and annihilation, and it was followed by the first shots fired.

Rifle fire commenced soon after the artillery, and the valley suddenly erupted with a thunderous wave of bullet shatter and shell explosions, biblical in its symphony of cries and decimation. Xiang ordered for the shields to be drawn up as the infantry used pulleys to raise them from the ground. Rows and rows of large, hexagonal, diamond-encrusted plates rose up, holding the enemy back while cavalry units attempted to flank the outside edges of the enemy. But there was no edge. The line of enemy troops seemed to traverse the spine of the mountain ridges and the Mongol army's horses and riders were gunned down with each attempt. With too much ground still between them, the Mongols hid behind their shields and the Luciferian infantry returned to their trenches, carrying their wounded with them. Artillery became the weapon of choice, prompting a hellish game of long distance shelling which continued for what seemed like days as the divine leaders began their true task.

Devonia watched the battle from her perch in the mountains but was not content sitting idle.

"We should be down there!"

"You're too young, Devonia. A battle is no place for children," the guard said.

"Not me dummy, you! Uli and I can take care of ourselves. You should be fighting with your friends!"

"We have strict orders to protect you two."

Beside Devonia, Uli shivered in the cool autumn air, despite her thick coat. The sky swirled above with a subtle turbulence, a sign of things to come.

"What should we do?" Uli asked Devonia.

Devonia sighed. "Wait for General Yu to come up here and get us, I guess."

They sat together under a blanket as the distant pops and booms echoed across the steep canyon.

Melody's song could not be heard over the immense noise of the battle, but its frequency sustained, protecting her troops from Fraus's ability to melt human minds and bend them to her will. Safely hidden behind a shield, Melody stood beside Xiang as the general coordinated attacks, only taking her eyes from the battle when she saw Tala fly into place over the palace.

Hurry, she thought as she watched the souls of the dying lifting into the sky with each shell blast.

Tala predicted Michael would lead his forces into battle from the front, that he was so prideful and arrogant he couldn't transcend dishonoring his men. But she was wrong. He was nowhere to be seen. Instead, at the top of the palace's high tower, Fraus stood in a battle-ready stance, carefully pointing her staff of sharpened black onyx at Tala's face. Seth lay behind her on a blanket atop the stone rise, crying and squirming with the erratic winds blowing around him. A thousand snakes slithered at the witch's feet, detecting the Aradian's every move; channeling them towards their Gorgon mother. Tala hovered in the air before the demon seductress, her armor shining with the fires of Armageddon below, and they wandered into each other's minds, searching out their intentions in a telepathic game of cat and mouse.

Suddenly Michael rose between the two Immortal women, his massive bat wings pushing the dust into cyclones rivaling the northern winds. All the pieces were now in place, but Tala did nothing but levitate and gaze into both the white eyes of the cornered witch and Michael's fiery irises, unquenchable in their perpetual conflagration.

Down on the battlefield, all hell had broken loose. The allied cannon operators were having issues ranging and were getting torn to pieces by the far more experienced Luciferian

Army artillery squadrons now zeroing in on them. Xiang had separated from the empress to get closer to the fighting. Her radio was an uproar of incoming transmissions, so clogged with traffic she could hardly hear herself think.

"Bravo company come forward…"

"We need more medics at the front of the line…"

"Zero-Zero Alpha, what is your status?"

"There isn't a single enemy officer in range, we need to push our sniper teams forward or else they're going to be pulled toward the flanks…"

"Lilith Actual, this is Air Operations, do you copy?"

"Go ahead Air Ops…"

"Bus those rigs up the line and bring fifteen crates of ammunition…"

"Enemy movement on the ridge…"

"Cease fire on the left flank, we're gonna focus fire on the ridge…"

"Copy that, sir."

"General Yu, Air Ops is trying to get hold of you…"

"It looks like there's a small opening we could plug them in…"

"WHERE ARE THOSE MEDICS?"

"They'll be with you shortly they got held up helping Alpha…"

"Spot weather forecast for twelve hundred hours: weather warning for Lake Geneva area, high winds with gusts up to eighty miles per hour from the north and thunderstorms expected at thirteen hundred hours, bringing large hail stones and rain with a cold front…"

Finally, Xiang picked up the radio amidst the blaring of guns around her and spoke into the mic.

"CLEAR CHANNEL ON COMMAND! This is Lilith Actual. Go ahead Air Ops."

"General, we have multiple reports of incoming enemy aircraft, break."

There was a pause. Rifles and cannons fired all around her as she wrote on her colonel's sleeve so she could still relay orders while committing her focus to higher tasks. The explosion from a shell blast showered them with dirt and shrapnel. The colonel winced as a shard sliced his leg but nodded to her that he was okay.

"I'm not quite sure of the nature of the crafts, General, but it's looking like hundreds of small entities, possibly flying human-like creatures my sources tell me. They look like Sararans."

"Copy, Major. What is their orientation and ETA?"

"You should be seeing them flying in an informal V from the west and northwest of your position within fifteen minutes. All of our drones are shot down so you probably won't get anything else until we put more in the air. I'll let you know when that happens."

"Got it. Shiva Actual, did you copy direct?"

"Affirmative. We've held them off but can't push forward currently. What are your orders, General?"

"Cease artillery fire. They've already stopped theirs. Send in the first ten divisions."

The sudden absence of shelling blanketed the battlefield in eerie quiet, until the Luciferian Army leapt back up from their trenches. Shiva responded by lifting his rifle and pointing it towards them. With a wild war cry he charged forward, thousands of allied infantry and cavalry behind him, hooves and feet once again at war with a common foe. Bullets zinged through the air, toppling whole lines of men as the running soldiers behind them jumped over their fallen comrades. The two sides clashed in a sickening display of hatred and brutality. A wave of Luciferian infantry penetrated the mass, wiping faces clean from skulls with shotgun blasts, their weapons torn from the hands of one dead soldier only to be handed to the next. The armies' combined arsenals were an expansive anthology of the history of the world. The Luciferians had gatling guns from the 1870's and pistols from the early 20th century, but they also employed modern carbon-barreled rifles that were dead accurate. The allies tore them apart with an even more diverse arsenal, with rail guns, ceramic armor, and swords passed down for twenty generations, limbing the men like trees and beheading them with vigor just as their ancestors had.

Rivers of blood flowed in every direction and no one officer could direct the madness. The Luciferian Army fighters were ruthless and primal, but the Mongols were a worthy adversary, using poison tipped blades modified by Melody to exact their vengeance. Elephants with plated tusks rammed enemy tanks, crushing the lewdly welded machines and tossing men into their own lances with their trunks. Apollo galloped riderless along that plain of death, biting the heads off Mongols as if they were fruits from a bough and trampling everything before him. The bodies stacked faster than medics could treat them, and they too found themselves being targeted and shot and forced into the fighting for fear of dying themselves. Every rule of war was broken on that once-neutral ground.

A stupefied Luciferian Army soldier stood up in the chaos and looked around, his face drenched in blood, his wounds unknown to even himself. He looked about as if he were an observer visiting from beyond the grave, unable to believe what he was seeing; unable to fathom the amount of bloodshed boiling in that valley of unholy crusade.

○

Xiang looked up from her shield and the wall of machine gunners she hid behind. A cloud of pink dust rose from the valley floor and her heart sank with the horrible waste of it all.

"FUCK! I'm going to need air support soon. Tala better hurry the hell up with stealing this damn baby."

She clipped her radio to her belt and began rattling off orders to two of her majors.

"We might not get another face to face, General," one of them said. "We'll be too far extended..."

"I know... we just have to hold off on certain transmissions until we know the witch cannot hear them."

"When will that be?"

"When Tala kills her. Which should be any minute now."

They ran back to their ranks as Xiang unclipped her radio and began untangling and re-routing the transmissions pouring in.

○

Tala held the gazes of the two demons. Her eyes were alight with the fires of memory, from when she herself had scourged the Earth, and she matched Michael's enraged stare as he slowly flew backward and landed next to his illicit spouse among the cobras and constrictors, both of them hard set on preventing Tala from reaching the child.

"Look at her. She's a carnal hell beast," Fraus snarled, her tattoos bubbling up on her neck. "Feel that hate in your eyes, Aradian? You are what you kill."

Tala levitated – as silent as her motives. The standoff continued as the battle raged on. Off in the distance, hundreds were dying by the minute on all sides of the battlefield. Michael smiled, the sounds of violence coaxing his stolen spirit.

"You want to drag this out, don't you?" He chuckled and shook his head, never taking his eyes off the Aradian's hands. "Perhaps you're more like us than you'd care to admit, content to let the last humans kill one another off until the species devours itself. Are we not the chosen creatures you had hoped would prevail? A divine Sararan couple to begin the world anew? Is that not the sole principle of your master's doctrine, the one you were instructed to protect? Or perhaps your sister knew the truth. She always seemed to be the more favored of Shakti's infamous Aradians. The one who became a privileged student to the most powerful man on Earth while you suffered in the brothels. How long did it take Shakti to find you? Three? Four years? I'm sure you were violated by many men during that time. Men like the men in my army. Men like the men in your army. Is this really about revenge for you? Is it balance? What stake do you have in this fight? Were you so abused as a child that you need to take out your abuse on the whole world?"

Michael grinned as he bore his eyes of hatred deep into Tala's stare. She didn't budge. Seth continued to weep quietly behind them as his mother kept the staff pointed at Tala and yet the standoff continued as a shift on the battlefield emerged.

"FALL BACK! I REPEAT, FALL BACK!" someone screamed

over the radio.

Xiang looked up over her shield and watched as the enemy cut her forces to bits, using the building momentum against them and bulldozing the corpses to make paths for reserves. The shrill sound of artillery shells cut through the air and rockets began falling heavily in a series of skull cracking explosions. The Luciferian Army were shelling their own troops in order to overcome the allies, and it was working.

"Melody, this is Lilith Actual. Is Tala available for air assault? Do we have confirmation the child is in her possession?"

"Negative, continue with defensive maneuvers."

"Do we have ANY air resources available?"

No answer. The wind was raging and lightening bolted through the mountains. One such bolt struck a lookout tower and destroyed an enemy machine gun nest, killing scores of men. After a few moments of empty radio traffic, Xiang looked up at the sky and saw a flock of what looked like large bats coming from the agitated storm cell. The black cloud of creatures got closer and finally Xiang could see what they were. Harpies. Hundreds of them. Winged women who had once been Michael's sex slaves, now tainted with polluted derivatives of his DNA, giving them feathered wings and metal teeth and nails, their breasts empty and sagging, their singular brain hemisphere connected to one cycloptic eye. They screeched and vomited blood, diving down upon the left flank of the allies like darting hell-hawks. Xiang warned the division, but it was too late. Men were picked up and dropped, crushed by their own weight if they were not shot out of the sky by increasing enemy fire. The Mongols battled back, cutting the harpies down when they reached the ground, keeping them tethered while others chopped and skewered the fiendish abominations.

Xiang looked around at the battle, and what a sight it was: a fleet of demon Sub-Sararans descending the slopes while enemy shells lit the sky a darker shade of red, thousands of warriors clashing in a battle larger still than the Somme or Cannae or Stalingrad. The storm increased in viciousness as the winds seemed to lift the Luciferian Army's bullets and lances into the retreating allies. Just when Xiang was about to officially call for a full retreat, however, she heard a familiar voice crackle over the radio.

"General Yu, this is Galen Fox, at your service."

"Galen?" she asked herself without keying the mic.

"I've got forty-four big fellas an' enough machine gun ammo to make it rain hell. So… where d'ya want me?"

Xiang quickly set aside her emotions to approximate him to the primary targets.

"I need you to strafe the enemy artillery positions on the north end of the battlefield. They already pulled their reserves so you should get limited return fire."

Galen's gunship circled high overhead, its roaring engines a dreadful sound to all.

"Which end of the valley shall I hit first?"

"Doesn't matter. Light them up and don't stop until you hear back from me. If I don't answer, your contact is Air Ops, copy?"

"Copy that, General!"

The old gunship swung down over the mountains and launched a cascade of bombs and machine gun fire, obliterating the enemy artillery positions. Galen's 'big fellas' were a mixture of napalm canisters, high powered explosives and grenades filled with metal darts that sliced human flesh like butter. He came back around twice more until the line of long-distance cannons were nothing but a smoking pile of metal and blackened bodies.

Xiang watched the retreat as the Mongol troops fled south past her. She felt like a rock in a river, a rock that would be tipped by the coming flood if she didn't leave with them soon.

"Lilith Actual, this is Melody. Fall back to the rendezvous point a quarter mile south of your position."

"Moving now."

Xiang clipped her radio to her chest rig and went to move, but was met with the sight of her colonel's head popping like a melon. Wiping the blood from her eyes, Xiang discovered that she was surrounded by enemy infantry and harpies. She had only two other soldiers with her, each of whom tried the same move to cover the general and achieved instant death. One was shot through the teeth, the other in both his legs and heart in rapid sequence. Xiang expected the enemy to be only a hundred yards out. She was trapped. She watched the last of her retreating troops scamper back, some getting hit with sniper rounds, some barely making it out of harm's way, swaying half dead on the back of their panicked, galloping horses.

"Galen?"

"Go ahead, General."

"What do you have left for ordinance?"

"I have ten bombs left. Sylvia is shot up pretty good. I'll have to land after this next one."

Galen circled above, his plane emitting a thin puff of black smoke.

"Put them all on the coordinates I'm about to give you. Standby."

She put her radio down and could already hear the voices of Slavic Luciferians closing in as she wiped blood from her GPS screen. Xiang got back on the radio as the plinking of bullets rattled the shield behind her.

"Galen? Are you ready?"

"Go ahead!"

"Commit your next bombing at 42.2044 N / 6.1432 E. It's my current position. I'm overrun by enemy troops and will be captured within seconds. Do not let them take my body. Do not let them make a mockery of what we stand for. You have to destroy them."

There was a pause. Somewhere on the battlefield, Ali and his sisters gave a dying Igor their last syringe of morphine as the fellowship listened to the disheartening transmission.

"Xiang…" Galen said, his breath stolen from him.

"Do it now! That's an order."

"Did you read the letter I left you?"

"Whatever it says, you can tell me in the afterlife."

Xiang dropped the radio as the enemy soldiers appeared from behind the shield. She leveled her pistol with a diving harpy and shot it though the mouth, the vile thing clawing at her with only a nerve stem to guide it. One of the soldiers held a gun to her head while the others grabbed her hair and neck and pinned her to the ground. They cursed her in their sharp tongues as they sliced her throat, and her last vision was of the nose of a plane coming towards them, bombs barreling end-over-end, incinerating the company on impact: harpies, soldiers, princesses… all.

Miles away, Devonia watched in horror as the retreating allies fell back.

"This can't be happening," Uli gasped. "Why hasn't Tala rescued the baby yet? What's going on?"

"I don't know, but I'm not waiting for permission to involve myself any longer," Devonia growled.

A soldier stood up as if to intervene.

"Don't worry, she's not an Aradian yet. She's just a kid," another guard told him.

The twelve-year-old prodigy set down her tortoise and stood up on a tall rock, her little dreadlocks collecting sleet as they waved in the wind. She took a piece of charcoal from her pocket and drew a series of symbols onto the stone.

"What are you gonna do?" Uli asked.

"What I should have done twenty minutes ago. Get your mirror out."

Uli took out the scrying mirror and stood ready, holding the silver plate up to the smoky yellow hole in the sky.

"The clouds will part, and when they do, the sun will show. Shine it on the rock when I say."

Devonia stood, concentrating as hard as possible on the symbols. She reached into her boot and when her hands came up, she held Ezra's knife. She cut her own hand and spilled the blood onto the illustrated stone.

"Now!"

The storm's fake eye split open and the light from the mirror hit the stone.

It was in this way the Immortal's standoff reached its zenith. A distant yet vivid memory shot into Michael's head like a golden bullet. He broke from Tala's gaze and turned his head to some glistening star in the mountain's gut, where Devonia and Uli had projected their spell into Michael's third eye, breaching the dimension that gave Michael his soul back.

Fraus snapped at him.

"Michael? No!"

He turned back to Tala in a whirl as if waking up from a daze. Tala distracted him with a false motion of attack, and he reacted. In an act of impatience, Michael called her bluff and leapt towards her, sword first and teeth clenched.

"YOU FOOL!" Fraus yelled.

Tala deflected his sword with her arm and elbowed his head, sending him spiraling downward as he reached frantically for the ether. Fraus's mouth opened to commit some heinous spell against the Aradian, but just as she inhaled, a still very much alive Avestan jumped up from the palace stairwell wearing a golden shroud and shot a single arrow through the witch's mouth and tongue. Tala disarmed the witch telekinetically, pulling the staff from her hands, then froze her where she stood as she tipped a massive stone boulder onto her head, smashing Fraus's devilish brain upon the reptile infested ruins. Avestan quickly hopped over the serpents and swept up the baby before quickly disappearing back into the halls of the palace.

Tala spoke to Melody with her mind. "The demon is dead and the infant is safe with the messenger. Retreat or be annihilated. I leave this world in your hands, Melody. Do not repeat your mistakes."

"What about Michael?" Melody asked.

No answer was received.

Melody collapsed in the company of her officers.

"Empress! Empress!" they yelled as they examined her.

She breathed heavily and slowly stood up, having finally been relieved of the labor of casting the protective spell she'd been emanating for almost two months. As Parvati and Melody stood together, they watched with their troops as Tala rose up into the sky holding a spherical white object in her hands and dropping it. Melody saw the bomb slowly float down and determined it would detonate on impact. They didn't have much time.

"We have to go now!"

"What about Michael? Is he dead too?" Parvati asked.

"He's no longer possessed, but he has the memory of everything he did while he was. If the atomic bomb doesn't kill him, he'll probably kill himself." She yelled to an officer, "Retrieve Devonia and Uhlanga from the mountains. Let's MOVE!"

"How can this be victory?" Parvati asked, a flashback to Japanese drones over Beijing resurfacing in her memory as the storm of black clouds swirled behind them.

"Because it is the will of the Earth," Melody reminded her.

"And the mothers of our new world? What will they do? What did we come all this way for?"

"To survive."

The severed allies retreated southbound as the Luciferian Army pursued them. Due to the legion's ignorance of their own fallen leader, the men of that stolen land stopped at the valley's edge and foolishly reveled in their premature victory. They watched the ominous ball of light float down and thought it to be some kind of glorified entity; a gift from the heavens. They congregated about its base like blind worshippers, just as Tala had intended.

In the dusty, windy ruins of Geneva, Avestan crept along with Seth tied tightly to their chest. They crossed the empty streets one by one, keeping to the shadows.

Then Avestan saw him.

Michael, the demon king, now demoted to less than a foot soldier.

His ear was bleeding and his broken wings dragged against the ruins behind him. Avestan stopped in the middle of the street and watched him. His eyes glowed a dull blue like flames struggling to find fuel. He looked at Avestan with interest as the sound of Galen's plane crashing to the ground echoed through the valley.

Avestan went to draw their bow. But as they looked down at Seth, they un-knocked the arrow again before darting back into the shadows, heading south to join the rest of the allies and leaving Michael to whatever fate awaited him.

When the guards rejoined the retreating army, Devonia was excited to tell the empress what she had done.

"Empress! Did you see it? Me and Uli used the mirror and my knife to turn Michael's gaze! He remembered the knife and that's what distracted him!"

The empress looked blanky at her officers, as if she could not hear her, but Devonia continued.

"Who would have thought? Just a bit of nostalgia was enough to pull him out of his curse so Tala could end the standoff. I knew I could do something to help, I just knew it!"

Devonia looked around at the wounded men and women jogging or limping away from the battlefield and was suddenly hit by the horror of what had befallen them; the immense waste of life.

The empress finally looked at her apprentice. "You did well, Devonia, but we are not out of harm's way yet. I have to help the others. Please, excuse me."

"Empress?" Uli called after her. "Where is General Yu?"

Melody merely smiled and turned away, not yet willing to give the news of Xiang's death to the young girls.

Suddenly, a flash of white light shrunk their pupils and vandalized their irises with an onslaught of gamma rays and electrons. They were only four miles from the battlefield when the bomb went off, and Devonia shuddered as the multi-life memory of the Tar Sands palpitated through her being. A shockwave hit the army as their pace increased, and those who had never understood the terror of what thermonuclear weapons were capable of were stunned by the curtain of pyrocumulus suddenly hanging over them, the winds pulling the mushroom cloud upward, rupturing the sky. The Luciferians were incinerated instantly.

"At least the worst is over…" Uli said quietly as she and Devonia rode ahead of the main army.

"I'm afraid this is only the beginning of something worse," Melody told them solemnly as her horse galloped beside theirs. "Tonight, the moon will seem smaller than before. Tala is leaving the planet and taking it with her."

"Tala's taking the moon?" Uli stared wide-eyed at the empress in confusion.

"Are you sure that Tala is on our side?" Devonia muttered.

"She was never on our side, only that of the prophecy. There will be some radical changes to our planet. But I shall be with you all the way."

"Where are we going now?" Uli asked.

"To your home, Uli. To Africa."

Uli nodded as they watched the smoke and dust climb high behind them, the blackened sky dripping with an appalling rain, the radiation already pulsing through the clouds and spidering its way into the soft flesh of the survivors; deleting cells, rewriting them, exchanging electrons involuntarily. This created conditions ripe for energy dispersal, and the souls of the dead were allowed to wander free in their new realm. It was the beginning of a new chapter for Earth and nothing would ever be the same.

CHAPTER 55 – TITANOMACHY

The road south offered no relief for the retreating Mongol Army. Though they had been victorious, the survivors hung their heads and stumbled forward with wounds both seen and unseen, having left parts of themselves, their souls and the bodies of their brethren behind. Tens of thousands had died, and even more were wounded or missing. The harpies followed and antagonized any stragglers as the storm itself pushed them south, accompanied by the smell of death and rot.

Melody and Parvati did their best to maintain control of their forces but the broken and shell-shocked soldiers began to disperse east, desperate to be reunited with their families. The division commanders tried to convince them otherwise, citing the daunting task of crossing the mountains alone, but the need to escape the horror was too strong, and many soldiers stumbled blindly towards the unchecked route into winter's volley.

Those loyal to the Mongol queen and Sararan empress continued south to the Italian coast, where ships from Turkey had been sent to retrieve them. On route, they passed the wreckage in Milan where the Zurvan campaign had committed the onslaught of Michael's troops a month prior, many of the bodies still decaying where they had left them. In the killing fields, passing soldiers sifted their hands through the dirt and burnt bones and salvaged supplies from ash pits of unmarked mass graves until the storm hurried them on again, carrying with it those reptilian-skinned, feather-winged monstrosities that sniffed the air for open flesh and scavenged like vultures.

After four days of constant bombardment, the haggard Mongol forces descended into the city of Naples, the harpies having finally withdrawn. The sky remained toxic, thick with grey smog as the army dropped below the foothills of the infamous Mount Vesuvius. The city bustled in preparation for a mass exodus from the nuclear fallout. People packed their things and moved with urgency, preparing to abandon their livelihoods once again after just returning from their escape that summer.

Melody stood on a cliff overlooking the ships being loaded in the harbor. The ocean churned in the distance as black clouds crept over the flat horizon. She spoke to Shiva.

"Make sure one of those ships is for us and the next twelve are for the wounded. We need to get them loaded with all the doctors and medics first. And I'll need to be ahead of the armada in case we need to clear a path."

"You'll manipulate the weather at sea, yes?"

Melody nodded. "It's looking like I will need to."

"The ships will be secured, Empress," Shiva assured her.

"Queen Parvati is staying with the rest of the army and will take the next round of troops when the ships get back from Africa."

"Africa? Are we not going to Turkey?"

"We need to get across the Mediterranean or else we'll be stuck in Northern Almuruna. There is a new mutation out there and our forces are not equipped to contend with the harpies. Prepare for the worst. This retreat will be arduous."

They walked on, and as Ali and his sisters caught up with them, Melody tipped her head toward them graciously.

"Igor fell," Ali said.

"I know. I see him when I close my eyes. I see all of them. Their last moments. Their last words. You made peace with him?" Melody asked.

"He made peace with himself, Empress."

Their moment of silent grief was broken by Shiva.

"Something isn't right," he said, smelling the air like a cat. His horse turned, shaking its head and whinnying uneasily.

"The Earth is spinning faster on it's axis," Melody explained. "When Tala left the battle, she left our world and took our moon with her."

"What? Why?" Ali asked, bewildered. "To punish us again?"

"She is evening out the playing field. Without the moon's gravity pulling at the planet, our climate, environments, oceanic currents, fault lines, core magnetism, air and water composition and life cycles will be drastically affected. Days will become twice as short. Plants will wilt rapidly. People will be forced to adapt quickly or die."

"How do you know for sure?" Ali asked.

"I have felt its absence. Can you not? When the sky is clear, just look up."

Just as she spoke, a rumble echoed beneath them and shook the Earth's crust all the way to the fiery mountain looming over the city.

"Incoming! Prepare for impact!" Shiva yelled.

"That's not artillery..." Melody muttered gravely.

Suddenly, a small puff of black smoke erupted from the peak of Mount Vesuvius and an invisible shock wave swatted the clouds away in a growing sphere of plunder, followed by a brilliant sonic blast clapping against their gunpowder-stained faces. Boulders the size of small buildings were blown upward as if hurled from the arms of giants, and they fell slowly down into the ravines in the distance.

"Everyone to the gulf!" Melody yelled to the troops as she sped their pace.

The army funneled into the city and warning bells were rung. Militants and town folk alike raced to the ships, many disembarking pre-maturely as the dark column of super-heated gases mixed dangerously with the storm's growing volition. Melody's division raced into the streets as Parvati's coalition split onto another route. Melody made eye contact with her before they parted.

"God be with you, faithful sister."

"God be with you, Empress. Beware the angry sea and fly the Mongol flag on your foremast when you arrive to indicate your queendom."

"But my empire is Almuruna," Melody said, confused.

Parvati looked at Melody, her aged eyes carrying a wisdom Melody could not know. For though the Mongol queen was a decade younger than the empress, the passing of time showed in her grey hair and crow's feet, her acceptance of mortality having already shaped her empire; her blueprint for the new world destined for greatness upon her demise.

"Almuruna is no more," she said at last. "It is now an empire that lives in our memory and in our hearts. But... it is a good memory. Be well, sister."

Melody walked her horse along the streets, the townspeople looking at the warriors with sorrow and regret as they whispered prayers. Many came out of their homes with flowers and fresh food for the starved army as they emptied their homes, preparing for the wall of ash and lava spilling toward them.

The harbor was near riot as thousands gathered to embark on the ships, but there was not enough room for everyone on board. Quarrels between locals and troops trying to return to their families commenced. No matter their country of origin, they all were about to become refugees.

Melody nodded to Shiva to go ahead of the forces and secure a vessel. With a nod of his own, he took his unit into the thick of the exodus.

From seemingly nowhere, Avestan came up behind the empress, still cloaked in their 24-karat gold shroud, a useful tool for hiding from Sararan detection, unidentifiable and mute on their swift Arabian horse.

"Where are you taking the children?" they asked, the infant hidden and making small noises under their shawl.

"Africa. You really shouldn't be here. Seth could be detected," Melody said.

The volcano cracked and boomed behind them, ash falling like snow as Melody reached her hand over to Avestan's shawl, eager to look upon Michael's son. Avestan slapped her hand away.

"You can only take one of the children with you, and you know which one. "

"I know what the prophecy says," Melody said. "But it was you who took them and made them Aradians."

"Regardless, one of them has to die before their transformation. You know what will happen if they don't. I would do it myself if I had softer means. I'm sorry for giving you this cursed task. Once I deliver Seth to the Zurvan temple, you may kill me, if you wish."

With that, Avestan slunk back into the crowd, blending in with the masses.

Melody turned back to her troops and called over to the two girls, her next words hesitant.

"Uli... come, I must speak with you."

Devonia and Uli looked quizzically at one another. Since they had been kidnapped, the girls had never been separated. They were bonded by more than friendship; they had cast a spell together, a strong one at that.

"Take her horse, Devonia. We'll catch up soon."

"But where are you going?" Devonia asked.

"We'll catch up soon. Go on now. Please, Devonia."

Devonia walked reluctantly towards the harbor, looking back over her shoulder as Uli and Melody headed back into the city. They walked for a few minutes though the crowds of people until Melody was no longer beside the child but following Uli, who quickly became isolated at an alleyway's dead end.

"What's going on, Empress? Don't we have to leave soon?" she asked, turning to face her mentor.

Melody was crying. The blood on her cheeks dripped down onto the stone ground as she held out her hand and touched the child with trembling fingers, bringing her in close and hugging her and stroking Uli's head.

"I wish it could have been him... I wish it could have been him," Melody sobbed as Uli slumped silently in her arms, her once bright eyes, now blank and lifeless, staring unseeing at the darkening sky.

○

What was left of the fellowship loaded onto an ancient wooden ship. The modern vessels of the age had been hijacked by Michael's troops months before and sabotaged upon his landings. All that was left were pre-industrial ships that creaked and dipped in the fluctuating tide.

Devonia ran over to the empress as she climbed aboard their vessel. Melody's face was splotched with red and black streaks; her eyes a shade of dark verdure.

"Where is Uli?" Devonia asked, her eyes darting around for her friend. "Where is she? What did you do to her?"

Devonia ran towards the ramp but Melody grabbed her by the arm and held her.

"We aren't leaving without Uli!"

"She is going a different way. We have to go, Devonia."

"NO! I'm not leaving without her!" Devonia screamed, kicking against Melody's hold.

The empress held firm, tears once more cascading down her cheeks.

Behind them, the mountain was purging its innards; great plumes of dark grey ash polluted the turbulent skies, and rivers of magma filled the canals and aqueducts, once again burying the city and mummifying its history. The people of Naples struggled to find vessels, even though most of the ships belonged to them, as the troops – driven by their own fears and hopes – used their weapons and intimidation to command the ships. Melody watched the crisis from the deck as they cast off, the Mongols leaving the locals to suffer while they stole the only way out.

Ali acknowledged Melody's look of disgust as Devonia cried on the other side of the ship.

"The mountain... it is a spell cast by the witch upon her death, or Tala to spite us?"

"No. The eruption was caused by the Earth herself," Melody explained. "It is another reaction to the absence of the moon."

They stood watching the chaos as the boat's sails were opened and their motion out to sea commenced. Ali read the empress's emotions.

"God will ultimately judge us. It is not for us to command God's will," he said.

"This isn't the work of God. This is madness. Synthesized violence made by irreversible consequences. The creation of Sararans was the worst thing that could have happened to our planet... treasonous to existence itself," she said, looking at her own bloodied hands as she trembled.

"But Sararans are God's answer to keeping the human race from destroying itself," Ali argued.

"No. Immortals can outlast time, and that is the greatest violation of nature's process. In turn, man has made us titans, and we will be hunted to extermination."

That night, heavy weather congregated above the ocean's rolling waves, and there was no rest for the emaciated survivors. They were now a maritime armada, attempting to navigate the rough and rising seas amidst driving rain and gale force winds. Those who were strong enough struggled to retrieve the sails from the masts and there was no direction. Voices screamed orders in all different languages and men foolishly cut ropes that might have saved them later on. Lightning became the only source of effulgence, and each time the scene was illuminated, one could see the horrible panorama, the clouds growing more deciding against the armada every minute.

Devonia held Boris close as she sat near the rear of the ship, turning her cheek as the empress approached her.

"Uli is going to be okay," Melody told her.

"Oh yeah? And what about General Yu?"

"Xiang is dead, Devonia. She died in battle."

"Why didn't you protect her?"

"Thousands of people died on the battlefield that day, not just Xiang. Stop trying to find someone to blame for your hardships, Devonia. There were sacrifices made that cannot be undone; that were committed for the betterment of humankind. One day, you'll understand that."

"How is killing my friends helping mankind?!" Devonia choked on her own tears and clung to Boris.

Melody stepped over her charcoal pentagrams, the failed markings of aeromancy spells now washed away in the rain and splashing sea water. Shiva approached her in the commotion.

"Empress... if the moon is no longer in orbit, how can there still be tides?" he asked.

"These waves are the result of high winds and deep oceanic earthquakes. If it wasn't for these conditions, the ocean would be glass."

"Can you do nothing to hinder the storm's might?"

"I've done everything I can, Lord Shiva. This is... out of my control," she admitted.

A fire started inside a nearby ship and with the illumination of the engulfed vessel they could see everything around them. Four ships capsized, their crew members screaming and struggling to stay afloat as they reached for ropes and buoyancy devices thrown by men standing rail-side. Those in the water had hardly enough strength to swim, and many drowned before they could get help. Melody prepared to dive into the water and start saving them when something stopped her.

A deep moan from beneath them was heard by all; the moan of a great beast circling the armada from the depths and somehow able to amplify above the wailing storm; the yelling and horror.

"It can't be..."

"What is it?" Shiva asked Melody, the surrounding soldiers likewise looking to her for answers.

"Ali! Take your rifle and climb up the bird's nest! Let me know what you see!"

"Aye aye, Empress," he said as he slung his rifle over his shoulder and scaled the rickety mast to the cork basket at its apex.

"Empress?" Shiva asked again.

The groan grew louder. Melody gazed at the fire's reflection in the wounded men's blood rising and falling on the shimmering tide, almost dazed by the sublime insanity of it all. She spoke to them as her eyes became entranced by the burning ship.

"A leviathan," she said, almost too quietly.

The moaning continued as the crews edged the railings with their weapons in hand.

"Shiva, get your men on deck with their guns and wait for my command," Melody demanded.

"You heard the empress! Get up here! Topside!"

"What is it here for?" Devonia asked, grabbing onto the railing, the storm still swaying the ship.

"It's hungry."

In the light of the fire a massive tentacle burst up from the waves and wrapped around the flaming ship, pulling it under with a furious smash and once again leaving the armada in darkness.

"Hold your stations! Our ship is much larger than theirs. Do you see it, Ali?" Melody shouted about the raging storm.

"Got her in my sights now... here she comes!" he yelled back.

The tentacle suddenly wrapped around the mermaid carving at the bow of their ship and snapped it off as another wave crashed against them. The ship jolted and those not thrown overboard or onto their backs opened fire, blowing bloody holes into the creature's dish-sized suction cups and slimy gills. The beast let go of the ship with a lurch, shrieking like a drowning elephant. Lighting struck nearby and they could see the monster's great bulbous eye turning over, glistening like a pale jewel in the foam. It was in this moment that Ali took his shot, his bolt-action rifle cracking off a round from the bird's nest, blinding the angry sea-beast.

"Wait? Where's Boris?" Devonia cried, standing up after being tossed against the railing. "BORIS! Where are you?" Devonia crawled around the ship's deck desperately searching for him. "No, no, no... what if he's gone overboard... Empress!"

She turned to find Melody sitting half-lotus with her eyes closed near the base of the mast, as if in meditation.

"You CANNOT be for real... seriously?"

"Look! The empress has conjured something," one of the soldier's shouted.

Everyone looked down into the water. A myriad of grey figures were just about visible under the surface.

"Hold your fire!" Shiva yelled.

Schools of Great White sharks called in by Melody's subtle song surrounded the injured squid and shredded it, leaving nothing but tentacles and opaque flesh floating on the surface. But they did not stop with the sea beast. The sharks began a feeding frenzy, feasting on the people in the water as well, their screams undying in the storm's cacophony. No one said a word as they helplessly watched the grisly scene unfold.

"Those in the water are beyond saving," Melody explained. "The armada must stay intact no matter what. Keep to your stations."

No one spoke, frozen in place as they observed the massacre unfold amongst the turbulent waves. Blood and guts began to splash up onto the deck and the crew members traded their weapons for buckets and began scooping out the muck. Their ship was being greased with the innards of men, squid and shark alike, and the smell became unbearable. Soldiers who had stomached the battle of Geneva could no longer hold in their rations as the slop sprayed over them.

"Animals will be able to smell this from miles around," Melody stated.

Her crew were too busy vomiting over the side to heed her words. Melody shook her head and looked east.

"Empress! Look! Starboard bow!" Ali called out.

Lightning struck behind the ridge of a cresting wave and they saw in the foreground a giant tail with sharp razorback fins dipping silently through the crashing water. A great bellowing reverberated from below, louder and more guttural than before.

"Guns up!" Shiva ordered.

Everyone ran to the bow of the ship, perhaps ready to die at last. The great whites had vacated the area, knowing well that Poseidon himself would not dare spar with such a creature. The beast breached: a Jurassic relic, millions of years in the making and still dominating the food chain, with teeth like porcelain swords and eyes like petrol. Its iridescent scales reflected the lightening as it dove back down.

"Prepare for impact!"

The great sea monster rammed the side of the ship as soldiers held tight to the railing, many losing their grip as the waves continued to crash against them.

"Everyone get to the life boats!" Melody commanded, grabbing a harpoon and charging it with all the built-up solar energy she could muster, until the tip was red hot and glowing and crying sparks with some malicious hex.

"Empress, we'll drown!"

Melody stabbed the harpoon into the wood of the boat and lit a fire beneath her, despite the rain and wash. The soldiers all gasped and stepped back.

"Devonia, go with Shiva!" Melody yelled.

"But Empress—"

"Go, now!"

The soldiers jumped onto the lifeboats and dropped into the raging waters, abandoning ship seconds before Melody burned the entire surface of the vessel and walked calmly amongst the flames, their bright glow a worthy sight for so many strained and night-blinded eyes.

"What is she doing?" Devonia asked Shiva as they drifted away.

"She's luring it towards her."

The beast moaned and breached the surface, its black fins shining in the orange glow as it built up speed and bolted towards the ship. Melody ran toward it and jumped, landing on its back and stabbing the megalodon in the head with her glowing harpoon. It roared, half out of water, throwing Melody into the wash, its long tail whipping the water, it's disgusting howl a furious sound culminating four hundred years of distilled hatred toward mankind. Melody was just surfacing when it turned around and jumped out of the black water, diving straight on top of her harpoon. She quickly emerged from the waves as its dying groan faded into the depths.

"I think she killed it!" Devonia cried.

"God let it be so…" Ali said as he wrapped himself in a wet blanket, his body shivering in the gale.

Melody began to swim over to the lifeboat, but before she could reach it, the giant creature came up behind her and stretched its massive jaws.

"Empress, look out!" Devonia screamed.

Melody turned just as at the beast snapped its mighty jaws, cutting the Sararan into pieces, swallowing her legs and torso and leaving her arms and head to float away upon the ceaseless waves. The Sararan goddess had sung her final song, giving her life for the sake of Devonia's, the monster satiated by Melody's god-flesh.

The storm finally broke the next day, and Shiva, Ali and Devonia saw at last what Melody had meant. The ocean was glass, so unblemished that it reflected the sky with a lazurite elegance, the distant flat horizon like a partition of realities wherein the weightlessness of space opposed the deadly burden of the sea with some silent blue tempera-ment. Peace had found the remaining fellowship at last, though their cannon-damaged ears still rang from the hor-rors of Geneva. All were silent and filled with sorrow. The Zurvan. The Kurdish fighter. The golden child. Their small boat was but a splinter of wood floating on a vast chrome desert where no moon rose over the outpaced stars, and yet the smallest ripple was an echo from the deep.

CHAPTER 56 – ARTEMIS

A light wind blew over the Sahara. Nothing moved save for the billions of fine rounded stones swirling across the floor of that arid ocean of air. The sun rose fast beyond the planet's edge as distant lenticular clouds evaporated like vast specters fleeing the light of day. The burning star seemed to stand on its own, the Earth spinning so rapidly on its wobbling axis that each day was halved; each dawn and dusk a linear defect never to be repeated. The teetering world was a sweeping agent of discourse and traumatic temperature fluctuations, causing famine and steering the migration patterns of giant insects not unlike those that thrived with the dinosaurs, re-routed by hellion hordes of nameless mutant derivatives too genetically disgraced to classify.

With the human species now classified as threatened, most territories of Earth were free to claim by stronger creatures willing to take them. Twenty revolutions around the sun had passed since the fall of Fraus. Villages had been decimated. Cities emptied. Entire deserts boiled to lakes of liquid glass. The tropics were ravaged by snowstorms, and yet Antarctica thawed. The seas rose, then dried slowly, and mountains cracked open with new paths to Hell. The old gods were not called upon but rather hunted for their treasured blood, so the Immortals had gone into hiding in the far corners of the world, each for different reasons: for sanctuary; for solace; to wallow in self-hatred; to build strength. But for one of these deities, their deep hibernation was about to come to an end.

Below the crest of one of the desert's dunes, the sand began to cave in. Only a few grains to begin with, then a dish full, until a crater opened under the sinking sediments, a figure drawn by its recession as if caught in the neck of an hourglass; a forgotten angel, still and pale as if sculpted carefully from the dust, a beautiful young goddess made by pain and time's disregard; a creature whose singular purpose, to desecrate and propagate, was derived from the environment in which they were cast.

She opened her eyes.

The sun cut into her segmented purple lenses as she affixed those pupil-less irises on the advancing star. The sun-gazer did not move. The wind pushed softly around her feet. For two hours she did not sway her stare, until the heat had turned her skin a darker shade, and her naked body was once again warm with pumping blood. She looked down and wiped clean a heptagonal sandstone slate she had buried there. She turned the dial twelve degrees west, looked down at the movements of the arrows, and let her eyes follow the projection to where the new sunset would occur. She stood, her Aradian body steaming in the one-hundred-and-fifty-degree heat. The air was deceiving in its quiet, blazing state. The simmering horizon gave no hint of life, but as she sniffed the air, the distant groan of some insidious monster sounded in the distance.

"Can't go west today," she whispered to herself.

The groan faded. She concentrated her hearing. A slight ringing trembled against the drum of her ear as she focused her senses.

"Sixty-eight miles away. That smell... it must be a female in heat. I can't go west today," she said again.

She reached into the sand and lifted a large spear and a knife, as if she had spawned the primitive tools from nothing, then walked northeast at a rapid pace, making small prints like lizard tracks that were covered quickly by the shifting winds.

She ran north for a while, through canals of hardened sand and onto salt flats where entire seas had dried and only the fossils of fish lay strewn over the broad pearl surface. No fixation stood in that traceless enclave, save for deceptions made by the mind.

Then she felt it. Not the grumbling monster. Something smaller. She scanned the horizon. Her eyes stopped as she turned east. Miles across the flats she saw a coruscating figure coming towards her through the baking slates of ether. She stood and watched, driving her pilum into the ground, the small white feather at its tip fluttering softly in the breeze.

At first, the figure appeared to be a person riding a horse. But she knew no human could survive in those deadly temperatures. She slipped the dagger into her tightly wound bun, hiding the blade neatly between the pulsing strands, ready to kill if necessary. She studied the creature as it approached. It had the head, arms and torso of a woman, but the body of a horse, standing tall with a bow and quiver of and arrows slung on its back. They looked at one another for a moment, each just as curious as the other.

The centaur spoke. "What is an Aradian doing out here… and a flightless one at that?"

The young goddess stood still with an eyebrow raised, the white feather spinning around her spear tip in the wavering, radiant heat.

"Were you the one who woke me?"

"Yes."

"How?"

"The same way you sensed by presence, just via a different medium."

"You're an enchantress?"

"I dabble."

They watched each other. The centaur seemed to be amused by her confusion.

"How long were you asleep, Devonia? You should know better than that."

Devonia stepped back. "How do you know who I am? And who are you?"

"I knew you long ago," the centaur said. "Long before you became an Aradian. When you were just a young girl."

Devonia looked into the creature's eyes. She saw in them something irretrievable.

"Too much sleep is bad... even for an Aradian. You'll start to lose parts of your memory."

"Meditation can rid the brain of damaging details, or connections that are insignificant," Devonia argued, not to be out-witted.

The centaur laughed, her hooves drawing half-moons in the baking salt. Their voices were suppressed by the emptiness and by the heat rising from the brilliant white sea floor.

"No memory is insignificant. Every act of favor or dissent, even the most seemingly inconsequential moments, have led to this. Life's path is chosen not by your trajectory, but by the obstacles you endure, escape or destroy. Like a coin spinning on a wood floor, retaliating against the grain so that only one side may be chosen; even the slightest altercation might ratify its fate." She paused. "Twenty years ago, a great travesty took place here. But you know that, don't you? You were there that day, Devonia. When Empress Melody's body was torn apart in the sea that once filled this basin, her blood creating another blasphemous array of creatures." She looked out in the distance, as if eyeing something beautiful but unattainable.

Devonia suddenly realized where she had seen the creature's face before. "General Valor?"

"I was wondering how long it was going to take you. I go by Artemis now," the centaur replied.

"But... how? It's been so many years. How did this happen to you? We all thought you died in the war..."

"I almost did. We were cut down in the Appalachians. Michael murdered my troops and made sure to humiliate me in front of his succubus and his soldiers. He instructed his demon horse to turn me into pulp with his hooves. The horse crushed nearly every bone in my body and the Luciferian Army moved forward, spitting on me and kicking my mangled corpse as they went. The pain was indescribable. But somehow, when the last solider passed, I was still alive. My legs were in pieces, but I could use my shattered arms and elbows to crawl. I moved over to where a horse had been killed and beheaded, and reached for a canteen of water. When I woke up, the metamorphosis had already begun. I was probably seconds from death, but Apollo's blood had dripped from his leg onto my body as he crushed me and that sour version of Sararan blood mixed with mine. The blood cells remembered both the man and his steed's DNA, allowing the creation you see before you. I am Sub-Sararan. I do not have the defective genes the harpies carry, but consequently have an acute bipolar disorder. And as you know, I cannot speak telepathically."

"But you can sense other Sararans and Aradians?"

"Yes."

"I think I've finally lost my mind," Devonia said, shaking her head in disbelief.

"You'd have to be crazy not to lose your mind in a world like this. Though from what I hear, you've made something of a name for yourself these past twenty years. I'm not surprised it took me this long to find you if the stories are true."

Devonia waved her off. "Tall tales and tavern jargon is all it is."

"The tallest tales are usually true. When I first met you all those years ago, I never could have imagined you would one day be traversing the Earth as a famous Aradian... Melody never had the stomach to be a true predator. Only the heir of Pavonis could be both merciful and violent."

"I'm not Pavonis."

"Yes, you are."

"I'm an Aradian."

"I'll forgive you for being grumpy since you just woke up, but remember, Devonia... Tala, Mayari, Shakti... all of them had decades of training that allowed them to transition into their Immortal roles with ease. You're still very young."

"So I keep being told. Why didn't we see you after the fall of Almuruna? Were you captured again?"

"It took some time to heal and to get across the ocean without drawing attention. Which, I might add, isn't easy if you're half horse."

"Naturally," Devonia said, studying Artemis with curious eyes.

"I was making my way through the northern theater of the war during the battle of Geneva when I tried to intercept and meet with the Mongols on the retreat, but I was cut off by harpies... nasty things... and when Tala stole the moon and the war ended, everything changed. The Immortals went away. And I was left wandering... trying to pick up the pieces of what had happened to the world. For a while I was looking for Michael, but his energy level is so weak he is impossible to locate, then I heard the stories about the return of Pavonis. Now, here you are."

"Why were you looking for Michael?"

"To kill him of course."

"Michael isn't a threat anymore. His curse was broken. Everyone's looking for his son now, the only pure-blooded Sararan. I started searching myself after Melody died, but Avestan kept him hidden well."

"His son Set? Set is in Egypt."

"What?"

"You'd be surprised what you miss after a four-year sleep. He's the talk of the Mid-East; the pharaoh keeps him as his prized gladiator. He's a slave, Devonia."

"A slave? We need to rescue him—"

"Rescue him? He's the demon spawn of Fraus! Set will die like every other fighter in the arena and the world will be better off for it. Besides, I have an unsettled dispute with Michael. He is my priority."

"But the Michael under Fraus's possession wasn't the Michael who ruled during the Age of Peace. He regrets everything that happened during that time. He is more of a threat to himself than to anyone else now. Forget about Michael. We need to get to Seth and then return to Queen Fatima in Iraq, she's a trustworthy ally, and a close friend of mine."

"We?" she laughed. "You're on your own. I can't go anywhere near Cairo. They'll throw me in a cage and put me on display with all the other captured mutants. I'll die before I'm paraded around in their fucked-up pony show. I intend to make my way to South Africa, to find your friend and counterpart, Uhlanga."

"Uli died two decades ago. She's not in Africa. You'd be entering some very dangerous territories for nothing."

The centaur nodded and pursed her lips, unconvinced by

Devonia's story.

"I will consider your advice. For now.... Go find Set, perhaps he can be turned away from his father's path. I will begin my descent through Africa to find Uli. May we bring these Immortals together for one last insurrection against the evils of the world. Peace be with you, Pavonis."

Devonia watched the centaur depart until the general faded into the desert air like a mist that had never been. She looked east towards Cairo and the stark calm of night, then back west to the fiery amber dusk where the groan of a great monster bellowed from the bosom of the sun's descent, lifting its elongated tail high into the sky and cracking at the rim of the beaming red disk with a single incredible lash. The great fish roared with a supersonic shriek of anger as it shifted mountains and fault lines in its slithering catastrophe, feeding on locust swarms like a whale swallowing krill in its gaping inescapable mouth. It moaned once more before diving its way beneath the sand, hidden once again like so many other emissaries of that disputed kingdom.

CHAPTER 57 – PHAROAH'S FLOWER OF DEATH

Devonia arrived on the outskirts of Cairo two days later. The lights of the city coated the moonless night with a milky glow like a trove of crystals leaking from the desert's thin veins. She looked upon the pompous maze with probing eyes. The city had doubled in size since her last visit. New money and wealth had arrived from the east, and the Pyramids of Giza gleamed with delicately placed gold and silver mirrors mounted upon those crumbling steps with white lights pointing at them day and night to please the heavens with their beauty. Below sprawled thousands of buildings, set in fractal patterns that wove their way beyond the Earth's edge into the Sinai desert.

"There must be ten million people here," she said to herself, knowing only a small amount of the population had the means and toughness to withstand the conditions of the wilds, being otherwise dependent on the state for their needs.

She stepped toward the bubonic sprawl before stopping and realizing she was still naked. She looked around her. She knelt and put her hand in the freezing sand, digging around until she pulled up a dung beetle, setting it down on the ground. The insect walked stiffly at first then stretched out and began to scuttle quickly across the sand. She watched it. The beetle darted from rock to rock as if looking for a new place to hide. Devonia stood ready, holding her spear cocked at an angle. Her breath steamed silently in the cool evening air. Suddenly, a viper sprang from beneath the sand and snatched its prey, only to receive a spear through the head moments later.

Devonia skinned the body of the snake with her dagger and proceeded to burn the flesh slowly with her charged fingertips until it was a sort of leather; callous and moldable. She fashioned a top and skirt with the skin and used the spinal fibers and a fang to sew it all together, adding a wreath of half-moon shaped bones clinking like subtle chimes below the hem of her skirt. Since she'd surely be recognized, she let her hair down and wore the tail bones of the snake clawing up from beneath her hair like a crown, with the tallest bones near her forehead like small horns, the fangs piercing her ears and still dripping venom. She put care into her attire; whether she liked it or not, the clout of Pavonis hung over her everywhere she went. It was no longer acceptable to avoid the festivals held in her honor, and despite Devonia's extended leave from her occupation of terminating trophy mutants, she had nothing to be modest about. For once, she would indulge her worshippers. She needed all the support she could get. Her aim was to save the planet, but she needed the humans help in order to do it.

The Nile ran clear as ever, sanitized upstream to the point of sterilization for fear of toxins and diseases from the south. And rightly so. Everyone who entered the city had to be vetted for sub-Sararan contamination. Even Devonia, heir to the throne of Almuruna and the reincarnation of Pavonis, the Earth's savior.

As she reached the gates of the city, she flipped her spear to use as a walking cane, and slowly approached one of the guards.

"Name and intent?" he intoned, evidently bored. His felt hat tipped sideways on his head as he looked at her from head to toe, curious about her strange attire.

The guards behind him whispered to themselves.

"Devonia Ketevan. I'm here to see Pharoah Ramadan."

The guard at the gate stared at her, wide-eyed; suddenly frightened as he realized who she was. "Can I see your eyes?" he asked warily.

She leaned in towards his torchlight. Her purple eyes shrunk and expanded again, the murky dark color moving like smoke over the orbs. She receded back to the shadows, and he nodded rapidly.

"It's been a while, Lord Pavonis…"

"I've been busy."

"Doing what?"

"That's myself and Pharoah's business."

"What's with the snake-skin outfit?"

Devonia shrugged. "I had no clothes, so I killed a viper right over there just outside the city. Now stop stalling. If you want me to keep the megalodons away – the kind that could wipe out this city overnight – I suggest you let me inside."

He nodded and quickly opened the large steel gate. The streets were busy with movement and chatter. Make-shift scooters, horse traffic and Sub-Sararan creatures intermingled with the shoeless poor, who walked helplessly insane among the circulate of thinly clothed industrious undead, for beneath the gold mirror plated pyramids and lavishly designed white buildings were still the ruins of old. The impoverished workers were but modern slaves made to build luxury housing, with the threat of severance and family separation instilled in them daily.

Devonia walked by the rows of vendors and merchants selling molecularly modified foods by the bushel to those who could afford them. The lies of promise were all around her.

People saw her and began bowing, some shouted to

their friends and some even hugged her. Devonia couldn't help but blush as the crowd flattered her with showers of flower petals and music.

"Pavonis has returned!"

"Look, it's Pavonis!" they shouted.

Devonia lifted her hand and suspended the flowers in the air, the children jumping and grabbing for the levitating pink petals as they laughed.

She passed an elderly blind man who knelt with his prayer beads held tightly between his withered fingers. She crouched beside him and cupped his hands in hers. The crowd grew quiet. For a moment, Devonia spoke to him with her mind, the old man's beard quivering with the divine sensation of their connection. They knelt like this for some time, the crowd amassing around the divine healer to watch her work. Suddenly, the old man's lashes split open and he gasped, wet cataracts spilling from his skull like white gristle, pouring into his hands as he wept away the opaque obscurity. The crowd gasped with him and all leaned in to witness his transformation. Devonia pulled her hands away as he cried and breathed sharply. He looked up, his blue eyes darting around at the crowd and colors and lights.

"You have the gift of sight once again, old man. Do not go out into the light of day or you will be blinded forever."

"Thank you, Pavonis! Thank you, blessed Lord!" he wheezed as he gripped her arm.

A woman behind her grabbed her as well. "Please help my husband! He has a terrible disease!"

"Pavonis! Our savior! Let my daughter live! She is dying from cancer!"

"Pavonis!"

"Help us Pavonis! Please!"

The crowd clamored for her to save the sick and dying,

and in the midst of the uproar she had caused, she darted under their legs, disappearing from the desperate humans.

The doors of the palace closed loudly behind the Aradian. She shook her head as the voices of the peasants dissipated behind her, the guards shoeing them off with machetes and whips and threats of lashings.

"Welcome back to Cairo, Pavonis," one of the Pharaoh's advisors said. The finely dressed man approached her, his eel-skin boots tapping lightly across the white marble floors, weaving between wild animal rugs and high columns with torches rounding about their bases. "You're just in time for breakfast. Pharaoh eagerly awaits you."

She looked out the window, watching the sunrise chasing the night away. "So I am. How are you, Allabin?"

The middle-aged man smiled and bowed. "Much better, now that you're here. Please," he said, escorting her.

They walked through the corridors of the palace. The walls held large paintings of the Fall and all its inglorious chapters. Devonia saw her child-self painted in one of them, and painfully remembered those dark days of the Fourth World War.

"And how is Pharaoh?" she asked.

"He has not been well since you left, I regret to say. I suppose you could call him love sick... he has a strong affinity for you, you know?"

Devonia rolled her eyes. "Well he had best get used to that feeling. Once I've spoken to him and seen who I've come to see, I'll be on my way."

"But you've only just arrived! What's the rush?" "Our

world is dying."

"Oh… right. This way, Your Lordship."

Pharaoh stroked his long black beard and smiled wide as he watched Devonia enter his chamber.

"Well, if it isn't my favorite Immortal in all the land! I was beginning to think you didn't like me anymore."

"What could possibly have made you think that?" Devonia asked in a facetious tone. "Oh yes… last time I was here, you got drunk and tried to take my apprentice to bed with you."

He laughed. "I remember that. You sedated me and strung me up naked as punishment. How is dear Helen these days?"

"She died in an accident. For a human, she was very strong, but apparently not strong enough. I will miss her."

"I'm sorry to hear that. Very sorry." He paused, and Devonia could see that he was trying to shape his expression into something more solemn. It wasn't working. "You have been away too long, the celebrations for the Year of the Dragon will begin soon. Is that why you have returned?"

"No. I've come to meet the child."

His false solemnity was replaced with a façade of confusion. "What child do you speak of?"

"The Sararan."

"Set? Why, he's no child, but a sharp young Sararan man now. The city's new mascot. A real ringer! With him here, we might not even need you anymore, Pavonis."

Devonia raised her eyebrows.

"I'm joking!" he chuckled. "Set is a great asset to us, but

he does not have your purity of heritage. We have to keep him starved of light or else who know's what he'll do."

"Is that your choice to make?"

"Tell me, what besides the sacrifices of Pavonis has an Immortal ever done for the human race besides destroy it? Hmmm?"

Devonia sat silently, blinking without emotion.

"This is my kingdom, Devonia. I rebuilt this great city from its ashes. These lands were ravaged by tribal warfare and vicious beasts until you and I united the Egyptians and crushed those evils fifteen years ago. You've helped us achieve what I could only dream of as a young man. But when you abandoned your headhunting expeditions four years ago and did not return to civilization, we needed a new form of security. To allow Set to roam wild... that would be suicide for this great city and its inhabitants. You can understand the risk, can't you? People all over Africa were trying to kill him, so I took him under my wing just as he transitioned into a full Sararan."

"That doesn't justify his captivity. Do you think I'm going to just let you keep him here?"

"He's not caged. Go see for yourself. He loves his life as a gladiator. He lives for it."

"Perhaps I'll do just that."

"There will be a fight tomorrow night at The Lotus, and I'd be ecstatic if you'd join me for the festivities," he said, grinning seductively at her.

"It would be my pleasure," she said, vomiting internally as his gaze lingered on her body.

"Perfect. Enjoy your stay, my dear, and please, do not hesitate to bother me for anything."

"Of course, Pharaoh."

She walked out twice as fast as she had entered, drifting

through the slums and back to her old quarters to watch the sunset and charge her cells. Of the two species she healed on her way, rats and humans, she knew not which one she felt greater sympathy for.

The next day, Devonia walked through the streets half naked in the razing heat. Most people had gone into their homes to hide from the sun, save for the hooded middle-class civilians who wore gas masks and bulking canvas ice-robes that melted and steamed and left no trail of drips on the baking road. Eventually, she arrived at The Lotus; a great stone monument that had been built over thirty years prior, at the height of the Almurunan empire. It was a massive maze built in the shape of the Flower of Life, once a beautifully sculpted palisade with gardens now stripped of its soils and scraped into a flat bed of rocks and clay where the bones of the unworthy lay against the stone walls in near perfect skeletal composure, allowing one's imagination to provide the details of their dying moment. The hollow walls stood tall with plush seats at their edges to view the grounds from above. Small arches were built between the passages, giving the fighters strategic options while providing the audience with the ability to nearly touch the massacre from above.

Workers prepared the stadium by erecting flags and torches and vendors were already setting up their carts outside as Devonia walked past them. She dropped into a shadowy passageway that snaked beneath the structure until she arrived at a door with a guard. He halted her.

"What business do you have down here?"

Devonia stepped into the torchlight so he could see her eyes.

"My apologies, Pavonis," he said, as he fumbled with the knob and opened the door.

The hall was filled with blades clashing and men yelling, and the air was stuffy and smelled of ironwork and sweat. The scarred-up gladiators watched her walk through their training hall like wolves watching a lion enter their domain.

A young man with unblemished white skin and a short, messy red mohawk sat by the wall, his eyes hidden by sunglasses. Devonia felt the man's energy as she passed. He looked up and smiled as she turned her head, then went back to staring into the fire next to him. At the end of the hall, a ring of men stood in a circle playing some twisted game of wits with a vicious black lizard hissing and flaring its gills at the center of their degenerate mandala. They laughed and spoke roughly to one another in Arabic. When Devonia approached, they stopped what they were doing. The lizard crept away as they looked her over.

"Min 'ant?" one of the men asked in his sharp speech.

"'Iinaha eahira," said another. "Hal labisat mithl hdha balnsbt li?"

They all laughed.

The tallest one walked over, puffing his chest out and smirking. He went to touch her breast and she smacked his hand away.

"Ohhhh!" they all jeered, surprised at the defiance of the short young woman.

The man tried again and she pulled his arm in and twisted and broke it, tripping him with a swift kick to his ankle then pushing him down onto the disgusting floor with her knee, her sharp elbow digging into his cheek while her other arm pushed on the shattered arm. The lizard came up and licked his crushed face as he squirmed.

"Do you want to die down here or up there?" she asked, nodding to the ceiling.

He looked up in anguish and pointed at the ceiling with his eyes full of fear. She released him. He crawled back to the other men, who stood fast and waited for her to move. She fake lunged at them. They flinched and put their fists up. Others who had been watching this unfold laughed and nodded in quiet acceptance of Devonia.

"Thought you could take on an Aradian, did you?" the young man with the mohawk chuckled from the corner.

The men put their fists to their sides and moved on to other tasks sheepishly as he stayed sitting. Devonia turned to him and saw that, unlike the others, he had no chains tied to him or guards watching him.

"Seth, I take it."

"Tis I."

"Do you know who I am?"

"Sure do. You were an accomplice to the one who murdered my mother."

Devonia watched him closely. Her hand crept over to her dagger slowly. His pose stayed fixed on the outcropping of the sandstone wall.

"Thank you," he said.

"Thank you?" She let go of the dagger's hilt.

"Yes. Thank you for killing my psycho-bitch mother."

"It was all Tala... I didn't really have anything to do with it."

"Ah, come on. We both know that's not the whole story. You're one of my heroes, you know? I heard you killed three thousand harpies in a single fucking day."

"It's not like I was counting wings," she rolled her eyes.

"You're a fucking savage, everyone knows it! Pavonis in

the flesh," he said, standing up and grinning with excitement.

"Quite the mouth on this one," Devonia muttered to herself.

He paced behind the fire, shadow boxing as he did so, his subtle mohawk flopping from one side to the other like a murderous rooster. He was just barely an adult, trapped in a god's body.

"Why do you live here?" Devonia asked. "Why do you stay?"

He kept fighting the air as if not hearing her.

Devonia went on. "You're the only pure Sararan in the world and here you are cooped up in darkness. You say I'm one of your heroes... why aren't you out there killing harpies for the liberation of people worldwide, instead of for this city's entertainment?"

He kept on ignoring her. She spoke to him with her mind to catch his attention. He stopped his training and looked over at her, removing his sunglasses. His eyes glowed like twin suns, the very arrogance of their brightness assaulting those without eye protection. The entire chamber was illuminated by them.

"Because I don't have to seek out the Devil's apostles. They are brought to me. I confront them here, and I do it for the people because they want to witness evil being destroyed. It gives them hope. Giant crustaceans. Sand serpents. Harpies. A sphinx even. I've fucked 'em all up."

"Sphinxes are an endangered species and an ally in the fight against the harpies. There are less than ten left and you can bet your ass they'll remember what you did. It won't be as easy to kill one when they haven't been drugged or had their flight feathers clipped."

"Who needs them?" he spat. "Wannabe immortals who

govern vast stretches of wilderness like it's been theirs all along."

"It has been there's all along, fool. They're part lion."

"So am I. I was raised by lions."

"So what about a megalodon?" she asked.

"Never had the chance to fight one. Bit big for the stadium," he laughed.

"Do you know why they keep you down here in this dungeon?"

"To hide me from the light, so that I can't absorb too much of the sun's energy."

"No. It's because they knew that if you were given enough girls and fame and weekend lights you'd stay their watch dog."

"Look around you!" he exclaimed, his arms open to the kinetic forms around him. "These men... these creatures... this place... this is my home. We don't need to fight wars for territory or resources. We do it for the sheer sensation of it. Because it is honorable to live and die as a fighter! My attraction to war games runs heavily in my blood line. Unless you have something better to offer than this, I don't see myself leaving Cairo."

Devonia nodded and sighed. She walked over and set Ezra's dagger at his feet. Seth picked up his grandfather's blade and his eyes brightened with luminosity as he smiled.

"Remember Seth, you're a sovereign creature. Do whatever you wish, but know that Pharaoh does not see you as he once saw me. He's just using you. You've been fed so many lies. Starting with your name. You're not an Egyptian god. You're Seth Beller, the abnormal reproduction of a genetically modified human. Your food is the sun. I dare you to step outside. You've been eating breadcrumbs under these halogen lights. Imagine if you had a whole meal."

"I know what it's like, Pavonis. But a bit of fasting is good for the soul, is it not?"

She turned away and walked a few paces, before looking back at him. "You said if I had anything better to offer, you'd consider my company. Well I do, so consider it. See you tonight, Seth."

She walked away, leaving the Sararan alone to ponder as he stared into the reflection of the old steel blade, with the faded initials EEB.

That night, the people of Cairo poured into the stands at The Lotus. Thousands stood on the walls and around the rim, filling every area possible as they awaited the weekly games. Devonia joined Pharaoh and his advisors on the high rise, with a full view of the games, city and shining pyramids in the distance.

"What is the finale tonight, Pharaoh?" one of the advisors asked.

"You'll have to wait and see, Prince Shakir," he grinned, his cup half empty as he motioned for more wine.

A servant came over and poured his glass as he greeted people, splashing it on his seat. The servant shook her head and turned to less inebriated folk.

Devonia sat with her lips pursed. The sheer spectacle of what was about to happen made her want to vomit. All the advisors had their wives and mistresses with them. One of the wives turned to Devonia.

"It has been a while since we last saw you, Pavonis. Have you been well?" she asked, her gold and black gloves pristine in the cool evening air as she tapped her cigarillo against the balcony, flicking ash onto the lower-class spectators below.

"I've been giving the Earth back the calcium taken from it by the bones of the living."

"So... you've been mining?" she asked.

Devonia smiled and shook her head, sliding her thumb across her neck: the universal symbol for headhunter.

The woman's eyes widened as she nodded slowly, turning away.

While Pharaoh and his advisors were arguing about what to do with the partisan Arab tribes in the desert, the games began. The torches were lit. The flags lifted. An uproar of music and cheering erupted as the gladiators walked out from the dungeons, holding their spears and swords and axes high.

"Do they always fight together as a team?" Devonia asked. "Last time I was here they were killing each other."

"Most of the time they do, unless the jails get overcrowded. Then it's a free-for-all," one of the advisers said. "There are three rounds. In each round they face a different series of beasts. They are allowed to move throughout The Lotus, in whatever formation their team leader chooses. Oh look, there he is!"

The crowd stood and screamed with delight as Seth walked out, his head freshly shaven, wearing a steel-plated kilt and drawing a half circle in front of him with his sword. Devonia saw the knife under his belt. He looked up at her with his beaming eyes. Something had changed. He neither smiled nor acknowledged the crowd.

"Where's the bravado?" Pharaoh asked as he shook his head.

"Oh, I wouldn't worry, Your Majesty. Has he ever disappointed you?" an advisor asked as they clapped.

They all sat and watched eagerly. With the blast of a gunshot, Seth began yelling out orders.

"Positions!" he declared, and they began their march forwards through the maze of stone.

The quiet was eerie and not long lived. The southernmost gate screeched open and out crawled a great ugly creature. The legs of the thing stretched wide and it punched the ground with its massive mandibles as it chased the scent of the men. It was a massive Sub-Sararan crab that scuttled sideways under the arches between the clearings. Seth motioned his men with hand signals. While a runner distracted its senses, they looped around behind the beast, using the walls to hide their scent. One of the men jumped through a small archway and stuck his sword between the fissures of its hard exoskeleton. The beast screamed and stabbed him through the neck with the point of its saber-leg. The rest of them came up behind and began their assault, sticking their spears under its shell and hacking at the legs with their axes. The crowd cheered and yelled with vigor.

Seth approached the creature from the front, dodging its snapping claws and lunging at its face, slashing its left eye, black goo splattering his arms. The crab screamed and bucked with rage, knocking a group of men back against the wall and severing another's legs in half with one swipe of her colossal pincers. The man rolled in the sand, blood spurting from the stumps as he crawled away screaming.

The crowd laughed and cheered. Pharaoh and the prince chuckled and clinked their glasses. Devonia kept watching intently.

The men reconfigured in a circle around the wounded animal, their lances pointing inward as they herded it around the yard, wearing out the beast as it spewed blood and fluids. Seth watched it suffer without emotion, without action or regret. The men lunged forward, one of them distracting it with their swinging while another lacerated its other eye, blinding it at last. The crowd reared forward as they chanted in unison: some warrant of death. The pincers of the beast clasped wildly at the empty air as the men dug their spears under one side of it like a fulcrum and flipped it on its shell, its soft blue underbelly exposed. Axe wielders approached and chopped vigorously at the legs and paunch until the beast was nothing but pieces of bloody shell and entrails.

People cheered and hollered, loving every moment of the gruesome performance. Seth pulled the survivors back together and realigned.

"He's really something, isn't he?" Pharaoh asked Devonia.

She sipped her wine and did not answer.

With the end of round one came round two. Several men had taken slates of the crab's thick shell and fashioned them into shields. Before long, they were back in their regiment, christened with new blood, their hearts throbbing with the pace of the drums and the crowd hailing them. The high-pitched shrieking of one hundred demons crying sickly through the night air shattered the applause. People gasped as the sound amplified.

"Harpies! Eyes up!" Seth yelled to his men. They paired up and stood against one another's backs, looking around in all directions. Even the crowd looked up, expecting the beasts to swoop down at any moment, but none could see their descending.

Without warning, the trap doors beneath the sand flung open, throwing bones and dust into the air as the revolting creatures sprang from their cages like angry wasps. They attacked the men with ferocity, ganging up on them one at a time until they had pulled them apart and combed their flesh with mutilating slashes. They used their wings as shields and their talons and fangs to disarm the gladiators and tear at their soft skin. Seth entered like a weaving needle, his charged blade yellow with atomization as he slashed at the winged furies. The crowd whooped and cheered for the warriors, though the harpies were quickly overtaking the gladiators, despite their Immortal leader.

"What happens if the cage fighters lose?" Devonia asked the Pharaoh.

He laughed. "Then we get more. Don't be I, Pavonis. The world is full of criminals."

The battle continued as blood of all sorts spilled onto the ground. Soil that had once held a botanical oasis alongside the world's longest river was now barren of all life but the blood of fallen monsters and men.

As Seth shifted the battle back in favor of his gladiators, they pushed the last few demons against the wall, the spectators standing above them yelling and leaning over to watch.

Only six men remained with Seth, the prodigies of Michael's illicit sex slaves screaming and spitting their infectious mucus at them. The men taunted the creatures with their blades until they at last lunged toward the fiends and stabbed them to death, raising their gristle covered arms in victory. The crowd erupted in delight, the mess of blood and steam rising into the cool night air. Spectators puked drunkenly over the edge of the wall as they cackled at the awful pandemonium.

Devonia shook her head as Pharaoh and his advisors hollered behind her.

"What a show! What's the plan for round three, Your Majesty?" one of the advisors asked.

"Something special..." he said as he rubbed his greasy

hands together, his tall white atef crown tilted on his head.

Round three began with a drum roll and the announcer's voice booming through the stadium.

"Tonight! For your amusement... from the jungles of the Congo... a creature so dangerous that it took one hundred men to bring it here... ROUND THREE!"

Everyone stood and clapped and cheered for their fighters. This was the climax of the weekly games and they had all been eagerly awaiting the big reveal. The East Gate opened as Seth stood ready with his men behind him.

"Line it out!" he yelled to them as something stirred in the shadows beyond the gate.

Everyone held their breath with anticipation. Devonia leaned forward in her seat, unable to sense anything from that dark corridor. Then, out they walked. A few dozen gladiators, just like their belligerents.

The clapping stopped as the crowd murmured and exchanged confused looks.

Pharaoh stood, enraged. "What is this?!" he yelled.

"What's going on?" an advisor asked.

The gladiators walked up to one another, shaking hands and forming new ranks, turning now towards the pharaoh, with Seth standing at the forefront of his forces.

Someone gave Pharaoh Ramadan a microphone.

"Good people of Cairo, it seems our champion fighter has something on his mind. Please, Set, hero of the new world, what words do you have for us that were worth interfering whatever magnificence you were about to perform?"

Seth stared at the pharaoh and dropped his sword. The crowd booed.

"I can give you anything you want, Set, there is no need for this!"

Seth addressed the crowd as a whole. "I will no longer fight for Ramadan's regime or be this city's protector. There are people starving beyond these walls and you're here gambling on the blood of my brothers with the gold of yesteryear!" he yelled.

His men behind him gave the pharaoh their middle finger and spat, shouting harsher criticisms. The crowd continued to heckle them. They threw objects at the gladiators, unsettled by the sudden end to their entertainment. Devonia stood and watched Seth, then turned to Pharaoh.

"What a turn of events, eh?" she said, smirking.

"What?" He gasped. "You did this, didn't you? You treacherous witch! Guards, take her away!" he yelled as he pointed to the Aradian.

The guards stood motionless.

"What are you doing? Go! Get her or I'll have your heads!" he ordered.

They stayed still as ever.

Devonia laughed. "Maybe they respect someone with integrity, you bloated old man."

"What the hell is going on?" he shouted as his advisors were apprehended by the guards.

Two of the guards grabbed Pharaoh to reseat him.

"You evil bitch! I'll kill you! I don't care if you're an Immortal! I'll kill—"

Mid-sentence, Seth's dagger flew like a steel missile into his forehead, his crossed eyes following the trickle of blood down the bridge of his nose as he slumped. The advisors screamed and stepped aside. Seth climbed up the wall and stood watching the man's veins secrete onto the stone as people filtered away from the stadium in anger and unrest.

"Another successful assassination," Devonia said, nodding with satisfaction.

"Can we do more shit like this?" Seth asked her as he watched the old pharaoh die.

"As much as you can handle," she said, pulling the blade from Pharaoh's head and handing it back to Seth.

That night, they left the city together, apathetic to the fact they'd left a power vacuum for half the continent to surmise. It was, after all, the human's job to stabilize their own habitat, as Devonia would later teach the Sararan. There was more important business for them to attend to in the wild lands, for the creatures featured in The Lotus Games were just a taste of the horrors that existed beyond the knowledge of those ignorant and sheltered children of the moonless world.

A few hours after they left Cairo, the sun began to rise. Seth stopped walking.

"It's been a while since I've done this," he admitted.

"You're going to feel stronger and healthier than you have in a while… and hopefully smarter. The way you talk makes you sound like another man-slave. Too much time with humans altogether."

"You really hate humans, don't you?" he said, looking at the coming dawn.

"I love all organic creatures that existed naturally before the pandemic of Sub-Sararan creatures. It's just a constant challenge to respect humans. They're so stupid and greedy."

They watched the sun break over the horizon. The light combed Seth's face, like the face of God smiling upon him. His skin thickened over the strange scars now healing before his eyes, the very composure of his being shifting as the cells in his organs and bones multiplied and aligned. His body shook and seized, adjusting after months of malnutrition, the rays penetrating him and invigorating his senses.

Devonia walked up next to him, stripping off her snakeskin garments and standing beside him, giving her body to the sun as well. He looked at her, surprised by her boldness. He had seen plenty of naked women during his time in Cairo, but never quite like this; never in the bright light of day. She was beautiful, her skin radiant as her cells shimmered, absorbing the energy from the burning star above them. She glanced over at him and gestured to his remaining clothing.

"May I?" she asked.

Seth nodded, a heat that had nothing to do with the sun's warmth enveloping him as she knelt down and unfastened his belt. He tensed subtly, trying to keep himself from revealing his attraction as his kilt dropped to the sand, leaving him standing naked as she on that warming desert dune. She looked up at him, smirking as she stood, but said nothing. The wind picked up with the drastic temperature change and they stood and sun-gazed for a few minutes longer before walking out onto that plain of nothingness. They moved north, across the dried canals of the delta and toward the holy lands, on a path similar to that of the old prophets.

The days passed quickly as their pace slowed. The Immortals walked side by side a quarter mile apart, widening the range of their impeccable senses and scanning the desert for lifeforms. For the first week they found only feathers and hints of movement in the sand, but nothing worth tracking. They moved east, crossing the red dunes of northern Saudi

Arabia and zig zagging back through the ruins of Jordan, walking under Petra and wondering at the meaning of the statues of ancient gods, who looked upon them like fathers holding out their hands, empty of omens or declaration.

They were near central Lebanon when they finally spotted a coven of harpies gathering in an abandoned military bunker. The night gave the nocturnal creatures better eyesight and the dark made the air cool enough for them to maneuver. They were scattered about the cracked and crumbling base, hunting for insects to eat and mating with their dominant Incubus lord, their disgusting screeches of lust echoing for miles around. When dawn came and the harpies went back underground, the Immortals moved down to the bunker.

With a concussive boom, Seth stomped his foot as they neared the door. The Earth shook and cracked the ground beneath them. They watched the entry. He did it again. The hinges loosened and the sounds of livid wretchedness grew. Suddenly, the door swung open and the beasts flew out. The Aradian and Sararan moved through them like wind through tree branches, murdering them with methodical ease, slaughtering the beasts as they rushed at them screaming and gnashing, their flesh smoking in the rising heat of morning, firing guns at the Immortals from above like mercenary angels. The last one fighting dropped its empty shot gun and attempted to fly away in retreat. Devonia threw her spear through its chest and it spun to the ground like a dead bird.

With their enemy defeated, the two of them entered the compound and found the infants. They slaughtered them as well, taking the bodies of the savages and stacking them on the abandoned tarmac. They soaked them with the chemicals and jet fuel left by the humans and let the rising desert heat combust the pile of corpses. They kept hunting. The burning remains could be seen smoking far behind them as they moved north.

"How many would we have to kill to make them go extinct?" Seth asked.

"At least four thousand a day," Devonia answered. "That's why we need to find a queen."

"We could really use another Immortal," he admitted.

Devonia said nothing but had similar thoughts. For what harpies lacked in intelligence and strategy, they made up for in numbers and ferocity. With flocks as big as fifteen thousand, and colonies much larger yet, another Immortal would be crucial. But their options were limited.

They moved across borders, following the wake of the harpies' devastation as they hunted them. In Syria they found a thin canyon with mud fixtures built into the overhangs like giant swallow nests and used their sorcery to pull in torrential downpours, drowning the flock and killing thousands of harpies in the raging floods. They murdered another flock in Tabriz, where the heathens had found refuge in the city's abandoned houses and hotels which the Immortals simply leveled with earthquakes before cutting down the wounded one by one. But although the number of dead harpies rose with each battle, Devonia desperately wanted to find a harpy queen.

They hunted for weeks, the two of them fighting without sleep or stagnancy, the sun's unlimited energy providing them with the perfect mental and physical edge. Tala had surely meant to make the world uninhabitable for humans and the rest of the Earth's creatures who relied on the moon's gravitational forces. But the conditions were often ideal for the more highly adaptive versions of Sub-Sararan mutants. There were days when the Earth flipped and digressed into abstract patterns, inverting its poles and hiding half the world in darkness for what seemed like weeks, spurring blizzards that made finding those cold-blooded abominations difficult in the towering drifts. But when the sun rose in the west, the snow melted and carved the desert with temporary rivers which steamed and evaporated by midday, leaving the hibernating wretches to scatter like cockroaches.

The Immortals moved into northern Iraq, setting fire to old oil wells to draw out more harpies. But none fell for the trap. Seth became concerned for the air quality as the sky turned a darker shade of black, but Devonia continued lighting the wells in vain, masking the sky with a gaseous filth as she angrily tried to smoke out the creatures. On the sixth day of their unsanctioned scorched-Earth policy, they finally spotted a lone Incubus darting through the smoke. Had it not crossed in front of the sun's fouled light, they might not have discovered the retreating demon.

"It's alone," Seth said.

"Then it's trying to lead us into an ambush. Let's take the bait," Devonia said as she began running after it.

They followed from afar as the harpy led them upwind of the burning fields, to an ancient delta of dried canals. Suddenly, several harpies came streaming over the dunes with giant scorpions running right behind them. They were immediately flanked by more mutant scorpions and Seth dodged a stinger as it slashed at him like a dagger. Sand was kicked up in the stampede and soon dozens of the Sub-Sararan creatures had swarmed them as the harpies cackled from above like flying hyenas.

Devonia swirled her spear around in the sand, jumping up and over the scorpions as they charged, creating a massive sink hole and burying the creatures in a suffocating enclosure. Seth faced each of the massive arachnids one at a time, slicing their claws and stingers off with his sword before moving to the next one, leaving the beasts belly-up and screeching in pain. The elite incubi fired crude single-fire rifles at the duo as they retreated to their nearby colony.

"They're going to try and hide their queen! We have to stop them. Remember the canyon in Syria?"

"Yeah, but good luck pulling up a storm at this time of day," Seth said, looking up at the blazing sun.

"We're not using water this time. Go to the colony and try to keep them as close to the ground as you can."

"They have wings, Devonia!" Seth yelled at her as she ran back towards the oil fields.

Seth rolled his eyes and turned, following the incubi to the edge of a huge waterfall's remains. He looked down into the hollowed canyon before him in awe.

"You've got to be fucking kidding me," he muttered to himself.

The air vibrated with the beating wings of over twenty-five thousand harpies. The colony had dug hollow nests into the walls of the deep crevices and they flew in large spirals, buzzing the very air he breathed. He looked around at the incestuous swarm and then directly below him. As the harpies spotted him and began circling closer, he dove down to an overhang on the cascading rock face and backed himself into a small fissure. The devilish beasts dove at him and slashed at him with their weapons. He fought them off as Devonia spoke to him from the astral plain.

"Incoming ordinance. Make sure you're on high ground

or tucked out of the way."

He kept to his defensive maneuvers, angering the heathens and inviting more and more harpies to hover below the fall's fringe. A rumbling could be felt through the rocks, and after a few seconds, a river of petroleum splashed over the cliff and onto the harpies, covering them in thick oil while filling the infested canyon. A wall of black muck poured in front of Seth as he climbed out from under the torrent and back up to the cliff's edge.

Devonia stood there watching the harpies drown in the oil while struggling to save their young. She snapped her fingers together to make a spark and lit the river's edge as the whole channel became engulfed in flame. The fire dropped into the canyon, lighting the smothered harpies and the canyon walls, causing a firestorm to erupt in the enclosed space. The screams of thousands of harpies filled the air and Seth and Devonia watched with satisfaction as the burning demons died in the fires or attempted to climb the walls slowly with melting wings. Those who had escaped the hellish canyon flew up and away and Devonia watched them retreat. Seth looked at her, then to the survivors getting away.

"We're not gonna go after them?"

"I'm waiting for her," Devonia said, watching the harpies closely.

A few seconds passed until she saw a pregnant harpy and twelve large incubi flying south behind the smoke. Devonia made her move. She ran along the cliff's precipice and leapt across the canyon. With quick feet, she chased down the small contingent until they had no choice but to face her.

One of the muscular incubi yelled something scathing before charging Devonia spear first. She cut his chest open and moved forward, taking on the royal guard single handedly. The elite warriors managed to cut the Immortal along her left shoulder and leg, but fell all the same to her violent maneuvers, until only the queen remained. Her pink and green feathers were ruffled, and she lay sweating and breathing heavily, but she made no sound. She just stared at Devonia with her large yellow cat-eye, trying perhaps to find some similarity between them, with the hope Devonia would recognize their unsaid bond.

"What is your name?" Devonia asked.

Adriel, the harpy responded in her mind.

"Where are the other queen's, Adriel?"

Adriel neither spoke nor thought, placing her mind into deep meditation to block Devonia's probing clairvoyance.

"If you tell me where they are, I'll make your death less painful," Devonia threatened.

The harpy queen spit a greasy wad of saliva onto Devonia's foot before insulting her in some ancient tongue. In half a second, the Immortal huntress reached out and gripped Adriel's jaw and tore it from her skull, leaving the moaning creature and her unborn baby to bleed out on the sand.

Devonia walked back towards the edge of the canyon and Seth nodded in approval. They left the canyon to smolder and moved south, continuing their campaign with higher hopes than ever.

One evening they stopped at the edge of a small sea and looked out over the strange body of water, for it glowed with yellow and blue algae as if reflecting an invisible aurora in the night sky above. Deadly to the touch, Devonia knew it couldn't be the only insolent organism in their midst. They rounded the shore, spear and sword in hand, crossing a massive swamp where they waded to their hips in a foul primordial soup. The water was black and thick with a strange oily texture.

"What is this shit?" Seth asked.

"Ink from a Sub-Sararan octopus. The animal expels it to keep its eggs warm. Keep your eyes out for them."

Seth bent down and held up what seemed to be a spherical gem, with blue lights swimming at its center.

"What in the actual fuck?" he murmured, the large slippery ball dripping a clear syrupy goo.

"Collect as many as you can."

They stacked the eggs in a pile on some dry rocks above the bog, laboring all night in the muck and fulfilling the tedious and disgusting task of finding each one. They remained vigilant, their senses keen, for the location of the mother was somewhere in those silent waters. But she never came. They lit the eggs on fire that morning, their skin dyed blackish purple with ink until the inevitable scorching dawn cleansed them of their old skin altogether. The Immortals molted like arachnids and threw their shells into the burning ovum, moving south once again.

They continued to kill whole flocks of harpies in their war path to central Iraq, and although they'd made headway, Devonia felt less than accomplished. The fight seemed endless. She knew they could do this forever and so could the harpies. Something had to change or else they would be doomed to coexist with the overpopulated hoard indefinitely.

On February 38th in the year 2120, the Immortals walked through the golden gates of Bagdad, naked save for the sashes of scalps hung over their shoulders and covered in the dried blood of their prey. Adriel's jawbone dangled from Devonia's neck like a barbaric medal as children rushed to touch its steel teeth, their small faces smiling as they welcomed the Immortals with flower necklaces and prayer beads.

CHAPTER 58 – THE SURGE

Baghdad had returned to being the gem of the Mid-East. The streets were teeming with people at all hours, the air protected from toxins and relentless ultra-violet rays by utilizing higher technologies. The queen of the progressive state was Devonia's primary client and close friend, and she happened to be the grandniece of Queen Parvati.

Before they entered the lavish Iraqi palace, the Immortals washed themselves in the bath houses of Queen Fatima's Royal Fountain and were measured and fitted with fine clothing made from Sub-Sararan silkworms, whose fabric could react to temperature and weather changes. They declined a meal and requested to go to the queen's chambers instead. Devonia wore her hair down but kept the snake bone crown she had been wearing. Seth wore a red and black three-piece suit and large sunglasses to keep his eyes from blinding the humans around him.

"She'll be right with you," an advisor said to them.

They waited in the hall for a few minutes; a meeting with foreign diplomats was underway. Seth tapped his foot impatiently as Devonia looked at the paintings on the walls. The queen's fascination with Christ was displayed from one end of the hall to the other, some of the paintings a thousand years old. They'd been somehow saved from Shakti's decimation of all religion during the Post-Eruption Wars.

"All I see are pictures of Christ's punishment. None of his miracles." Seth commented.

"He was a martyr for his people during a very troubling time. His followers believed he gave his life for our sins; that he was the Lamb of God. That was his miracle. Had he not been sentenced to torture and death, he may have been the first Immortal."

"He gave his life for OUR sins?" he said, his eyebrows raised.

"Well... yours... mine... all humans."

"So now you're a human again because you sympathize with Jesus Christ?"

"What I'm saying, fool, is that he was a symbol for all that is good and righteous, and through his seeking he became something more than human, regardless of what came after."

"Yet what came after meant everything, surely? He had the power for far greater accomplishments. If he had the tools to be an Immortal and chose not to, I think he blew it. Big time."

"Now you're just being a dick," she sighed.

"What did his sacrifices actually do for this world?," he said, stepping back to concentrate his thoughts. "His true disciples fled to the desert because they knew what was coming. Then the Church began their two-thousand-year conquest of systemic persuasion, convincing god-less tribes that this 'creator' would provide for them. Most people could never actually comprehend the idea of a singular divine entity. It was all about control."

"But you can comprehend such an entity," Devonia said.

"Yes, I can. Which is why I would never give such a thing a name. To these people who blindly fall into the trap of Christianity, anything done in the name of God is 'righteous' because that is how their god intended it. Where does the spiritual enlightenment end and the child slave syndicate begin? You have to throw it all out. God. Paradise. Forgiveness. Look at what humankind's fear has done to the world; we angels have been made flesh. And we're bitter. As were Lucifer and the others who quickly understood the mistake that was the creation of Sapiens."

Devonia looked at him with a tilted brow. She had never heard him speak so passionately before. After travelling together for so long, she had grown used to Seth's steady presence, but listening to him now was compelling in a way she had not expected. She could sense the trauma in him. "Where did you learn so much about Christianity?"

"We had a chapel at the Lotus. Anyway, I'm just saying the guy wasted his talents," he went on. "His whole life he could have been killing Romans and slaying tang."

Devonia rolled her eyes. "I'm sure that's what you would have done... but that would have defeated his message of compassion," she said as she gazed at the cracking old paint, the crucified man looking back at her with tormented eyes.

The door opened to the queen's hall and people funneled out, bowing politely to Devonia as they went.

"How do they know you?" Seth asked.

"I'm a goddess, remember?" she smirked.

"Are you going be a martyr like this asshole?" he asked, nodding to the painting.

"Watch your language, Seth. And don't be disrespectful in front of the queen. In fact, just shut up for a while."

They entered and the queen ran to greet them.

"Hello my darling!" she said as she hugged Devonia and kissed her on the cheek.

"How are you, Queen Fatima? It's so good to see you," Devonia said, kissing her in return.

The petite young queen was beautiful, her ears and eyebrows pierced and adorned with golden hoops.

"I'm well. Busy, but well. Please, sit!"

They all descended to the plush couches where the queen took her less formal councils. Seth dropped his shades and stared at her with his beaming eyes until Devonia pinched him to disarm his attraction. He put his glasses back on and leaned back, trying to act relaxed.

"This is Seth, who I'm sure you know from the stories."

"Of course! It's an honor to meet another Immortal. You're finally of age, I hear?"

"I was seven when I killed my first human," he said brashly. "Took me a few more years to get into the harpy business."

"He's fairly new to all this," Devonia laughed awkwardly. "I came to apologize."

"For what?"

"For being gone four years and not being here for you. I know how hard it can be to keep the peace."

"Well, it hasn't been easy, but things are going surprisingly well. My engineers have completed the Tesla-Helix machine and the city is now livable at all hours. Our water and food is tested regularly and security concerns are steady but manageable. We have built up a formidable army, and their readiness has been tested with great success."

"I'm glad to hear it. You will be pleased to know that we have recently relieved Pharaoh of his command."

"Really? How?"

Devonia slid her thumb across her neck.

"I suppose the old man had it coming," Fatima sighed. "He had become a bit of a… is tyrant too strong a word?"

"No," Seth and Devonia said at once.

"Anyway," Devonia continued, "there's eventually going to be a new ruler in North Africa, and I thought we would warn you since you're the next closest empire. The region will be unstable. I doubt whoever comes to power would want to expand their territories and attempt to overthrow you, but your city is indeed a jewel, and the greed of man will eventually turn its ugly head this way."

"I appreciate the warning and will do what I can to prepare. Unfortunately, other humans have been the least of our worries," she said solemnly. "At least people communicate and sometimes bring an ounce of reason with them."

"Those people that left here a moment ago, why were they here?" Seth asked.

"I've assembled a war council. Despite the enduring efforts of Devonia and other headhunters, the harpy problem is getting worse. Whole regions of Central Asia and Siberia are becoming infested. We know of twenty-two harpy queens, many with nests deep underground that are difficult to find and even more difficult to breach. The summit today was to discuss the use of new weapon systems for large-scale eradication."

"Biological?" Devonia asked.

"Nuclear," she answered as if the word were cursed.

"The last nuclear weapon detonated was over Geneva. I'll never forget that day..." Devonia shook her head solemnly.

"I'm very aware of the horrors of such a weapon, and want to avoid dropping any until absolutely necessary. But we're running out of options."

"What about all the people living within reach of the fallout? There would be a devastating amount of collateral damage."

Queen Fatima leaned in and spoke plainly. "We have to view this from a mathematical standpoint. If twenty thousand people die from radioactive poisoning, we'll still be saving the rest of the human population. We'll do our best to warn them ahead of time, but these days, even harpies have spies. I'm just letting you know that it may become the only option."

"What stage are you at in production?" Devonia asked.

"The war heads will be ready in a month's time. But we don't plan to use them until the trigger point is reached."

"What's the trigger point?" Seth asked.

"A census conducted last month placed the population of harpies at one-hundred and eighteen thousand, with projections climbing into the millions by 2125. If that number rises to a quarter of a million before the locust season, that's our trigger point for reassessment. The dominant species of this planet will be harpies if we don't act quickly."

"I understand your predicament, Queen Fatima, but please allow me to come up with a plan. If we cannot curb the numbers before the locust season, do what you must. We won't get in the way. But until then, I believe that if Seth, myself, and any other mercenaries out there all worked together, we would be able to accomplish the task from the inside out."

"What do you propose?" the queen asked.

"I'll gather up the best headhunters in the city and form a solid team. We'll recruit others along the way and move deep into enemy territory. From there, we'll perform as a strike team of operators working with local militias. Do I have your permission to use type three spells and hexes?" Devonia asked.

"As long as you don't possess anyone, or anything, I don't see a problem with that. You have both my clearance and my praises. Just don't get yourself killed, my wonderful Aradian friend."

"Don't worry. The harpies are no match for us."

"It's not them… it's the leviathan I worry about."

"Otodus Gigantis Megalodon. The most revered monster of the desert. We'll be sure to maintain a safe distance from the breeding grounds."

"Very well then," the young queen smiled.

"I'll return in a day's time to present my contingent."

"Please, stay as long as you need to. I know you're eager to get back into the thick of it, but I can tell Seth here has a lot on his mind. Why not take a few days and rest? You'll be busy soon enough."

They left the palace and split up, Devonia heading right as Seth walked left.

"Where are you going?" she asked him.

He looked at her and she read his deviant mind.

"You've got to be kidding me."

"Is there something better I should be doing? You heard the queen, we need to relax," he said.

"I know you don't act like you are the son of royalty, but try to understand who and what you are, Sararan."

He smiled and saluted mockingly at her, walking towards the city center with a swinging stride, his thick sunglasses barely holding back the glow of his gleaming eyes.

Devonia took a different route, going to a club in the western district where mercenaries commonly stopped to drink. Bluish green lights lit the black-walled room as low-fidelity instrumental beats thumped against the ceiling. The place was busy, mostly with middle to upper class humans, but in the corner there was a large circular table of mercenary headhunters. Some were clean shaven and dapper, with tattoos of foreign gang symbols branded on their knuckles;

others were heavily scarred with black ash that had sunken into the creases of their rough faces. Two were wearing turbans and sashes symbolizing their service in the war against the Luciferian Army. Handsome African tribesmen conversed with Mongol ex-patriots, a pair of lovely escorts at either's side as they spoke of simpler times. Only one was not human, but he hid his identity behind a copper mask like some foregone deep-sea voyager. They drank and smoked laced hukkah, paying little attention to the Aradian as she walked to the bar.

"Vodka and mint, please."

"Right away, Pavonis."

The bartender plucked a bottle from the shelf of worldly spirits as she conversed. "Haven't seen you in a while, dear. How are you?"

"As well as I could be, I suppose. My apprentice died in an accident, so I hid away for a few years to meditate, only to wake up to the same nightmarish world."

"I'm sorry to hear that."

Devonia continued. "Four weeks ago I met a centaur, overthrew the North African government, and found the child that World War IV was fought over."

"Woah… sounds like you've been busy. Did you say you met a centaur? What's that?"

"Half horse, half man. In this case, half woman."

"What was the gender of the horse half?"

"I didn't bother to check," Devonia laughed.

The bartender poured the vodka into a fine crystal glass and dropped a hollow sphere of ice inside, poking a hole in it with a needle to allow a nitrogen and mint infused fog to slowly leak out, before garnishing the drink lightly with dried opium leaves. She wiped the rim of the crystal with a cloth soaked in benzoic aloe and placed it on the counter over a green cotton napkin, ending the performance with a 24-karat gold-flake web draped over the surface.

"A new rendition, using freshly spun web from a sun spider. On the house."

"Thank you. I love the web." Devonia sipped the flavorful concoction and smiled.

"I'd heard about Seth being discovered after all these years. Such a shock."

"Indeed... there are a lot of unanswered questions. I'm still learning his story myself," Devonia said.

"How's the drink?"

"Delicious, as always."

"I like the smooth feeling the opium adds to the vodka, it's a nice change of pace from all the stimulant cocktails people are into these days," the bartender said.

"Well, neither chemical will have much of an effect on me, but I'll need it to act the part while I'm recruiting."

"Oh, you're working right now? You need to take a load off, girl."

"I just did, for too long it seems. Thank you, darling."

She left three gold coins on the bar and took her drink over to the table of mercenaries, the smooth guitar trills playing over a crackling pocket beat. The room was seven flavors of smoke, all legal under the queen's mandate of somatic freedom, all ravishing yet diluted enough to provide the customer with a steady intoxication: libra perfectus.

Devonia approached the table of mercenaries and held out her drink.

"Good evening gentlemen. I'm looking for a few dedicated headhunters. The pay is good, and you would start work immediately. I don't care if you have criminal histories, debts, or even current charges against you."

They looked at her as if waiting for a punchline. Two of

them chuckled to themselves. A large man put down his glass of liquor and wiped his black beard with his sleeve.

"Who is it for?"

"Queen Fatima."

They all laughed. Some uttered their skepticism.

"And the pay?"

"Thirty for every kill."

They all laughed harder and slapped the table, pointing at her and shaking their heads.

One of them settled down and explained to her, "Listen lady... I can get fifty a head working for my brother, why the hell would I take a government contract for twenty fucking less?"

"Because we will be killing over fifteen thousand harpies a week. That's thirty for each kill per man in my company. Do the math."

They looked confused. One of the dapper men in suits nodded and smiled sadistically, enjoying the conversation immensely and leaning in for more.

"How?" the large copper-faced mutant asked in a low, gruff voice.

"By going into their territories and operating from strategic locations. By finding nests, one by one, and killing the incubus guards and their queen. We won't all be engaging directly. Specifically, I need operators who can call in air-strikes, train local forces, and coordinate joint attacks on large hordes of harpies. Entire colonies will be decimated."

"Yeah all that's great and everything but you said government contract... that means rules of engagement and all that other bullshit," one of the men grunted.

"You are mistaken, friend," Devonia said, smiling and swigging her drink before setting it down on the table. She scooted in next to the nearest mercenary and wove her fingers together delicately. "This will be a free-fire on all targets, baby-killing, bloodline-ending murder spree. The humans of these areas have either cleared out already or will be forewarned to leave for risk of being in harm's way."

"We're allowed to kill children?" one of them scoffed.

"Harpy children, yes. They are a blight upon the land that cannot be tolerated in any merciful sense. Complete, overwhelming force is now being fully supported and implemented by twelve nations, eager to crush the species in a final push. We'll have open passage to all borders, moving fast and freely wherever the objective lies."

"And who's leading this new order?" one asked.

"I am."

They laughed again.

"And who the hell are you?"

"I'm Devonia Ketevan, reincarnation of Pavonis."

Then men raised their eyebrows.

"Prove it," the large man with the beard said as he squinted at her.

Devonia lifted her arm and slapped it on the table. Everyone looked at her hand. She turned it over. A dead fly lay in her palm. After a moment, the fly twitched, and from its belly, a green bud popped out and grew a stem. The stem lifted up towards the light and bloomed into a little white flower.

"Touching. And how does that help us kill harpies, flower girl?"

"Yeah, can you even fly?"

"Ha-ha that's a good one!" one of them cackled.

"No seriously, aren't Aradian's supposed to be able to fly or something?"

"Hey, where are you going cutie pie! You scared her off,

asshole! I was just getting to know her!"

They continued howling as she stormed out of the club, off to more bars and gambling hideouts and watering holes all filled with the same sort of dumb brutes mocking her, believing neither her identity nor her proposition. She went from place to place, buying rounds of drinks and downing shots to try and impress potential recruits, but each time they would just try to make a move on her or wave her off as crazy. After being disgusted by the swine around her, she finally left the bars, staggering through the city. Though she thought herself immune to the effects of alcohol, the half-gallon of liquor inside her managed to give her a slight buzz. She walked her way through the vibrant light displays; the green and blue paper peacocks dancing above cauldrons of fire. Dancers in feathered costumes twisted and spun through the streets, honoring their mother deity Pavonis, their Lord and divine prophet. But were they honoring Devonia or Ingrid, the one who saved the world sixty-seven years ago? These questions troubled her, so she hid herself behind her shawl and ignored them, hiding her eyes to avoid recognition. She ducked into a theater where a play had just started.

"May I?" she asked, handing the doorman a stack of gold drachmas. He stared and said nothing as she passed, his jaw hanging as he felt the weight of the coins in his hand.

She went in and stood near the back in the shadows, finally away from the men and the noisy festival. The lighting was low as the show began, and she smiled as she listened to the string instruments meld softly with the actor's romantic motions. She stood for some time before she felt something in the air. She turned to the man beside her.

"What are you doing here?" she asked, looking at Seth from head to toe in disbelief.

"I love a good show. Especially these old-timey ones."

She smiled. "Aren't you just full of surprises? And where did you see this, in the training halls of Cairo?"

"I've been all over. The gladiator thing was just a phase. I was planning a coup and it just so happened you were of the same mindset, so I pulled the trigger. All that stuff about me starving myself was true, but I knew about it of course."

"Then why did you do it?"

"To feel empty, weak, on the verge of collapse... that's how I train and learn. I wasn't faking my reaction to my first sun-gaze in a while. That was much needed."

"You're such a moron."

He grinned. "Have you seen this play?"

"Yes, once, a long time ago. Dramas and movies are some of my favorite things, next to natural wonders. I love stories from the past."

She watched the actors for a few seconds.

"How did recruiting go?" he asked.

"Terribly. How did your 'massage' go?"

"It was okay. The masseuse wanted to give me a hand job at the end and I had to tell her to keep working on my shoulders," he whispered.

Devonia rolled her eyes. "Yeah, like I'm going to believe that. Why else would you get a massage? Our muscles are regenerative."

"Sometimes it's just nice to feel the touch of another person," he said, sipping his drink.

She looked over at him in surprise, then up at the play again.

"Why are we whispering? We can speak telepathically," she said.

"It's rude to talk with the mind. It's lazy and elitist."

"And all that cussing isn't rude?"

"Well, when you surround yourself with the kind of scoundrels I did over the last few years... by the way, thanks for rescuing me from my own vanity. I admit, that place was getting to my head."

"Oh, so now you admit to it? You're welcome, though no gratitude is needed. Besides, you rescued me."

"From what?"

"Retirement."

"You're far too young to retire, even if you already deserve it." The audience began to clap as the actors filed onto the stage for their final bow. "Right, I'm off to bed. Wouldn't want to miss out on a good dream cycle before the next deployment, right?"

Devonia smiled at him as he held up his glass and mouthed the words goodnight, striding off with a saunter of confidence. She was quickly learning the deceitful tactics of Seth, and just how dangerous he could become the more he was exposed to the world.

The next day, Devonia stood ankle deep in water on a rooftop infinity garden. The cool water flowed around her as she inspected the plants rising from that oasis in the sky. The sweet-scented flora were set into circular patterns that rounded the building's rooftop. When the folds of sunlight passed beyond the torque of the Earth's rotation, Fatima appeared, her slender silhouette making love with the dusk in a contrast of burgundy and black, as if she were a window to the abyss and something of dense matter still. Something in Fatima reminded Devonia of Avestan, but she couldn't frame the relation. She smiled and hugged the young woman. But it was Fatima who sighed with relief as she held Devonia close.

"I wish it could always be like this. This peaceful. This protected. When this is all over, you will stay here, won't you?" Fatima asked.

Devonia stroked Fatima's hair, silken threads catching between her fingers.

"I'm afraid this may never be over," she whispered. "But I will do everything I can to keep evil away from here. And I'll always come back. I love this place. I love you."

Fatima clung to her tightly and sobbed into Devonia's chest. "I hate myself for what I ask of you! It's not fair!"

Devonia shook her head. "Shh, don't blame yourself. I would be doing this even if you weren't here; it just makes everything better knowing I can help someone as amazing as you."

Fatima looked up and smiled, her eager lips trembling as Devonia cupped her face, brushing away the remaining tears on her cheeks. Their faces drew closer, seemingly pulled by some gravitational force, until Devonia's lips met the queen's and she kissed her softly.

The Aradian quickly pulled back once she realized what she'd done.

"I'm so sorry," Devonia gasped.

"Don't be," Fatima replied, reaching towards Devonia and kissing her deeply.

Melting into one another's touch, they explored each other for a few moments until Devonia once again pulled back, her eyes a glowing violet sprawl. They looked at one another for a moment longer until Devonia broke from Fatima's gaze, a blush creeping up her neck and onto her cheeks.

Fatima smiled. "Here... I want to give you something,"

she said, pulling a small, polished rock from her pocket. "It's a moonstone, like the one Pavonis used in the Post-Eruption Wars. You can call upon animal minds more readily with this piece. Queen Parvati gave it to me before she died."

"Queen Parvati is dead?"

"She died of cancer three years ago, didn't you… oh… you were asleep…"

"This is why I fear nuclear weapons, Fatima. She was poisoned from the fallout."

"I know…I just… I'm so scared. I don't know what else to do," she said, weeping again.

"My Fatima," Devonia whispered, placing her forehead against the queen's.

They held one another close as they watched the night drape softly upon them. The sky was a dripping wall of eyes lending their old light and the lovers watched on with theirs, as all energy in all things does acknowledge itself with the least encounters, like planets longing for a deeper orbit, or comets running supreme on the friction of heavenly catastrophe, diving ever towards the sun.

The morning dawned quickly over the glittering megapolis, the sun's light reflecting off Baghdad's massive shield of hexagonal, ozone-enriched nano tubes, woven spherically over the city like a sunken hive. Protecting it. Isolating it. The burning desert around the city was smeared with the blackened carcasses of those who had committed felo-de-se by exodus, their flaked remains but ashes to the wind in that infernal paradigm of Hell on Earth.

Devonia stepped out of the gates, her thin golden armor

covering her whole body. Her purple dreadlocks were tied into a thick knot, in which she tucked away her magickal instruments of war. Harpy feathers. Magazines with crystal bullets. Meteorites. Poisonous Darts. She wrapped a small red flag around her spear and stuck it into the ground, looking out over the waste with squinting, magenta eyes. She glanced at the rising sun.

"You're late, Seth," she said to herself.

She waited for a few more minutes, tapping her foot until Seth arrived at last. He was clad in Roman-style armor with a longsword on his back, his muscled chest on display; his mohawk regrown – spiked and dipped in blood; his bright eyes relentless and eager for the hunt.

"No help, huh?" he said, stretching out his arms to absorb the light's sprawl.

"There were a few who might be considering the offer. I'll wait another hour, no longer."

"Right on," he said, pulling a grapefruit from beneath his metal kilt and eating it, skin and all.

Devonia looked at him. "Did you get laid last night or something?"

"Ha. You can smell her on me, can you? Guilty as charged." He leaned towards her, sniffing the air. "You too, huh?"

"Don't be gross," she said, shaking her head.

"Wait..." He drew in a deep breath through his nose. "And with a woman? You really are full of surprises."

"Not another word or I'll skin you alive!"

He laughed, but before he could respond, the sound of hydraulic machinery cranked into being.

Seth smiled. "Fatima has a surprise for you," he said, his mouth dripping with the pink juice.

Just then, a convoy of tanks drove out from the bunkers

below the city. Twelve of them in all. Massive and thunderous and clinking heavily against the ground, their cannons bearing the same red flag as Fatima's palace.

They rolled up one by one and sat idle, their diesel engines chugging loudly. One of the tank operators climbed out from inside the belly of the painted steel machine and waved. It was one of the mercenaries. The rest of the hatches opened and there were more of them. It was the group from the bar, now dressed in desert camouflage, mostly sober, and ready to stack bodies. The masked Sub-Sararan called out to her.

"Pavonis! We're ready to fight! Provided you supply the bullets, of course," he said, chuckling.

Devonia looked back at Seth.

"They said they would come if I led the surge," Seth told her over the rumbling engines. "But don't worry, they'll know who the boss is soon enough." He winked.

"Is it because I'm an Aradian?"

Seth shook his head, his expression uncharacteristically serious. "No. It's because you're female."

Turning towards their troops, Seth walked over and jumped up onto the lead tank, looking to Devonia for orders. Nodding to him, Devonia headed to the rear of the convoy and was handed a headset. She stood tall on the turret of the last tank and adjusted her mouthpiece, looking back towards Fatima's palace. She blew a kiss to the queen one last time before switching roles from lover to commander.

"All right, listen up. Half speed to save fuel, split on the southeast road toward the gulf. I'll notify Seth when to break off east. That's where the hunting grounds lie."

They rode out, the deadly convoy of death machines riding fast over the blazing earth towards zones no sane human would enter.

◯

They broke pace at noon to let the engines cool and hid behind the shade of a rock spire. Seth was quick to pour water on the hot tanks while the men stayed inside the air-conditioned capsules.

"Quite the machines," Devonia said, pacing around one of the tanks as rolls of steam hissed into the air.

"We're going to have to move during the night to keep them cool," Seth remarked, watching the sun teeter over them, a pendulum at zenith. "With that in mind, when do we fight?"

"We'll fight during the night for the time being."

"Hit and run tactics?"

"Exactly. There are no large nests until the mountains anyway. We'll go through the gulf zones, then east and veer back north near the old border of Iran and Pakistan.

"Why don't we just go through Yazd?"

"Dangerous things lurk in that desert. Things not even you are prepared for, Sararan."

They waited until the sun had set and continued on, through ravines too dry to contain water and over shelves of sandstone erosion. The clear night sky held a syzygy of Jovian entities, with Jupiter and Saturn near alignment in the eastern sky, their many moons aglow as they blinked in the eyes of Perseus, mocking Seth's gaze as they tumbled along their wide descent, the Andromeda Galaxy in silent tow, its nebulous smear hurtling towards him at a quarter of a million miles per hour, barely visible beyond the Milky Way's strewn treasures.

They refueled before the morning came, and hid the

convoy in a caved-in area tucked into the slope of an abrupt plateau. All day Seth scouted the area ahead of them while Devonia briefed the men and went through introductions, denoting each an expertise. There was a medic, an explosives specialist, a weapons expert, a navigation and weather man, a sniper, a scout, an advisor, a tracker, a thief, and a mechanic. Devonia and Seth would be performing each of these specialisms as best they could, though certainly not at once.

Many of the mercenaries had worked together before, headhunting all over the Arab world and performing small operations with various militias and vigilante groups. Their ability to speak different languages and train locals was partly the reason for Devonia's recruitment. Two of the sharply dressed men ended up being dejected syndicate agents, their pasts mired with conspiracy and criminality. They were the advisor and the thief, one black, one white, their resumes beyond proficient for tasks ranging from counterintelligence and tradecraft to hacking and even EMP jamming.

The large, bearded man was Oden, an orphan from the North raised by a family of hunters. He was the tracker, and had near as good a sense of smell as Devonia on her best day. The navigations expert was a man named Emul, from the wreckage of Yemen. He was an aspiring geographer and scientist who'd been fighting harpies ever since his survey outings began to be disrupted by the vicious creatures.

The masked Sub-Sararan was the mechanic, with a thousand tools around his waist belt to solve any issue arising from the endless labyrinth of cables and machinery in their gargantuan cavalry. The turban-wearing Sikhs were WWIV veterans who had served as a sniper team. They were a seasoned duo who'd fought in countless conflicts since the fall of Almuruna, and were as deadly from afar as they were close. The medic was a Japanese man who rarely spoke. He was a doctor of holistic medicine who had worked on the front lines in the Harpy Wars from Western China to Ukraine. The bomb specialist was a Gurkha fighter, and Zurvan student of Avestan, who paid particular attention to detail in all things. Devonia was confident in his abilities and trusted only him with high-energy explosives.

Only one of the team was a gunsmith. The Mongol had been an artillery operator during the battle of Geneva. He would be their weapons specialist, and serve as the communications and logistics coordinator when the planes came in to refuel them and when the rest of the trucks and aircraft arrived for the main push. Devonia had ordered the resources before leaving Fatima's palace, and the request was granted so long as they could secure a route for the reinforcements.

When Seth returned, he reported a flock of harpies bedded down nearly forty miles south. They waited until dusk, then moved out as the coming clouds of a cold front whisked across the lowland sands.

The convoy stopped a few miles from the flock and shut off their engines. Seth and Devonia conversed in front of the lead tank then drew their plan in the sand to show the others under the dim starlight. The mercenaries wore night vision goggles and had rifles equipped with holographic infra-red scopes and suppressers. Fatima had outfitted them with the most advanced weapon systems, built by engineers who had picked up where such technologies had left off nearly a century before.

The sky was cloudy and dark, the air brisk and blustery upon the blue sand as they walked in silence. Two incubus sentries stood idle on the crest of a dune, one leaning on its rifle, half asleep. The other one turned. Seth's dagger found its throat while the tracker covered the other creature's mouth and sliced its chest, spilling its beating heart onto the sand. They hurriedly pushed heaps of sand over the bodies to cover their scent, then went on. When they found the rest of them, the sickening fiends were mating in an orgy at the pit of a crater, hiding from the wind while they sucked and fucked one another violently. The mercenaries surrounded the pit and peeked over, biding their time.

"Oh my God," one of the mercenaries said.

Seth was the first to open fire, his suppressed shots not even heard through the wailing sandstorm. Everyone else followed his lead and hundreds of rounds descended into the pit, until the dripping creatures slumped in their spunk, full of bloody holes, dead before they even had time to scream.

Devonia chucked a grenade into the center of the massacre and let the sinkhole devour the bits of bodies. Some smoke came up from the blast and flew away with the wind, leaving little trace of the abominations.

They watched the hole for a moment before Devonia roused them.

"Good work! Back to the rigs!"

Devonia led the convoy towards the next flock while Seth and the tracker went ahead to scout out more of the area. The sands had nearly filled in the trails of the cretins as the two hunters walked the subtle depression that lay under the cascading sand. The storm winds blew hard and loud against their ears, yet both man and Sararan were keen to the tones of the desert. A screech and a whimper came from under the sand.

"Is that what I think it is?" the man asked, pulling out his shotgun and racking a shell into the chamber.

"Stay where you are. I'll lead it out of the area."

"How far are you gonna go?"

"Not far. It's just a hatchling," Seth said.

"What if there's a den below us?"

"Then we're fucked."

Seth took off running as fast as he could into the desert, his tongue flicking at the air like a lizard, probing the clamorous night. Behind him the sands rose with a suspicious movement and after a thousand meters the subterranean creature had caught him up. It burst through the sand and screamed like a tortured infant, the incredible fish as wide as Seth was tall, and long enough to hide its razor tail far beneath the dunes it parted. Seth lunged at the scaled serpent but it snatched his sword in its shark-like jaws and shattered the metal to bits, the metallic shards shining between its bleeding teeth like crowns. The eyes of the thing were caked with sand and bloodied; it had been stabbed and blinded by the harpies, left to suffer in the wasteland for want of its dead mother.

The megalodon extended its jaw and snapped at Seth as he rounded the neck of the beast with a small leather ribbon. Seth pulled the ribbon tight and grasped the beast's spine as it whipped and flopped and slapped against the sand. Eventually, the creature grew tired, giving in to the sedative liquid that dripped from the ribbon. In dawn's quiet light, it lay peacefully upon the sand, breathing deeply. The storm drifted off to the south in grumbling retreat as Seth lay next to the serpent, petting its head and crooning to it as if it were a loving pet. The tracker stood watching the sun's coming light uneasily as the temperatures rose, observing the two mutants engaging in some concomitant truce beyond his understanding. Seth rubbed the serpent's cut-up face with a precise motion and as the sun came over the horizon, it leaned its heavy head toward the warmth as the burning orange light cracked open its grey opaque eyes. Seth released the beast from his grasp and it licked his leg, before slowly slithering away into the desert.

"Why did the harpies blind it?" Oden asked.

"To broadcast a distress call. The harpies wanted to cut us off using the baby as bait. Must not be any other leviathans in the area to answer it."

"Why'd you leave it alive then?"

Seth smiled. "A poet once said 'a snake's poison is life to the snake; it is in relation to man that it means death'."

Each night they continued similar operations; hit and run methods that kept them moving while clearing the route for support forces coming in behind them. They were a strike team reconnaissance group but each night they found themselves going deeper into harpy territory, forcing them to coordinate larger attacks, sometimes hiring local humans to help with cover fire and support. It wasn't until they arrived in Pakistan a month later that they finally found a worthy nest, and just in time for the supply chain to catch up.

One hundred surface-to-air missile trucks, fifty support vehicles, and a team of highly trained air-traffic combat controllers on motorcycles established a base camp at the foot of the Surman Mountains. Devonia had located a whole colony of harpies in a high mountain valley and she didn't waste any time in planning. On a cool March morning, the Immortals, mercenaries and airmen met in a white tent at the center of their fortified outpost. Fatima's red flag waved brightly against the snowy peaks as the men and woman entered.

"We've killed nearly four thousand harpies in the last four weeks," Devonia began, "but we're about to double down in a single day. We'll be upping the operational tempo and taking a more indirect approach, utilizing air support thanks to our new friends from Baghdad."

The men saluted and stepped forward, identifying themselves in a rigid military fashion. A few of the mercenaries smirked.

"These men are qualified operators and will be calling in air support for us. Order what you need and know you have the Nation of Iraq behind you. We have long range bombers, multi-use fighters, and cargo aircraft. We also have a variety of helicopters and a few Almuruna-era gunships to help us as well. We're going to have a tight communication plan so no one gets left in a bad spot. The last thing I want is collateral damage. As long as all the pieces are in place, we'll make the sky rain fire upon them."

They all nodded in agreement.

Seth smirked and shook his head. "That's a full size colony you'll be attacking."

"And?" Devonia questioned.

"Sure you can defeat a few thousand harpies overnight… and maybe even the next twenty or thirty thousand in the caves to the north, but eventually word of our genocide will spread through the demon world and we'll have the hordes of Asia on us faster than we can resupply ourselves."

"This is exactly why Queen Fatima has approved this insurgency. We need to move quickly, forcefully and without hesitation. It may be our last chance before such tactics become inadequate. We need to kill them all."

After more formalities and planning, the group ended their evening with a cask of arak brought in by the locals. The mercenaries wagered their livers with the fermented yak's milk and became drunk and loud; by midnight they had initiated the air corpsman with drinking games and fathomless jest.

Devonia left the group when she'd seen enough and made her way back to her yurt. Just before she entered, she stopped and tasted the air. A smile came across her face. On her ibex-skin floor lay her lover, Fatima, naked and alluring in the dim firelight.

"You didn't think I'd send my best without making sure the delivery arrived safely at your feet, did you?"

Devonia reached for her, capturing Fatima's lips and trailing her hands down her lover's body, the queen's stolen breath sucked into the lungs of the tempered Aradian and then returned. Fatima swiftly divested Devonia of her clothes and flipped them, pinning her down and exploring her naked form with eager fingers. They made love for hours, their warm kinetic movements oblivious to the freezing air outside.

A while before the sun rose, they lay by the fire and spoke softly to one another.

"How far into the mountains are you going?" Fatima asked as she nestled her body into her lover's.

"As far as we need to."

A minute of silence passed. They stroked one another's skin.

"Do the killings ever get to... do you ever regret the suffering you cause, even though it must be done?"

Devonia sighed. "I have killed men and I have killed

harpies and I have killed creatures not yet coded into the index of life on Earth. Humans kill with a passion separate from all other creatures, yet to wound one and watch it die is a grim affair. Since I'm still just an augmented version of a human, I am transformed by their emotional responses regardless of my ability to filter the immediate effects. I love all animals, and think most creatures deserve to live. Just not harpies. What the world ultimately decides, however, will be what is best for it. Natural selection supersedes all laws by our hand."

"Then why hunt them?"

"Because I am entitled to ensure the propagation and protection of my own species."

"But this isn't about territory or food shortages... you're just exterminating them. What other species does that?"

"Humans do."

Fatima laughed.

"What?" Devonia asked.

"I'm trying to imagine what an Aradian population would be like..."

"Perhaps more of us will exist someday. But it's not likely."

"Why not?"

"Because no one wants this. There is nothing lonelier than being an Immortal."

The tent flap rustled softly. Devonia turned towards the sound, listening intently to the light, near-silent footsteps walking away from them.

"What is it?" Fatima asked.

"Nothing," Devonia lied, not wanting to reveal that Seth had heard their conversation. "Just the wind."

That morning things moved quickly. The trucks were in position and the mercenaries had already crawled under the overhangs like canyon wolves, sniffing lines of amphetamines to keep their edge while they glassed their target areas. The mountains of Pakistan wore icy capes that shed their snow in great vapor trails shadowing their western faces. It was time. The morning air was good for flying, and the demons were still asleep in their caves. In an hour, they'd be swarming the hills like blasphemous wasps conjured from Hell's depths.

"The F-22's are inbound. Better to kill them in their sleep," Devonia said to the operators.

She was right. Destroying a whole colony of harpies was no easy undertaking. The devilish creatures were tougher than humans and this particular sub-species had skin the color of the pale granite around them. Just finding them was a constant task, left chiefly to Oden and Seth, who had traded his broken sword for a scepter that held an orb of red tiger's eye at its forked end. The operators allowed Seth to give the first order, since he'd be their contact when traveling ahead with the tracker.

"What do I say?" he asked as they stood on a precarious perch.

Devonia watched the rows of mountain ranges with shifting eyes. The operator knelt next to Seth as they looked at the map.

"Think of it from their perspective. How would you want to be oriented? What would you want to know?"

Seth closed his eyes then opened them and spoke into his radio. "Phoenix Two, this is Air-Operations."

"Go ahead Air Ops."

"I'd like to request a full run on objectives alpha through

hotel for starters. The winds are light and out of the east. Visibility is good. No clear hazards at this time. You're cleared hot."

"Copy that Air Ops, we'll be there shortly. ETA ten minutes."

Devonia smiled. "That wasn't so hard, was it?"

"I'm not used to using machines in a fight," Seth admitted.

"Welcome to a whole different game, Sararan."

The jets shook the valley with a thunderous roar, their engines built by engineers who'd been taught the rare power of fission. The bombs tumbled onto the hillsides and seemed to crack the mountain open with new fissures and chutes. Smoke lay flat over the terraces in the aftermath of the bombardment and the screams of the wounded rose from the aquamarine glow. Harpies clamored above the rubble, their charred lungs choking for air.

"God damn," Seth said, impressed with the results.

"Call in another, same targets," Devonia ordered.

Seth called in another airstrike and the entire range seemed to cough up grey phlegm as the jets screamed overhead and their roar echoed along the canyons. Avalanches drowned the wounded in rushing rivers of snow, and thousands of harpies lay dead and dismembered as the smoke cleared.

They watched the scene dissipate and let the jets return for refueling. They waited several minutes. A few rifle shots rang out. Then confirmation came.

"That's all of them," one of the Sikhs said over the radio.

"Copy that. Meet us at the next rendezvous."

"Okay. Let's move north. There will be more," Devonia said to the others, grabbing her spear and hiking back down the mountain as the team followed her.

They moved from range to range, continuing with the same tactics and often leaving the bodies to rot in those stone towers of silence. After becoming highly efficient at executing air strikes and training local militias to ambush escaping legions, the team soon became a well-greased machine, able to move fifty miles a day and obliterate the enemy before drones could be sent north to warn other colonies. Once the pilots had built up enough trust in Seth, he began abandoning protocol altogether in order to direct bomb runs from the actual target zone for more accurate delivery. He weathered furious harpies, explosions and raining boulders alike and kept himself protected by understanding his environment and concentrating his energy on making his Sararan bones ultra-resilient to the shock waves.

    The operators found their place in the mountains with the mercenaries, and after many battles they deviated from regulation and fell into rank with the clan of savages, dismissing their crisp fatigues for fur robes cut from the three-eyed snow leopards they'd killed. The creatures stalked the men at all hours and cried terribly at the pale sky like shrieking babies. The coalition began to fear these sly creatures more than death itself after a man was pulled from a tank and found toyed with and skinned alive to scorn the human's usage of their offspring's coats. No one slept after the incident, and they couldn't afford the stagnancy anyway. They began to acclimatize to their sleep-deprived state, conducting full scale attacks by day and hunting Casanova incubi at night. As they fanned through the blasted scree, each collected harpy talons and flight feathers as trophies of war and wore them around their necks or sold them to merchants on the treacherous silk road.

As the coalition moved north through the valleys and mountains, they annihilated innumerable monsters, sometimes accidentally bombing small communities of humans where Devonia would turn a blind eye as the men threw the carcasses of families in the same pits as the dead harpies. Despite the collateral damage, they made great progress in those first few weeks of the surge. Devonia eventually discharged the support chain due to Himalayan obstructions, and the Immortals led the mercenaries and operators on camelback into strange lands.

When they arrived at the Gobi, all geological distinction dropped away, and the hills suffocated the flora and rose in a vast red plateau. Even the air was red. The barren desert wheezed with a ceaseless wind as the dust swirled and blew the shells of locust larvae across the waste, where the thin altitude gripped their veins and the air burned with a rusty haze over the dissolving edge of the world.

Devonia had prepared the men for the severe environment, outfitting the mercenaries with protective suits and oxygen tanks as resident cosmonauts of a writhing iron age, the tubes coming from their flat-faced masks making them resemble outcast sons of Ganesh turned wasteland storm troopers. They carried only what they could, mostly ammunition, water bags and dried ibex meat tucked in their satchels. They'd commandeered Almuruna-era solar panels for shields and hid glass weapons in every article of clothing.

At that point in their deployment, they had developed such a taste for savagery that they'd ornamented their rifle stalks with the teeth of infant harpies, which glowed like pearls in the corroded light, and the clinking black scalps of their victims, which hung from their battle-worn scepters still flying Iraq's crimson flag.

Devonia scented the evening air as she led the group onto open ground.

"Looks like Mars," Oden muttered through his mask.

"And how do you know what Mars looks like?" one of the Sikhs asked.

"I've seen pictures."

The others laughed.

"He's right! I've seen them too!", one of the operators exclaimed. "Space programs have been landing rovers on Mars since 1997, and there were even colonial missions in the early '30s before World War III. The first humans on another planet... wow... I wonder what happened to them."

One of the ex-patriots chuckled. "By now they're just a pile of bones waiting to be considered false martians by whoever finds them."

They walked for miles in silence, wondering when their own species would become some archeological discovery for alien life to question.

After a while, Seth sensed something and whistled to Devonia. She looked back behind them. Far to the west was a mirage of cloud forming over the sun. The men turned their animals to gaze at it as well. None could rightly describe the sight. They watched and waited.

"What if its locusts?" one of the operators asked.

"What if it's not?" another answered.

A few seconds passed, and once the things were within sight of the Aradian, she whistled loudly to the team.

"It's a flock. Prepare for attack. Take cover behind that rock fixture to the east. Air-Ops, come with me."

"Where would you like me?" Seth asked Devonia.

"See that ripple in the sky to the north?"

Seth squinted in the direction and nodded. "About thirty miles out?"

"Yes. I need you to go to it. It's a hole in the ozone layer. There was an M-class solar flare on the sun recently and its currently pounding the planet with charged particles. Absorb the ultra-violet rays to near combustion, then come back and help us."

He nodded and put his hand on her shoulder. "Hey," he said, meeting her gaze. "Be safe."

"You too," she said, offering him a rare smile.

He winked and walked away, pointing his scepter forward like a spear and sprinting deftly over the rocks and dunes.

Devonia made sure they were far enough away from the rest of the group before she ordered the operators to halt.

"There's at least ten legions of harpies coming this way, and fast. We need to slow their advancement. We don't want them going any further east."

"Lord Pavonis."

"What?"

One of the operators pointed back east, where another flock had risen above the darkening horizon. Devonia focused her eyesight on them.

"How many are there?" one of the operators asked as he set up his communication instruments.

"Another twenty thousand."

"Shit!"

Devonia telepathically spoke to Seth to relay the new information.

"Ready for your orders," the operator claimed.

"First thing's first," Devonia said, looking around frantically as she improvised a plan against the heavy ambush. "Let Command know this is a prairie fire emergency. Bring in bombers from the south and have them strafe the harpies advancing toward our position from the west. I want strategic long-range fighters to engage the legions to the east and get me some air cavalry to come in behind them. Deploy all available aircraft immediately."

The operators went to work, ordering resources.

The skies grew dark with the death of the day, and an eerie wind played softly on their still bodies. Nearly an hour passed.

"How long until support arrives?"

"Twenty minutes, Lord Pavonis. What are those harpies doing?"

"They're still coming. The closest one is still fifteen miles out from either legion. We'll have a small buffer but not a very good one. Be prepared to drop some close ordinance."

"Copy that, ma'am."

They waited. Devonia ordered the snipers to prioritize shooting male drones, since they were the key to the harpy queen's propagation. The sound of thousands of flapping wings came within range and the men hid their fear behind their silent motions of preparation. Devonia continued looking from west to east, watching the massive legions close in while scanning the dark for signs of Seth or the bombers. There was nothing.

"Hurry up, dammit!" she whispered.

"Bombers are inbound!" the operator said.

A rumbling came from the south and the bomber fleet arrived high above them. The combat controller got on the line.

"Skipper, this is Air-Ops. About two thousand meters off

your port side, you'll see the targets closing in on our position. We'll be pretty close but go ahead and begin your first run five hundred meters to our west, you're cleared hot."

"Copy that, Air-Ops. This one's gonna be danger close."

The harpies were within an eighth of a mile and their screeches filled the night air with a sickening echo. They neither retreated nor broke formation when the bombers unleashed their ordinance. When the bombs exploded so did the rifles of the mercenaries. The line of fire lit up Devonia's face as she took her spear and cast a rejective wave of energy to block herself and the operators from the billowing flames. Their temporary dome of sanctuary became wrapped in fire and the operators held their heads frightfully as the soles of their boots cooked and smoked.

"Call in another!" Devonia ordered as the enemy formations collapsed and quickly re-aligned.

The scent of burning flesh filled the air as the bombers turned around and flew in lower, moving faster, dropping more bombs than the first run. Another whoosh of fire swept past them and the Earth shook and cracked. The sound of fighters roaring overhead was followed by more bombs and machine guns, until the harpies alas came through the smoke and fire and made contact with the mercenaries.

Devonia closed her eyes and spoke through her third eye. Please hurry, Seth. We need you now.

They were being attacked on all sides. The fires from the bombings illuminated the night air, and the scene was a horrific masquerade of murder. One of the mercenary's oxygen tanks exploded and turned him and three others into pink dust. The rest dropped their suits and masks for fear of further incidents and faced the seething creatures naked like Greek heroes sent to expel Hades' minions.

Devonia used her spear for its primitive purpose and

began skewering the screaming winged demons by the dozen. They attacked her and slashed at her but she became meaner with each blow. Heavy machine gun fire opened up and when the helicopters arrived, no sound could be rightfully distinguished in that unraveling bloodbath. Helicopter propellers hit the flying monsters and crashed, torn from the sky by the weight of the clinging cyclopes.

Bombers continued their runs on the outskirts of their position as more creatures poured into the region. The concentration of hate and anger and pain seemed to be unearthed from the core of the planet, and the mercenaries were being overrun by the heathen horde, that disdainful plenty who were joined by an array of behemoth spiders and rows of python-like centipedes who shared an obscene armistice with the slack-jawed devils. One of the mercenaries ran out of bullets and started lighting harpies on fire with a torch until he himself was caught up in the conflagration as the enflamed demons smothered him, laughing as they burned to death with him.

Devonia looked around at the overwhelming violence. The air operators had been halved as giant centipedes fed on their guts. The mercenaries were fighting for their lives in cornered positions and piling bodies around them with no break in the blitz and no ammunition reserves to sustain their counterattack. The bombers were crashing in the distance like falling stars and the fighter jets had all but left the atrocity for fear of what may come.

In the middle of the madness, Devonia swung her weapon through a mass of spiders and harpies, sending bodies in all directions as more came piling in. She kept killing, the blood and gore of the animals pouring on her like a gruesome rain as she screamed and fought with ferocity. When Seth arrived, the creatures looked up with sunken eyes and began to fly or crawl away. Devonia looked up from her kneeling position panting, her skin dripping with blood and gristle. The almighty Sararan levitated over the atrocity, shining with a bright yellow glow above the scattering fiends.

"Do it," Devonia said, burrowing deep under the sand.

The army of harpies retreated madly as Seth closed his eyes and raised his hands. The ground shook with a coming energy, and from his hands and feet and torso an emanation of blue bolts followed a blinding white blast in every direction; a gamma ray burst on a small scale, his Sararan circuits accommodated by the atoms around him, bringing total incineration to all mortal life within eye's grasp.

When Devonia awoke from the explosion, Seth was watching her sleep, reclining on the baking, shattered glass. It was midday, and the scorching sun fell upon the still burning black bodies that covered the desert around them as far as the eye could see. Wrecked aircraft smoldered on the horizon and a fog of black smoke had settled over the bombarded crust of the Earth. Fifty thousand harpies lay smoldering, their stench far reaching and already changing the climate.

"Well, that got out of hand quickly, didn't it?" Seth announced, chewing on a blade of wheat grass.

"How long was I out?" Devonia asked, wondering where he'd gotten the wheat from.

"A few hours. You haven't slept since you woke up in the Sahara, have you? That's not healthy, you know."

"Yeah well, neither are celestial events inside the

atmosphere. You're lucky the black hole you created collapsed at its onset," she said pointedly.

"I tried to be subtle but you know how these things go. It's like dropping acid. Sometimes you get a hit, sometimes you get four or five." He shrugged.

"You accomplished the task. That's all that matters for now."

Devonia stood up, the glass cracking like ice around her feet. She grasped her spear and twisted it in the ground, breaking the red glass in spiraling ripples that spread throughout the land in great fractal formations. She coughed up some spores and seeds and threw them into the wind, finishing her spell with a short, whispered mantra. Her eyes opened.

"By nightfall this place will be a forest."

"Won't that bring locusts?"

"The plant and fungal species are hybrids. Completely unsusceptible to the insects."

"What will the seeds take root in?"

"The bodies of the dead."

Seth nodded approvingly. "So... what now?" he asked, spitting out the wheat and standing wearily.

"We keep hunting."

Devonia looked at the rot and devastation, the bodies of the mercenaries nearly indistinct from the corpses around them. Aircraft wreckage lay in the distance like ancient capsized ships in a dried up sea.

Sighing heavily, she gestured to Seth and they headed south, continuing their conquest as if nothing had happened. It was just them again. No support units. No mercenaries. No air force. Just two Immortals wandering the old world in search of a greater purpose.

They walked for three days before Seth said something. The rough flat ground sprawled in every direction, and their voices were hollow in the featureless wasteland.

"Devonia," he called out.

She continued walking ahead of him silently.

"Pavonis. Lord Pavonis. Whatever you want to be called. Where are we going?"

She looked over her shoulder as she kept on. "Does it matter? We're exterminating a creature that has crept into nearly every crevice of the planet. What else do you need to know?"

"I don't know," he shrugged. "Perhaps confirmation that the harpy queen in that flock was killed since, you know, our whole team was destroyed along with half a squadron of aircraft? And don't forget those bitching camels you traded the tanks for. I'd also like to know how you plan on telling your girlfriend what happened—"

"Do you want to lose your skin?" Devonia said sternly, turning around and glaring at him with her gem-like purple eyes.

Seth grinned. "I don't care if you're a lesbian."

"I am not... ugh! God damn you, Seth," she muttered as she turned and walked away from him, picking up her pace as she sensed him following her.

"Talk to me, Devonia, what's going on?" he asked as chased her down.

She looked back but kept going, swiping her foot along the ground and creating a sand trap behind her. Seth was following too close and dropped into the invisible pit. A puff of dust rose as he coughed and climbed out quickly. He caught back up to her.

"What did I do? Was it the flying? You're Aradian, Devonia, I bet you could fly if you—"

Seth stopped abruptly as she turned and levitated several feet off the ground, a purple flame ghosting past her eyes as her aura suddenly brought in high winds behind her.

"Seth, if you don't shut the fuck up, I'm going to sell your skull on the silk road for the price of a fig pit!"

She dropped to the ground and kept walking. Seth smiled and chased her, his adrenaline still pulsing from the aftermath of his signature quasar.

"So you can fly! Why did you hide your talents for so long? I thought I was the con-artist. It's because you really are divine, isn't it? You know you're better than everyone but you want to be humble... I get it. That's noble of you. Look at us. We're learning a lot about each other. What else haven't you told me, Devonia? Are you really the last Aradian? I heard that your old training partner came out of hiding; that she's an Immortal too. I wonder what turned her. It takes some sort of resistance or arduous undertaking for the transformation to take place if you're not a natural born like myself... what made you come out of your human cocoon to become the exalted creature I see before me?"

Devonia stopped and turned so quickly that Seth almost stumbled into her. Tears of blood were running down her cheeks.

"I was tortured," she said quietly, before walking away again.

Seth finally ceased his questioning and followed her as she scented the air, following some old tracks. The desert winds blew and swept a wave of locust eggs between them.

"Devonia," Seth said timidly.

"What?" she snapped.

"Look at the eggs."

They were alive. Unhatched. Ready to open and lay waste to whole swathes of the Earth, from the low fields to the high mountain gardens. They watched the small white eggs swirl in the wind and drift off again. Within minutes they could hear a swarm approaching. A low droning from some inexplicable origin. The buzzing amplified and shook the small rocks on the ground like rolling dice. It was a chaotic cadence, the symphony of the century. A sound no one wanted to hear. Seth looked at her with a blank expression.

"What do we do now?"

Devonia shook her head and shrugged angrily. "What am I, God?"

"I just figured you had more experience with this. I'm less concerned about the bugs than what eats them."

"Yeah… no shit."

They stood motionless as the mutant insects came forth, their millions of wings flapping in a tenacious rhapsody as they blocked the sun and turned the sky black with their seemingly infinite stream. The Immortals cooled their bodies and hardened their skin to make themselves both invisible and impenetrable to the hellacious bugs. Still they clung to them and investigated the lone beings with their fiberglass antenna and stereoscopic eyes. The mass flew by, screeching through the sky, their hand-sized bodies taking up almost every space for miles in that desolate zone.

Then they heard it. A soft moan beneath them. Devonia put her hand out for Seth to stay, but he was eager to take action.

"Don't move, Seth. Just let it feed."

The locusts changed their course as the moaning grew louder, but they could not escape the beast. Suddenly, a rumbling came from beneath them, an earthquake made from collapsing caverns where the megalodon was carving its way through the dirt and bedrock. An explosion of rocks erupted as the incredible serpent rose into the air, it's black eyes haunting in their lidless gaze. It opened its incredible mouth and swallowed the insects by the millions, roaring and gnashing at the them as it slithered along the ground, cracking the crust of the desert as if it were a fragile shell.

Devonia and Seth stood and watched as it fed from the outer edges of the swarm inward, its mile long body circling them widely like an ouroboros nearly swallowing its own tail. The creature crushed entire landscapes and rock formations and depleted the locust population with jaws that could bite the tip off a mountain and spit it into space beyond the planet's orbit like a titan throwing back the osseous culmination of God's triumphs, defiling the very essence of creation in its insatiable rage. The great fish came back around towards them as the locusts dispersed into smaller factions. Seth stood fast.

"Just. Stay. Put," Devonia whispered.

The leviathan dropped down to the ground and barreled its way toward them. It slowed just meters before the Immortals and smelled the statue-like beings. Devonia held her moonstone and whispered some calming spell. What effect it would have on such a creature, she didn't know, but the creature seemed unthreatened, its hunger met. Its large eyes darted between the two as it studied them. Seth's hand found his grandfather's dagger, but Devonia shook her head slowly.

"Let it happen, Seth," she whispered as the creature smelled their bodies still stained with gunpowder and the blood of harpies.

When its curiosity had been satiated, it moved away from them and returned beneath the ground, shaking the Earth as it went until the end of its tail disappeared and the pebbles and dead locusts rattled no more on the mired plateau.

CHAPTER 59 – DOOM ASCETICS

When their tracks had circled the heart of the Gobi twice over, Devonia finally gave up. The harpies had mocked her in their counter-tracking, and with the arrival of the locust season she was out of time anyway. She, along with Seth, the mercenaries and the Iraqi coalition, had killed a quarter of the harpy population in two months. But it wasn't enough. Soon, Fatima and the other world leaders would be fueling the bombers for a whole different kind of assault.

It was a calm evening when Devonia sent the message of defeat to her lover. She wrote a heartfelt note on her device and pressed send, smashing the transmitter on the rocks immediately after. Seth came up to her as she gazed at the vast empty desert gleaming blue under the stars. He sat down and looked up at the sky.

"No matter what they say, you did one hell of a job. Had we taken a different route or planned things any other way, I don't think we would have been as successful. It was a valiant campaign, Pavonis. One that will be remembered for all of time."

She scoffed. "Remembered by who? Humans don't care about what we do anymore."

"But we do it for them anyway, because we must."

"Sometimes I ask myself why I even bother."

"Because you used to be human," he said.

"And yet you never were. Why do you involve yourself in this fight, Sararan?"

Seth chuckled awkwardly. "You knew my father, when you were younger, right?"

"I was very young and saw him seldomly at the palace before his possession."

"I've been told he was a noble king before the witch seduced him. And even though he was a Sararan, he held true to the virtues that make men great, having been trained by those with a reputation for honor and strength. Maybe it's my desire to be something similar that drives me to do what we do."

Devonia nodded. "Before his possession, Michael seemed like a good man. I loved Melody like a mother since I never had one of my own. But when Michael left, everything went terribly wrong."

"What did you do after Melody died, out at sea?"

"What could I do? Her blood was in the ocean. The creatures that consumed it turned into malicious beasts and we had to adapt quickly. Myself and a few others who survived the storm landed in Africa and hid as best we could. We were in Libya at first, then West Africa, where my company came under attack by raiders and I was kidnapped. I lived with my captors for three months until one day my Aradian genes kicked in. In the hell holes of South Sudan is where the tales of my headhunting began."

"Yeesh. I bet those were some sorry bastards."

"Not very many humans have challenged me since then. They know better. I live to heal the Earth, but I'll kill any man where he stands. What about you... I mean... the battle of Geneva happened over you. You're going to tell me you were raised by merchants in Cairo after so much effort was put in to save you?"

"I must have gotten separated from Avestan somehow since I never met them... only heard stories. Tala meant to deliver me to the Zurvans. Instead, I had a series of pseudo-parents after living with lions for the formative years of my childhood."

"It's amazing no one wanted to kill you for fear of your heritage."

"Oh, they did. There are anti-Immortal folks all over the Savannah. I killed my first assassin at the age of seven with a pitchfork. Luckily no one expects a kid with super strength to throw a farm tool through their chest and a have pride of lions behind them to finish the job."

They laughed and sat for a moment in silence.

"What the hell do we do now?" Seth asked.

She looked at him and smiled.

"What?" he asked.

"Nothing," she said, seemingly very happy all of a sudden. "You're just very... I don't know the word."

"Charming?" he winked.

"I wouldn't go that far, but it's something," she laughed.

They looked into each other's eyes intimately for a moment, until Devonia could feel his burning desire, and she quickly looked toward the horizon.

"Let's fly to Tibet. Something tells me we should visit the Zurvans, since I doubt the coalition even considered them in their council for nuclear war."

"Oh so now you want fly?" Seth asked.

They took to the air as floating deities, soaring high over the mighty Himalayas, far above a harpies limits, where the thin icy air played lightly against their arms. They watched one another as they twirled and dove, the cusp of the Earth shadowing their angelic figures. They laughed like children in a dream as the sun's light cascaded a thousand shades of ultra-violet over them, their bodies a morphing scape of changing temperatures and organ adjustments as the brutal conditions of space set in. They were high above the Earth and thrust themselves upward until they were completely free, floating in the ether. Devonia looked longingly into the void. Seth floated over to her.

"What is it?"

She reached her hand out and held it up as if presenting something. "That's where it would be now. Our moon. It's hard for me to even describe it to you. I thought about replacing it, but the task would take centuries."

He nodded and tried to imagine.

"The Earth will be doomed if its rotation isn't slowed," she said.

"Do you mean the Earth, or life on Earth?" he asked.

She closed her eyes and remembered it; the luminosity of a full moon shining down like a divine mirror for all the world to admire.

She looked back toward Earth. The planet was no longer the brilliant blue world it had once been. What seas remained had sunken into the trenches of the ocean floor with giant islands of trash sloshing between their toxic shores. Between them, brown and red deserts stretched across the surface; only the high elevation temperate zones, far above the mutant aphids and scorching lowlands, could maintain any greenery. Cobalt clouds swirled thickly in the western half of the world, which had been choked with countless cyclones for years, some a thousand miles wide, fixated in their turbulent regions while the polluted air came alive with veins of green lightning.

Seth was looking at her intently when she turned back to him.

"You really are Mother Earth. I can tell you care a lot for what's going on down there."

"I always have."

As they watched their planet in turmoil, they slowly descended, the air thickening as they dropped through the clouds and down further into a fog. Eventually, they touched down on the steps of an old monastery, perched on a cliffside in the mountains of Nepal.

An old man sat at the foot of the temple steps with his legs crossed. He breathed so slowly he seemed dead. Vine-laden statues of the Buddha stood behind him, and the dharma wheel hung in midair between them, suspended by magnets buried in the mountain. Devonia approached him and knelt formally. She closed her eyes. Seth watched her, and he could tell they were speaking telepathically. The old man opened his left eye and watched Seth for a moment before closing it. He stood. Devonia stayed kneeling but watched him closely.

He opened his eyes and smiled. "Nga-to delek."

He turned and led them up the steps. Seth asked Devonia what he'd said, and she shrugged. They could hear the monks humming like holy toads in the stone halls of the temple as they climbed. Dew drops fell quietly from teetering leaves and bent flower petals, for what had once been a snow-covered region was now a high mountain garden, suspended in a perfect ecosystem on the plateau's monolithic peaks. The air was fresh and smelled of wet earth, carrying an essence of tranquility with it.

They walked to the top of the steps where the old man led them to the entrance of the temple. The stone hall was massive, with hundreds of monks kneeling in a circle. Candles were lit between them, and a ring of suspended fire licked the ceiling and illuminated a forty-foot tall tortoise, its shell glistening with gold paintings as it rested its massive head on stacks of yak hide. The monks continued their mantra as Devonia ran to it. She knew immediately the identity of the creature and hugged its neck as she wept.

"Boris!"

Seth watched from afar, unsure of exactly what was going on. Devonia cried and embraced the creature, looking into its eyes and smiling and laughing as if it were her own child reunited. The monks quieted their mantra and left the hall.

"My sweet Devonia," the tortoise said loudly, his deep voice bellowing through the halls.

Seth stared wide-eyed at the talking reptile but watched and listened as Devonia spoke.

"You can talk!"

"Many Sub-Sararan species can, we just choose not to. It's good to see you again, Devonia."

"I thought you died when you were cast off the ship!"

"I almost did, but I held my breath for a very long time and was thrown onto the jagged shores of Cyprus, as was the empress. My cuts had absorbed some of Melody's blood, and it was enough to transform me. But, of course, along with my own transformation came those of hundreds of other creatures, many of them far more dangerous than I. After many years of avoiding captivity I was rescued by the Zurvans, protected in this tranquil mountain pass."

He looked to the back of the hall. "Come, Prince. Let me see your face."

Seth walked forward and bowed. Boris looked him over with his massive eyes and chuckled.

"So you're the one they call Seth. I could sense your energy long before you stepped onto the mountain. I had thought you would arrive sooner."

"With all due respect, I'm not sure what you're talking about."

"Can you not feel the energy of another Immortal vibrating along the plane that connects all our subconscious?"

"Well... yes, but only at certain distances—"

"My young Sararan... there is a Zurvan here who has been waiting a very long time to see you. But it will have to wait until morning. We take the time of day here very seriously, no matter how contorted the day may be, for to reach harmony is our one and only objective."

"I will abide by your wishes, and look forward to the morning."

Devonia kissed her tortoise good night, hugging him for a few minutes until Seth finally coaxed her away.

The old man stood at the door and led them along hundreds of twisting cliffside steps until they arrived at some ruins half swallowed by the moss and mountainside. The old man turned and bowed.

"Sleep now," he said quickly, smiling. He looked at both of them before disappearing into the cloak of darkness.

The night took them, and for whatever reason the Immortals did attempt to sleep for those few short hours of night. Perhaps it was the exhaustion of war, or their bodies adjusting to the vacuum of space and back again, or their desire to hide in their dreams as they longed for a fantasy apart from their dissonant world. They laid there a while as they closed their eyes and synchronized themselves to the placid night. Seth opened one of his star-like eyes and watched Devonia. She opened one of hers and looked back at him.

"What do you want?"

"Sorry," he said, turning back over.

"No, seriously, what is it? Are you okay?"

"Yeah... I mean... I just feel like we've shared a moment

like this before. It's strange."

"Oh don't be getting all sentimental on me," she sighed. "I thought I was supposed to be the one sleeping more."

"Maybe it's déjà vu, or memories from a past life. I've been told that I'm the reincarnation of Ezra, my grandfather. What would that mean?"

"Well, I've been told I'm the reincarnation of Ingrid. What would THAT mean?"

"I'm not sure. But if I could ever be with a woman as incredible as you, I'd feel pretty lucky."

"Thanks Seth. You're sweet."

He smiled and she laughed. Before long, Devonia was sound asleep, her neck muscles pulsing lightly as her body morphed subtly, a motionless reconfiguration to the untrained eye, like tracking the heavenly bodies arcing against the spinning cusp of the world. Seth lay awake for some time, processing his thoughts as he aimed his bright eyes upward into the cosmos, wondering where the moon was and why Tala had taken it, and why she had killed his mother, and why she had killed his father's godmother, and yet not him, a golden prodigy of a befouled generation, not yet spoiled by the treachery of false allies; knowing only the camaraderie and belonging war provides, like each his fathers before him.

Seth looked over at Devonia, who was sound asleep, and yet her eyes opened wide, those binary purple green orbs of gelled nebula looking back at their ancestry as if frozen in time, delaying the details of those stars providence as they churned a noble reckoning. Devouring the dust of old worlds. Seizing the void silently. Her gaze had been vested in these proceedings and hence called out to them, inviting the universe to indulge in their approaching exchange like some grand anti-sacrament, befitting for a congregation of dying gods.

When they awoke, the sun had not yet risen over the massive peaks as the monks lined up on the ridge for morning meditation. A bell was rung to signify dawn's coming, and the old man appeared again to greet the Immortals. He gave them fermented yaks' milk, which they drank appreciatively, before he took the cups back and opened a hidden door into the old ruins.

"Yesterday, you arrived. Today, you leave. But first, you must go inside," the old man said before bowing and walking away.

Devonia turned to Seth, who seemed apprehensive.

"I'll go," she said.

She stepped confidently into the dank old temple. Dim light snuck through the doorway, illuminating the rows of columns that lined the black abyss. From behind one of the columns, a voice spoke quietly.

"Melody?"

Devonia stopped and scanned the room for the creature, but her sensory abilities saw only a faint heartbeat pulsing behind the stone pillar.

"It's okay, I'm not going to hurt you."

"The door! Shut the door! I don't want the light!" the voice insisted.

Devonia nodded for Seth to close the temple doorway, and he rolled the massive circular stone over it, shutting out the last bit of light with the sound of scraping rock. The creature appeared, but Devonia could only make out it's thin profile with her echolocation. It crouched and kept its distance.

"What are you doing here?" it asked in a shaky, weak voice.

"I'm Devonia Ketevan, Princess of Almuruna, reincarnation of Lord Pavonis. We've come to visit you."

"Devonia?" it asked.

"Yes. May we speak with you," she asked as she walked towards it.

The creature scampered back behind the column. "What do you want? Are you here to kill me?"

"No. Please, come out. We can help you."

The creature tiptoed slowly out from hiding, revealing its eyes: small blue flames suspending the smallest array of sparks in their depths. The creature was malnourished and starved, with pale white skin and scars on its back where wings had been hacked off. It had no hair on its body and its face had been mutilated, its ears and nose sliced off and left to heal. The being's ghoulish appearance was striking to Devonia in the cold blue light, and she gasped as she saw him for who he was.

"Michael..." she whispered. "How long have you been here?"

"Many suns," he said, moving backwards just out of the way of a thin yet tempting beam of light. "One day I awoke from a terrible nightmare. A nightmare where I killed and tortured millions of innocent lives. But it wasn't a nightmare. I did those things."

"You aren't accountable for what you did, Michael. You were being possessed by Frau—"

"DON'T SAY THAT NAME!" he shrieked wildly.

They stood in the dark together while the echo faded eerily through the long hall.

"She'll hear you," he whispered. "She's dead but she will

hear you. Curses linger in the wounds of the world. I am one of them."

"Why are you here? You need light to survive, Michael."

"I am empty of desire; devices; energy… I have made myself pure."

"No, Michael. You're hallucinating from starvation and on the cusp of death. You need to step into the sunlight."

Michael shook his head rapidly.

Devonia stepped forward cautiously and reached for him. "Take my hand."

"What if I don't?"

"You can't stay here forever."

He reluctantly reached out to her and a short spark arced between their fingers.

"You tricked me!" he yelped as he reeled back and held his hand up to his face like a wounded child.

"It's okay, Michael. Your body is so hungry for solar energy that it's borrowing some of mine. Please, come outside. It will feel good and make you healthy again."

"Why should I? So humans can take me away and torture me for what I've done?"

"You have the right to be afraid, but we need you, Michael. You are one of the last Immortals. Deep down, you still have the heroic heart to do what is right. You've lived your life as a warrior, a king, a tyrant, and a monk. But there is one role you've yet to fulfil, a powerful role perhaps more crucial than any before."

Michael looked up curiously.

"Come to the doorway, there's someone you should meet."

He crawled behind Devonia and she told Seth to open the door. The rock scraped open again. She stepped behind him and nudged Michael forward as the orange glow poured in. His anemic skin was instantly assaulted, and his eyes burned bright with fire as he gasped and shook. He clenched his fists and coughed as smoke rose from the skin on his thinly wrapped spine and ribcage. A shadow came between him and the incoming light and he looked up, his eyes flickering as he struggled to see the articulations of the creature before him.

"Father?" Seth asked.

Michael grasped his son's hands in his, weeping with streams of blood as he knelt like a blasphemer begging his redeemer for forgiveness. By the grace of the sun, golden halos rounded their heads like transient evidence of a higher power; an exhibit of holy rites any script would have embossed eternal, yet no chronicle sufficed its capture. The emperor in exile, his Sararan prince, and the goddess of the world stood together, now a triad of Immortals relinquishing their fears of mania as they emerged from the temple: prophets in a God-hating world.

Michael pulled himself up weakly, still sickened by his own wickedness. The Immortals ushered him out of the door as if he were a halfwit transferring asylums. He hid his eyes from the light and stared down at the ground, away from the trees or sky or air, fearful now of everything before him, as he would discover the grim effects of his undoing which consisted of horrors beyond righteous explanation or catalogue. The Immortals said goodbye to Boris and the monks, promising to relay the Zurvans' plea for denuclearization amid rising tensions between humans and the dominant harpy hordes.

Seth watched as Michael stumbled down the mountain in his saffron robes, wondering what was going through his father's mind.

"Will one of you carry me?" the former emperor asked. "My legs are in so much pain."

"That's because your nerve endings are waking up. You need to exercise your muscles," Devonia reminded him.

Seth shook his head and spoke under his breath. "Some Sararan he is."

"Your father has been through more than you can imagine. He was possessed for an unhealthy amount of time," Devonia said sharply.

"Uh huh... and how much is a healthy amount of time?"

"Possession under fifty seconds usually won't inflict any long term damage. Your father was possessed for ten months."

Michael hung his head as they walked. After the death of his lover, the death of his empire, his defeat in the war which was fought over his heir, and all the torture and gloom and isolation he'd been subjected to since, he couldn't look his son in the eye.

They stopped after a few miles and Devonia took counsel with Seth while Michael scrambled to a creek edge for a drink.

"His healing process is taking longer than it should. We won't get anywhere at this pace," Devonia whispered.

"Why don't we fly?"

"We will. I just wanted him to get his legs under him, but it seems there's more work than I had expected."

"Why won't his body heal like a Sararan? His nose hasn't even grown back."

"I'm not sure. Perhaps he is as cursed as he claims to be."

"You really think we're going to be able to utilize him as

an asset? As of now about all he's good for is a distraction."

"It's about more than that now," she said as she watched Michael sip the crystal clear water in his shaking cupped hands. "He's a symbol."

"For what?"

"I don't know yet."

They kept on for a bit longer, the young Immortals trying to coax Michael to increase his pace, if not at least walk straight. Years ago, his legs had been broken by an angry mob, the same group who had cut up his face and dragged him through rocks behind a pair of oxen. Although he'd escaped and healed, his body hadn't mended as it should have. Seth made his own conclusions as he watched his father from afar.

"It seems not even Sararans are immune to melancholia."

Devonia didn't respond.

They continued their trek, following the panophobic creature like scientists observing the customs of a lost primate traveling back from the recesses of extinction.

That evening, Seth picked up his frail father in his arms and the Immortals flew over Pakistan, where just a month before they'd slain colonies of harpies. The caves had already filled with new vermin, their fires widespread, their nests deeply rooted as they swarmed in the base of the valleys, unafraid of bombers or Immortals or any form of resistance to their advancing front. Seth and Devonia watched the build up with heavy hearts but said nothing.

Devonia scanned the horizon and watched the swarms move below like locusts. Then it hit her. She smiled and looked at Seth as they zipped through the air.

"Seth, take Michael to the canals where the Tarnak river used to flow."

"But that's in the heart of leviathan territory."

"I know. I'm going to try something. I'll catch up in a few minutes."

Seth flew to the base of the mountains and touched down on the flats where the desert spread out wide from the canyons westward. Michael was shaking from the cold of the mesosphere as he knelt on the ground.

"Do you need more than a robe, old man?"

"Perhaps," he said weakly.

Seth walked over to a dead olive tree and spit fire, igniting it like a beacon on that lonely plain. Michael walked over to it and put his hands up to the flame.

"Thank you, son," he said.

Seth nodded and put his hand on Michael's back. "No problem. You'll get better soon. Don't you worry."

Michael attempted to smile, but his anxiety seemed irrevocable as his eyes sagged with woe.

Devonia arrived soon after carrying a creature of her own. She touched down, holding in her arms a harpy child, bound with barbed wire and bleeding on the sand as its gagged mouth collected tears.

"What is this suffering child?" Michael asked as his eyes darted between the Immortals and the bound prisoner being dropped on the ground.

"This particular being is an adolescent female of the species Homo harpia, a creature made by you and your succubus mistress during the height of your indulgence. You spliced birds with humans and gave them only one brain hemisphere too keep them mortal and vicious," she said to him bluntly.

Michael shook his head in disbelief. "Why are you torturing this poor creature?"

Seth stepped towards his father. "Because in a few months this poor creature will be a bloodthirsty killing machine. The whole reason we pulled you from self-imprisonment was to help exterminate them, so you better get on board with our operation, dig deep and remember a time when you gave zero fucks for the lives of the enemy, because this is the new reality."

Devonia pulled the improvised steel muzzle from the thing. It screamed at the setting sun, yelling its parents' names as it wept in anguish.

"How does it know the language of God?" Michael asked.

The Immortals did not answer, instead watching the thing squirm. The child shrieked proverbs and spoke ill of the Immortals, casting them as hypocrites and traitors to God, all in perfect Hebrew, cursing them to die alone.

"We'll be inviting more than harpies if this keeps up," Seth said nervously as he looked out over the megalodons breeding grounds.

"That's the idea," Devonia said. She rested her foot on the child's back, turning the harpy over with a kick and looking at its terrified expression as it pleaded for its life.

"This isn't right what you are doing!" Michael cried as he knelt and watched the pain in the child's eye as if he were experiencing the sensations himself.

Devonia kept her foot on the chest of the creature as she looked east, the sparks of the burning tree wafting over her hardened face. A black cloud rose behind the mountain, and she could hear the humming of thousands of beating wings.

"Colony, inbound. Be ready," she said as she lifted her spear and sunk it into the child's skull, a glug of blood coming out of its mouth as it seized like a dying insect before exhaling its final breath. Devonia didn't shift her gaze from the approaching swarm as she pulled the spear from the harpy's head and dug the bloody pilum into the sand.

"How could you do such a thing?" Michael sobbed as he held his bald head in his hands, clenching his gauzy skin helplessly as the ferocious beings approached.

Seth shook his head. "You're gonna have to harden up or you will die out here like this one. Hell... the way you look, you'd easily be mistaken for an ailing incubus."

Devonia tipped her head east. "Time to go."

They took off in a sprint, Seth carrying Michael since he couldn't keep up, leaving behind the dead harpy child to enrage the colony and lure them out into the open desert. Night had come but the clear skies and light winds made for perfect conditions. Once they were out in the middle of an old canal, Devonia stuck her spear in the sand and twisted it. She spoke quickly in Latin as she churned the sand with her right hand and held her moonstone in her left. After a few moments the spear lit red hot and they heard a roar from below the glassy deep.

"Whatever you're doing, make it quick," Seth said as the first waves of the swarm came upon them.

He used his scepter as a bludgeon and struck the incubus' skulls with each forceful swing, their limp bodies falling at Michael's feet as he cowered on the ground. Suddenly, a giant megalodon burst from the sand, sending the three Immortals into the air as they toppled over the dunes. The beast swallowed whole hordes of harpies. It was an elder leviathan, probably one of the first generations to be mutated; aged and pale like moonlight; hungry and ferocious, with decades of hunting experience. As the Immortals stepped quickly away from the madness, they watched four more leviathans erupt from their underground den, following the first one into the feeding frenzy as they devoured the invading creatures like a hydra, rooted in the underworld and yet far reaching.

The harpies quickly shifted their focus from the Immortals, fighting the megalodons directly by trying to gouge their eyes or retreating back to the mountains. As they watched the massive creatures snap at the fleeing savages, Seth and Devonia nodded and smiled, agreeing wordlessly that Devonia's new harpy-killing strategy was both effective and efficient. Michael breathed quickly and watched with wide burning eyes in horror as the giant fish dove back into their den far beneath the bed rock of the desert. They widened their stances to stay balanced as earthquakes shook the ground and receded just as quickly, with silence permeating the air at last.

"Let's go show Queen Fatima your new secret weapon. You think she will be receptive?"

"We'll find out soon. Michael?"

Michael had passed out from fear. Seth took him in his arms again and they ascended into the night, flying above old Iran where an unusually bright light was glowing from Mecca. They changed their course in that direction, and Devonia felt the aura of another Immortal approaching, a frequency she'd not felt since she was a human.

CHAPTER 60 – THE MONARCH

They arrived in Mecca just before sunrise. The lights of the metropolis shone in tremendous fluorescent green hoops, reaching far and wide over the Arabian Peninsula. Skyscrapers with walls of sheer black glass erupted from the desert floor at the city's blinding center, and small blinking antennae sprouted between the fields of solar panels like a mechanical forest rising over the desert sands, creating a modern day neon city. Many changes had taken place since Devonia had been there last. She'd thought the region too large for any one organism to claim suzerain, no matter how imperious their reach or lasting their loyalties. And although she'd made headway with the Arab prince on her visit a decade prior, his flag flew no longer, torn down and replaced with the red cloth of the New Republic of Iraq.

The Immortals floated down slowly and landed a half mile outside the city gates. Seth set Michael on the ground as he sniffled in the cold night air, his face iced with snot and saliva as his flat, triangular nose trickled.

"We can't take him in there with us. They'll kill him," Devonia said.

"What should we do?"

"Stay here with him."

"I'm not staying here," Seth disputed.

"He can't be alone."

They looked at Michael, who looked back at them sadly.

"I don't want to burden you... but I don't want be here alone either."

"Stay out here for just a day or two, Michael. If you stand

in the sun, you'll regenerate a bit," Devonia said.

He nodded and knelt down under a solar panel. "Don't forget about me. And don't tell anyone where I am."

"We won't, Michael, just stay right here, okay?" she said in a soft voice.

He curled up and lay in the sand, wrapping himself in his robes to stay warm as they walked off toward the gates. Seth looked back.

"You think he'll try to run off?" he asked.

"He's too scared. He has the mind of a child. Who's to say what he remembers and what he doesn't, or what infectious ruination Fraus planted in his brain. I think whatever curse is in him has since lifted, but its aftermath has thrashed his ability to regenerate."

"But he's still a Sararan. I don't understand."

"His mutation keeps him strong enough to stay alive, but the damage of the curse constantly weakens him. It's probably excruciating just to exist."

"Fucking hell. It's a miracle he hasn't offed himself."

"He's too timid. Fraus left him with the 'perfect' balance of mental and physical disability to make him live forever in his suffering: a perfect curse."

Seth shook his head, his eyes alight with anger. "The Immortals of the time should have killed Fraus after the fall of Shakti."

"But... she was your mother, Seth. You wouldn't have been born."

He spat and answered harshly. "She made it so this world isn't even worth being born into."

They kept on and arrived at the large gates at sunrise. They identified themselves to the guards and the massive steel doors swung open. The nobles were already standing in a line to welcome the Immortals. They stepped forward and suddenly Devonia stopped.

There stood Queen Fatima, the centaur Artemis, and between them, the tall and stunning Uhlanga, whose beautiful white dress shone brightly in the morning light against her dark skin. Her eyes were a rolling blue wash like the waves of a furious sea, her Aradian transformation complete. She stepped forward, smiling widely. After a moment of hesitation, Devonia ran up and hugged her.

"My dear sister," she said, holding her friend close.

"How are you, Devonia?"

"I'm alive. And so are you! Where have you been?"

"I was hidden for a very long time. But I'm here now, ready to do what we were trained to."

They stepped back and smiled at one another, their third eyes matching, speaking their own language beyond the ears of the mortals. Seth rolled his eyes and waited as they laughed and hugged again. Queen Fatima stepped forward slowly, unable to hold back any longer.

"Fatima!" Devonia said as she hugged her. The lovers embraced as best they could without giving themselves away. Uli approached Seth and introduced herself, as Devonia said hello to Artemis and the other nobles.

"Seth Beller. I am Uhlanga. You were very young, but I knew you when you were an infant."

"So it seems."

Seth shook her hand and nodded emotionlessly. She waited for a moment for him to say something else, then broke the awkward silence.

"You're quite the headhunter I've been told. How was your last deployment?"

"Good fun. You should join us next time."

"Maybe I'll do that," she smiled. "Welcome to the city of Mecca."

He nodded again as she turned and met with the others. Fatima and Devonia held hands as the lot of them walked into the city center where curious inhabitants watched the Immortals pass, Seth trailing behind the powerful women as if he were subordinate to their matriarchal clan. Whether it was their intention to make it appear as such or not, Seth's clout was being drowned out by their voices before he could even speak, and he was more than a little skeptical of the African diviner.

They went on through the city, passing wealthy, clean-cut Arabs who wore suits and luxurious clothes, their faces glued to their web devices as they ran their errands or directed their businesses from marble cafes and buildings designed to dazzle the eye. Nearly everything was a dyed glass, and the warped high-rises glistened like dripping icicles in the heat. They went to the palace, where painters were erasing the former prince's legacy and dropping long red flags from the awnings and displacing statues with new erections. Seth stopped at the foot of the monstrous structure and watched them climb the steps: the two Aradians, the centaur, the queen of Iraq and her dignitaries, all walking tall like an assembly of female dictators eager to carve the rotten flesh from the world. Devonia looked back at Seth, who stood silently, leaning on his scepter, his grandfather's knife fixed to its base as the tip spun slowly on the cracked marble.

"Aren't you coming?" she asked.

"I'm not invited," he replied.

"What do you mean?"

"Go ahead. Ask her," he nodded to Uli.

Devonia looked at Uli.

"Devonia, you are a trusted cohort and have been an ally with us for years. We do appreciate the amazing work Seth has contributed, but this is a council of national leaders, not headhunters. I hope you don't take offense."

"Not at all," he said, putting his scepter on his shoulder and turning away.

"Where are you going?" Devonia asked.

"I think you know," he said, smiling.

Devonia turned and they kept walking towards the gate.

"Seth might not be an expert in sociology or policy, but he's a worthy asset and could help us immensely. He might be aggrieved by this exclusion and drift to another place as he's known to do."

"Then let him," Artemis said, shrugging as they walked inside.

They met in a large room at the height of the palace's rise, overlooking the city that sparkled like a rolling ocean as the industrious peoples drove hovercrafts between the sharp gridlines. They sat around a circular table, save the centaur who paced slowly by the window, watching the motion of humans below as she clopped lightly on the stone floor. The massive skull of an African elephant hung from the ceiling, plated with a mosaic of gold and brilliant jewels, with rubies at the tips of its massive tusks. They sat and Uhlanga looked carefully at Devonia. Artemis continued looking out of the window as if she were on watch duty.

"It seems a lot has happened since I left Baghdad," Devonia said, looking at Fatima who smiled and winked.

"Yes it has. While you were making headway with your operations, we planned and executed an invasion. The entire Mid-East is free from tyranny thanks to Iraq, and you as well. After the fall of Cairo, I moved my army north, one

I'd secretly been building for a decade, and took all of Africa, then helped Queen Fatima liberate the Arabian peninsula. We now have enough resources between our two empires to be sustainable and, eventually, to thrive."

"That's all good and well... but Prince Abadallah was not the same kind of person as Pharaoh Ramadan. He was a good man and friend of mine."

"He ran slave camps in Yemen and had total control of the market. Typical male dominancy. Now there is a true free market and those who choose to work in the oil fields are paid well and have been provided suitable living conditions."

"Where is he now?"

Fatima smiled and looked at Uli, who smiled in return.

"The crimes the prince had committed allowed us to gain enough public support to allow the transfer of power to Fatima. Foolishly enough, he resisted, and now he's dead."

Artemis laughed sinisterly as Uli moved on to more demanding subjects.

"I'm truly sorry again about the death of your team. I'm sure they were good men."

Devonia shrugged. "Not really. But they did their job none the less."

Fatima leaned in. "You did tremendous work out there in the deserts. Both Uhlanga and I are beyond appreciative of how much you accomplished."

"Seth had a lot to do with our progress as well, but it doesn't matter anyway. We flew over the desert on the way here. The nesting grounds have returned. Everything we did was for nothing."

"Don't say that." Fatima shook her head. "You still pushed them back long enough for Uhlanga and I to establish a cohesive society. Yes, we'll have to consider other options now regarding the harpies, but however the turn out of your endeavors, you still fought bravely for our people, and that we are thankful for."

"You're welcome," Devonia said, biting her tongue about how she truly felt.

"I know these wars have been hard on you Devonia," Uli began. "I can see how it's tearing you up inside. I would recommend retiring from the battlefield to join us in more diplomatic affairs. Shed the armor and don the royal gown of Pavonis. The prophecy calls for a trinity of sisters to bring a balance back to nature. There have been others who have attempted this sacred coven, only to be ridden back to their primeval selves. But now the world needs a different kind of sisterhood. What say you?"

For a moment, Devonia just sat and stared at them. Artemis looked over, then turned to her post again.

"You act like Seth doesn't exist. Like he's just some headhunter wandering from town to spend his spoils at the tavern."

"I mean... he's probably on his way to do just that," Artemis muttered.

"But he's also a tactical genius and a Sararan prince and the offspring of two of the most powerful sorcerers on Earth. What is your issue with him?"

"He's a man," Artemis interjected.

"Artemis, please," Fatima warned.

"Why starve her curiosity? We're all thinking the same thing. Leave him in the wild to be an animal as he was born to be, as his body was designed to be."

"I thought you said you wanted a different kind of sisterhood, Uli. What she's saying sounds a lot like the sexist talk of Shakti that led to the genocide of billions." Devonia turned to Artemis. "You don't like him because he's the son of your enemy, admit it."

"I will, and more," Artemis scoffed.

"The Sararan is a liability and I'll tell you why," Uli said, putting her arms out on the table, her soft skin dark against the blue glass. Her eyes were like Vishnu's: midnight-cobalt and gyrating ceaselessly in her reinforced skull as if hundreds of years of wisdom hid behind them. "There's no way to control him. He has no parents or masters. He was raised by savages. If we let him take his natural course, he could end up like his father—"

"He's nothing like Michael! He's an honest soldier and a sharp thinker. You really don't give him enough credit."

"Regardless, for now we'll keep him out of the circuit. You can keep these talks between us at least, can't you?"

"As you wish. I'm not trying to make him your king. I just think fearing him will do more harm than good. He just wants to be accepted and respected, like everyone else."

The Aradian nodded. "I'll see to it that he is made welcome here, and I will personally thank him for his efforts in this war."

"As will I," Fatima assured her.

Artemis kept looking out of the window and said nothing.

"Uli…" Devonia asked warily. "What happened on that terrible day? Why did Melody leave you behind?"

Uli stood. "Fatima… Artemis… will you please excuse us? You both know this story and have other business to attend to, I'm sure."

"Of course," Fatima said. "You will stop by my quarters after your meeting, won't you, Devonia?"

Devonia smiled and nodded, pulling out the chair beside her so that Uli could join her once the others had left.

Uli looked out at the horizon, as if drawing the scene with hollow eyes. "When Seth was born, there was a rip in space-time. Not even Tala saw it coming. The Zurvans... they made a huge mistake by kidnapping me and giving me the Aradian gene. They thought I was the reincarnation of Ezra, but I wasn't. Avestan knew it the moment they rescued Seth from his gorgon mother. That's why I didn't even make it to the docks in Naples. Avestan asked Melody to do it, since she could kill me gently. But Melody couldn't bring herself to end the life of someone who didn't deserve it, so she sedated me instead. When I woke up, I was so scared. Avestan found me and took me with them, unable to finish the task of killing me since the priority was getting Seth to safety, at least that was their excuse. It was a sordid affair, that only one of us could live simply because Tala had ordered it. Even to Melody and Parvati, Seth was the preferred Immortal. So, when you and Melody and the other Zurvans set out to sea, we headed east, towards Turkey. The fallout followed us all the way down, but luckily the harpies hadn't spread there yet. We tried to continue east but the conflicts and storms were to such a scale that no way was passable. So we went south, deep into the wilds of Africa. Avestan met with the Zurvans there but when they found me alive, they tried to kill me. So Avestan defected from the order, a motion punishable by death. For a while they tried to start anew in a small village in Botswana, hiding the Sararan toddler's identity with sunglasses while they continued my training, raising me as their own. But I think the grief was too much to handle; the years of unchecked depression, both war and the absence of war, the lack of friends or communal identity outside of combat, with only a life of sedentary living while hiding two Immortal children like prisoners. When I transformed into an Aradian, they knew I could be trusted to take care of Seth, and Avestan took their own life. They left a note, and wanted Seth and I to continue on, to disregard the prophecy as ancient religious dogma.

"But unlike those before me, I did consider ending the child's life. I stood at the banks of the Nile as he stumbled around its edges, picking flowers and already mimicking their genetic codes and replanting them like a tiny gardener. The Sub-Sararan hippos were hungry that day. I was going to push him into the current and walk away. But I couldn't do it. He was innocent. His mother and father deserved a thousand tortures, but they'd been dealt with. Who was this child, so special that Tala uprooted herself to save him before spinning the world like a top and sending us all into havoc? So I did to him what Melody did to me. I abandoned him. I left him in the savannah when he was four years old, and used what magick I knew to convince a pride of lions to take him in. Luckily, lions are a perceptive and wise species. I washed my hands of his fate and let the pride raise him in an environment that would have pleased any of his would-be masters. From there I used my skills and body to unite Africa, and I've been working diligently to establish order in this chaotic world. You can see now why I'm concerned about letting the continent be torn apart."

Devonia's eyes were squinting as she studied Uli. "You regret not killing Seth now, don't you? Even after you've seen him rise into the great Sararan that he is. He doesn't even know most of this."

"He doesn't need to. What he learned on the savannah was essential to his destiny. I just hope he isn't contracted by the same foul forces his father was. Just because he is a Sararan does not mean he is a virtuous creature."

"The same could be said for Aradians."

Uli nodded and sighed. "These are uncertain times. I wish some things were clearer, but we don't have the resources to delay what's coming any longer."

"See, that is where you're wrong, Uli. I found a way to exterminate the harpies. All of them. Naturally. Using the leviathan. They eat them up like locusts. It won't even result in any collateral. No one else has to die."

"I'm impressed, really. But that's the trouble though, isn't it?"

"What do you mean?"

Uli walked back over to the table. "The nuclear program is a business, like any other, and Fatima and I have already invested too much into this contract to back out now. This way is just as effective as your plan, but will provide the good people of this empire with wealth and opportunities not seen in a hundred years."

"Humans don't need wealth, business, and a global market. They need community, purpose and a culture not rooted in technology. That's why Vishnu did what he did. You're repeating humankind's mistakes all over again. I don't think we share the same interests, Uli."

"Which is why I need you in our council! Trust me, I want different views, I want a balanced governing body. Those checks and balances are what make democracy work. I'm willing to listen, Devonia."

"Then trust me when I say the leviathan can do the work for us!"

"It's out of the question. I'm in no position to rely on such a despicable creature."

"Despicable? Humans are the ones that are despicable. The only thing the megalodons ever did was become involuntarily mutated and outgrow their evaporating habitat to find a new one on a fairly desolate slab of Earth no one gave a shit about anyway. Our relationship with them is neutral. But that could change."

"Are you threatening this nation with some unwarranted

pact with the leviathan?" she asked.

Devonia shook her head. "You care about humans so much you've already forgotten the lessons you were taught so painstakingly. But what would I know, I'm just another headhunter heading for the tavern."

Devonia walked out and Uli sighed, tapping her crystalline nails on the glass in a quick rhythm, contemplating the value of her relationship with her old friend, and what it meant to be a queen in the modern age.

"Pavonis, keeper of the wilds. And I, keeper of civilization… the embodiment of each entity, concentrated to their most saturated states of being. Sisters from childhood… now impossible allies. What am I to do?"

Devonia entered Fatima's chambers. The queen was sitting on her bed, anxiously wringing her hands. She immediately rose to meet Devonia and they fell into one another, kissing passionately on the bed as their legs tangled.

"Your skin… is so… soft," Fatima panted. "Even after all your travels and bloodshed."

"I molted before arriving. It's better for public relations."

Fatima giggled. "I love you."

They made love all afternoon, the fast-moving sun taking them right into evening as a blanket of stars fell over the bright city. They lay on the bed naked, covered in sweat and each other's liquids, caring not for anything but their own company as they drew small constellations over the contours of each other's skin.

"When do you go back to Baghdad?" Devonia asked.

"Whenever you agree to come with me."

"Let's leave now!"

"Don't be silly. I have to sleep."

"Sleep on the way. I'll be your magic carpet."

"Oh yeah?" Fatima raised her eyebrow sensually.

"Stop it," Devonia giggled.

"Seriously though, I have to stay here for a few weeks, then I'll go back to my city."

"Because Uli said so?"

"Because it's good for the campaign. Voting starts this year. The first election in ages."

"I'm proud of you."

"For what?"

"Everything."

Fatima laughed and smiled wide.

"Well I'm proud of you too. I read the note you gave me, about the leviathan eating the demons, about coaxing them out just before locust season when they're most hungry. It's a genius strategy. I'll bring it up with the council tomorrow morning."

"Uli doesn't seem to share your enthusiasm."

"I'll convince her, don't worry."

Devonia smiled and combed Fatima's hair with her fingers, staring longingly into her eyes before kissing her and turning off the lights with a charm. When Fatima was asleep, Devonia crept away into the night. She navigated the miles of panels and took a long, confusing route to diffuse the interest of any onlookers. When she found Michael, he was sitting on the sand alone by the panel where she'd left him. He reared back like a fawn.

"Don't worry, Michael, it's just me."

"Oh... you frightened me."

"How are you holding up? Did you charge your cells at all?"

He shook his head violently. "They won't charge."

"Why not?"

"My cells won't take it. It just burns."

Devonia frowned. She could see the pain and weakness gnawing at him. "Seth didn't come back to visit you?"

"Why would he? He's ashamed of me."

"He's just having a hard time matching the Michael who saved the world with who you are now. But Michael, you're still the same person. You're still Ezra's son. You're still a man of many walks. You can be there for Seth in other ways. I'm sure you two would get along fine after a formal reunion. Maybe I can convince him to go on a trip with you."

"You would do that for me?"

"Yes, of course. I'm sorry you have to stay out here, so far away from everything. But you understand, don't you?"

He nodded, shivering in the cold.

"Here, I brought this for you." She pulled out a large deel, its soft fur coat glowing in the starlight. "This should keep you a bit warmer. Are you sure you don't want any food or water?"

"Spiders and dew are fine, thank you."

He wrapped himself in the fur coat and curled up in the sand, sleeping soundly under the panel as the blue light of dawn approached. Devonia watched him for a while, studying his breathing patterns, trying to diagnose whatever curse plagued him. She left after a while and made her way to the gate. When she arrived, Artemis was standing outside the gate with her arms crossed.

"Midnight hunt?"

Devonia laughed. "Hardly," she said, walking past the centaur as she stood tall, looking over the desert.

"We're expecting an attack today."

"By who?" Devonia asked, turning back to her.

"Loyalists to the former government. They come out of the canyon every so often to try and sabotage the city."

"I'll make sure to be on my game then."

"Will Seth be available, or is he at the brothels again?"

"Your guess is as good as mine. He's disguised his aura from me."

"Hardly the actions of an 'ally'."

"He's a sovereign creature, like everyone else."

Devonia entered the gates as Artemis remained, tracing her eyes along the mysterious path on which the Aradian had come.

Just as Artemis had warned, the raiders attacked at noon. They wore thick armor made of vandalized solar panels and masks that made them look like reptile hybrids as they charged across the wastes on camels and horses. The animals were kept cool with ice coats and the dripping water from the coats' hems turned the dust behind them into a vapor trail between the mirage of black glass panels. Hundreds of them charged in as the security teams assembled. The first shots rang out and alarms sounded throughout the city. Civilians made their way into bunkers and to other sanctuaries as panic caused yelling and disorder. Devonia met with Uli at the east wall where a slew of snipers were lined up in prone positions, their muzzles poking between the marble railing and already cracking away at the attackers. Uli smiled as the occasional incoming bullet zipped past their heads or ricocheted off of a column.

"They come through the panel fields because they know we won't bomb our own energy sources. It's harder to pick them apart. They'll come in, cause a panic, maybe shoot a soldier or civilian if they're lucky, then retreat, and come back in a few days or a week."

"Why doesn't Fatima take the offensive instead of just waiting for them to attack. It's a small contingent. I'm sure a strike team could manage the mission."

"These savages are better at hiding than you think. Besides, it's good to keep a few enemies around before elections. You can always turn the violence up or down depending on public opinion."

They watched as the gunners blasted away, careful not to hit the panels as men began dropping like sacks between them, their horses standing dumbly under the panels in the insane heat. The contingent retreated, pursued by an assault team on dirt bikes, chiefly to ride them off rather than engage them.

"Venus platoon, stay here and finish off the ones you can see," Uli ordered. "Jupiter, get down there once they're finished and execute the ones you can't."

"You don't keep prisoners?" Devonia asked.

Uli laughed and waited to see if Devonia was joking.

Her Aradian sister remained silent.

"No, I don't keep prisoners. Do you?" Uli looked out over the desert and breathed deeply, waiting for Devonia to respond. When she didn't, the African queen turned away.

Devonia watched her before looking back down at the panels of glass. A man was crawling for cover, his guts spilling onto the sand. She could hear him wailing. A shot from a rifle rang out and he lay dead, his innards cooking on the barren plain.

That same evening, Devonia knocked on the door of Fatima's quarters. No answer. The door was locked but she picked it and let herself in. There were clothes strewn across the bed and Fatima stood on the balcony in a see-through gown.

"Devonia? Is that you?"

Devonia looked around the room. She smelled the air. Something was different. Fatima walked in and hugged her, but Devonia didn't return the embrace.

"What's wrong, my love?"

Devonia stood back, looking intensely into Fatima's eyes. She shook her head. "How could you?"

"How could I what? What are you talking about?"

Devonia's eyes lit with purple flame like a supernova blast and she drove her fist through the mirror on the wall, shattering the glass over them as Fatima collapsed onto the floor with a scream.

"Uhlanga was here! You've been sleeping with her!"

"No! I wouldn't!"

"I can smell her on your clothes and sheets. How could you be so heartless?" Devonia cried, bloody tears falling down her cheeks. "You were my last tie to the human race! I trusted you! I gave you my everything!"

"Please... please don't kill me," Fatima cowered, blood running along her forehead from the shower of glass shards.

"Kill you? I fucking loved you!"

Devonia stormed out and slammed the door, leaving Fatima sobbing on the floor, rolling in the clanking glass like a bloody doll with no strings as her former lover raced out of the city and across the desert, raging at the sand with frustrated kicks.

"Who the fuck does she think she is? And with my old

training partner? Fucking humans!"

She cursed at the sky as she made her way to Michael, crisscrossing through the rows of panels. Unable to find him, she made sure she was in the same place they had left him, looking at the angle of the constellations and the city. But Michael was gone. She walked for many miles during the night, searching for him, but to no avail. As the thin light of dawn beckoned, she saw an old man collecting the bodies of raiders in a cart. She approached him.

"Have you seen an odd creature in amongst the bodies?"

The thin old man looked at her with a curious gaze.

"He's about this tall... looks like a heroin addict... probably would have tried to run away from you."

"No, ma'am. I've not seen anyone but dead tonight."

"What are you doing out here at this hour?"

"I come to collect the bodies so they may receive a proper burial."

"So you sympathize with the raiders?"

He chuckled. "There's more to life than taking sides. Sometimes, you just have to do the work that needs to be done."

She looked at the old man's hands. His skin was cracked and worn like an aged pachyderm. He continued picking up the charred pieces of human flesh and placing them in his cart.

"Do you work for the city?"

"I do God's work. And my payment is knowing these souls may finally be at peace. The queen leaves them to burn in the merciless day until they are ash in the wind. No funeral, no epitaph, not even towers of silence to commemorate them."

"I'm inspired by your nobility. Lately, I'll admit, I've been having trouble seeing humans as anything but stupid and selfish."

He chuckled. "Stupid... selfish... is that what I am?"

"Not at all."

"Then why do you group me into that description? What if I was to say all Immortals are reckless murderers, just because most of them are?"

Devonia hung her head in embarrassment.

"I was born in 2025, not far from here. I have lived through the oppression of Shakti, when the tribes were allowed to behead aristocrats and the Aradians leveled whole cities. I was here during the reign of Michael, as the Luciferian Army went through the streets like dogs and committed atrocities you couldn't imagine. And now I see these new leaders come in, claiming they will bring peace at last with the same rhetoric as those before them. My gracious Pavonis, you must remember that humans never had a chance to evolve on their own trajectory. We've prescribed our sick little world a host of favored gods to fix these problems, not realizing these angelic creations are a defiant breed. We humans keep setting traps for ourselves. And yet, amazingly, we have reached a new enlightenment since the creation of the Immortals. I believe your species is a great example of the extremes of what it means to be human, and I hope you understand that as a compliment. The universe unravels beneath our feet. One day, you will be a grain of sand washed away in a tidal wave, lest you become the wave itself." He smiled. "I do this job because of who I am, not because of what happens afterword. But you? You desire to be rewarded for your sacrifices."

"Only with victory."

"Your victory will not be achieved, for you are making the wrong sacrifices."

"What should I do then?" she asked earnestly.

"We are only meant to be what we are. If I could be anything, I'd be everything! But a human life is shaped by the time prescribed to it. And even as an Aradian, a dire fate awaits you. Immortals are not immortal – they're amortal. Did you know the life expectancy for an Aradian is the same as a human? And they are expected to save the world with that amount of time? There are human kings and queens who have lived longer. At the end of our restless day, the work you do is no less important than the work I do. We are included in the membrane of this world. The convergence of language and magick has opened a new dimension; even the smallest and most insignificant people can conjure a desired outcome. In the Zurvan scriptures, I read about a twelve-year-old girl who changed the course of a great battle by raising a dagger to her enemy's gaze. Show us the true essence of Pavonis again and the world will be revived."

"That's not exactly what happened. I would take what you read in the scriptures with a grain of salt."

He smiled and looked her over as if he were her father, proud of the woman Devonia had become. Devonia couldn't help but feel guilty that he was out here doing such back breaking work alone.

"Can I help you?"

"Nay, your majesty. If you helped me, you'd be displacing both our purposes. Go look for your friend. It sounds like he could use an angel."

He smiled and wiped the sweat from his brow as the heat rose and Devonia walked on, her headache mounting with the old man's words still playing in her memory.

After an evening of strippers, cocaine, and heavy drinking, Seth stumbled through the desert singing into a bottle. He couldn't find where he had left his father, so he waltzed onward. The night was cool as he danced through the sand, acting like a front man to a swing band as he meandered through the hills far away from the plain of mirrors and painted women dressed up like tropical birds for noble charlatans. His baritone voice echoed off the canyon walls as he walked along an unknown path, unafraid of whatever might lurk there. Suddenly, a gun barrel came poking through the shadows at his ear. Seth tipped his head back drunkenly and looked into the fissure from where the shade was hidden.

"Have you come here to kill us?"

"No, man," Seth shook his head calmly before taking a swig from the bottle and handing it to the shade. "I came here to have a good time."

Seth soon found himself sitting around a huge bonfire with the tribe of raiders. The fire was hidden well from the city's lookouts, the canyon's walls of stone surrounding them, projecting the shadows of dancing men and women. The tribe played ancient Arabian music on improvised instruments as children ran laughing through the crowd, playing some invented game. Seth lay next to the fire and looked around and smiled at what he was seeing. He spoke with one of the elders, who lay equally lazily next to him, smoking a pipe.

"What brings you here, Seth, son of Michael?"

"Not sure. Got sick of the city I suppose."

He chuckled. "Why do you think we're out here?"

"Because you liked your old government better than this one?"

He shook his head. "That's what they're saying, is it? Lies

and propaganda. It's because we lived a simpler way of life, and we were gentrified as money and growth and industry replaced our kind. My tribe... we are close. We share things. We make time for one another. We are egalitarian. We grow together. But the city disconnects us from this way of being. That's why people in the city do drugs and become addicted to sex... they forget what the meaning of life is."

"Which is?"

"To become something greater; to complete self-metamorphosis. Perhaps our battles to take back Mecca are for nothing. But it gives us purpose, to fight for what we believe is right."

"You'll never defeat them though. You'll just die out here."

"The point was never to defeat them, but to show them how alive we truly are."

Seth nodded and tipped his bottle to the man. They watched the tribe dance and laughed through the night.

At some late hour, Seth felt a strange essence in the air and left without saying goodbye. He walked back out of the canyon. For miles he wandered, not knowing the meaning of his meandering, until he saw a strange figure standing on the dunes before him. The stars were being swallowed by dawn's coming light and his drunken eyes found it difficult to make sense of the creature's cat-like outline over the blue sand. He walked toward it and suddenly his heartbeat quickened in his chest. He was sober in a second.

Standing there was a sphinx, its muscular lioness legs standing tall, its massive falcon wings folded over its back as its gorgeous human face staring intently into Seth's eyes. For a time, they just watched one another, the wise yet deadly goddess stirring the sand with her tail, her only motion in her solitary state. She, like Seth, was raised by a pride, and thus they shared an unmistakable bond which could not be denied by history or vendetta, their anther oleo roots entwined. But, unlike Seth, the sphinx knew the Sararan's weakness. Her face was more beautiful than any he'd ever seen, and she spoke without fear or doubt, like a being who'd experienced all things and had finally been enriched by the spectrum of the universe's totality.

"Tell me, Sararan, is it better to be a king in a land of men, or a king of a desert which is empty, but by all means peaceful?"

He knew the creature spoke in riddles. "It's better not to be at all," he said. "For existence is pain and love is the bite to its venomous sprawl, and yet I am not worthy of its grace."

"Am I supposed to pity you for this plight which all life must both endure and desire? You deserve nothing short of torture for your secession from the truth."

"What is your name, sister?" he asked solemnly.

"Hathoraeon. You will remember it." There were splinters in her words.

Seth could sense her animosity but was unsure of her intentions. "If I fulfil what I owe to you now, may I offer you my body and soul forevermore."

Seth spoke sincerely, knowing well the sphinx could steal his ghost before his heart ever stopped beating, if she so chose.

"So willing to offer your eternal spirit… as if you were not amortal. As if you were so oblivious that you couldn't reach immortality through discipline alone and undo the evils of this world." She sneered. "Have you no dignity?"

"I've done… terrible things," he said.

"You were a child when you killed my sister, so I would have forgiven you for your recklessness as a juvenile, but she was pregnant with the last of our kind. Poachers killed the rest of us when the North African government collapsed. Only I remain."

"I regret... so much...." He sputtered. "What can I do to remedy this?"

"Remedy what? At any moment you may choose to value your life and the actions you commit to. Your punishment is to witness my ascension, that you may understand the glory of duty when eternity comes to you at last."

The sphinx turned towards the walls of Mecca and began lumbering towards the guard towers.

"No... please!" Seth said, chasing after the magnificent beast.

He gripped onto the Sphinx's tail and pulled her wing, but nothing would turn her.

"Please stop! You don't have to do this! Pavonis will save you, she'll save us all!"

The sphinx kicked him in the mouth and ran faster as Seth knelt on the sand, defeated and crying hysterically, his face bloodied from his tears and the sphinx's wide dewclaw laceration across his chin.

"STOP!" Seth shrieked. "STOP!"

When she reached the panels, a burst of gunfire turned the rare goddess into a heap of smoking fur and feathers and Seth watched in horror as the last of the great sphinx's fell dead before him, his weeping and moaning audible to the guards standing in the high towers, hundreds of meters away.

"Should we engage the Sararan, ma'am?" one of the snipers asked Ulangha, who stood in the shadows next to him.

"No... not yet. Never destroy all your enemies at once. It's better to let them devour one another."

It was morning when Devonia approached the gate. There, Artemis and Uhlanga stood with forty armed guards behind them. The guards lifted their rifles as she approached. Devonia stopped and put her hands on her hips and spat.

"Hands where we can see them," Artemis ordered.

"I'll put my hands wherever I damn well please, nag. What's all this about?"

Uli stepped forward. "We found the fugitive you've been harboring. The world's most wanted. I'll waive the charges against you since you practically handed him to us."

"Charges? You've got some nerve after having my partner in bed last night. I should remove you from power."

The men clicked their safetys off.

"That would be a huge mistake, Devonia. Popular opinion rules in favor of myself over you, so I think you should calm down and just watch the show."

"Show?"

"The execution of Michael Ian Beller for his crimes against humanity. This morning at 11:11. Many people will sleep better knowing he's finally dead."

"Like I said to the talking horse, he's not possessed anymore! Get it through your fucking heads already!"

"That's irrelevant, Devonia. Some things just have to happen for the future of our species."

"Which species? Our species or humans? You're just a puppet master. You use your clout and pretty eyes to seduce politicians when they're alone and susceptible but really you're not as powerful as you think. I wonder what kind of campaign money Fatima's going to bring in after last night's affair."

"Watch your tongue, Devonia. Will you be joining us for the execution peacefully or not?"

Devonia looked at the soldiers and the centaur and at Uli. "He might as well be dead anyway. He's a castrated imbecile. Do what you want with him."

"That's better. You don't know where his son wandered off to, do you?"

"Still haven't seen him," Devonia said, attempting to hide her anger as she ground her teeth together.

"I have a feeling he will be arriving very soon," Uhlanga said.

With that the guards and their rulers turned around and entered the gates, leaving Devonia looking back at the endless waste beyond the solar farms and then at the metropolis, wondering which way was best to go. One way was best for her, another best for humans, and another best for Seth, her last friend in that lonely world. Still, she didn't know the answer to these questions. She knelt and wept under the lights of the gates, letting the drops collect on the white and brown pebbles as she gripped the sand with her fists and cursed the harshness of the world, and at the same time, became it.

CHAPTER 61 – OBLIVION

That morning, the city gathered to witness a tyrant's execution. They came by the thousands to the open aired Mosque of Makkah, crowding around the sacred Kaaba that glistened black and brilliant in the center of the mass. A platinum guillotine had been placed on top of the sacred cube where the centaur volunteered to be the executioner and wore a black hood and clopped around on top of the granite structure inviting people to gaze upon the surreal spectacle, that place which had been the center of Islamic practice for centuries but was converted to a chopping block for a disgraced god.

The humans came with their families, ready to witness history as the eighty-six-year-old ailing emperor was publicly denied his life. The nobles came and stood on raised glass monoliths next to the Kaaba, the crowd cheering for their soon to be rulers. Fatima smiled as she waved, with Uli next to her raised on a higher platform still, as if already overshadowing her power. The masses yelled and hollered, creating a swelling applause that sounded like a sustained wave crashing endlessly upon a formidable shore.

Devonia arrived in full battle dress, crouching high on the mosque wall as she viewed the mortal drove from above, her spear held tightly in her hand as it pointed up to the eternal blue sky. In her other hand was her moonstone. She moved it between her fingers as she stared at Uli.

Her Aradian counterpart stared back.

From that distance, in the rising heat, through all the commotion, they attempted to read one another's minds, but they'd already blocked their own thoughts. The very powers that separated them from humans now denied their aim as Immortals, reduced them to their simplest emotions rooted in passion and hatred and strange feelings not yet known by name as they studied each other's faces from afar. Fatima raised her arms to silence the crowd. After a moment, they settled and quieted as she spoke.

"There have been many dark ages in Earth's history," she began, her voice booming through the loud speaker. "But today, we see the end of one, as we bring hope for a new generation. People of Mecca, I give you the tyrant of our age: Emperor Michael!"

They clapped and cheered and whistled, the sound filling the large square. A corridor of people made an opening at the east end of the square and they shushed one another. Devonia watched on as the door opened.

Out walked a ragged, lifeless creature. He'd been beaten, his half nose now bleeding as he stumbled into the light. He wore his tattered saffron robe and chains on his hands and feet. The guards walked him out as he trudged jangling over the ground, whimpering with fright, his fingers shaking like leaves. People watched with eyes wide, expecting a tall robust man they could humiliate. But the creature could not have been more humiliated as they stared in awe. He moved like a skeleton wearing clothes, the guards prodding him along as he gazed around at the people ready to see him die.

He saw the centaur standing tall on the black monolith, and the heavy blade shining in its rectangular frame like a mirror to the rising sun, sharpened and dripping with a cell-deforming cyanide compound. He looked at the guards as if expecting some form of mercy, but they moved him forward just the same, up the steps as he tripped and labored his way to the platform. He cried and mumbled some improvised prayer.

"Please God... have mercy... please Father..."

He cried tears of blood that splashed atop the granite and sizzled in the baking heat. The crowd remained quieter than if the area were empty as the centaur coaxed him over, fixing his neck into the clasp where the blade would fall and behead him. The guards cinched him down with chains and stepped back into the crowd, so that only Michael and Artemis remained. The general he'd tried to kill all those years ago was now ready to exact her vengeance. She leaned over and lifted her hood so he could see her face.

"Do you remember who I am?"

"Whatever I did... I don't remember... I'm... I'm sorry for whatever it was!"

She spit in his eye and put her mask back on. "Goodbye Michael, son of Ezra."

She reached over to the rope that would release the block of steel with the slightest tug. Uli and Fatima turned to watch, their arms behind their backs as they spoke no more regarding the nature of the execution. Everyone looked on as if the entire world were about change. A child wept. A crow cawed. But other than those distinct sounds nothing was heard as Artemis pulled the rope and let loose the shearing blade in its predetermined arrangement with gravity. Down it fell, and Michael shrieked. To everyone's surprise, the blade was stopped only inches from Michael's throat as a white spear sunk into the stone cube and halted the edge's fall, after being flung like a missile from above.

Everyone looked to where the spear had been thrown and saw their savior Pavonis, standing high on the wall, her purple and green cape flowing in the breeze as she let it loose to the wind and dropped down to the dirt lightly. A corridor of the crowd split wide as they viewed the mighty Aradian and stepped back quickly. Artemis went to dislodge the spear but Uli stopped her with a motion of her hand, not losing sight of Devonia as the goddess came walking up to them, with no other weapon save the moonstone held tight in her fist. The crowd knelt and lowered their heads to their true queen; that global enforcer and biophilic-healer who carried the essence of Ingrid and all other reincarnations of Mother Earth before her. She raised her arms to Uli as she stopped a hundred yards from the Kaaba.

"If we're still basing authority off the people's trust, take a look around you," Devonia said.

"You're just delaying the inevitable," Uli said to her.

"Perhaps, but I also don't think you have the right to kill this creature, for it would be a crime to execute a falsely accused man. I'm sure you skipped his sentencing since all of your judges agreed on immediate execution, but may I testify in his defense before you end his life at this once holy site?"

"So that he may be forgiven?" Uli asked.

"Nay. So that he may be received," she replied.

Michael panted where he lay as he stared at the sharp blade hovering over him.

"Alright, Pavonis. Plead his case," Uli said.

"When Michael became possessed, the demon completely replaced his soul with another. He was only Michael in the flesh, but the person directing him was Roman Emperor Gaius Julius Caesar Augustus Germanicus, or Caligula, as most knew him. When Fraus died, the power of his possessor left him as did this lustful spirit, making him Michael again, but a fearful, ignorant and docile version. Killing him here, like this, would be just the same as doing nothing at all, or perhaps worse."

"Even so, it must be done."

They stood and stared at one another. Someone lifted their head from their impromptu worship and pointed.

"Look!"

The crowd stood again and watched as Seth walked up behind Devonia and stood beside her. He'd shaved his head and wore his battle outfit, wielding his grandfather's knife in his left hand.

"At last, the Sararan has come to witness the end of his father's legacy. I hope you've come chiefly to spectate," Uli said.

Seth looked at Uli and Fatima, then to Devonia. She read his expression as he walked solemnly towards the Kaaba.

"No, Seth. You don't have to do this," she said softly.

Uli saw it in him too and smiled. He walked past the Aradian and Queen Fatima and up the steps, the guards pointing their muzzles at him all the way, the crowd watching on with confusion and excitement, yet all remained observant. Artemis stood in front of him as if to stop him.

"I won't hurt you, centaur, but I will end your life in a blink if you don't let me have one last word with my father."

She stood aside reluctantly, watching his every move. All eyes fell on Seth as he lifted the blade to its highest position and tied it off. He then threw Devonia's spear back to her. The captivated audience of humans and Aradians watched as Seth knelt down and stroked his father's blood-stained forehead under the bright sun.

"I know this isn't how you imagined your life ending: that you'd rather die in some glorious battle, or perhaps lying next to Melody in old age, looking back on a life of great achievement... but at least you can die next to your son, and a fellow comrade," he said. "Once, long ago, you helped save the world, and for a while, people knew the meaning of peace. That's something to be proud of. And I am proud of you."

Michael wept crimson, shaking his head. "I wish you had known the man I once was," Michael said.

"I know him, for he is with me now. You have not forsaken me."

"I love you, son."

"I love you too, father. Do not fear the great darkness before you, for you are as one with the sun. See you in the next life."

He sunk Ezra's blade into Michael's heart as the old Sararan wailed, twisting the blade and pulling it back out of his chest as dark blood spewed over the edges of the cube. Michael's eyes stayed glued to Seth's as he bled out, and his to Michael's, both fathers and sons to one another at once. Artemis reached over but Seth warded her off with the knife. After a few moments, Michael stopped gargling and lay still, his son holding his heavy head in his hands as it dropped. The crowd erupted in applause.

"At last, we are free from the pain of Michael's oppression!" Uli's voice boomed through the court.

The people began converging towards them and some clambered to the top of the Kaaba as Seth pushed them away.

"He deserves a proper burial!" Seth yelled.

"Did my mother get a burial when she was impaled?" one woman yelled as she slapped him across the cheek.

People started undoing the chains as Seth pushed them away, but he couldn't get to all of them. They tugged Michael's body from him and Seth watched in horror as his father's body was dismembered and sent outward into the masses, each of his limbs diverging in the cardinal directions, with his head on a spike bobbing through the crowd: a communal trophy.

"You savages!" Seth cried as he started punching people in the face indiscriminately.

The humans fought back futilely and when Artemis attempted to strike him, he took his knife handle in both hands and swiped her through the torso, halving the rare beast. She fell from her mount as her guts poured onto the crowd.

Devonia, meanwhile, was now being faced down by Uli. Fatima had already fled the scene with her guards.

"What are you going to do, Devonia?"

"Make sure the only friend I have left knows he has one too," Devonia said.

"This whole queendom just bowed to you and you complain about loneliness?"

"Loyalty rather, of which none of these ungrateful humans harbor any!" Devonia yelled over the chaos.

Uli screamed. "Enough! You and Seth are banished from this queendom! Get out and don't come back! Spend your useless lives in the wilds where you belong!"

Seth dropped from the structure and walked away quickly as people clung to him, biting him and punching him as though he were Michael, as if the execution did nothing but rally their candid desires for violence and a misplaced sense of retribution. He expelled them like a water buffalo shaking off flies and walked on.

"Let's go before I kill every human here," he said to Devonia.

The riot they started did not subside, and guards were pulling people from the Kaaba when suddenly a loud shot rang out. Seth turned in a whirl and caught the bullet in his fist, spinning with the object's momentum then stopping to study it. It was made with a crystalline complex that would have killed him and trapped his soul in time, an illegal form of magick not used since the reign of Fraus. He looked back. Uli's pistol was still leveled at him as she stood as still as stone, shocked that Seth had sensed the projectile mid-flight.

Seth looked at Devonia, then back to Uli. "Our whole lives, people have been killed, wars have been fought, thrones decimated... all over which two of us three should live. She still thinks it's up to her."

Uli kept the pistol leveled at Seth, but Devonia shook her head.

"You were my best friend, Uli," Devonia said softly.

Uli began to cry but kept her aim as her face streamed with blood. "Why can't you just live for the common good? Why can't we work together to save this world?" she shrieked.

"Because you think humans are the world," Devonia said. "And we believe the Earth itself dictates what is and what isn't worth saving."

"Let's go. This woman is a coward," Seth muttered.

Another shot rang out. Devonia gasped. She looked down at her bleeding lung and chest where a bullet had gone through her back, then back at Uli, crumbling into a pile of silk as her old friend sobbed with regret.

"Look what you made me do!" Uli cried, her mind more compromised than ever due to the Immortals short proximity.

"She betrayed us," Devonia wheezed in disbelief, her lung collapsing. "How?"

She could already feel her spirit drifting from her body. Lights flashed before Devonia's eyes, her entire life escaping her. The very magnetism of her being vibrated with instability and a fearful reckoning. Seth's eyes burned white with anger and he leapt into a full sprint toward Uli. The Aradian stood up quickly and parried his knife thrust with her pistol. They stood opposite one another and a group of people made a circle to watch the dueling gods as Devonia knelt in the distance, trying desperately to fight whatever curse grew inside her as she turned and watched them square off.

Seth rounded Uli in a spiral formation and lunged again as she fired three shots. He stuck the knife through the trigger guard and cut off her finger while tossing the gun to the side. Uli kicked him in the chest and knocked him hard against the side of the Kaaba, the black stone crumbling over his shoulders. It was clear to everyone the fight leaned in the Aradian's favor. Seth coughed up blood as he looked up in a concussed daze.

"You should have killed me when you had the chance," he said quietly.

"I will kill you now," she panted, "and finally put an end to you and your fucked up family." She took out her scrying mirror and cracked it in two.

Time skipped strangely like a lagging screen on a monitor as Uli discarded the larger half and held the crescent high above her as she sliced it downward at Seth's skull with a shrill cry in that psychedelic haze of false dimension. But Seth saw through time's coagulation and caught the blade in his hands and used her own momentum against her, pulling her down and kicking her chest so that she flipped up and over onto the Kaaba, her head landing half-cocked under the guillotine. Devonia watched this unfold with her fading eyes and rubbed her moonstone as the Aradian began to rise, pulling the rope telekinetically and dropping it onto her forehead, scalping her. Uhlanga's arms dropped to the side lifelessly as the super-concentrated cyanide killed her faster than her frontal lobe could reconstruct itself.

Time returned, the humans around them unfazed by the realm-scattering sequence that had taken place.

Seth stumbled over to Devonia and pushed away the concerned citizens.

"The life in me is leaving," she said. "I think I'm going to die, Seth."

"Shh don't talk like that," he said, cupping her face in his stained hands and looking into her fading eyes. "I need you now. Stay with me. Come on, stay with me Devonia."

Devonia's heart stopped and her eyes fell dark and as they lay in the middle of that riotous mass. Seth leaned down and began kissing her, his blood mixing with hers, his Sararan cells reinforcing the fight to keep her alive. He poured his energy into her being, trying desperately to keep her heart and mind strong while the poisonous curse battled her nervous system.

A few dire seconds passed, then, miraculously, the color returned to her eyes and her heart began to beat again. But all this came at the cost of Seth's strength. He was so exhausted from his healing methods he needed help getting to his feet. The crowd stood back as they helped one another limp out of the mosque, leaving behind a smoking riot and bodies of both gods and humans halved and murdered. With the fall of Uhlanga, people began a free-for-all, fighting over the limbs of Michael, burning buildings, and licking the Aradian's blood off the walls of the black monolith, clawing at each other like feral beasts in that once pious place.

The Immortals stood on a slight rise overlooking the city, realizing nothing could stop the new wave of mutant beings that would undoubtedly rise from the city in upheaval.

"You have that stone Melody gave you?" Seth asked.

"Yeah."

"You wanna see if your new friends can help us?"

Devonia nodded. "We don't have a choice anymore."

She rubbed the stone and conjured a spell of vast broadcasting. A deep moan cut through the Earth. Soon, earthquakes shook the ground and crumbled the city's highrises. Shattering glass fell to the city streets below, chopping people to bits as the quakes rumbled incessantly. Then they came, from all directions, entire dunes and fields of panels ripped to pieces as the desert suddenly rose like a sandstorm with the oncoming leviathans. The megalodons sounded off like sirens of a hellish realm, shrieking with hunger as Devonia awakened them with her singing stone. They entered the city with crashing explosions, debris flying high into the sky as people screamed and fires started and ripped through whole districts. They fed on the humans. They fed on plastics. They fed on anything that would sustain them. And when their skin had been slashed up enough by the jagged steel beams and they'd feasted on all the humans, they descended back underground, leaving behind a city so reduced that its glass had nearly been made sand again.

The Immortals stood motionless on the rise and looked on at the smoldering scape. Millions of people had been silenced. And yet they felt nothing, as if the people were another colony of harpies left to burn in the broken walls of their nests.

"Fatima was my last connection to them, my last hope of binding my destiny to the human race."

"Your destiny was never bound to the human race. It was bound to me."

Seth took her hand in his. She looked into his starry eyes and smiled.

"I don't want anything but you," he said. "That's how I've

felt this whole time. I went on the headhunting expeditions because, well, that's what you wanted. Truthfully, I just wanted to be by your side."

She held his chin and gushed to him, "Oh Seth, our love would offset the stars."

"Then let it."

He leaned in and kissed her, and she kissed him in return, and as night fell upon them they created a genetic strain of bacteria between their two species blood types, letting it loose upon the Earth, destroying nearly every living thing from animal, to Sub-Sararan, to parasite, disease and beyond. And thus the Immortals walked away from Mecca, never looking back, just holding hands and admiring the sky of possibility before them, cosmic lovers, together at last.

CHAPTER 62 – GENESIS

The global extinction took several years, but when the last animals had been pinched out by the Immortals, they reveled in the Earth's simple Devonian beauty. They lived inseparably, flying through the air like birds of paradise and exploring their love for one another and their quiet world. They meditated by the hanging gardens, floated in the mists of great waterfalls, and flew like nighthawks over the deserts and grasslands. They explored the canyons, the low valleys, mountain peaks and high into space, where they absorbed nutritious unfiltered sunlight.

They dove down through clouds birthed from the old oceans vapor, just as souls bleed from a place of epic elongation and come into being before falling back down into that cradle of ethereal magma. And when they'd at last mapped and memorized the surface of Earth, they came unto the artifacts. The Immortals wandered into people's houses and found interesting antiques and guessed their origins. They looked through photo albums and saw what kind of people used to live there. They read love letters, tragedies, and enjoyed the humor that strung it all together. They learned the languages. They read books and performed plays for one another, going through the classics and beyond. They listened to music and played whole record collections and world instruments as their tastes matured and changed. They visited cemeteries of famous artists and leaders, paying their respects to those who'd inspired them. They explored what intrigued them, rediscovering the lost history of what made humans special, beyond the bloody history that deformed their truly great legacy.

    Centuries passed. The Immortals wandered the lonely planet without regret or grief. They had become shepherds of the elements and soon forgot their arbitrary pasts until only their divine love remained. Then, one night, Tala brought back the moon, returning that glowing friend of Earth. The planet was empty and desolate, nearly void of intelligent life. But somewhere in a valley of South Africa, two lovers gazed at the beautiful dancing orb with feasting eyes and felt Earth's rotation slow at last. And it was there the Immortal's eyes met and they decided with mutual embrace to begin life anew. They made love under the moonlight, a wave of green blossoming over the surface of Mother Earth; a rendering of two beings to propagate all life from a dueling entity, their love far reaching. Beyond time. Beyond atrophy. Beyond broken lineage or death itself. Their love had held. It had held tighter than any fist held Ezra's knife. And as the mushrooming world came to be, Seth tucked the blade into the folds of sand, like the folds of time, never at once where they were or will be, and at the same time always there, awaiting a new wind.

ACKNOWLEDGMENTS

Firstly, I would like to sincerely thank my parents and sister for supporting me through the arduous, transformative, and wild decade I spent writing this trilogy. Your patience and compassion did not go unnoticed. A very special thanks to my mother for being my first editor, and for encouraging me to read at a young age. It's because of you I've made it this far. I'd like to thank my father for making me a mountain man and teaching me about how live in congruence with nature in a world where such knowledge is nearly lost. And thank you sister for believing in me but also being a hard teacher when you needed to be. You are my bestie.

A huge thank you to my grandfather who has been a constant inspiration all my life, and to my grandmother who is a saint. Thank you to my uncle Shannon, who has since passed, but was a superhuman in my eyes and had the spirit of a warrior. He lives on through his siblings and niece and nephews.

Thank you Dillon Sleichter for being my biggest fan, blazing through the books each time one came out, and giving me honest feedback as a revisor. A sincere thank you to my ex-girlfriend and life-long friend Alex James, who the character Ingrid was loosely based on (Alex is a bit gentler), and for showing me the value in all life forms, even the smallest sapling. A huge thanks to those on the Hotshot crew who read my books on the down days between firefighting adventures, offering ideas and advice as I was formulating the plot. Thank you to the combat veterans who I know closely and who were able to give me a better idea of what it's like to be an operator in the post GWOT world.

Thank you to my publisher Cranthorpe Millner for believing in my writing, and to Kirsty Jackson and Victoria Richards for being my editors, and to Shannon Bourne for helping with marketing.

Lastly, I'd like to thank my teachers who encouraged me to write more; without them, I would never have become an author. A big thanks to Beth Beaulieu, my high school writing teacher who let us read books beyond the average high school's limit of controversial works, Ray Boksich, who let me fashion my own curriculum based on my interests, and Matt Halloway, for showing me that poetry is the voice of counter-culture.

Thank you to all who have found my writing thought provoking and worth a read. I appreciate all my readers and look forward to meeting many of you someday.

With love and fortitude,
Parker

www.ingramcontent.com/pod-product-compliance
Lightning Source LLC
Chambersburg PA
CBHW031255300925
33374CB00054B/1424